Counting Coup

JACK DANN

Counting Coup

A Tom Doherty Associates Book
New York

COUNTING COUP

Copyright © 2000 by Jack Dann

This book was originally published under the title *Bad Medicine* by Flamingo, an imprint of HarperCollinsPublishers, Australia.

A Forge Book
Published by Tom Doherty Associates, LLC
175 Fifth Avenue
New York, NY 10010

www.tor.com

Forge® is a registered trademark of Tom Doherty Associates, LLC.

ISBN 0-765-30185-7

First U.S. Edition: October 2001

Printed in the United States of America

0 9 8 7 6 5 4 3 2 1

ACKNOWLEDGMENTS

The author would like to thank the following people whose support, aid, and inspiration were invaluable:

Theresea Anns, David and Anna Beers, Susan Casper, Sean Cotcher, Patrick Delahunt, Lorne Dann, Jim Demetriou, Gardner Dozois, Ford Drake, Andrew Enstice, Jim and Louise Feeney, Linda Funnell, Christine Farmer, Jim Frenkel, Bryan Furlong, Gordon Van Gelder, Richard Gilliam, Jack C. Haldeman II, Joe and Gay Haldeman, James Herd, Barrie Hitchon, Merrilee Heifetz, Jim Holly, Phil Klink, Pat LoBrutto, Angelo Loukakis, Barry Malzberg, Shona Martyn, Midge McCall, Paul Montaut, Rod Morrison, Sue Page, Richard Parslow, Steve Paulson, Pamela Sargent, Lucius Shepard, Johnathan Strahan, Norman Tiley, Jeanne Van Buren, Bob and Karen Van Kleeck, Albert White, John Wilkinson, Sheila Williams, Kaye Wright, George Zebrowski, and my partner Janeen Webb.

CONTENTS

If I had the balls of a bison,
And the prick of a bull buffalo
I'd stand on top of Crazy Horse Mountain
And piss on the bastards below.
—Korczak Kiolowski's favorite song

1 .

BOOZE AND FROGSKINS

Goddammit, but they wouldn't leave him alone. Charlie stood in the bathroom, looking at his wrinkled, ruddy, burn-scarred face in the mirror over the sink, and mumbled to himself. His daughter Anne was listening to the rock-and-roll crap again, and his wife Joline ... well, she didn't have to say *anything*, goddamn her.

But she's right, he said to the mirror, you *are* a selfish sonovabitch. Then he ran his large hands through his thinning gray hair. Satisfied, he opened the bathroom door and stepped into the kitchen, which was next to the bathroom. It was a 1930's railroad apartment.

Joline sat at the newly purchased red Formica table and glared at him.

"I'll be back later," Charlie muttered, avoiding her eyes, and walked stiffly out of the apartment into the hallway.

"You're a selfish sonova*bitch*," Joline shouted after him. "Go ahead then and get drunk, let your daughters know what they have for a father . . ."

Charlie started coughing halfway down the hallway stairs, but he didn't stop to rest until he was outside. The street stank of garbage because collection had been reduced to once a week, thanks to the new Republican mayor. It was one of those warm Indian summer days in late October; somewhere in the '50s, although it seemed warmer than that. But even with his jacket on, Charlie was cold . . . he was always cold. He didn't know how he was going to get through another hard winter.

He stopped near the edge of his building, which was a red brick six-family, and started hacking again, coughing and wheezing and spitting up that whitish-yellow phlegm. Then the spell was over, and he took a deep breath. He hadn't even needed his asthma inhaler. He still had the tickle in the back of his throat, but that would stay with him all winter. It was the dry air, Joline had always said. The dry air . . .

Anyway, he wouldn't cough anymore for a while, he told himself as he lit a non-filtered cigarette. He watched the neighbor lady across the street bundle her baby into a carriage. She lived with her bastard child and Hell's Angel boyfriend in a tiny ground floor apartment next to an empty bar. The boyfriend wasn't a bad sort: big, fat, and always smiling through crooked teeth. He called his girlfriend "Momma", which was what Charlie called Joline.

Suddenly, Charlie started to cough again, and he let his cigarette drop to the ground. The emphysema was worse this year: *that's* what kept him from holding down a decent job.

But fuck the emphysema, he thought when he stopped coughing. He felt in his pocket for another cigarette. Fuck everything. He had fought in the goddamned war.

He had a right to get drunk.

Charlie always kept a bottle of wine and a few cans of beer hidden in the cellar below Nathan Isaacs' office. He had a key to the office, which was on the ground floor of an anvil-shaped brick building; the office was situated next to a small bookstore. On the window of the office door was painted in large block letters

LAW OFFICES

NATHAN ISAACS, ESQ.

and in the lower left hand corner was painted in much smaller letters: BEST REALTY, LTD. Although Nathan liked to keep up the pretense that he was still in practice, he had retired to Florida, both physically and spiritually. His son Stephen took care of his upstate income properties, which supported the whole family. Charlie was certain that Nathan had salted away enough money for himself and didn't need the income from the properties. But the old man took a good share of it for himself, nevertheless.

As Charlie paused in the narrow, crowded office before going down into the cellar, he remembered the old days when Nathan had four other lawyers working for him, and his offices had taken up the entire second floor, which Nathan had converted into furnished rooms for middle-income transients. But instead of letting Charlie have the work, he had brought in "professionals" to convert the offices into furnished rooms. After all the money I've saved the sonovabitch, Charlie thought, the humiliation still grinding away at him.

Nathan could afford to hire "professionals" . . . he could *afford* to let them overcharge him, the Jew bastard!

Now Charlie didn't have anything against Jewish people. His best friend Avram Kanckle was Jewish, and Charlie had grown up with him. Avram became a millionaire. But goddamn, Charlie had been a good friend to Nathan. He deserved better than this. Nathan had *promised* him that he'd never have to worry about money. Well, Nathan was even tight with his own son.

Now that was unusual to see among Jewish people . . .

Charlie went down the cellar stairs, past the bathroom and the metal shower stall he had installed. It had been his idea to build a furnished room at the other end of the cellar, which had windows. The added income would help pay Nathan's expensive winter heating bills. But the fire marshal had told Nathan's son that the

3

room couldn't be inhabited unless a fire wall was built around the old converted furnace. Well, Charlie had offered to build the goddamned wall, but Stephen demurred, saying, as he always did, "to wait until we get some money in." Like father like son.

The cellar, which was filled with oddments, plumbing accessories, sheets of wallboard and marlite and paneling, old desks, chairs, couches, office equipment, cardboard files, bed frames, and moldering mattresses, consisted of six rooms. With the exception of the furnished room, bathroom, and furnace area, the cellar was filled with all the junk Charlie had collected for the firm over the years. Charlie boasted that he could find a use for everything, such as the boxes of used carpet squares at the foot of the stairs, and thereby save . . . and make . . . money.

But fuck that. Let them pay a premium rate now, Charlie thought. He'd keep his ideas to himself.

He passed the cubby where breaker-switches lined the low-ceilinged wall; it looked like the control room of a space-ship in an old 50's movie. Charlie noticed that one of the black breaker toggles had snapped to the off position, breaking the neat double row, and he switched it back on: someone was using too many appliances upstairs. Then he checked the furnace. It was hissing away cozily, but he made sure there was enough water in the boiler because the automatic feed didn't work. A new mechanism would cost over two hundred dollars, and Charlie had advised Nathan and Stephen that a new one would foul-up just as this one did. So they paid him to check the water-level. It was the least they could do, the bastards, he told himself.

Then he retrieved his already opened bottle of sauterne, which he had hidden in the drawer of a desk with three legs, which, in turn, was hidden behind a section of sheet-rock that had been water-damaged and was curved and bent, as if it were kneeling. He'd have to get rid of all this stuff one day, he told himself, before the whole fucking building goes up in smoke.

Nathan would like that . . . he'd make some *more* money.

Fucking Jew-bastards . . .

He suddenly felt guilty for harboring such thoughts . . . after all, Stephen always tried to do right by him. Taking a sip of wine, he apologized to Stephen, as if Stephen was sitting right there with him in the furnace room. He raised his bottle and then spilled a few drops on the floor in Nathan's honor. "And to you, too, Nathan. You're a cheap Jew-bastard, but I love you. That's more than you've ever done for me."

He got up and paced back and forth in the crowded cellar hallway, maneuvering around the piles of junk. He looked into his work room, with its shelves neatly filled with jars and tins of nails and screws and bolts and washers. There were several five-gallon drums of paint along one wall. Arrayed upon his workbench were the various tools that he had bought for the company. He had always thought of himself as part of the company, as if somehow he too were an owner. When Nathan used to go off on business trips or vacations, Charlie was always the one in charge. He would sit at the desk and make the decisions and handle the money. He did the same thing now for Stephen. He could still handle anything that came up. But he had to pay rent just like any other tenant.

Goddamn, if Nathan shouldn't have at least given me a rent-free apartment. In the old days I didn't pay any rent . . . and there were always the bonuses.

But where the hell else could he work "off the books" and still keep the paltry allowance Social Services gave him to support his family?

Goddamn, every five minutes his daughters had to buy something else. They were like little birds, their mouths always open, and every day, every *hour*, they had to get dressed up in a different color. No, Daddy, I can't wear those slacks anymore because *nobody's* wearing bellbottoms, they're out of style, *Daddy*, you can understand that, can't you?

Charlie mimicked his daughter's voice in a gravelly falsetto, and talked earnestly to the green couch that Stephen had stored in the cellar until such time as he could afford a larger house. Well, that sonovabitch will get his larger house, Charlie thought, and what the hell will I leave to my family? Diddleyshit, that's what!

Charlie was almost sixty-six, and his wife was only in her late forties. He'd shown everyone that he still had the stuff, the jizzum; and now he had to somehow support his late-born children.

"I love those kids," he said to the couch. "God knows I do. But I can't afford all the shit they want, I just can't afford it." He turned to a cardboard box that had once housed a large appliance and said, "And I'm *not* buying another shitbox of a used car that'll fall apart an hour after I've paid for it. If I'm going to get out and *do* something with my life, I need a truck." He turned toward the furnace, as if speaking to an old and trusted friend. "But they won't listen . . . Joline certainly won't listen. Once that woman gets something into her head there's no talking her out of it. But she's *not* getting her way this time. I'm not buying another car, and that's final. There's just no *money*. And I won't go into debt for it."

As if in response, the furnace roared into life.

Charlie felt tipsy from the few swigs of wine. Lately, just the smell of booze seemed to make him drunk. Joline belittled him for getting "shitfaced" on a glass of beer, but it was because of the medicine he had to take for his emphysema, he supposed. In the old days, he could drink *anygodamnbody* under the table!

But that was long ago when his arms were the size of most people's legs, and he had a chest like a bull . . .

Suddenly a voice asked, "Do you always talk to the furnace and these broken pieces of furniture, my friend?"

Charlie jumped and turned toward the furnished room where the voice came from. He made out the figure of a man in the shadows. "Who the hell are you?" Charlie demanded. In the wan light he could see that the man had a shock of white hair that was long enough to be a woman's.

"Myself, I often talk to the rocks," the man said, chuckling.

"Goddammit, who the hell are you, this is private property." Charlie took a step forward and reached above his head to pull the chain of a light bulb fixture. In the sudden bright light Charlie immediately fixed upon the man's deeply lined, craggy brown face. That face looked like the earth itself, as if it were baked and cracked; and Charlie thought for an instant that he was looking at some indecipherable road map of the man's past. He was wearing a woolen shirt over a white T-shirt that was torn at the neck, faded dungarees, worn boots, and a vest with lines of bright beads worked in geometrical patterns. "I meant no harm," the man said, extending his hand.

But Charlie wasn't going to shake hands with this overaged hippie until he found out exactly what he was doing here. Probably a goddamned tramp—he'd had trouble several years ago in his own building, what with the damn kids sneaking into the cellar and setting up house so they could fuck their brains out and smoke their pot.

The man lowered his hand and said, "I rented the furnished room down here." He turned his head slightly, indicating that he meant the room behind him, which Charlie had remodeled.

"Well, that room is *not* for rent, so you can just—"

"You're Charlie Saris, aren't you? The landlord told me I'd be meeting you. You're in charge of all the maintenance, right?"

"That's right," Charlie said, unmollified.

"I know all about the fire wall business," the man said. "The landlord told me all about it when he rented the room to me. At first he told me I couldn't rent it until the spring, when you turn the furnace off. But I told him I just needed a place to lay my head, and that if there's any trouble at all, I'll pick up and move the hell out and he can keep any leftover rent. It was a gentleman's agreement."

"Well . . ."

"Come on and have a drink in my room," the man said. "Nobody should have to drink alone and talk to himself."

"I wasn't talking to myself," Charlie insisted, embarrassed. "I've got work to do, and I'm *going* to check all this out with Mr Isaacs. This is all very irregular." But it's just the sort of thing that Stephen—or his father, for that matter—would do, Charlie told himself. Neither one could bear to give up a dollar.

"My name's John." Again he extended his hand to Charlie.

This man doesn't take no for an answer, Charlie thought. He shook hands with John and asked, "You got a last name?" John looked almost Asian, but that wasn't quite right: Charlie had seen enough gooks during the war. God forgive me, he thought, for his son was married to a little Vietnamese girl, and he, Charlie, was a grandfather, and sonovabitch if he shouldn't be struck dead by lightning for even thinking such a word.

But goddammit, the man did have that pushed-in kind of face. Maybe he was part Negro, or Phillippino . . .

"The name on my driver's license says 'John Stone.'"

Charlie laughed and said, "With a name like that I can understand why you talk to rocks." Then he followed John into the furnished room, which measured about nine by twelve. There were high, narrow windows on one wall, a stairway leading to the street above, a single bed, a desk and chair, and a curtained closet that Charlie had built. The ceiling squares were old and cracked and torn, but Charlie had tacked up the sagging ones and then painted the ceiling white, just as he had painted the floral-papered walls. It had certainly not cost Nathan or Stephen anything much for materials.

John sat down on the bed, which was covered with a beautiful star pattern quilt. He reached under the bed and pulled out a bottle of inexpensive Scotch. "Glasses on the desk."

Charlie sat down in the chair beside the desk. He couldn't

8

help but notice a rather large worn pouch trimmed with leather fringe on the desk; beside it was an Indian-style wooden pipe with a red stone bowl.

"I've known some Indian people," Charlie said.

"That so," John replied noncommittally.

"You're not from anywhere around here, are you?"

"Originally from South Dakota," John said. "But I live just about anywhere now." He chuckled.

"I mentioned knowing Indian people because of the pipe on the desk here," Charlie said, feeling uncomfortable . . . and curious.

"That's a social pipe," John said. "Supposed to be smoked with friends, it isn't a holy pipe. That's put away in the bag there."

"Ah," Charlie said, wondering if John was going to ask him to smoke the pipe. Might do him some good, smoking the peace pipe. But when John didn't say anything further, Charlie asked, "What do you smoke in them. Tobacco or something else?"

"I thought you said you know about Indian people," John said, a hint of sarcasm in his voice. "I don't smoke dope in them, if that's what you mean."

"No, that's not what I meant."

"Maybe you were thinking of *kinnickinnick*. Indian tobacco. That's what you probably meant."

"Sounds familiar, but it's been a long time, as I said."

"No, I smoke Bull Durham nowadays," John said. "Hard to get real Indian tobacco. In fact, it's hard to get Durham anymore, most of the stores don't sell it. Just that cheap-shit chewing tobacco. I'll tell you what I do like, though, I like a good cigar."

Charlie nodded, although cigar smoke made him gag. "I guess you don't smoke the pipes much then," he said, hinting.

"I won't smoke the sacred pipe when I'm drinking," John said. "And I don't even feel right about smoking the social pipe." He finished his drink and poured another round. "I'm all wrong

9

when I drink, like somebody who walks around backward all the time. I've got no business with anything holy, can you understand what I mean?"

Charlie nodded. "Goddamn straight, I understand."

John started laughing; it was a good, infectious laugh, and Charlie caught it easily. "And, man, I've been *wrong* for a good long time."

"Hallelujah," Charlie said. "Here's to being shitfaced wrong." They made a toast, and Charlie found himself talking about Joline and the kids and his whole goddamned life—about the three service stations he owned in Los Angeles when he was thirty-one years old, about his women and cars and the beautiful *Lady Lorelei*, a sailboat he had won in a crap game. ". . . I had a friend who owned the service station across the highway from mine, and we used to save our money until we each had a thousand dollars, and then we'd buy food and booze and take three or four girls out on the *Lorelei* and just stay on the water until the supplies were gone. Those days are gone . . . Jesus, are they.

"But, Jesus Christ, you know I can't really blame Joline or the kids. They don't want any more than they ought to have. They've got to have decent clothes, for Chrissakes. And we needed a new kitchen table, the leg kept falling off the old one. When I think of how I blew everything I had on fast broads and slow horses . . . and now I'm struggling just to buy my little girl a dress or buy a fucking second-hand pick-up truck. It just don't make sense . . . Well, my old Momma used to say 'There ain't no such thing as a second chance.' She sure was right about that."

"You know what my father used to call dollar bills?" John asked.

"What?"

"Green frogskins . . . when I left the family to see what the world looked like, he called me a fat-taker, a white man, one who chases the green frogskin. He was right, too, I suppose, although I think I was more interested in rodeo riding, pretty girls, and getting drunk; and I needed the frogskins to get the last two."

"Are you trying to tell me that Indians don't need money?" Charlie asked. He didn't like slurs about white people . . . or any people, for that matter.

"No . . . most do." John said something under his breath that Charlie couldn't hear, and there was an ugly tension in the air.

They drank in silence. Charlie listened to the cars swooshing by. An argument started outside The Trot Line, one of the neighborhood bars; and a woman was shouting and swearing at her husband who answered her back word for word as if he were an echo. Then everything was quiet again, and Charlie wondered about what kind of an argument he was going to get into with Joline when he came home. Christ, if he tried mimicking Joline, she would bite off his goddamn leg!

Suddenly there was a sharp rapping at the door, which was the outside entrance to John's room. The knocking was persistent.

"You wanna get that?" Charlie asked.

"Shush," John said, holding his finger to his lips.

"Well, it won't fucking stop."

"Yes, it will," John whispered. "I know who it is."

"John Stone," shouted a voice, "I know you're down there. It's Sam, and I need to talk to you." After a pause, the pounding started again. "Damn you, John, answer the goddamn door!"

Charlie looked at John, but John put his finger to his lips again.

"I'm vision-questing Saturday," the voice said. "And I need you there. You promised me that, remember? Damn you!"

Charlie could hear cleats clattering against pavement when the man finally walked away.

"You see," John said, taking another drink, "I told you it would stop."

"Who was it?"

"A friend of mine."

"What'd he want?" Charlie asked tentatively, knowing it was none of his business.

"Poor bastard has to vision-quest, just like he said. The spirits told him to do three days."

After a time, Charlie asked, "What's this . . . vision-quest?"

John laughed and said, "It's sitting naked with no booze or food on top of a hill and either freezing or sweating your ass off . . . It's what crazy fucking Indians do when they're not chasing frogskins."

"*What?*" Charlie asked.

John's tone and mood seemed to change suddenly. "It's sort of an Indian bar mitzvah . . . a coming-of-age, except traditional people usually vision-quest more than once in their lives. They do it when the spirits tell them to . . . or when they get lost and need to find themselves again. You vision-quest to find your name—your *real* name. You learn what you're supposed to do with your life, according to the wishes of the Creator. You find out where you come from. You talk to the spirits—or maybe they'll kill you. It's dangerous to have those kind of visions because they're real. They can come back and bite you. But it's only up on the hill that you find out who you really are."

"So what's he need you for?" Charlie asked.

John laughed. "To tell him what he saw." Then John put his glass on the floor and fell fast asleep on the bed, leaving Charlie to his thoughts and questions and memories and the street noise above. He thought about his daughter Stephie, who took after him. She was brash and sweet and big-boned like her mother, but she had Charlie's wildness. It was in the eyes, those cool gray defiant eyes. But she was a good girl, and she was his girl. When her appendix burst, and she almost died from peritonitis, she called for Charlie, and he lay beside her every day and night on the hospital bed that smelled like witch-hazel and combat-sweat.

He could smell witch-hazel and sweat right now—the very same acrid, sour odor—as he nodded forward into stupor ... into alcohol dreams and peace pipe visions; but he was wide awake and on his way home an hour later.

Joline didn't argue with Charlie when he got home. She had his favorite dinner on the table: shrimp chow mein. The chow mein came out of one of those large cans, and Charlie had bought a bag of frozen shrimp, the tiny ones, on sale at the supermarket last month. He preferred soft foods, as he had no teeth. He kept his dentures in a drawer under his socks. Although he looked nice with teeth, the damned things never did fit; and he wasn't going to be uncomfortable just to look pretty.

He ate like a trencherman, which he often did when he had been drinking. Joline made small talk, and had evidently told the children to stay out of his way because there was no rock-and-roll noise or pimply boyfriends wandering around, raiding the icebox, looking for handouts.

Charlie apologized to Joline for the harsh way he had spoken to her earlier and swore that he wasn't going on a binge. He had had a few beers, and that was it. Then he lay down on the couch and watched television. Joline joined him after cleaning up the kitchen, and they made love quietly right there under the blanket, and the children weren't the wiser.

He was gentle and tender and comforting. He was old enough to be her father, and strong enough to satisfy her; but he wouldn't leave the couch to come to bed with her afterward. He was choking again, and the wine and food had made him nauseated. He slept fitfully, coughing, breaking out in cold sweat, and dreamed about vision-questing on a hill.

But when he woke up, wheezing, in the morning darkness, he couldn't remember the dream.

2 .

SMOKING THE PIPE

"You've got to get up, Charlie, it's almost noon and Steve's on the phone, he says it's an emergency."

"How the hell would he know if there's an emergency?" Charlie asked, squinting up at Joline—he hadn't even napped for an hour and was still groggy. After all, he had been up coughing half the night. "He never budges off his ass to check anything. He's just like his goddamn father."

"Well, he's waiting on the phone," Joline said and walked out of the living room. She was still wearing her pink house dress; her natural blond hair was frizzy, as she hadn't brushed it yet.

Charlie answered the phone, which was on the wall in the kitchen. "Yeah?" he said, his voice slightly slurred. His mouth felt dry, and he felt the insistent tickle in his throat that always came before a coughing spell.

"Charlie," said the voice, "I've got a real problem and you're the only one who can take care of it."

"What's wrong?"

"I got a call from Leslie Becker on Union Street about the tenant downstairs."

"Cindy Kahn, she has the little baby," Charlie said. "A nice girl."

"Well, Leslie Becker said she heard a lot of noise last night, as if Cindy was moving, which was exactly what she was doing. The door was open, and Leslie looked inside, and Christ the place is a complete disaster. The woman was hysterical, so I drove over to take a look, and Jesus I couldn't believe what Cindy has done to that apartment. She was living in complete filth—feces on the walls, bugs crawling around—I couldn't believe it."

Joline brought Charlie a cup of coffee, which he poured into a saucer so that it would cool faster. "Hard to believe, her place always seemed tidy whenever I was there."

"Well, she must have gone over the deep end," Stephen said. "Leslie showed me where the kids must have slept . . . in garbage. I called Social Services—she was on welfare. Frankly, I'm afraid for her kids."

"I can understand that," Charlie said, taking a sip of coffee from the saucer.

"Well . . ." Stephen said, "we've got to do something. If the housing code people see that place, they'll close it up. And Leslie says something's got to be done right away or she's going to move. I promised her we'd take care of it."

"What about that new man you hired . . . Tom, I think that was his name. The one with the beard. Let him take care of it, he's been doing your work for you." Joline gave Charlie a nasty look and shook her head. "See if he can do the job first . . . if he can't, then maybe I can help you out."

There was a pause on the line, and then Stephen said, "Well, quite frankly, I'd feel better if *you* took care of it. If I give the job to him, he'll take three weeks on it, where you'd take three days."

"I am going to need someone to give me a hand," Charlie said. "I can't do the heavy work and lifting like I used to." He felt the tickle again, which erupted into a wheezing cough. He quickly handed the phone to Joline who told Steve to wait a second, and Charlie hacked and coughed and finally spat into the green bag inside the plastic garbage can. Joline handed the phone back to him. "If you can get Tom over to meet me, I'll try to get over there and see what has to be done."

"I won't be able to get ahold of him until Thursday . . . the asshole's gone to his cottage at the lake."

"I've been trying to tell you all along," Charlie said, "none of them guys gives a shit about you or the operation. And I don't *like* that Tom, anyway. Thinks he knows everything, and he don't know shit."

"You know, I rented the basement room that you fixed up to an Indian guy. He told me if I had any work to just ask him. He needs the work. Maybe you can train him. Can you help me out?"

"I met him yesterday," Charlie said, interested. He was curious about that vision-quest or whatever you call-it business, and he suddenly remembered that he had dreamed about John Stone having a vision on a hill. In that dream a bunch of goddamned buffalo or steers or *something* jumped right out of John Stone's vision and came right down the hill after Charlie. Just thinking about it scared the hell out of him.

"Well . . . ?"

"If I can get my rust-bucket started, I'll pick him up later and have a look," Charlie said. "But remember, I'm doing this just to help you out." And Charlie gave the phone to Joline to hang up.

It was another warm and sunny day, and all the neighbors were out bustling around. Charlie always felt better when the sun was out; he felt younger and his autumnal depression seemed to fall away. Joline acted differently, too; Christ, they'd made love last night for the first time in weeks. Maybe she was learning . . . finally. If she just wouldn't constantly grate on him about taking a drink once in a while, he wouldn't drink—except for maybe a beer here or there.

Some of the neighbor kids were playing on the rusting swing-set that Charlie had erected on the back lot. He waved hello to everyone and then got into his car, which started without any trouble. It was the warm weather. The choke was defective, and on most cold days Charlie had to stick a screwdriver into it to get the car started.

It was a good day for a ride … even a good day to work, although he dreaded what he was going to find on Union Street.

He found John sitting on the metal steps that led up to Nathan's office. Stephen had already talked to John, who was ready and waiting. He had on the same clothes he had worn yesterday, and he held a soft white and blue rolled-up blanket on his lap. It was thick and obviously wrapped around something.

"I stopped being wrong today," John said as he got into Charlie's rusting, four-door Plymouth. Charlie looked perplexed. "You know," John continued, and then he raised his hand to his mouth as if he were drinking from an invisible bottle.

Charlie laughed and said, defensively, "Well, I only have a few beers once in a while, anyway."

"Aha," John said, turning away from Charlie to look out the window. "I figure I owe it to Sam—the guy who was knocking his brains out at the door last night—to help him with his ceremony." After a pause, John asked, "Did you have any trouble last night when you got home? You seemed worried about the wife."

"No trouble," Charlie said curtly. "Everything's fine." Goddamn nosy Indian.

"You know, I think I like you better when you're *wrong*," John said, chuckling.

"We've got work to do. It's not going to seem so funny once we get into that shitbox apartment," Charlie said. He remembered most everything he had told John last night, and he was embarrassed about it today. He had talked too fucking much, and to a total stranger, who was getting off on it. He'd lost face, and Charlie felt certain this Indian was going to continue busting his balls about it. "Which reminds me, we've got to stop at the supermarket and pick up trash-bags and cleaning material."

17

Charlie made no mention of the rolled blanket on John's lap. Maybe he carries his goddamn lunch in a blanket . . .

Charlie parked the car in the dirt driveway of 71 Union Street. The two-family house was an eyesore: flaking blue paint, a front yard devoid of grass, and the porch itself had settled differently from the rest of the house. The front door was open, its glass broken-out.

"Jesus Christ," Charlie said as they entered the first floor hallway. The stink was overpowering. Upstairs a door opened and Leslie Becker, a short, dark woman in her mid-forties, peered downstairs. "Charlie," she said, "you've got to do something. I can't stand the smell."

"Don't worry, darling," Charlie said. "Charlie's here and everything's going to be taken care of. This place is going to be good as new."

"You haven't been inside yet," Leslie said, and then softly closed her door.

"Let's go inside," Charlie said to John.

It was worse than Charlie had ever imagined. In all his years with the Isaacs' family, he had never seen such filth. There was garbage everywhere, and the floors, which he had painted white last year, were gray and grimy. There were rags strewn about and unwashed clothes, and Steve was right, she had somehow brought in cockroaches. John followed Charlie into the kitchen, where the stink was the worst. The bathroom door was open—the bathroom was off the kitchen—and Charlie could see that indeed feces had been smeared on the wall behind the john. Used sanitary napkins were strewn around the floor as well as toilet paper. But it was the kitchen that made him sick. The smell of rotting food and mold combined with sour milk and old dirty diapers. The odor was overwhelmingly sweet. Charlie tried to get to the sink, only to find that it was completely covered—filled with mold. He gagged and ran out of the apartment for some fresh air. Outside, on the porch, he thought he was going to throw up, but he just coughed. He finally had to use the inhaler.

John, who had followed him out, said, "Maybe this is a job for professional cleaners or something."

"I *am* a professional," Charlie insisted. "And I've seen worse than this, you can bet on that. Now let's get the windows and doors open and start hauling out the trash. Tomorrow's garbage day, thank Christ."

It was hard work, and Charlie had lost too much strength to the booze; at least that's what he blamed it on. He was getting too old for this kind of manual work, and although he would readily admit it to his family and friends, he could never admit it to himself.

John, however, worked like a steam-shovel. He didn't mind getting filthy dirty, and he remained cheerful, regaling Charlie with stories of his rodeo days and old girl friends and about how he used to get himself liquored-up and walk around backwards for days on end, as if he were a *heyoka*, a crazy person. When he couldn't stand his wife and job and kids and neighbors—when he became so depressed that everything seemed to take on shadows—then he'd become *heyoka*. Although he was just playing at being crazy, no one believed him, and he was humored and given the respect due the contrary, or sacred clown. Then everyone else would take over his responsibilities for a while, and would even cover for him at work.

"Now that's the way to do it," John said. He demonstrated for Charlie by carrying out the garbage bags backwards and walking backwards up the stairs to Leslie's apartment and, standing with his back to Leslie, asking her if he could wash up and have a glass of water. Charlie shouted for him to stop acting crazy and tried to explain it all to Leslie, who thought that his explanation was even funnier than John's antics.

She invited them into her apartment "for good strong coffee and sugar cookies."

After they washed, they sat down in her large, tidy kitchen. John complimented Leslie on her coffee and cookies, apologized for smelling like a goat, and then went on talking to Charlie. "It didn't usually take but a few days of walking backwards and getting drunk and being contrary and talking nonsense before I'd begin to feel better. Nothing like being crazy to make you sane . . . and vice versa, as they say. The one thing I didn't like about playing *heyoka* was after that I'd have to stay sane for a while and work like a white man."

"What kind of work do you do?" Leslie asked, topping up his coffee. Charlie could see right away that Leslie liked this Indian . . . she wasn't a bad looking woman, and he certainly had her schmoozed. He hadn't lied about having a way with the women, Charlie thought a little jealously.

Of course, John didn't tell Leslie about his whoring around the country as a rodeo clown and rider; instead, he told her that he had worked as a railroad brakeman and was a fair to middling electrician.

Well, that might come in handy for the firm, Charlie thought, forgetting once again that the firm could go fuck itself.

They went back to work, and now that a good portion of the debris had been cleared out of the downstairs apartment and put into bags and boxes which lined the curb, John seemed to sniff about, going from one room to another, hesitating, as if in mid-step, as if he were listening to something, or someone. Charlie washed down the bathroom with liberal amounts of ammonia and cleanser, and his hands tingled and his throat burned, although he didn't do more than cough and sneeze a few times. Under the filth in the sink, tub, and toilet were the inevitable lime scales; the water was very hard in these parts.

"What the hell are you doing?" Charlie asked, slightly out of breath from the exertion of scrubbing and bending over the tub. He watched John, who was just standing in the kitchen.

"This is a very sad place, and will be for a while, even after we clean it up and paint it," John replied, coming into the bathroom, which was long and narrow. He took a wire brush and began to clean the toilet vigorously. "The woman who lived here, what was her name?"

"Cindy . . . Cindy Kahn," Charlie said.

"This Cindy went down very hard, fighting."

"What the hell are you talking about?" Charlie sat on his haunches beside the tub, his arms resting on his knees.

"What did she do . . . for a living?" John asked.

"As far as I know she was on welfare. Her husband left her with two babies, she's a housewife, and I think Steve told me that she wrote songs. I think some singer or another actually sang them on her records. Steve seemed excited about that, but he's always excited about something."

"The things won," John said matter-of-factly. "It's a wonder that she didn't kill her kids."

"It makes you wonder, by the looks of this place . . ." Charlie stood up; his legs felt numb from crouching. God forbid those little children should be harmed, he thought.

"I think the kids are probably all right," John said, leaving the bathroom to walk aimlessly around the kitchen.

"How the hell do *you* know?" Charlie asked, feeling suddenly angry. All this mumbo-jumbo crap. "And why would she want to kill them anyway, even if she was crazy?"

"See this?" John asked, kicking some broken bits of plastic away from the molding on the filthy hardwood floor. "Everything we took out was broken. She broke everything. It wouldn't've taken much for her to think that her children were things too."

Charlie laughed a bit too hard and said, "You are one crazy fucker."

But that didn't break John's mood. He walked into the living room, surveying.

"We've got work to do," Charlie said, but their work day was over, and he knew it as soon as he had spoken. They had broken the back of today's work and were tired . . . and damned if John wasn't right about this place. It made him feel depressed, unfocused somehow, and he wondered what Cindy was doing right now . . . if she hadn't done herself in. That wasn't impossible. Or was she breaking up another apartment . . . or maybe she was up on the hill in the sanitarium? He'd have to talk to Stephen, make sure he had called the proper authorities so the children wouldn't be abused.

"Hey . . . Charlie," John said after a time, waking Charlie from his reverie. "You want to smoke the pipe?"

"You mean the peace pipe?"

John laughed.

"Well, I told you it's been a long time since I . . . smoked the pipe, I was a kid . . . what's so funny?"

"Nothing," John said as they walked out to the car.

It only took about five minutes to get into the country. They drove along a winding old state road that cut through autumn colored trees; goldenrod, red clusters of sumac, and tiny blue asters grew wild on both sides of the cracked and patched macadam. They stopped the car and walked into the woods, where John pointed out a good place to smoke the pipe: a copse of white elm surrounded by thickets and pine. The elms were tall and still held most of their crisp orange and red and gold leaves, but there were bare spots where wind had blown away the leaves to reveal skeletal branches interlocked like witch's fingers. In contrast, the pine trees were full and green, oblivious to the seasons.

John spread out his star blanket in front of a large, double-trunked elm, which he called "the Chief" of the elms, and sat down on the edge of the blanket. He motioned to Charlie to sit down. Then he connected the red pipestone bowl of the pipe to its wooden stem and waved a smoking piece of braided hay called sweetgrass over the pipe, tobacco, and a large beat-up eagle feather. Using the feather as a fan, he waved the smoke around Charlie and himself. The smell was earthy, and delicious.

After he filled the pipe, he stood up and lit it. Then he prayed, smoking, and facing in the four directions.

"To the East where the Sun rises.

"To the North where the cold comes from.

"To the South where the light comes from.

"To the West where the sun sets.

"To our Grandfather the sun.

"To our Grandmother the earth."

Then John sat down and conversed with the Great Spirit as easily and as comfortably as if he were talking to Charlie. He seemed to be praying for everyone and everything, even the birds and the bugs.

He prayed for Charlie's emphysema. He prayed for his own family and everyone he had wronged. He prayed for his enemies. He prayed for strength and asked for pity. His knuckles whitened as he held the bowl of the pipe tightly with both hands, as if trying to keep it from flying up into the sky like an arrow.

Charlie found himself staring up into a clear, crisp, cloudless sky. Leaves fell from the trees. A breeze tickled his face and ruffled his hair. He shivered, feeling the autumn chill, and took a long, deep breath. It was as if he were a balloon floating upward, drifting through the sky, expanding into pure, cold daylight. Charlie had never thought much about God; in fact, he didn't really know if he believed in Him. But he felt something here and now ... something that breathed power and truth. It was as if Charlie could feel everything the earth felt. But he still couldn't say if he really believed. He knew one thing, though. He wasn't ever going to find God in a goddamn church where he couldn't do anything but sit still and sing psalms and listen to the preacher who got to do all the talking and praying. How the hell are you supposed to find God when you're wearing a goddamn suit and tie and pretending your shit don't stink? Charlie asked himself.

Charlie wasn't paying attention to John's prayers. He was practicing his own. In his mind, these prayers were perfection itself. He was Billy Graham talking to the sky and the sun and the trees . . . and the whole world was listening, absorbing his words like light.

But when John handed the pipe to him, Charlie forgot everything he had planned to say. He was nervous just holding this old stone and wooden pipe now that the pressure to pray was upon him. It wasn't easy just to sit here and recite like a minister. "Do I have to pray out loud?" he asked John after trying once again to form a prayer that would sound good.

"Whatever makes you comfortable," John said, distracted. He glanced upwards as if he were surreptitiously searching for something in the sky. Then, turning to Charlie, he said, "Either way, the Creator will hear you."

Charlie closed his eyes and intoned what he could remember of the Lord's Prayer. He thought about his family and felt the warmth of the sun on his face and arms and smelled the lingering sweetgrass and sage that John had burned and sprinkled as offerings . . . and he wondered what the hell he was doing here in the middle of nowhere praying with an Indian over a peace pipe. But nevertheless for these few moments he felt at peace. He opened his eyes, as if just waking up from a trance, and John lit the pipe for him.

When they were finished smoking, John prayed over the pipe and cleaned it and put it away. Charlie helped him roll up the blanket and they both sat with their backs against the double-trunked elm. Charlie remembered feeling this good once before after he had gone to a public steam bath in California. That was some thirty-odd years ago, he thought. But right now he felt as if he were twenty years old again. He felt strong as a bull. As long as he didn't move his old bones too much . . .

Suddenly, unexpectedly, Charlie burst out laughing. It had just occurred to him that maybe praying was like sweating.

"What's funny?" John asked.

"Nothing . . . I dunno," Charlie replied, embarrassed.

"That sometimes happens after praying. I knew a guy once who couldn't stop laughing after he ceremonied. Said that once he washed all the shit out of his mind, everything would look funny as hell. Poor bastard would also get the giggles at funerals. Said the spirits of the dead did it just to piss everyone off. I wonder if he's still alive . . . haven't seen him for years."

"I guess it's something like that," Charlie said and, unable to control himself, he started laughing again.

"I guess it is," John said, glancing upward. He seemed nervous about something.

"What's the matter?" Charlie asked, having regained his composure.

"Nothing. Why?"

"Because you keep looking at the sky . . . as if you're looking for something."

"Are you *sure* you're not Indian?" John asked, smiling sadly. Then after a pause he said, "I was looking for eagles."

"I don't see any," Charlie said, craning his neck.

"You won't," John said, standing up. As they walked to the car, John explained that he had been given the gift of eagles when he became a medicine man.

"I didn't know you were a medicine man," Charlie said.

"I haven't been for a while. Booze and medicine don't mix."

"What'd you do when you were a medicine man?" Charlie asked.

"Same things I do now, mostly . . . except for the drinking, and I used to help people out."

"How do you mean?"

"Just help out."

"Like curing sick people?" Charlie asked as he unlocked the car door for John and then walked around to the driver's side.

"Sometimes," John said, getting inside the car.

After Charlie turned the car around in the road, he asked, "You mean you give people herbs and stuff like that or do you dance around and . . . I'm sorry, I didn't mean no disrespect."

"None taken."

"Is that what you carry inside that little bag on your belt— your herbs and medicine?" Charlie asked.

John laughed and said, "Yeah, something like that." Then he lit a cigar. Charlie coughed, but didn't say anything; John opened his window. "You should smoke a good cigar once in a while," John said. "A good cigar has no filling, none of that artificial crap like those cigarettes of yours."

"They make me choke," Charlie said, swallowing hard. The breeze from John's open window felt cold on Charlie's neck.

"That's in your mind . . . all in your mind." After a long pause John said, "If I ever get the eagles back, I'll show you some stuff about medicine. Even water if it's treated right can be medicine."

"What do the eagles have to do with anything?" Charlie asked.

"They're my medicine."

"What the hell does that mean?" Charlie asked, curious, even though he knew that John was full of shit. Turning water into medicine . . . what bullshit. Christ he's not.

"You're thinking bad thoughts again," John said.

"What?" Charlie asked.

"Your face wrinkles up like a goddamn prune when you're thinking bad things, and every time you make that prune face you say something nasty."

"I wasn't thinking about *anything*, and you're out of your fucking mind."

"See what I mean?" John said. When Charlie didn't laugh, John said that he'd lost the gift when he'd started drinking. "I always went on binges," John continued. "My downfall was always the booze and the broads—"

"Hallelujah."

"—but I'd pray my ass off and try to be right and sooner or later the eagles would come back, I'd look up and there'd always be one or two just circling around, way the fuck up, and, man, those eagles would keep me on the straight path, keep me good, until I just couldn't stand being right and I'd get fucked up and leave all my responsibilities behind. I've been paying for that ever since."

"I still don't understand any of that stuff," Charlie said. They were back in the city now, and it was difficult to concentrate and drive in the traffic at the same time. "I'm not disrespectful to any man's religion, but it sounds crazy as hell to me. You mean wherever you go there's eagles flying around . . . even in the city?"

"I've seen them in the city . . . once. It was my first time in New York, and I was scared shitless of all those cars and concrete and people. One of the people I was with—we went to do some politics and ceremonies—pointed up to the sky, and sure as shit there was an eagle making a circle over one of those skyscrapers. I wasn't afraid to be in that city anymore . . . I mean I was no more afraid than the next guy."

Charlie just shook his head. "I'll believe it when I see it."

"Maybe when we do a sweat . . . maybe one will fly into the sweat lodge and bite your pecker off," John said. "Then would you believe?"

Charlie laughed. "Yeah, I guess then I'd believe it."

When Charlie pulled up to the office building, beside the private entranceway to John's room, John just sat and stared out the window.

"I'll pick you up early tomorrow," Charlie said. "We're not nearly done with Union Street. And I think that crazy broad upstairs likes you . . ."

John didn't answer for a time, and then he said, "You told me you had a dream about vision-questing."

"Yeah, I dreamed something . . ."

"My friend is vision-questing this weekend, the one who knocked on the door. You want to go with me?"

Before he even had time to consider it, Charlie heard himself say, "I'll go, what the hell. I'll do anything once."

"Might be dangerous," John said. "Sweating your ass off in the sweat-lodge with a bunch of crazy fucking Indians that don't even like white people and those eagles flying around, going for your pecker."

"Don't you worry about me," Charlie said. "I'm a bull . . . but what the hell do you want me there for? I'm not an Indian."

"You're a friend, that's enough," John said. He got out of the car, but before he closed the door he said, "One other thing, Charlie. Don't touch any booze until after the ceremony. No matter what happens. It's important."

Charlie nodded and drove off. He was feeling just fine, not even a tickle in his throat. This could be counted as a good day . . . even if there were no fucking eagles in the sky.

3 .

HOW THE LAWS WORK

Charlie didn't have to be a medicine man or a nuclear physicist to understand how the world worked. He had figured out a few natural laws by himself. Although he didn't have much education beyond the fifth grade (except for the time he'd spent in the *Andrew Jackson Second School Library* when he was a sanitation engineer and night watchman), he'd been around and done pretty near everything a man could do in a lifetime.

Charlie's First Law was that, good or bad, everything always happens in "threes". So once you started the karma in motion (he had learned that word from his son) by, say, breaking a leg, then you had to expect two more disasters to follow. Of course, they might be *little* disasters . . . His mother had always told him that, but he never took her word for it. (When he was young, he never took anybody's word for anything.) Like everything else, he had to find out for himself.

The Second Law was that you pay for any happiness with a double helping of grief. He'd learned that law from his dear friend Nick Aristoxenos, who had lost his beautiful blond twin daughters in an automobile accident on their birthday. Charlie had gotten a call from Nick's wife that Nick was going to do away with himself unless Charlie could come and help him, so Charlie took the train to New York City and spent the weekend with the family. Twice Nick had tried to shoot himself. It was when Charlie got Nick drunk that Nick stood up and told Charlie the Second Law as if he were Moses on the mount.

Of course, Nick got it wrong because he was so upset. He exaggerated and said that for every day of happiness, you get four days of grief. But what could you expect from a man who just lost almost everything he loved in the world?

The Third Law everyone learns too late. Charlie's mother had tried to tell him, just as Charlie had tried to tell his son Louis: You get only one shot at success. If you screw that up, then you're finished. Now, of course, Charlie had read and heard about people who had failed once or twice and then made their money, but they didn't count because they hadn't really made it yet. What counts is once you lost it, then can you make it? And you just can't, no matter what anybody tells you. And those people in the stock market who lose all their money and then regain it don't count either. That's gambling, and different rules apply.

Charlie was the perfect example of the Third Law. He'd had his service stations and money and a good reputation, and he lost the whole thing by gambling and whoring and being a nice guy and giving his money away to every Tom, Dick, and Harry. Charlie had tried to have a man-to-man discussion with his son last year; he told him the story of his life in the hope that Louis wouldn't have to make the same stupid mistakes as his father. That was when Louis was thinking about quitting the Navy. Charlie told him not to quit, that civilian life was shit . . . but, of course, Louis wasn't hearing any of it. Charlie had been a Marine, and in a way he couldn't blame Louis for wanting to get out of the Navy—it sure as hell didn't have the history or the respect of the Marines.

So Louis got a discharge on account of having back pains, and then he scraped around the west coast and saw other women and now he's divorcing his wife.

He'll pay for that, sure as shit, Charlie thought. But as he hadn't really ever "made it" yet, he still had his one big chance with the Third Law . . . if he didn't fuck up like his father.

Charlie was still paying his dues . . .

He knew there was bad news as soon as he got home.

Joline had prepared spaghetti and meatballs, and was sitting at the kitchen table waiting for him. His baby Katherine, who was seven years old, was in the living room watching "Mash", and his two older daughters must be at the YWCA or something because the house was quiet. Christ, he hated that rock-and-roll crap. Joline listened to country all day, and he could hardly stand that.

"Where's the children, Momma?" Charlie asked, after he kissed Joline.

"Anne's in her bedroom, and Stephie's over at a friend's working on a school project . . . the baby's watching TV, *but she's going to go to bed right after her show's over*," Joline said, raising her voice so Katherine could hear her.

Charlie showered and shaved the stubble on his face, then came out to eat. He didn't care for spaghetti, but Joline didn't know that. The kids loved spaghetti, and they were harder than hell to please, so Charlie pretended that he loved it too. The damn kids wouldn't eat fish of any kind, nor anything that smacked of being outré, such as Chinese or Mexican, which were Charlie's favorites . . . as well as stews and spices, which the kids wouldn't eat either.

At least spaghetti was easy to chew without teeth . . .

After he finished eating, Joline brought out a chocolate pie, his favorite, and coffee. After the coffee cooled down so Charlie could drink it, he said, "Now tell me what's the matter."

Joline looked tired, although it was obvious that she had bathed and dressed before Charlie came home. Her hair was loose, the way he liked it, and she wore a touch of rouge and lipstick . . . Charlie liked to think of her as his little girl, the awkward but pretty teenager he had married. He could remember the first time he saw her, as if it were yesterday. He had lost his gas stations and had drifted east, when he found her working in a country store, which also functioned as a post office, in Davenport Center, New York. She was wearing pegged jeans and a white blouse. Her face was full and smooth, except for a pimple on her chin, and her hair looked just as it did now. She used too much lipstick and make-up then to suit Charlie's taste, and she looked her age—seventeen. But he remembered how he had wanted to kiss her full mouth and fondle her large breasts. He had felt the heat in his crotch that first time he saw her, never mind that he was twenty-two years her senior and robbing the cradle. They made love that afternoon; two weeks later they were married.

All told, it had been a good marriage, Charlie thought. Joline was a good woman, loyal as the day is long. Goddamn it takes something to be able to live with me all these years . . .

"Why do you think anything's the matter?" Joline asked.

"Because the house is quiet, the phone's not ringing off the hook with boyfriends, and the rock-and-roll crap isn't on full blast . . . and the pie is a dead give-away."

"It's Stephie," Joline said.

"Well . . . ? Did she break up with Joey? Christ, I figure that that wasn't long in coming. We shouldn't have ever let her get engaged, she's not even out of high school and she's engaged."

"She is a senior, and they're in love, and he's going to college . . ."

"Well, if they're still lovey-dovey, then what is it?" Charlie asked.

Joline turned to fuss with a pan on the stove; in a quiet voice she said, "Stephanie's pregnant."

"She's *what?*" Charlie asked. "Jesus fucking Christ Almighty!"

"Watch your damn mouth and lower your voice, your daughter is in the next room."

"This is *my* house and I'll say whatever I goddamn please. Why didn't you tell me about Stephanie before?" But Charlie didn't give Joline a chance to answer. "I'm going to break her ass when she comes home, the little slut. God *damn* her!" Charlie struck the table with his fist, spilling his coffee.

"You're going to do no such thing," Joline said. "You're her father, you should be wanting to help her."

"—And that fucking little wimp of a boyfriend of hers, that eighteen-year-old snotfaced bastard, I'm going to punch his pimply face in.

"Christ, Stephanie's not even of age, I'm going to have him put in fucking *jail* for raping my daughter." Charlie had worked himself up to the verge of tears. That little bastard had violated his daughter . . . and would pay for it dearly.

"Stop it!" Joline said. "Or you'll start coughing again." But it was too late, for Charlie was already hacking, the veins on his forehead standing out. Joline pulled the plastic garbage can over to him, and while he coughed and spat, she wiped the table and poured him another cup of coffee. "Okay, Kathy," she said loudly, "it's time to get washed up and go to bed." Kathy had obviously heard every word her parents had said and seemed delighted. She didn't even argue about bedtime, nor did Joline make her wash up and clean her teeth. It was sufficient for her to kiss Daddy and disappear.

When Charlie finished coughing and spitting and caught his breath, he said, "Christ, we don't even know who knocked her up, for all we know—"

"Just stop it right there," Joline said. "You know better than that. She's in love with Joey, and what she did was natural, no different from what *we* did, and she wouldn't've got pregnant if . . ."

"If what?"

"Nothing," Joline said.

"I want to know what you started to say, and you fucking well better tell me."

"Don't talk to me like that, I'm your wife."

"What were you going to say?" Charlie asked in a gentler voice.

"We didn't tell you because we thought you'd only get upset," Joline said, sitting down at the table beside Charlie. "Stephanie's on the pill, has been for a few months."

"She's *what*?"

"She came to me with her problem," Joline said. "She said she loved him and couldn't wait any longer, and I took her to the doctor to get the pill so she *wouldn't* get pregnant."

"Well, she did get pregnant, didn't she. You had no right to sneak around my back . . . and how the hell did she get knocked up if she was taking the pill?"

"Remember when she was sick and had to stay home from school? I think she vomited one of her pills . . . that had to be it."

"She's sixteen years old," Charlie said, "and you're getting her pills so she can fuck her boyfriend. Damn you! You should have told *me*!"

"What would you have done?" Joline asked.

"*I* would have told *you* . . . and I certainly wouldn't have told her it was okay to screw Joey, that little sonovabitch. I would have kept her home where she belongs."

"You couldn't watch her all the time."

"I'd tan her ass if I thought she had those ideas in her head."

"And she would have run away . . . like you did when you were a kid. Is that what you want for your daughter?"

Charlie had stopped shaking enough to take a sip of his coffee, which was cold. "That was different . . . Pop was . . . it was just different." He stared into his coffee cup for a time, thinking about Pop. Goddamn if he, Charlie, still wasn't angry at him, after all these years. Charlie had caught him cheating with a whore, caught him right in the act. Pop tried to explain that it hadn't meant anything, but Charlie was young and raw and couldn't, or wouldn't, forgive him. Later, during a particularly nasty family argument, of which there were many, Charlie lost his temper and accused his father of being a whoremaster ... accused him in front of Charlie's mother, who cried right there at the dinner table. Pop ordered Charlie out of the house. He left that night, and never came back. That was the last time he ever saw his father, who died two years later. His mother blamed *him* for his father's premature death. It wasn't right, but he never could shake the guilt, which had been slowly eating away at him over all these years. He never heard from any of his brothers, either; they probably blame me for killing Dad, too ...

"What the hell are we going to do now?" Charlie asked. But he wasn't talking to Joline; he was talking to himself. "The damage is already done. I suppose she could get an abortion, they're legal, but that's no way for her to start out her life. She's a baby ..."

"You just shut your mouth about an abortion, Charlie Sarris," Joline said. "I don't believe I'm hearing this from you ... what the hell's gotten into your head? It's bad enough she's pregnant, now you want her to have the baby killed?" That caught Charlie, and he started coughing again. She gave him a new cup of coffee and waited for the coughing to subside. Then she said, "Stephie's a good girl. She's going to have a proper wedding and have her baby ... and you're going to be a grandfather again."

"Yeah, I've got two granddaughters in San Diego that I'll never see again because my son was too busy screwing around with—"

"Watch your mouth ... and lower your voice," Joline said. "The girls don't have to know about their brother's business, for God's sake. And they can hear every word we say."

"Stephanie's too young to get married," Charlie insisted. But he had already lost the argument, even though he felt that right was on his side. How could he have even let it enter his mind that

Stephanie should get an abortion? Yet he had said it aloud. He would pay for that, too, he thought, ashamed of himself.

"I wasn't much older than Stephie when I married you," Joline said. "And I didn't see my parents for five years after that, remember? Is that what *you* want?"

"What the hell are they going to live on . . . love?" Charlie asked. "Well, that little bastard Joey is just going to have to forget about college and get himself a real job and support his family . . . that's what I fucking had to do."

"Jesus, you've got a foul mouth . . . and Joey won't have to do any such thing. His parents know all about it and they agree—"

"They *what*? Does everybody know what's going on around here but *me*?"

"—And they're going to help the kids out so Joey can get his education," Joline continued. "In the meantime, Stephie can stay home, so you'll get to enjoy your granddaughter, or grandson, whichever it is."

"I don't care what they think they're going to do, I'm not taking any goddamn handouts from anybody, much less Joey's parents." Charlie stood up. He felt shaky, and his face was burning. "What the hell am I around here, just the fucking asshole who puts bread on the table, that's who! But I might as well be invisible. *You* might just as well wear the pants in this family and I can get the hell out of here right now." Charlie wanted to shut himself down, close off his anger as if it were gas leaking from a pipe, take Joline and Stephanie in his arms and comfort them . . . he wanted to be the man, the father; but the part of him that had been angry all his life had taken over. As it always did.

"Charlie . . . for Christ's sake," Joline said, but she didn't approach him, not when he was this angry. "I just did what I thought was right . . . it all happened so fast."

"Yeah, but it was slow enough for you all to make plans without *me*," Charlie said. He had been right about everything in the first place, he told himself. And if Joline and Stephanie hadn't snuck around behind his back, Stephanie wouldn't be pregnant right now.

"Look, honey, I'm telling you everything now, it's—"

"It's too fucking late is what it is," and Charlie stormed out of the apartment, slamming the door behind him.

He needed a drink, and he didn't feel like walking all over Hell's half-acre because it looked like rain, so he took the car, which he had trouble starting. Maybe there was something wrong with the starter, too.

Goddamn laws are taking over again, he told himself as he drove to the office. He felt helpless. A few drops of rain spattered on the windshield, and the wipers squeaked and made a long smear out of a tiny speck of birdshit. He had paid dearly for having a good time smoking that peace pipe and being with nature. Maybe Nick Aristoxenos was right, after all. Maybe you did pay four-fold for any joy. One thing he was certain of though: he'd be paying out some more. The violation of his daughter was just the first bad thing; there would be two more to follow.

At least she wouldn't be having the baby out of wedlock. That was something. But Joey was such a little asshole. Charlie dreamed of beating the crap out of him.

He went through the office and then down into the cellar to have a drink, but John caught him. It was as if he was waiting . . .

Charlie certainly wasn't going to tell John *why* he needed a drink. That was none of the Indian's goddamn business. All Charlie could do was try to explain the immutability of the Laws to John, but John wasn't having any of it. Charlie had promised not to drink until after the vision-quest, and that was that. A man's only as good as his word. The Indian bastard was using Jewish guilt on him . . . it was emotional blackmail.

"You'll see," John promised, "after you've ceremonied and been in the sweat-lodge, you won't need the booze."

After talking and smoking the pipe in John's room, Charlie left . . . sober. He was as strong as he wanted to be. He didn't need any goddamn crutches. He was the head of his household, and goddammit he was going to take control. *He* wore the pants in his family, not Joline. He had no one but himself to blame for what had happened. He had let things slip away from him. It must have been the booze and the emphysema and being so depressed and frustrated. That wreaks havoc with a man's life. But no more. He would handle his family and the Laws.

Maybe even beat them . . .

When he returned home—the night chill was giving him a sore throat and making his lungs ache—he found Joline and Stephanie and Joey sitting at the kitchen table having coffee and pie. They were surprised to see him, and Joey was so frightened that he wouldn't look Charlie straight in the eye. He was a good-looking boy, small and dark with curly black hair and dimples. But he was too short for Stephanie, who was big like her mother, and had her mother's wide fine-featured face and high cheekbones and pug nose. Stephanie wore her thick, coarse, blond hair cropped short and she used too much make-up, especially lipstick. Still . . . she was beautiful just the same, and Joey, that little wop bastard, just wasn't right for her. Just looking at Joey infuriated Charlie. How could a daughter of his even think about screwing such a little turd?

And Stephanie looked so *smug* . . . like a little goddamn whore.

But Charlie was under control. Maybe smoking that peace pipe and being holy did help. He nodded to everyone to assure them who was boss and told Joey that he, Charlie, could take care of his own family, thank you, and neither he nor his daughter nor his wife would accept any charity from anyone. Joline quickly asked him if he wanted coffee or something to eat, but Charlie saw her glance at Stephanie and Joey, as if they were all holding another secret from him.

Charlie got up from the table, grunted, "Nah," and left the room. He looked in on the baby, Kathy, who was playing *hearts* on her bed with Anne, and kissed them both goodnight. Anne was thirteen and sonovabitch if she hadn't already turned into a woman. Next thing, the baby would start growing tits.

Well, there wasn't anything he could do about that.

If he couldn't get blind drunk or punch out that little bastard Joey or slap the smugness out of Stephanie's face, he could at least get a good night's sleep.

Charlie dreamed that he was inside the sweat-lodge with John and eagles were devouring them, tearing off pieces of flesh and flapping their wings, blasting Charlie with waves of dry searing air. He woke up coughing at five o'clock in the morning and got out of bed without rousing Joline, who was snoring. He never showered in the morning, but washed his face and shaved. He didn't have to pick up John to work on Union Street until after nine. This part of the morning was going to be for himself alone. He didn't want to see Joline or the family. He just wanted to get into the car and be driving in the hills when the sun came high. He'd grab a coffee and eggs at the Open Doors, his favorite all-night diner. He'd read the morning paper and watch the men coming and going. He'd talk to the waitress and clean up his own table, which was a privilege reserved for old patrons; but he'd leave a quarter tip anyway. It was going to be a perfect morning away from all the emotional noise of his family. He was in effect sneaking out of the house, just as he used to do when he was a boy and would get up early to eat with the workers at the nearby factory.

But, of course, his car was dead.

He put a screwdriver in the choke to hold it open, as it was chilly out this morning. He tinkered, bitched, and became more and more frustrated, even though he understood that it was just the First Law working itself out, and there wasn't a goddamned thing he could do about it but accept it. He had always thought that the Laws went easier on you if you accepted them. His son had told him that that was the Way of the Cow, or something like that, but he'd known about it before. Goddamn, for someone without too much education, he knew more than most people gave him credit for.

His whole morning was foiled, and he couldn't accept it with equanimity . . . and he *wasn't* going to go back upstairs and face Joline. What he needed was a truck. This shitbox of a car had had it. At least Charlie had enough money to buy a new starter, which would alleviate his problem for the time being. He could take a bus to the parts store and eat at the diner on the way. But the store wouldn't open until 9:30. He could kill an hour and a half in the diner reading the paper and watching the weirdoes and maybe walk around a bit, depending on how he was feeling.

So he walked to the diner, sat down in a side booth, ordered eggs easy over with bacon and home fries, read the paper, watched everybody coming and going, and couldn't relax for a moment. The day was dead, and the times he had planned for himself, his *precious* few fucking minutes, were violated just as sure as his daughter had been. In some deep way which he had no words to describe, he was as upset about his car, about his time being stolen, as he was about Stephanie. He could rationalize that what happened to Stephanie was what was supposed to happen: he just didn't approve of the dumb sonovabitch she had chosen to do it with. But time was something different. He lost some of it with every hacking cough, with every day spent cleaning up shit for the firm, with every moment listening to Joline complain about how he was a lousy provider, a terrible father, a half-a-man; Jesus Christ, he couldn't even *drink* like a man anymore. He got drunk as quickly as a giddy schoolgirl.

As he looked around the room, he thought: What I need is a strange piece of ass. I haven't touched a woman other than Joline in . . . Jesus, it must be twenty years. Charlie, you're an asshole, he told himself. He didn't know why he thought of getting laid just now: there wasn't a woman in the place, except for Carol, the waitress. But she wasn't his type—too willowy, fragile, and she had that frizzy hair that made her look like a Negro . . . not that he had anything against Negroes.

He could have walked down Main Street and told John that he couldn't pick him up until later; but he didn't want to wake the man if he was sleeping, and he just didn't feel like seeing John and making small talk and making explanations. John would probably want to accompany him to the store and tell him stories about the old days and how the Indians lived and that sort of crap while he, Charlie, worked on the car. He couldn't work with people blathering on around him, and even though it was fucked up, this was still *his* time. At least he could have his own company and some quiet. Maybe the day wouldn't be so bad after all, if he could keep everyone away from him. Anyway, he was going to see John all day tomorrow at the ceremony.

He was having second thoughts about that, too. All that mumbo-jumbo. What the fuck had possessed him even to want to smoke the peace pipe, much less join in John's ceremonies? Christ, he could *die* in that sweat-lodge. With his lungs, how was he supposed to stand all that heat? Yet the whole idea fascinated Charlie. He wanted to see this stuff for himself, and to do that he'd have to fix the car. If he had his druthers, he'd let the junkbox rot until Joline relented so he could buy a decent truck. If the family could tighten its belt for just a little while, he could get a truck and find work and then nobody would want for nothing.

He took the bus to Binghamton, the next town, and bought the starter. He took the bus back and started to work on the car without going up to the apartment. He just didn't feel like talking. Was that such a goddamn crime?

But Joline called out to him every few minutes, checking on him, asking him if he was ready yet for coffee, or what he thought about this and what he thought about that. Although Anne and Stephanie were at school, Kathy, the baby, kept coming downstairs to play on the swing and beg Daddy to push her just for a little bit. She had a virus . . . a chronic condition, and Joline kept her back from school. If she's too goddamn sick to go to school, then she should be too goddamn sick to be playing outside, Charlie thought. But he kept it to himself. It wasn't worth a fight, and Joline would pull some sort of shit out of the hat so she'd win anyway.

Charlie could never say "no" to Kathy, who was quite well spoken for a seven year old; she was spoiled, but not whiny. So every time she came downstairs, he would push her back and forth on the swing and play house and carry her around for a bit. Then he'd tell her that Daddy had to go back to work. Although she was an arrogant little thing, she was the only one left who couldn't infringe on Charlie's special time. After all, Charlie's purpose in life was to take care of his wife and children. But Stephanie and Anne were almost women. They are women, he grudgingly conceded. He would do anything in the world for them, but they stole his time every bit as much as Joline did . . . maybe *because* they were women.

He installed the starter and checked the engine; but when he tried to start the car, there was just a clicking noise. The fucker was still dead. The First Law had won again, only this time Charlie wasn't going to fight it. He was going to go upstairs and have coffee. He would let the car sit until hell froze over.

Even as he walked up the back porch stairs—which needed to be repaired and painted, as they had some dry-rot—the phone rang.

Charlie hesitated, but it was too late. His nextdoor neighbor Clifford, who smelled bad and looked filthy (he had a crossed eye and wore wrinkled green pants held up with suspenders as if he were imitating a clown) opened his screen door and proffered advice on repairing Charlie's car.

Another county heard from!

Stephen never should have rented to the likes of Clifford. He sold his food stamps every month for beer money and encouraged his children to steal checks from the mailboxes downstairs. He had filled his apartment with so many rags and dirty clothes hung on makeshift clotheslines that you could barely walk through it. Charlie had told Clifford repeatedly to remove all his junk and clean up the filth, but it was like talking to a wall. And all Stephen and his father cared about was the rent. After all, the apartment was already ruined. They'd fix it after Clifford left, if he ever left. They had nothing to lose, the Jew-bastards! And Charlie couldn't do one fucking thing about it.

He ignored Clifford and walked through to his own back door, hoping that the call might be for Joline. But Joline was waiting for him and holding the phone. "It's Stephen," she said. "He says it's important that he speak to you." She covered the mouthpiece of the handset and said, "He sounds really upset."

"Tell him I'm downstairs . . . or in the john," Charlie said. He couldn't deal with Stephen right now; if Charlie called him back later, then he, Charlie, would be in control.

"I already told him you were coming right up," Joline said. She held the phone out to him as if it were an offering.

"*Sonovabitch*," Charlie mumbled and took the receiver. "Yeah."

"Jesus Christ, Charlie, where the hell have you been?" Stephen asked. "You *promised* me you'd take care of Union Street, and Leslie called and said you hadn't been there today at all and Jesus, the Board of Health called me and they talked to her, and they're going to condemn the building unless we take care of it *immediately.*" He sounded out of breath.

"Well, what the hell am I supposed to do?" Charlie asked. "I'm only one person, and my car is dead, and I've spent the whole goddamn morning going back and forth on the bus to get parts and trying to fix the goddamn thing. So it's going to be a while. I can't do shit without a car. I told you that something like this could happen, which is why I didn't want to take on the goddamn job in the first place. I told you that, remember? Now maybe you just ought to find some professional somewhere to just take care of it and—"

"Look, Charlie, cut the bullshit, will you please? I don't mean to sound upset, but I'm right up against the wall. I can't get anyone else . . . I'd need more time, and then they'd probably only fuck it up anyhow. Look, I'll lend you my car, if you need it. It's the company car anyway . . . how long will it take you to get the job done, do you think?"

"Jesus, you're just like your father, always thinking that everything can be finished in five minutes."

"Don't talk to the man like that," Joline said. "Keep a civil tongue in your head."

Charlie glared at Joline and then said to Stephen, "I don't know how long it's going to take. We got some of the crap out of there, but it's a holy mess, you ought to know that, you've seen it."

"I know, I know," Stephen said impatiently. "But the Code cited us, too. They're going crazy about the shit on the walls and the bugs, and they say that the garbage has to be cleaned up."

"Well, we got what we could out of there yesterday, we can only do what we can . . ."

"I know you're doing your best," Stephen said, but Charlie never fell for that appeasement bullshit, especially when Stephen talked to him in that I-really-understand-you tone of voice. "Well," Stephen continued, "they want the stuff around the yard cleaned up, too. And they want the shit off the walls and the garbage out of the house and out from around the house by tomorrow or I'm going to be in real trouble. If the newspaper gets hold of this, it's going to be terrible . . ."

"You'd need a team of able-bodied men to clean that shithole up by tomorrow," Charlie said. "You'd better face that fact."

"Well, if they see we're doing *something*, I think it'll be all right. Christ, they're threatening me with the newspaper, can you beat that?"

"That's the name of the game," Charlie said, thinking about his car and his daughter. Fuck Stephen! he thought.

"Can you try and get to it today?"

"Jesus, use your ears, man. I don't have transportation."

"I told you I'll leave you my car. I'm at the office now. I'll leave the keys on the top of the desk. All I can ask is that you try."

"How are you getting home?" Charlie asked.

"Don't worry about that, but, please, get started on it today. Okay?"

"I'll do the best I can," Charlie said firmly. "But Jesus it seems that I'm always putting my own work aside . . . and what do I ever get in return but a kick in the ass."

"Look, I can't help what happened between you and Dad, but you should know that I—"

"Yeah, yeah, I know," Charlie said. "I'll be talking to you," and he hung up the phone. Two peas in a pod, Charlie thought. Like father like son. And the little bastard couldn't even be bothered to come to my home and talk to me like a man. No, he'd leave the car at the office.

"So . . . what are you going to do?" Joline asked.

"I'm going to have my coffee, and then I'm going to lie down. There isn't anything that can't wait until tomorrow."

Joline was about to say something to him, but she checked herself.

Charlie took a sip of his coffee. Although it was a totally fucked up day, he didn't feel half-bad. He was going to take his time. He was in control. He was going to go to bed and think about that vision-quest and the sweat-lodge.

He would make a decision about that tomorrow.

In the meantime, everybody could just go to hell . . .

4.

BAD MEDICINE

Never one to give up easily, Charlie worked on his car the next morning. But it was no use—it was probably that bargain-priced, cheap-jack, reconditioned carburetor he had bought last month. So he walked over to the office after lunch to pick up John, and they took Stephen's late-model Chevrolet—the company car—to Union Street.

John didn't ask Charlie any questions. He seemed distracted, although he worked hard and methodically, and Charlie approved. They decided not to bother cleaning the bedroom walls—there were too many large holes to be patched. Better simply to tear them out and put up new wallboard. Charlie and John became used to the sickly-sweet, putrid odor of garbage and feces and mold, and Charlie had even stopped coughing. Soon he forgot about his car and his family. He liked the rhythm of work, the directness. When no one was distracting him, it was pure. Even working in shit was better than thinking and worrying.

John came into the living room and said, "The vision-quest is going to start in a couple of hours. We'll sweat, and then Sam will go up on the hill. Just before sundown. The purification sweat, it's a hot one. Hotter than a regular sweat. Anyway, I want to be up there early in case anyone wants me to take flesh. Are you going up with me or not?"

John climbed down from the stepladder. He had been removing the foam-plastic squares of the drop-ceiling. Although most people didn't know it, you could spray-paint them, and they'd look like new.

"Well . . . ?"

"I've been thinking about it," Charlie said, brushing dust and particles out of his hair. "I just don't know about my lungs . . . my emphysema. I don't know if I could breathe in there with the heat. Other than that, I'm strong as a bull."

"Don't worry," John said. "The spirits will take care of you. You won't die, I promise."

Charlie laughed and said, "I wasn't worried about *dying*, but I don't want to be responsible for screwing up your prayers and things."

"Well, then let's go. It can wait until after the weekend." John looked up at the ceiling, indicating that he meant the work on the apartment.

"I don't feel right taking Steve's car," Charlie said. "He loaned it to me to get his work done, and, Christ, we ain't been here for more than an hour."

"It's been longer than that, my friend—and you didn't pick me up until eleven-thirty."

"I still don't feel right about the car . . ."

"Well, I've got to get over there, one way or another," John said. "If you want to, we can just leave the car here and try to hitch a ride."

"How far is it?"

"I dunno, couple of miles in the country . . . good for your lungs."

Charlie had done enough for the firm in the last ten years. It could at least give him a free ride in the country.

They drove east on the main highway, and John read the directions from a wrinkled piece of lined yellow paper. It was an unseasonably warm day—close to 70 degrees—and Charlie and John had rolled down their windows to let in the warm, fragrant air. Ripe milkweed lined the highway. Their pods had already exploded, and the wind carried their plumed seeds, which looked like tiny, spidery parachutes. "I've been here once before," John said, "so I'll remember the house."

"Is it your friend's house?"

"Sam's aunt and uncle own it, it's a farm, and Sam is sort of living there now."

"How do you come to know him?"

"Sam came to learn some things from me," John said. "He was hoping to become a medicine man."

"Is he?"

"Never quite came around that way. Like most of us, he got sidetracked. Fell in with some kinds of people."

"What do you mean?" Charlie asked, as he drove uphill on a winding road. There were trees on both sides of the road. This was good country, gnarly and wild, and, although close to the city, thinly populated.

"He got medicine things mixed up with human things," John said. "All the people he was with were blaming everything on bad medicine instead of on themselves. When anything bad happened, they thought that somebody had done something to them."

"What do you mean?" Charlie asked.

"They blamed everything on sorcery."

"Do you believe in that crap?"

"Sorcery's real," John said flatly, quietly. "Medicine is just there, it can be used in good ways or bad ways. But I think that Sam just got himself messed up. He came out west for a sun dance, and stayed with me for almost a year. He started to become a pretty good sweat-lodge man, but he wanted to go too fast, he wasn't ready to be a healer, and I thought he should work and learn from someone younger for a while. So I sent him to study with a Sioux guy I know who lives down south . . . Joseph Whiteshirt. He's a young medicine man with a good talent. Anyway, Sam needed to study in a different place. Different places have different medicine, different powers. Well . . . he ended up screwing the guy's wife and almost got himself a knife in the belly for that. Was a lot of bad blood between Sam and Whiteshirt . . . maybe some bad medicine, too. Anyway, Whiteshirt blamed me for what happened with Sam and his wife. He thought I put Sam up to it or something. Everybody got sick . . . I guess I was responsible. When they needed help, I was drinking and didn't have any power to help anybody, including myself. But that's no excuse . . ."

"Why would he think you put Sam up to screwing his wife?" Charlie asked. "That sounds pretty off-the-wall, if you ask me."

"I slept with his wife once, too," John said matter-of-factly. "It was before he had married her, of course, but he must be still holding it against me, just the same. I guess I hurt his ego—he figured I was an old man taking advantage of a young girl. I guess he was right. But she was a pretty thing then. Women always seem to get me into trouble. Sam's the same way I am. And Whiteshirt, he's a little bit crazy. Always been that way. That's where his power comes from."

"If he's crazy, then why'd you send Sam to him?" Charlie asked.

"I said he's only a little bit crazy. And Sam needed to learn what Whiteshirt had to teach. Whiteshirt has considerable power. He's a strong medicine man. That's a rare and sacred thing."

"So where's this Whiteshirt now?" Charlie asked. The whole thing seemed fucked up to him.

"He's at Sam's . . . so is his wife, they got back together."

"What?"

"There's still a lot of bad blood," John said, "but Whiteshirt has to help Sam out on his vision-quest whether he likes Sam or not . . . if he's a real medicine man. Maybe doing some ceremonies together will help them all out."

"What about you?" Charlie asked.

"Maybe it'll help me out, too," John said, smiling faintly. "But then again maybe the ceremonies won't change Sam and Whiteshirt and the other people mixed up in this, maybe their hearts will stay hard. You'd better start slowing down now," he said as Charlie came upon a sharp curve in the road.

On Charlie's side of the car were hayfields stretching back to smooth, fir-covered hills. The fields were mottled green and brown. An old cannibalized mowing machine was rusting in the middle of one of the fields. On the other side of the road, on John's side, were a few modern, expensive houses owned by executives who worked in town, but they were outnumbered by farms and the ever-present country shacks, their front yards littered with old car hulks and ancient appliances, their porches filled with mildewed mattresses and torn couches and broken cabinets.

"There's the house," John said, pointing. It was red clapboard, set about fifty feet from the road. Behind it on higher ground was a dilapidated red barn and several storage sheds. The sheds were unpainted, and one was caving in.

Charlie pulled into the driveway, behind a green Ford truck, which had a poster in the rear-view window proclaiming that it was an Official Indian Car. On the back of the truck was painted AKWESASNE in large block letters.

"What the hell does that mean?" Charlie asked.

"It's a Mohawk reservation, not far from here," John said. "It got invaded, you might say, by white folk . . . poachers, and the Indian people had it out with the state police. Sam was there, so was Whiteshirt. But there ain't no more poachers."

"What about you?" Charlie asked.

"I was home getting blind." Then, after a beat, John said, "There might be people here who are really against me . . . do you still want to come?"

"Christ, I'm already *here*."

"Anyway, you don't believe in any of the superstitious nonsense like we were talking about, do you?" John asked, grinning, his demeanor suddenly changed, as if he had just put on a mask, or taken one off.

"You're fucking crazy," Charlie said.

They crossed the road and cut across a field, passing the rusting mowing machine. On the western edge of the field was woodland. They walked through the woods on a springy covering of red and yellow leaves. The woods opened into a clearing. John thought that the warm weather was a good sign for Sam's vision-quest, as Sam wouldn't have to freeze his ass off on a hill. But Charlie was getting nervous about the whole thing, especially when he saw the sharp decline they would have to negotiate if they were going to get over to the lowland on the other side.

"What the hell do I look like, a stunt man?" Charlie asked, as he looked at the riverbed below. A thin ribbon of water was flowing.

"Just follow me, it's not nearly as bad as it looks." John started climbing down, holding onto a branch, gaining a foothold, then taking a step and grabbing another branch or rock or outcropping.

Someone appeared on the other side, a man in his late twenties with jet-black shoulder-length hair. He waved up at John, and Charlie knew it was too late to turn back. He had his pride, after all.

The climb down wasn't bad, although Charlie's heart seemed to be pounding in his throat.

"Charlie, this is Sam Starts-to-Dance," John said when Charlie crossed the stream.

He doesn't *look* like an Indian, Charlie thought as he shook hands with Sam. Sam's features were fine and thin, almost Nordic; but he wore a beaded shirt and a headband . . . and he did have that black hair.

"I'm glad you came," Sam said to John, as they all stepped over riverbed stones onto a well-worn path that wound up a gentle incline. "I didn't think you were going to make it. I knocked on your door a day or so ago, but nobody answered."

"I told you I'd be here," John said flatly.

They talked, and Charlie followed a few steps behind. He was angry and nervous and embarrassed. What the fuck was he *doing* here? Christ, even John was ignoring him, after making that big deal about needing a friend to go along with him. The asshole . . .

"We got the sweat-lodge ready," Sam said, "and the women went and got the meat; they're preparing it now. Are you going to take flesh?"

"Didn't Whiteshirt take flesh?" John asked. He stopped walking just before they reached the crest of the hill.

"He said he thought it was proper for you to do that."

John nodded. "That's good . . . how are things going? Still bad blood?"

"Whiteshirt's doing what he's supposed to," Sam said. "He's helping me to do this thing. But it feels very bad between us. Most of the people that were with him at his camp have left. He's got new people now, too many Wannabees."

"What's that?" Charlie asked. Fuck them, he thought. If he was here, he wasn't going to be invisible. He could just as well turn around right now and go home if they gave him any shit.

But John laughed. "A Wannabee is a white who wants to be an Indian." Charlie felt his face grow hot. "You certainly don't have to worry about *that*," John said.

"Anyway," Sam said, "I hear that there's some bad stuff going down there at Whiteshirt's place."

"Is he back together with Janet?" John asked.

"Yeah, she's here with him. She's taking care of the other women."

"Well . . . that's good."

"She did a lot of sweats, and vision-quested, and the spirits told her to stay with Whiteshirt and help him out. That's what she says. But it's over between us. Even though she says she doesn't love Whiteshirt, what we did was wrong. It was my fault, and you were right, it was a human thing."

"Happens," John said. "Maybe it can be put behind all of you."

"But I still think something's going on."

"Bad blood doesn't mean there has to be bad medicine," John said.

Sam didn't say anything; he looked down at the ground. Then he said, "Janet told me some things . . . that Whiteshirt blames you for what happened. He thinks you sent me to him to bring him trouble."

"Why would he think that?" John asked.

"He says the spirits told him that you were using bad medicine on him because you'd lost your power . . . because you'd stopped being a medicine man. He thinks *you're* a witch." After an awkward pause, Sam said, "I think Whiteshirt's still jealous of you."

"Why?"

"Because most people come to see you when they have problems, even when you're drinking . . . most traditional Indian people don't have much respect for Whiteshirt. They call him a white man's medicine man."

"Maybe we'll talk about that" John said, "or pray about it."

"I think you should be very careful, anyway," Sam said. "Whiteshirt's changed. He's not the man you used to know. I think it's because of Violet."

"Who?" John asked.

"He's been living with a white woman who was always hanging around his camp. She likes to play mind-games on everybody. She thinks she's an Indian."

"How'd she get her hooks into Whiteshirt?"

"She hung around him," Sam said. "Made herself useful. She's got power over men; she always used to have somebody or another fighting over her. And Whiteshirt—he's like you—he sometimes has trouble saying no to women. He likes them too much."

"I don't know anything about that," John said, looking uncomfortable.

"She's dangerous," Sam continued. "She knows that Whiteshirt's got a strong power, and she wants to use it . . . or take it for herself."

"What about Janet?"

Sam shrugged. "He's made her eat enough dirt for what we did. She's been having to wait on them both hand and foot like a maid. She's doing it . . . because the spirits told her to stay with him."

"Whiteshirt may have his problems, but I've never known him to be sadistic or mean . . ." John said, as if thinking out loud. "I'm going to think right about him until I see otherwise."

"I'm glad you're here," Sam said. "It's going to be right for me now, I can *feel* it."

"Well, we're soon going to find out," John said; and then he turned to Charlie and asked, "You know how Sam got his name?" John had put on another one of his masks and switched moods. "He touched a rock in the sweat-lodge once and jumped around so much that he got a new name."

"It certainly beats being called Sam Smith," Sam said, and then he went on ahead to let everyone know John was here and going to take flesh.

"Sam likes you, I can tell," John said.

"How can you tell that?" Charlie asked.

"You think he'd talk like that if he didn't? You can feel right about Sam."

"What's this taking flesh business?" Charlie asked. And what the hell am I getting myself into? he asked himself.

"You got that bad face on again," John said. "You don't have to come along on this, I told you. If you're worried and—"

"Just tell me about this flesh business. What do you do, cut somebody up?" Charlie had already committed himself, and he was going to see this thing through, no matter what. He was a man of honor, goddammit, and he had fought in the goddamn war. Of course, he wouldn't just stand by and watch someone get mutilated . . .

"It's a ceremony," John said. "It's a kind of prayer, a gift . . . the only thing we really have to give of our own is our flesh. That's the only thing that's really ours. So everyone who wants to make a gift for Sam, that he should have a good vision-quest and find what he's looking for, everyone gives a little of himself. I usually take flesh off the arm, with a razor and a needle. I don't carve out steaks, if that's what you think."

"Are you going to do this to yourself, too?"

"I might have Whiteshirt take my flesh after Sam's vision-quest is over . . . if everything is okay. But not now, people might think I was following my ego and not my heart. After the vision-quest is a good time to do that; also, there'll be lots of food, Indian food . . . a good time. You'll see . . . maybe I'll even take flesh from *you*."

"The hell you will," Charlie said, and they walked down the hill toward the ceremonial grounds below. Charlie glanced up at the sky; there were certainly enough goddamn birds flapping around up there. Maybe some of those were John's eagles, swooping around, waiting for John to get to be a medicine man again. Christ, who the fuck knew *what* could be going on around here?

"Lot's of birds flying up there," John said matter-of-factly. He didn't tell Charlie that none of them were eagles.

John introduced Charlie to several people, one of whom was white: a young guy with shoulder-length dirty-blond hair who was wearing a headband, faded dungarees, and a T-shirt. He asked Charlie if he wanted to smoke his pipe. Charlie politely declined and sat down under a large oak to watch John take flesh from the men and women standing around him.

Although he felt awkward and out of his depth, Charlie could not help but be awed by this place. As it was in a hollow, it seemed to be completely secluded. The surrounding banks were covered with trees, and there was a moist, earthen smell that reminded Charlie of caves he had explored when he was a boy. The sun filtered through branch and leaf, giving the place a dusty, soft, almost magical quality. Charlie felt somehow secure here ... and it seemed quiet, even though children were shouting and playing games and running around on the blanket of leaves that covered the open ceremonial area, and men and women and adolescents were all busy doing something: attending the large fire, which would heat the rocks for the sweat-lodge; tearing pieces of cloth; carrying stones and blankets; or just sitting around talking in huddled groups, passing pipes back and forth.

But sitting under that tree, feeling the cool dampness of the ground, smelling grass and sage and the burning of the fire, Charlie felt as he had when he smoked the pipe with John.

He watched John, who was talking to a young woman wearing a sleeveless flower-patterned blouse. She had curly black hair and looked Mexican. She held John's pipe in both hands upon her lap and stared at it. Her mouth moved. She must be praying, Charlie thought. Then John began making lines down her arm with a razor blade. He gave her a yellow piece of cloth to hold in her palm, and began to remove tiny pieces of her flesh with a needle. She didn't flinch as John cut her, and Charlie noticed that she had scar-lines from previous cuttings—just as John did. Charlie had never noticed that before. Both of John's arms were scarred. Neat little indentations. Pieces of flesh removed. They made Charlie think of tattoos.

To Charlie's right, about thirty feet away from him, was the sweat-lodge, a small, squat, round frame of willow shoots covered with old blankets. Charlie wondered how the hell anybody was going to fit in there. A woman with soft frizzy red hair was piling up blankets and tarpaulins beside the lodge. She seemed to know when Charlie was watching her, for she turned around. Although she was pretty—rather pale and petite—she looked arrogant and hard-faced. There was also something very erotic about her. But she stared Charlie down as if she knew who he was . . . as if she hated him.

Charlie looked away from her.

About ten feet east of the sweat-lodge several men were attending a large, crackling fire, which had been prepared in a special way under the supervision of a scowling heavy-set man. Rocks for the sweat-lodge had been placed on the fire. "These rocks should be just about ready now," one of the men shouted to John, who nodded.

The heavy-set man squatted close to the fire and squinted at the rocks, as if he was reading the entrails of some sacred beast. The woman who had been piling blankets shouted something to him, and he looked at Charlie for an instant, then returned his gaze to the fire.

Charlie had a coughing fit. Maybe it was the smoke from the fire, which the wind wafted toward him, or pollen, but he felt as if he was going to cough his lungs out. He used the inhaler, but his hand was shaking so much that it took two squirts before he could feel the mist in his throat and then the tickle as he inhaled it. But he couldn't get any *air*. Jesus Christ, he thought, I can't buy the fucking farm right *now*, not *here*. Jesus Christ . . .

It subsided, as they all did, but, Christ, that was a bad one. Suddenly Charlie realized that someone was touching his arm, rubbing his back. He looked up, right into a woman's face: a dark, flat face, high cheekbones, large dark almond eyes, and a thin mouth. She was missing a tooth, but there was a feral beauty about her; it was as if she, like John, had come from the earth. She carried a different map etched across her face, but the lines were there, even though she looked to be only in her mid-thirties. There were laugh-lines and worry-lines on that face, which looked like it had never been touched by make-up. There was also a smell to her, the smell of the fire mixed with perspiration, a perfume like grass and mud, sweet and sour. She couldn't have been more than five feet tall. "Take some of this," she said, giving him a sprig of sage. "Cup it right in your hand and hold it over your mouth after you cough. It'll help you breathe easier. Use it in the sweat-lodge, too. You breathe through it like this"—and she showed him—"so you won't feel the heat so bad. It really helps."

"Thanks," Charlie said. He smelled the sage—and it did smell good—but his coughing spell was over, anyway. He turned away from her to spit.

"You came with John, didn't you?" she asked.

"Yeah . . . although I feel like a fish out of water."

She chuckled. "I'm Janet, Joe Whiteshirt's wife. This is a good place, been some good ceremonies here, good feelings, before . . . before a lot of things turned sour and people's hearts became hard to each other. But John is a good man . . . and so was . . . is Joe. Maybe Sam's vision-quest will bring them close again. I know Sam told you about . . . us. He likes you."

"That's what John told me," Charlie said, "but you couldn't prove anything by me. He hasn't said anything to me—he was talking to John."

"Before a vision-quest is a quiet time, you're not supposed to talk much or mingle around. A vision-quest is dangerous. Sam's getting ready. Sometimes people who go up on the hill don't come back . . . people have been known to just disappear."

More bullshit, Charlie thought. "Do you believe that?" he asked.

"Yes," Janet said. "I do." She smiled wistfully. "But you don't have to." She paused. "Hasn't John told you anything about this?"

"Yeah, he told me a little," Charlie said, feeling awkward. "I never felt right about pushing, though."

"I can see why he likes you. I once heard John tell Joe that we're like trees, all of us. But when you look at a tree, you only see the trunk and branches and leaves; but deep down in the roots is where we take our life from, that's where the dreams and visions are . . . that's where our life *comes* from. That's why we vision-quest . . . to go back to the roots . . . and don't you worry while you're in the sweat, no matter how hot it gets. Just keep some sage in front of your nose and pray. Everyone will take care of you. No matter what's between John and Joe, neither one will let any harm come to you." But she averted her eyes from his when she said that, as if she wanted to believe it, but somehow couldn't.

"Which one is your husband?" Charlie asked.

"The big one, tending the rocks on the fire."

Charlie looked towards the fire and saw Whiteshirt, the same heavyset man he had seen before. Whiteshirt had a large belly and huge arms. His shoulder-length hair was coarse and black, except for a streak of gray that fell across the side of his taut face; and for an instant, when their eyes met, Charlie felt a chill feather up his spine. The man seemed to be looking right through him.

"Those rocks have to be hot for the sweat-lodge; they glow like coals," Janet said.

Then there was a loud crack—an explosion—and something smashed into the tree just above Charlie. Charlie and Janet jumped out of the way. A glowing shard of rock fell from the tree onto the leaf-covered ground close to where Charlie had been sitting. The leaves under the rock began to smolder.

"It's those damn river rocks," Janet said apologetically as she kicked the rock over to a bare patch of ground. "They explode sometimes like that. The next time—if there is a next time—we're going to bring our own rocks."

But Charlie had the uneasy feeling that Whiteshirt had somehow *willed* that rock to explode . . . as surely and as certainly as if he had fired a warning shot from a pistol.

The women brought out bowls of raw heart and raw liver. Everyone took a piece, even the children. When it was Charlie's turn, John said, "Eat just a little. It's good for you, give you strength." Then John bit down on a large piece of liver.

Charlie had eaten raw fish before . . . but raw meat? That was disgusting.

John handed him a piece of meat—one that was rather smaller than the one that he, John, had eaten—and Charlie had no choice but to take it. He wasn't going to lose face over a piece of meat. If the goddamn little kids can eat it, than so can I, he told himself as he ate a piece of the chewy, slippery meat quickly. He didn't know whether he was eating heart or liver. He just hoped he wouldn't gag. God only knows what kind of germs are crawling around on this meat, he thought. He'd probably get food poisoning from it, or develop worms . . .

It was time to go into the sweat. The willow-stick skeleton of the lodge had been covered with old blankets and large tarpaulins.

John and Charlie took off their clothes behind a tree and left them in a pile. Charlie hadn't brought a towel or blanket for himself, but John got one for him. They walked around the sweat-lodge, careful not to walk between the altar and the lodge. The altar was a mound of dirt set back from the opening of the sweat-lodge; the ceremonial pipes were propped against it. John told Charlie to wait, that Janet—who was keeping the door, as he called it—would tell him when to enter. Then John crawled in through the low, narrow opening, and said, "*Pila miya*, thank you." Whiteshirt crawled in after him, but not before giving Charlie a look of pure hatred. It was as if he and the red-haired woman hated Charlie just because he was with John. But the others would no doubt interpret it simply as Whiteshirt's dislike for honkies. Two young whites and two Indians, who looked like brothers, followed Whiteshirt into the sweat-lodge.

Charlie stood back, feeling anxious and also foolish wrapped in a blanket and holding the sprig of sage that Janet had given him. He didn't want to sweat . . . not with Whiteshirt in there.

Sam walked over to Charlie and said, "Come on, your turn next." Then he smiled and said, "Don't worry, it'll be a good sweat, good ceremony. Jim and Larry, they're brothers, they know some old songs, and John, he's one of the best sweat-lodge men around. He says you and he are a lot alike." Sam laughed. "Both fucked up."

Charlie forced a smile and crawled into the sweat-lodge, trying not to crawl on his blanket and trying to keep it around his waist. Sage and sweetgrass had been scattered over the earthen floor, and their fragrant smell was overpowering. He already felt claustrophobic, even though the door of the lodge was still open, letting in some light. But he felt locked-in—the blankets and tarpaulins and willow sticks of the sweat-lodge might as well have been made of steel. He could hear the women standing and chatting outside. They would listen to the prayers and watch for the eagles to dive out of the sky into the top of the sweat-lodge.

"Did John ever tell you about his eagles?" Sam asked Charlie in a whisper. He was sitting on John's right. "Those eagles can really be something. We've had them right here inside the sweat-lodge . . ."

Charlie grunted something back to Sam and asked himself, What the hell am I doing here? He sat back against one of the willows, but the sweat-lodge was so small that he couldn't sit up straight. He looked at John, who looked back at him, but didn't say a word; then he looked at Whiteshirt, who was gazing into the pit in the center of the sweat-lodge, where the rocks would be placed. Everyone sat with his legs crossed, but even then, toes were almost touching the pit. Charlie would have to watch himself, lest he burn his feet.

There was a tension in here, palpable, growing stronger. Charlie felt a pressure on his eyes, and he looked up. He caught Whiteshirt glowering at him. Whiteshirt averted his eyes and stared once again into the pit.

But Charlie was certain that Whiteshirt was going to make trouble . . . for all of them. He felt the hair on the back of his neck rise. It was too late to get out now.

"Okay," John said, "let me have a small rock," and Janet handed in a glowing coal on the end of a shovel. John used a forked stick to push it into the hole. He asked for his pipe, which he purified over the coal. He sprinkled sweetgrass on the rock, and the sweetgrass sparkled like fireflies. Charlie was nervous, his heart beating fast, and he hoped he wouldn't start coughing. But he was going to do this thing . . . no matter what.

John passed the pipe around, and everyone made a prayer. Charlie just asked that he get out of here alive. Then John asked for more rocks, and Janet brought in a shovelful. John took a large rock and placed it in the center of the hole with his stick, and said "*Ho Tunkashila*," which everyone repeated . . . everyone except Whiteshirt, who seemed to be praying on his own, as if *he* had to purify the lodge himself, as if *John* was making them impure. But John ignored Whiteshirt and scraped the rocks from the shovel. Charlie could feel the heat already, and then John said, "Okay, close the door," and everything was darkness, except for the reddish glowing rocks. Every bit of light was blotted out, for the women outside stamped down the blankets wherever the men saw any light.

"Aha," John said, "we thank the rock people, the rock nation, for these good rocks which are sacred, we pray they will not break and kill us in the darkness. It is from your sacred breath, the breath of life, that we inhale, so that our people will live. Oh, rocks, you have no eyes, no ears, and you cannot walk, yet you are life itself, alive as we are."

Then John explained the ceremony. He talked about how the *Inipi*, the sweat-bath, was probably the oldest ceremony in Indian religion. "The steam brings friends and families and even enemies together. It heals. It is the strongest medicine. The sweat is a way to make ourselves pure, and it gives us much of our power. No matter what the ceremony—sun dance or vision-quest—we do this first. It binds us. Even though Sam here is going to vision-quest alone on the hill, we all sweat with him now. We pray together and suffer together. We'll help him now, and he'll remember when he's alone on the hill tonight facing the dreams and spirits." Everyone agreed, and there was much yea-ing in the darkness. Only Whiteshirt was silent.

John prayed to the Grandfathers and the Four Directions. He prayed to *Wakan-Tanka*, he prayed for the two-leggeds and four-leggeds and wingeds and everything else on the earth, but he also seemed to be talking to God as if He were a presence in the sweat-lodge. He prayed for everyone in the sweat-lodge, for Charlie who he said was walking a different path, yet they were all walking together . . . whatever the hell that meant, Charlie thought.

But in the blackness, you couldn't tell if you were cramped in a small space, or whether you were somehow suspended in eternity.

Charlie felt as if everything was being pushed up right against him, yet paradoxically, he had no sense of breadth or width or height here. He felt dizzy. He could hear the others beside him . . . he could smell them. It was already getting too hot. It was difficult to breathe. Oh God, don't make me start coughing now, Charlie prayed. He stared at the glowing rocks, and heard the water swishing in the bucket as John stirred it with the dipper . . . and he *felt* Whiteshirt's glowering presence, even though he couldn't see him in the dark. He felt that same pressure against his eyes and knew that Whiteshirt was watching him.

It was then that Charlie realized how frightened he was.

John prayed, but Whiteshirt was praying louder, trying to drown him out.

John poured a dipperful of water onto the rocks.

The exploding steam sounded like a gun being fired. Suddenly, Charlie couldn't breathe. He was screaming, bending forward to get away from the searing steam. Everyone was shouting, "*Hi-ye, Pilamaya,* thank you, thank you," and Charlie found himself shouting, too, but he didn't know what he was saying. He thought of his family—in one rushing, instant thought—and he started crying for Joline and his children, for the pain he had caused them; and in another instant he hallucinated that he was not drenched in sweat, but in blood.

He had to get out of here. He was going to die. He pressed the sage to his mouth, but it was still like breathing fire. He didn't know where he was; it was as if part of his mind knew, but another part was soaring, taking him miles into darkness, from where he might not return.

Another retort, as more water was poured on the rocks. This time, though, it didn't seem so bad. Charlie heard the brothers singing. The melody sounded strange and harsh and ancient; through what seemed to be a hole in Charlie's consciousness, he could hear John's prayers for them all.

"If anybody has to eliminate, that's okay," John said. "This is a place to get purified, to get out all the evil, to get all the garbage picked up from the world outside out of your system."

Charlie started wheezing and coughing. He spat up phlegm, which sizzled on the rocks. He couldn't get his breath, but he heard Whiteshirt say, "The evil's right here, inside the sweat-lodge."

"Well, if it is, then we'll just have to burn it right out," John said in an even, cutting voice.

Whiteshirt laughed at that. "Don't worry, John . . . if you get burned, I'll take over the ceremony for you."

After a pause, John said, "We came here to pray, remember? And to sweat." Then he poured water on the rocks.

Charlie felt the pain as a searing wave. He pressed his blanket to his face, trying to breathe, trying to find respite from the rising heat. After a few seconds, he could breathe again. He removed the blanket from his face and stared into the darkness. The rocks weren't glowing now, but he could swear that he could see something flickering in the blackness. John would have called them spirits.

Sam handed Charlie a bucket to cool him off, and automatically Charlie ran his hands through his hair. It was hot to the touch, as if on fire. He splashed water on his face. I'm not going to last, he thought. John had told them all that if anyone had to get out to say, "All my relatives," and the door would be opened for them.

Charlie would try a little longer.

More rocks were brought in, glowing red, and Charlie burned in the darkness. But he thought he was beginning to understand something about this ceremony, that if he was going to pray—and he really wasn't sure if there was anyone or anything to pray to—he had to do it like this. Prayers had to be somehow earned. You had to go through the pain and sit with your ass in the mud like an animal.

He felt the mud beneath him. He was part of the earth. He was connected.

John told everyone not to wrap their towels and blankets around themselves, but to let the steam sink into their bodies. "The pain is good," he said as he ladled more water on the rocks. Charlie heard the hiss of steam and felt the hot blast burn over him.

"The pain is only good if it comes from the spirits," Whiteshirt said loudly, belligerently. "Only the spirits can burn away bad medicine . . . only *they* can drive a witch out of the sweat-lodge . . ."

John began to pray, as if nothing had been said, as if nothing had gone sour. "Oh, Grandfather, *Wakan-Tanka*, we're sending you a voice. Please hear us . . . pity us for we are weak. Give us the strength and wisdom so that our hearts may soften."

Whiteshirt began praying, too. But he was praying as if he was fighting. He was mocking. He was accusing. He was trying to drown out John. He blamed John for sending Sam with a disease . . . bad medicine, a disease that had afflicted everyone at Whiteshirt's camp. But now the spirits were going to put things to right. He called them down from the heavens to destroy his enemy.

Whiteshirt worked himself into a frenzy.

But John didn't raise his voice. He was in control.

The tension was electrifying the steaming, boiling darkness.

Then John decreed that the first round was over and called for the door to be opened. Janet, who looked distraught, pulled the blankets and tarpaulins away from the sweat-lodge . . . letting in the blessed light and air and a cool, chilling breeze.

"You don't have to stay for the next round," John said to Charlie. John looked at Sam, and something seemed to pass between them. Then Sam, who was sitting next to Charlie, whispered,

"There could be some bad shit coming down. I don't think John wants you in here . . . just in case."

"Well, I'm *staying*," Charlie said. He'd come this far. He was going to see it all the way through. He was no coward. And he knew goddamn well what was going on. You didn't need to be an Indian to see that, for Christ's sake, Charlie told himself. This Whiteshirt was like a bible-pounder, like those guys who came to the door with their leather-bound bibles and black suits and short-cut hair. It wasn't that they all *looked* alike—that wasn't important. It was that they all thought they knew the truth, and there was only room for *their* truth, and they'd just as soon kill you in the name of love, if they couldn't save you.

There was no way that John was going to cure this fucker with love. He was going to have to punch the shit out of him, and even then the crazy bastard would just come up again for more. Charlie had a good thought and congratulated himself: These fanatics were like junkies, you just couldn't stop them. Charlie didn't need to be a medicine man to see that. You couldn't find that kind of knowledge in books either. It was experience that counted. That's how he'd discovered that the Laws were true; and the Laws, unlike poor John, didn't take no shit from anybody.

John had better get his shit together . . . and soon.

But all John did was pray softly, as if everything was all right with the world.

John explained that this was going to be a "hot" round. He also told everyone that this was going to be a "spirit round", and that anyone could ask the spirits for help, or ask them to answer questions, but they'd better be sure they really wanted an answer.

Then Whiteshirt said, "Just as long as it's really the spirits that's doing the talking."

"Let's just find out then," John said softly. He called for the "door" to be closed. Once again the women draped the blankets and tarpaulins over the lodge and it was pitch-dark inside. "We'll make this a short round," John said, and there was an ear-splitting cracking sound like an explosion inside the sweat-lodge. John must have ladled enough water onto the rocks to melt iron. And right after that there was another explosion.

"You bastard," Whiteshirt screamed in pain.

Charlie buried himself in his blanket to escape the burning steam. It's too hot, Charlie thought. He wasn't going to survive. He was a stupid asshole for even wanting to do something so crazy as sit with a bunch of fanatics and burn his lungs out. He gagged and coughed. For an instant everything went blank. Then he found himself crying and praying for his family, for every family, for everyone. He was praying and crying *because* of the heat and the pain. He believed in the spirits flickering all around him, and yet at the same time he disbelieved. Part of his mind seemed to shrink back, and he was left with the part that believed what was happening to him. He was in the center, he was praying for his own, for himself, for his family, for his dead mother and father . . . and for the trees and the rocks and birds and animals and every other goddamn thing in the world. Words were *things*. They could *do* things. They could help or harm. Magic was real.

And praying was something that was as practical as cooking food.

Then he caught himself . . . he was thinking crazy.

His lungs were raw, but he wasn't coughing. He saw things in the darkness; maybe they were words or spirits or just something like the patterns you see behind your eyes when you press them hard with your palms.

One part of him saw the trails of spirits. Another part dismissed them. He was fighting with himself, believing and disbelieving, and just trying to breathe . . . to stay alive so he could get out and know that he had done it. Know that he wasn't a coward. That he was still a man. Still a bull.

As the spirits flickered in the dark and left trails that looked like tendrils of mist floating in red moonlight, Charlie listened to John's prayers.

"Oh, Grandfather, *Wakan-Tanka, Tunkashila,* remain with us in this lodge. Send the eagle down to us to guard the sacred pipe and the life of the People. Send *Wakinyan-Tanka,* the great thunderbird, to cleanse us. Send us the one that has wings, but no shape. Send us the one that has an eye of lightning. Send us the one that has no head, yet has a beak filled with the teeth of the wolf. Send us the winged one to devour whatever is bad inside us, just as it devours its own young."

Charlie could feel John's power in the suffocating darkness of the sweat-lodge . . . what John would call his medicine. This was not Charlie's friend talking. It was as if John had become another man. Someone strong and sacred and implacable.

Maybe John didn't have to worry about Whiteshirt, after all, Charlie thought.

Then John poured more water onto the rocks, and everyone screamed with pain. Time seemed to slow down for Charlie, contracting hours and events into instants. In these flashing beads of time were buried hours of mistakes and cruelty, all the memories of his life. He screamed out against himself, for everything wrong he had done, for his failures as a man, as a father and a son and a husband, and he saw blood . . . he was breathing it . . . he was tasting it . . . it was the very steam itself . . . it was the rocks, which were of the same stuff, coagulated.

The questions began.

Almost everyone had a question for the spirits, and John seemed to be talking, but it wasn't quite his voice. It was somehow shrill, and it certainly wasn't John's personality. He was laughing at everything; he was cutting, witty, nasty. But always laughing . . . and Charlie really began to believe that it *wasn't* John who was speaking. He heard different voices, yet he didn't hear what the spirits were telling the individual people in the sweat-lodge. The words seemed mostly garbled, except for a phrase or sentence here or there. John had told him that usually happened . . . that you only heard what you were meant to hear . . . what was important for *you*. This was a private place, even with the others sitting and groaning and sweating beside you.

But when it came to Charlie's turn, he didn't ask the spirits any questions. Once the spirits gave you an answer, you had to follow what they told you to do, and Charlie wasn't taking any chances. Not on your life. John, however, asked for him. He seemed to appear in the middle of those spirit voices, and he asked that Charlie be helped with his emphysema and his family. The spirits thought that was funnier than hell, and it gave Charlie a chill to hear those laughing voices and see those flickerings in the dark. He wondered what had happened to John. He felt naked and alone. Vulnerable.

Did John just disappear? Or was he just talking funny . . . of course, *that* was it.

It was . . . and it wasn't. Something else seemed strange to Charlie. Even if the flickerings and the voices were phony, he found that he somehow didn't care. It was real even if it wasn't. That felt true, but it didn't make a fucking bit of sense, and Charlie knew that if he could manage to get out of this sweat-lodge alive, he was going to think that he'd been crazy as shit for even thinking these thoughts—that is, if he even remembered them, which he probably wouldn't.

Charlie wanted to get out of here. He felt something bad, sure as shit he did.

Then it was Whiteshirt's turn. Charlie had blanked everyone else out, just as John had told him to do. But he was going to listen now. He supposed everyone else felt the same way because the tension returned to the darkness like a storm.

As John poured more water on the rocks, the two Indian brothers started singing in Sioux. Those brothers were shrieking.

It was then that Charlie saw the coal move in the pit.

Whiteshirt had picked up a glowing coal, hot as it was, and put it in his mouth. It illuminated his face in red, as if that face was hanging in the darkness, disconnected. It was as if Whiteshirt had become a spirit himself . . . or maybe the spirits were *inside* him. Whiteshirt turned toward John and grinned; the coal was clenched between his teeth; its glow illuminated the hatred and frustration and sickness on his face. Whiteshirt was making a funny keening noise as if the spirits were speaking through him.

It's a trick! Charlie thought. It's got to be . . .

Then the coal moved toward John, as if Whiteshirt were embracing him. John screamed, an animal scream of pure agony, and the smell of burning flesh pervaded the sweat-lodge.

"Open the door, for Christ's sake," Sam shouted. "All my relatives. Goddammit, open the door!"

The women pulled down the blankets and tarpaulins from the willow framework of the sweat-lodge. The light was blinding. Everyone was silent, stunned. Charlie coughed and spat and vomited, and found himself lying half inside and half outside the skeleton of the lodge.

John had fallen forward. Blood oozed from large ugly gashes in his back.

It wasn't the glowing coal that had burned and cracked John's flesh; the coal was just a symbol of Whiteshirt's power. It was the heat that had torn him open . . . the heat contained in Whiteshirt's burning heart.

John groaned and sat up, shaking his head as if warding off something invisible. Whiteshirt stared at him in hard satisfaction. He might have been made out of stone, red pipestone . . . a wet, sweating statue. He didn't say a word, but his wife, Janet, applied sage moistened with her spittle to the gashes in John's back. John flinched every time she touched him.

"You were wrong to do this thing," she said to her husband.

"I didn't do it," Whiteshirt said flatly. "It was the spirits."

"You were *wrong*," Janet said again.

Whiteshirt didn't answer her. He crawled out of the sweatlodge, as did all the other men except Sam and Charlie.

Charlie crawled over to John. "What the fuck happened to you?" Charlie whispered, deeply frightened.

But John didn't say a word.

5.

BROKEN WINDOWS

John kept looking upwards, as if waiting for one of his eagles to appear and save him. He seemed to be in shock. Janet had bandaged his back, which was still oozing blood. He dressed himself, but remained beside the sweat-lodge. The blood was making designs that looked like little dots on the back of John's white shirt.

Sam sat beside him before going up the hill to vision-quest. "I'll pray for you, John Stone," he said. "I'll pray for this bad medicine to be removed. I'll pray for good spirits to return to the sweat-lodge. And I'll pray for the eagles. I told you Whiteshirt was dangerous," he said in a whisper. "I think he's a witch . . ."

John shook his head slowly, as if he were negating something he had said to himself. Sam told Charlie to take care of John and then left. Although John wouldn't speak, the others said their goodbyes to him one by one. Then they formed a line, a procession. Whiteshirt led the procession, as he was the medicine man. Sam followed, holding his pipe before him and moving his lips in prayer. Behind him were Janet and the red-haired, hard-faced woman . . . Whiteshirt's woman. Then the two Indian brothers walking side by side, and everyone else. They all carried something for Sam's vision-quest: a sprig of sage, a piece of yellow cloth, matches, tobacco, a blanket, yellow gourds filled with pieces of flesh, all the mundane yet sacred materials that would help separate Sam from the profane world around him.

They left the glen and disappeared over a ridge, leaving Charlie and John to the suffusing light and the whisper of leaves. It was as if there had been no sweat, no flesh-giving ceremony, no eating of raw heart and liver . . . just this, right now, Charlie and John sitting together beside the sweat-lodge, their clothes still smelling from the filthy apartment on Union Street.

It was as if they had dropped out of the sky and landed here.

"Come on, John," Charlie said, standing up. God, he was weak and shaken. He was so exhausted that he could barely keep on his feet. He looked around. There was an unreal quality about this place. What had seemed beautiful before was now somehow frightening. The place had taken on a different complexion. It was later in the day and growing darker . . . it felt dangerous, evil. This is crazy, Charlie told himself. "Let's get the fuck out of here," he said to John.

John led the way to the car.

"Are you just going to fucking sit there without saying a word?" Charlie demanded. That's what his father used to do to him— give him the silent treatment. Charlie couldn't stand being ignored; it was like being pronounced dead.

He pulled out of the dirt driveway, glad to be driving away from the whole crazy, superstitious mess. The whole thing is bullshit, he told himself. It's fucking bullshit. His hands were shaking. It must be the emphysema and all that sweating. He felt chilled and clammy, but his strength was slowly returning. Although it was warm in the car, he turned on the heat.

John didn't respond to anything Charlie said. He just petted his leather bundle that contained his pipe as if it were a cat on his lap.

"Well, I think you should be stronger than that," Charlie continued. "You're supposed to be a fucking medicine man, for God's sake. You're *supposed* to be strong. Nothing happened in that sweat-lodge, except that it was too hot for your skin and you got burned. Could've happened to anybody. But that's *all* that happened, it was natural. Same thing could've happened to you in a sauna bath." Charlie knew *that* was bullshit, and he shuddered thinking about the bleeding gashes in John's back. Then an image came back to Charlie again: he could still see that red-hot coal burning between Whiteshirt's teeth, turning Whiteshirt's face into something that wasn't human . . . turning it into a spirit. He tried to wipe the thought from his mind. You're going crazy, too, he told himself. But that face was going to give him nightmares. It was the kind of thing he would have dreamed about when he was a kid. It was a face right out of a nightmare, the kind from which you wake up sweating and screaming. "It's all bullshit," he said to John. "And look what it did to you. Fucking burned your skin and addled your brains. So this was supposed to make me stop drinking? Well, I can tell you what we both need—and that's a fucking drink."

John still wouldn't talk. It was like trying to have a conversation with furniture. What was Charlie supposed to do with this crazy bastard who thought a goddamn eagle was going to drop right into the sweat-lodge and eat up all the bad spirits? And what the fuck was he supposed to do if John didn't come out of this coma, or whatever the hell you call it? Well, that was his problem, wasn't it, Charlie told himself. If the fucker could get himself dressed and get into the goddamn car, then he could just as well get himself something to eat when he, Charlie, wasn't there. But what about those burns? Charlie wondered. Should he take John to see a doctor? Janet had said they'd be all right, but what the hell did she know? And what was he supposed to tell the doctor? Well, he could be like that broad in *Gone With the Wind* and just worry about it later. That usually worked.

"Goddammit, John, will you stop playing games and talk to me?"

But John just stared out the window. He didn't even look particularly upset. He was petting his sacred bundle with one hand, and his right arm was resting on the door cushion.

Charlie resigned himself to driving the rest of the way in silence. This car of Stephen's gave a nice ride. Charlie had always liked Chevrolets. But it was starting to get dark, and Joline would be wondering where he had been. Here he had Stephen's car and he hadn't done diddley-squat at Union Street.

Well, the hell with Union Street. The hell with Stephen and all his goddamn properties. The hell with this crazy Indian guru. And the hell with Joline . . . the hell with his whole fucking family, for that matter.

The whole day had been bullshit. But he *saw* that coal in Whiteshirt's mouth. He saw the slashes on John's back. He saw the flickers in the sweat-lodge. Maybe there *were* spirits, as everybody claimed. Bullshit! he thought, as if he were two people having an argument. It was all crazy . . . it was the heat. It felt like 200 degrees in the sweat-lodge. It's a wonder everybody didn't die. That kind of heat would make anybody crazy . . .

Fucking A, it will . . .

He parked Stephen's car in a back lot down the street because Stephen was probably in the office—Charlie didn't want to risk a confrontation with him. He just wanted to get piss-assed drunk, is all; and so he told John that he was going down into the cellar through John's apartment instead of using the office entrance as he usually did.

And sure enough, Stephen was in the office: all the lights were on, and Stephen had his wife's little orange sports car that was in the garage every other week for repairs. Her name was spelled out on the license plate: ESTHER. He had parked her car at the east end of the alley that ran between The Trot Line bar and Stephen's office building, thus leaving room for Charlie to park the Chevy.

Charlie didn't want to face Stephen, especially if Esther was there. Goddammit, he'd had enough things happen to him for one day. He didn't need another asshole humiliating him in front of a woman. Joline humiliated him enough . . .

They went down the stairs into John's room. Charlie retrieved his bottle of wine from his hidy-hole in the cellar and proceeded to get shitfaced drunk while John lay on his bed, not saying a word. Charlie figured that John's back would be all right; he didn't look like he was in any kind of pain. "Hey, John, you in any pain from your back?" Charlie asked.

John shook his head.

"Well, holy fuck and goddamn," Charlie said. "He's alive. Do you want something to drink? I got a little wine left."

But John turned over in bed and faced the wall.

"Well, fuck you, too, brother." Charlie had just about finished the bottle of wine—it had only been half-full to start with—and was feeling flushed and pleasantly fuzzy. But his hands were shaking, which was unusual. When he was drinking, his hands were quite steady; it was when he'd come off a binge and was taking his emphysema medicine regularly that he'd get so sick and have the shakes so bad that he could hardly hold a spoon. At least Charlie wasn't coughing: the booze cleared out his lungs.

Yet he felt as if someone were looking at him, staring straight at him from behind. It wasn't John because he was facing the wall, and there wasn't anybody else in here—nervously, Charlie took a quick glance around.

He listened for Stephen upstairs, but couldn't hear anything. But goddamn if he didn't have the distinct sensation that he was being watched, and it scared him. That sweat-lodge shit made you crazy, Charlie told himself. All he could think about was that coal in Whiteshirt's mouth, and John's bleeding back.

Someone outside dropped a bottle. Charlie jumped and said, "Jesus!" After a moment, still feeling shaky, as if he had just awakened from a bad dream and wasn't sure what was what, he asked, "Hey, John, you sleeping? You gotta come out of this thing now. It ain't healthy at all and I'm worried. I don't know if I shouldn't call the doctor."

Of course, Charlie had no idea what doctor he would call . . .

"I'm all right," John said, his voice hoarse and gravelly. "I just need some time to work things out."

"Man, I was worried 'cause you weren't talking. You want a drink . . . ?"

But John suddenly started shaking and shivering as if he were cold; then it seemed that he was having convulsions. He was making a whining noise and curled himself in a fetal position on the bed—as if that would stop the tremors.

"What'samatter?" Charlie cried, not knowing what to do. He sat down on the side of the bed and held John's arm tightly. That seemed to calm him a bit. "Jesus, maybe you do need a doctor."

"No!"

"Okay, just take it easy."

John pushed himself closer to the wall, as if he could press himself right into it and disappear. He began to cry. The sound was so strange and somehow out of context for someone like John that Charlie couldn't place it at first. Then John started crying louder, wailing, sobbing, his shoulders heaving, and he was speaking in Sioux or some other language Charlie couldn't understand. Maybe he was praying because he hushed, then mumbled in a monotone, pausing only to catch his breath; and when he drew breath, it sounded like a child who had been crying and couldn't stop the contractions in his throat, even though he felt safe and secure once again.

Charlie sat on the bed with his arms around John, and he, too, started crying, although he had no idea why. But the mood seemed to come over him like smoke from the pipe, just as it had when he had smoked with John under those white elms . . . and he cried and felt bonds of friendship and remembered thoughts and things he had seen and heard in the sweat-lodge. What the fuck am I doing? he asked himself. If someone came in right now, they'd think we were two faggots. Well, fuck them, too. And Charlie remembered something that John had said about those elm trees they had sat under. That one was the chief. What the hell did he mean by that? Charlie wondered, surprised at the thoughts that pass through your head when you're fucked up.

After a time, John fell asleep, although he still moaned and mumbled.

Charlie got up and paced around the room. He noticed that the small windows near the ceiling were now black squares. Charlie didn't know what time it was, but it was late. Joline was going to have a bird. Well, what the hell else could I have done? he asked himself. Just leave John alone here? Sam *told* me to stay with him and take care of him. I may fuck up on most things, but goddammit, I'm a man of my word.

He walked over to check on John, hesitated, and mumbled, "Oh, what the fuck. He won't care, not after I've fucked myself all up for him, anyway." Then he stooped down and fumbled under the bed for John's hidden bottle of Scotch. He pulled out a half-empty bottle of Chimes and sat down in the hardbacked chair beside the desk to drink and watch John's back. Maybe those spots of blood could tell him something, if he could only interpret them. They reminded him of those connect-the-dots puzzles in the coloring books Charlie used to buy for his daughters when they were little children. Charlie stared at John's shirt. The spots had turned brown.

He's going to be all right, Charlie told himself.

Charlie became dizzy and drunk and anxious. He kept imagining Whiteshirt staring at the back of his neck. He imagined Whiteshirt with the coal in his mouth, ready to burn him, just as he had burned John. But when Charlie turned around, there was no one there. He shook his head, angry at himself for acting foolish. Bad medicine . . . it's all a crock of shit, he told himself. It's all a crock of shit. Although he felt vaguely nauseous, he didn't want to leave John—who was snoring—because he, Charlie, was supposed to take care of him.

But who was going to take care of Charlie? Who gave one shit about *him*?

"I have to go home and see if the kids are all right," Charlie explained to his sleeping friend. "I've got responsibilities, you know. Man, if I were single like you, what I couldn't do." But I've got to be careful in case that little asshole's in his office, Charlie told himself. God forgive me, but Steve *is* an asshole. Like father like son. I don't need him and his bullshit tonight.

So Charlie left by way of John's private entrance; and sure enough, the lights were still on in Stephen's office. Maybe he just forgot to turn them off, Charlie thought. If I don't do everything around here, nothing gets done at all. Well, screw it, let the lights burn all night long for all I care. *I'm* going home.

He walked south on St. Charles Street, past the laundromat and the green and brown two-family houses that were rented to a bunch of illiterate assholes on welfare who didn't do anything but carouse and smoke their pot and live like pigs. It was chilly out now, and Charlie was cold and uncomfortable. Any day now the weather was going to change, winter would be here for good, and he would be cold all the time. He quickly and quietly went up the back stairs to his apartment; and of course his cross-eyed neighbor heard him coming and said, "Shitfaced again, hey Charlie." Charlie asked him if he'd like his other eye crossed, too.

"I'm home," Charlie said as he walked into the kitchen. Sitting at his table, big as life, were Joline and Anne and his baby Kathy and Stephanie and that asshole Joey, sitting right there in the kitchen drinking coffee.

"Okay, everybody, why don't you all go into the living room and watch TV," Joline said.

Everyone got up and left. They all averted their eyes from Charlie. You'd think I have the goddamned plague, he thought. It's *my* house. I pay for the food they eat and the coffee that little sonovabitch Joey was drinking.

"Where the hell have you been?" Joline demanded in a low, growling voice. "You took that man's car, and he's been calling all day because you didn't go to the job. Now you're going to call that man and tell him where you were."

"I'm not going to do any such thing," Charlie said, sitting down at the table. "This table looks like a piece of shit. I liked the old one better. But you've got to spend my money, don't you? Don't you?" he demanded.

"Keep your voice down," Joline said. She gave him a cup of coffee. "You're drunk. Steve told me you were working with that Indian. He said that *that* was a mistake. He didn't think that Indian was any good, but he thought he'd be able to help you out. Oh, he helped you out, all right."

"Enough, woman, shut up. I didn't come home to listen to you."

"Then what did you come home for? To go right to sleep, to sleep it off, is that it? That's all you can do is sleep anymore. You can't even get it up."

"I told you to shut your mouth," Charlie said. His hands were shaking again; he couldn't drink any of his coffee. But he was going to control himself. That's what he told himself. He should never have come back home. Why did he come back anyway? He was supposed to be looking after John.

"I want to know where you were all this time," Joline said. "I think you owe me that. And just look at yourself. Your hair's all messed up and"—she leaned over him and pulled a piece of sage out of his hair—"where did you get this? Working on Union Street?"

"Just leave me alone."

"What were you and your do-nothing friend up to?" Joline asked. "Did you find an old bag and gang-bang her in the woods?"

"I told you to shut up," Charlie shouted, feeling himself slip out of control, as the booze took over again, numbing him, refocusing him. He tried to hold on, but it was as if he were already in flight. He felt as if he were watching himself on TV and couldn't switch off the program. "And I want that little asshole who knocked up my daughter out of my house."

"Now *you* listen to me," Joline said. "There's nobody leaving this house—unless maybe it's you."

"Well, it fucking well is going to be me," Charlie said, standing up. He felt everything sloshing and spinning and almost fell; but he had come back home to do something. What was it? He'd come home to his family, that was all. But even here he felt as if Whiteshirt was staring at him . . . and he just wanted to run. He didn't deserve a family, he thought. He was a goddamn drunk, Joline was right. They didn't need him, his family didn't. Nobody needed him.

Well, then fuck them all! Fuck everyone. Fuck everything. And fuck that Joey, that little Italian bastard geek who'd spoiled it all, who had spoiled his daughter.

Charlie stormed into the living room and said to Joey, "Get the hell out of here, didn't you hear what I said?"

Joey was sitting on the couch with Stephanie, and he still wouldn't look at Charlie—as if by not looking at him, Charlie couldn't hurt him.

"Did you hear me?"

"Yessir," Joey said. "I heard you."

"Well, then get the fuck out of here."

"No, *you* get the hell out of here," Joline shouted, coming up behind him from the kitchen. She grabbed him, and he almost lost his balance. But he didn't cough, the booze saw to that. "You're a goddamn drunk and I hate you. Let your kids see you. This is what he is," she said, looking at the children. "This is your father. Probably spent the day banging some old whore on Clinton Street with his Indian buddy who lives in the cellar."

"I told *you* to get out of here," Charlie said, walking toward Joey, ignoring Joline. Then, surprised at himself, he pulled Joey to his feet and took a swing at him. But the booze had a mind of its own. He only grazed the boy's chin. Joey seemed more dumbfounded then hurt and backed warily away from Charlie. Stephanie was screaming hysterically.

And then Joline slapped Charlie squarely in the face.

Reflexively, he slapped her back hard, hurting her. He stumbled out of the apartment. Crying and swearing, he took the front stairs. I swore I'd never hit her, he told himself. That's it, I've spoiled it. But she don't need me. None of them do. I only stayed with her all these years for the kids, anyway. He knew that was a lie; but he paused on the bottom of the landing and shouted up the stairs, "I only stayed with you this long for the kids. You hear that? I should've left long ago. But I'm leaving you now, goddammit. Do you hear that?"

He was his own man, after all. If he couldn't have who he wanted in his own house, then he'd leave it. He'd finally be free after all these years. Joline would probably do better without him. She'd still get his checks. That's what she wanted all along, he thought.

But Charlie waited a moment longer. He expected her to come screaming out of the apartment. She should be crying her eyes out by now, he told himself. She should have been out here by now, calling him names and then asking him to come back inside for dinner.

Goddammit, I'm drunk, he thought.

Joline, get your ass out here. But he wasn't going to yell that, no matter how bad he was. He was in control, not her.

Quietly, reluctantly, he left.

The motorcycle people were across the street, fussing with their bikes and talking and drinking beer. They probably smoked their pot or took their heroin *inside* their apartments. Charlie's fat neighbor was out, too, wearing his black gangster jacket. There were women standing around with the guys. Some of them even had their babies out. Those infants shouldn't be out in this chill, Charlie thought. It's a crime is what it is. He couldn't imagine any of them having babies. What the hell did they do for a dollar? None of them worked. They probably robbed or dealt drugs. The women were probably all on welfare, supporting their babies and boyfriends. They were probably all stoned right now.

Charlie had tried pot once, but it didn't do anything for him except give him a sore throat.

The people across the street waved at Charlie.

Charlie waved back, thinking that at least they have some family. That's more than I have now, he told himself. He knew that he could just turn around and walk back upstairs. Joline would fight with him, call him every frigging name in the book, but she would fix him dinner and probably even screw him if she had a mind to. He wouldn't even have to apologize—not to Joline or his daughters, and especially not to that little asshole Joey. Of course, he would apologize to his daughters for the crude words that had passed between Joline and himself; but he'd do that tomorrow, after things quieted down.

That's all he had to do. Yet he couldn't. He just couldn't go back. Not after he had slapped her. That had done it . . . broken the sacred bond. It was as if he had severed one bond and formed another, as if he couldn't have a family anymore, except for John. John was all he deserved. He never should have taken on a family. He was always a loner and a drifter, even when he was a family man, because it was in his heart.

But he suddenly, wrenchingly felt his loss, felt it as he had in the sweat-lodge when he cried for all of them: for Joline and Anne and Stephanie and the baby, and for his son, too. God, maybe that's who I need to talk to, Charlie thought. Maybe Louis could set him back on the right path, tell him what to do, make everything all right.

Of course, he knew what to do. Go back home. But he just *couldn't* do that yet. Although he couldn't admit it to himself, right now he was terrified. He was afraid of what had happened in the sweat-lodge, which he tried to dismiss. He was afraid of his future, which looked hopeless. He was afraid of his fading health. He used to be a bull, and now he had trouble climbing stairs. He didn't have teeth, his arms were skinny, his belly was fat, he'd lost too much hair, and he was a failure. He had lost it all, and the Third Law had seen to it that he didn't get it back—none of it.

Maybe it's just the Laws working themselves out, Charlie told himself. Maybe that's it. He was paying dues, and there was nothing in the world he could do about that. Maybe this was what he deserved for not being a better father and husband and breadwinner. Maybe this was his payment for drinking and not being there when his daughter really needed him. If so, he was really going to pay for tonight, for slugging that little asshole Joey.

He tried to call his son from a phone booth on the corner of St. Charles and Main Street. Behind him was the Blue Moon Diner, a greasy spoon famous for its blinking blue neon signs; across the street was Stephen's office. The office lights were on, and, as Charlie watched, a grubby-looking young man and woman came out of the office. So that's why he's there, Charlie thought. He's renting apartments. He's doing it himself so he won't have to pay me to do it. No . . . he'll let *me* clean up the shit for him while *he* pockets the rental fees from his father. Very neat. Like father like son.

Charlie called Louis collect, but there was no one home. That's typical, Charlie thought as he stood in the phone booth and watched the office. Suddenly, everything seemed to come clear, even though he still felt a bit nauseated and dizzy. He had drunk more than he was accustomed to, but he could handle it, he told himself. He *was* handling it.

As he watched the office, it occurred to him that if he had no family, then he had no reason at all to suck up to Stephen or Nathan or anygoddamnbody. The firm owed *him*, owed him for all his time, all his ideas . . . and for all their broken promises. The Indians aren't the only ones who got broken promises, Charlie said to himself.

It was time to collect, and Charlie knew exactly how to collect what was due him.

He crossed the street. He wasn't steady on his feet—he weaved back and forth, but only a little. He picked up two fist-sized rocks from the curb—the city was always working on the gas lines or telephone lines or water lines right here at the corner, and the street seemed to be always broken up. Then he threw the rocks, one after the other, through the glass panes of the office door. "So much for LAW OFFICES, NATHAN ISAACS, ESQ., whateverthehell ESQ means, and so much for BEST REALTY, LTD, STEPHEN ISAACS PRESIDENT," Charlie said softly, calmly.

Stephen rushed to the door, looking out through the space where the window had been, looking directly at Charlie, who stood on the street with his hands on his hips, as he surveyed his work. Charlie tried to stand as steady as he could. He nodded to Stephen. I've made an asshole out of you, Charlie thought, gloating, feeling the piss and vinegar burning inside him as if he were eighteen again.

"What the hell happened?" Stephen demanded. "What the *fuck* is going on?" he screamed, opening the door. He was a tall man of about thirty-five with graying hair and a strong, rough face. He looked like his father—the same squarish face, widow's peak, and blue eyes. He always looked like he was squinting. He also resembled Charlie, as people had often remarked. In fact, Stephen's wife had actually thought that Charlie *was* his father when they first met. She often asked Charlie, chiding, if maybe he didn't know Mrs Isaacs in the biblical sense. Charlie would laugh and say he was the milkman.

But Charlie wasn't laughing now.

"Hey Charlie, you ever hear that you don't bite the hand that feeds you?" Stephen shouted. "You goddamn drunk!"

I'm *still* a bull, Charlie reminded himself, afraid that Stephen might try something. He regretted breaking the window. But fuck it. It was already done. "Neither you or your father ever gave me nothing," Charlie said. "Everything I got I got myself. I even had to give you a security deposit when I moved . . . after ten years of service. That's how you thank people who love you. Well, I can tell you—I admit it—I was an asshole. And your whole family can stick it right up your asses."

"I'm not going to stand on the street and argue with you," Stephen said. He acted contemptuous, but he also seemed nervous, wary. He knew better than to push Charlie too far: it wouldn't be worth a fight. "I'm going to call the police, and you're going to pay for this window. I'm sure Joline is just going to love this, as if you haven't embarrassed her enough."

"You just shut your mouth about my family," Charlie said, "and if you want to call the police, you just take your ass back to the phone and make your call."

"First I'd like to know what the fuck you've done with my car."

"I didn't steal it, if that's what you're getting at," Charlie said. "Your car's safe and sound in the Endicott-Johnson factory lot."

"I'd like the keys back right now," Stephen demanded, stepping out of the office and into the street.

"Well, here they are, your honor," Charlie said, tossing the keys to him.

Stephen caught them and said, "I'm not a judge, but you're too *drunk* to know the difference between me and my father." His voice became more condescending now that he had the keys.

"Jam it up your ass," Charlie said. He was going to say, "Jam it up your *Jewish* ass," but even drunk Charlie didn't want to step over that line. Stephen might come after him for that.

"Get the hell out of here," Stephen said, "and I want all your keys—the keys to the office, the keys to all the properties—and I'm giving you notice right now. Find yourself another apartment. Find another landlord whose windows you can break. But you're never getting the chance to do it again here, I can guarantee you that."

"It's a shithole, anyway," Charlie shouted, pulling his office key from his key ring. He threw the key at Stephen, who didn't even try to catch it. "I was going to move," Charlie said. "I've been looking in the paper for the last two months. You can rent your slum to some other dumb asshole, you and your father sunning his ass in Florida." Charlie was breathing heavily now, and every breath seemed to make him more dizzy and pull him farther away from Stephen. Why doesn't that bastard just go inside? Charlie asked himself. Fucking pansy. I could beat the piss out of him right now, even at my age, if he was man enough to say the word . . .

"And you can tell your Indian crony that he has until tomorrow to get his ass out of my building," Stephen said. Then he went back into his office, locking the door behind him.

Even if he had the will, Charlie was too drunk to get through that broken window in the door. "Get one of your other maintenance men to fix your door," Charlie shouted after Stephen. "I'm sure you'll find a 'professional' to do the job."

But Stephen had disappeared into the inner office, effectively cutting Charlie off.

Sonovabitch, Charlie thought. He probably *is* calling the police.

Suddenly Charlie felt something in his throat. He began retching right there in the street. Then he began to cough, gagging, kneeling on the cement, spitting; and even as he coughed his lungs out, a part of his mind was clear and steady and objective. It gave Charlie the true picture, as he called it. Charlie had humiliated himself—that's what he felt kneeling there. Joline had humiliated him. Joey had humiliated him. Stephanie had humiliated him. Stephen had humiliated him. But it was the humiliation of being who he was that was the worst of all. He had done it to himself . . . and to everyone he loved. He'd always known that. He knew the Laws, yet he was a loser. He was better off right here in the gutter. Fucking *A*.

Someone helped him to his feet—it was John. Charlie had drawn a small crowd.

"What the hell are you all looking at?" Charlie shouted. "Haven't you people ever seen a broken window before?"

6.

TURNING *HEYOKA*

Charlie felt drunker than ever after vomiting. He remembered John bringing him downstairs to his room. He remembered sitting in the chair; and it was as if the air was made out of water and he was just floating along . . . floating and belching and feeling sick and then feeling perfectly calm. Then there was the coolness of the metal desktop against the side of his face as Charlie leaned over to sleep. He remembered being a child in school, falling asleep at his desk on the hot, muggy afternoons . . . remembered the inkwell that always dug into his right arm.

He snapped awake, disoriented. It was still dark, and John's room was filled with shadows that jumped and danced with every passing car.

There was a pounding upstairs. For an instant, he thought it was rifle-shot or cold water being poured onto the hot rocks inside the sweat-lodge. After a few seconds, he mumbled, "So Mr Isaacs got himself a professional to fix his window." He sat up, still feeling the cotton-work of sleep and booze in his mouth, the itchy numbness in his hands, and the familiar tickle in his throat that meant an explosion was soon to follow. He looked around for a place to spit before he started coughing, and saw John as if for the first time. But he was busy looking for a waste-paper basket or a paper bag; he couldn't find either. He tried to ask John for help, but he started wheezing and coughing and his stomach was churning. He tried to get to the bathroom, which was at the other end of the cellar hallway, but he threw up as he stumbled past John's door into the cellar. He did it right on the floor—like a goddamn animal, he thought, mortified.

When he came back into the room—angry at John for not lifting one finger to help him—he suddenly felt that something was very wrong. He *smelled* something in that room, something other than his own sour smell, something other than vomit. It was as if he was smelling fear itself.

Charlie made his stumbling way back to the chair and desk, as if there lay safety. "What the hell's the matter with you?" Charlie asked John, who was sitting on the bed. John shook his head impatiently. Charlie began to tell John everything that had happened at home and with Stephen, but John didn't seem to hear a thing Charlie was saying. He was agitated. He kept curling and uncurling his large hands, and he would pace back and forth several times across the room, from his bed to the closet, and then sit back down on the bed. He mumbled, but wouldn't answer Charlie.

Even *here* it was as if Charlie didn't exist . . .

Charlie was nervous, anxious. He didn't like what was happening in here, even though he didn't quite know what it was. It had something to do with what he had thought was a smell. Maybe it was a smell. Maybe it was John, who looked like he was going to break up everything in the room. He looked angry and mean. He looked crazy. His face was all tightened up, especially around his eyes and mouth.

"Whatsamatter?" Charlie asked softly. He felt sober now. His voice was clear. "Everything's going to be all right," he said tentatively. "You just need a good night's sleep is all." The sound of Charlie's voice seemed to make John worse, and that feeling of fear began to build up in the room like bad air.

"They told me," John mumbled as he paced furiously around the room, looking down at the floor. "They *told* me, goddammit!" It was as if something was pulling him apart.

"Told you *what?*" Charlie asked, but John gave him such a nasty look that Charlie caught his breath. "I didn't mean you no harm, I—"

"They told me . . . they told me years ago."

Charlie didn't say a word. He just sat there and wondered what the hell he was going to do. He was certain that if he got up to leave the Indian would go for him. The fucker was crazy. Goddamn if the man wasn't losing it right here in front of Charlie. But what was Charlie supposed to do? He remembered stories about people going insane and killing their families or just shooting at people passing by. Jesus, he was getting so nervous, he imagined that *he* was crazy.

"Well, then fuck it," John said, and he kneeled before the bed and reached under it, felt around for the bottle, and not finding it, looked up at Charlie.

Jesus Christ, Charlie thought, caught by the hate and anger in John's face—he's going to kill me for a bottle of cheapjack hooch. "I drank it," Charlie confessed, and then he felt a wild anger take him over. He wasn't going to be pushed around by this crazy-assed Indian. He'd been pushed around enough tonight. He'd punch out the Indian's lights, just like he broke the windows upstairs. "All right," Charlie said, "so I owe you a bottle, but for Chrissakes, you were catatonic like a zombie and I didn't think you would mind."

John stared at Charlie, as if deciding what to do, and then he burst out laughing. Reflexively, Charlie grinned. Without saying a word, John went into the closet and pulled another bottle out of a wrinkled paper bag.

"Holding out on me?" Charlie asked.

But John was still lit with rage, and he paced around the room and chugged down the booze as if it were beer. Suddenly he started laughing again, and Charlie sensed something dangerous about it—not sinister, just plain crazy. "You were right," John said, as if responding to something that Charlie had said. "I should have left well enough alone. I should have taken this drink long ago. I shouldn't've stopped being wrong. Man, I was *right* when I was wrong!" He seemed pleased with what he had said because he started laughing again.

Charlie's face froze into a smile. Well, at least he's talking to me, maybe that means something. Charlie needed a drink.

John sat down on the bed, squarely in the center of his Indian star blanket, as if even now it was important for him to keep balance and order in the world. He took a swallow from the bottle without offering any to Charlie, who knew better than to ask, and then started to shake as he had earlier. Charlie started to get up, although he wasn't feeling so well either, but John shook his head. "Leave me alone ... don't even come near me ... I'm not holy," and then he sprang from the bed toward Charlie and snatched the leather bundle that contained his pipe from the edge of the desk. Surprised, Charlie fell backward onto the desk, almost losing his balance and landing on the floor.

Charlie thought that John was coming after *him*.

John took the sacred pipe from the bag, which he discarded, and connected the bowl to the stem. He held the pipe in both hands for a second, as if making an offering, caressing it, and then he threw it hard across the room. It bounced from the wall onto the bed without breaking, as if it were a living thing that was somehow attracted to the bright star woven into John's blanket, just as John had been attracted to the security the blanket represented.

"I'm not a pipe-carrier any more," John said in a low, dangerous voice, talking to the pipe across the room. Then he looked up at the ceiling, as if still looking for his eagles—as if they could appear miraculously to save him at the last. "Well, spirits, you were right." Now he was talking to the air, or to the ghosts, which only he could see. "I should have known better than to try to pick up the pipe again. You told me . . . you told me if I kept chasing the skirts and getting blind, I was going to die. Well, spirits," he shouted, extending his arms to them, wherever they might be, "you were fucking right." Then he turned to Charlie and said, as if he had just worked it all out, "And they *were* right . . . I am dead. Whiteshirt ate me alive, didn't he?" That more a statement than a question.

Charlie looked away. He couldn't hold up to that stare, to those eyes, which seemed to be on fire.

Then John started crying, right there in the middle of the room. He looked away from Charlie, looked down at the floor; and for an instant Charlie could almost believe that Whiteshirt was in the room with them. Charlie remembered how Whiteshirt had left the sweat-lodge after burning John's back . . . after humiliating John by forcing him to cry out.

He felt as if he were suddenly fixed to the chair, unable to move. He could almost taste John's anguish. He could feel John's anxiety. It was as if they were connected, just as they were when they smoked the pipe that first time. Charlie wanted to kill that sonovabitch Whiteshirt. That bastard *was* a witch or a sorcerer or whatever you call them.

And Charlie had the uneasy feeling that they weren't finished with Whiteshirt yet . . .

John started walking around and around the room; then he started turning, spinning around, as if he were dancing; and sometimes he walked backwards, moving faster and faster, becoming angrier with every step, with every turn, as if he was stoking himself up. Charlie thought that surely John must be under some spell or another. If Charlie hadn't been able to see the anger and humiliation and just plain craziness flushing John's face, he would have thought that John was doing one of those Indian dances that people pay to see at county fairs.

John stopped and looked around the room, his motions quick and jerky, as if he was terrified. "I've got to get out of here," he said. But he had enough presence of mind to pull a green canvas army bag out of the closet. He began stuffing his belongings into it.

"What the hell are you doing?" Charlie asked. John couldn't go out now—not in his condition.

"If I'm going to be dead, then the whole fucking world is going to know about it!" John said. Then he went back to his packing, stuffing his blanket into the bag. He nodded and laughed as if someone was right there telling him jokes, whispering in his ear.

Charlie sensed the change in John's mood and became bolder. "You're not dead, you're just a little drunk. It was all those others in the sweat-lodge that were fucked up. You were like a goddamn saint. And I'll tell you something else, you're going to be fucked up as long as you believe all that bull . . . all that stuff about visions and eagles in the sweat-lodge and the rest of that stuff. I don't mean to be disrespectful, but that's the way I see it."

John thought that was funny. He took a large swallow from his half-empty pint bottle of Chimes, which he then slipped into his back pocket. He grabbed the pipe on the bed and stuffed it into his bag, laughing all the while, as if the *pipe* were somehow speaking to him, only now it was telling dirty jokes. "You mean to tell me you didn't see *anything* in that sweat-lodge?" John asked Charlie.

"Like what do you mean?" Charlie asked warily, feeling as if Whiteshirt was watching him again. It felt like Whiteshirt was right behind him. Pretending that he had lost something, Charlie turned around and looked at the wall. He felt like a fool . . . but he felt better. Then he became nauseated again. He always got that way from drinking. It came in waves. He clenched his jaw, and John started laughing. "What are *you* laughing at?" Charlie asked.

"I'm laughing at you," John said. "Well ... did you see anything in the sweat-lodge?"

Charlie waited for the spell to pass. I've got to keep away from the booze, he told himself. "No," Charlie lied, "I didn't see anything in there. It was pitch dark, for Chrissakes. And it was hot, that's all."

"Charlie, you're a bigger asshole than I am," John said. He pulled tight the laces of his canvas bag and, holding it under his arm, rushed up the stairs, leaving the door open.

"Jesus, wait up," Charlie shouted, grabbing his jacket and following him. It was a chilly night, and even with the light from the surrounding buildings, a few faint stars could be seen. Everything seemed faint: faint music from the beer gardens on either side of St. Charles Street, the faint smells of food and diapers and garbage, the odors of leather and rubber from the factories across the railroad tracks, the murmur of traffic ... and a train whistle, probably blowing somewhere west near Endicott or Union.

John had cut through the alley behind the Isaacs' anvil-shaped building and into the parking lot where Charlie had parked Stephen's car. Stephen had the key now, Charlie thought. Good riddance. "Where are you going?" Charlie asked John as he walked beside him. John was walking hard, almost running. "Would you slow down a little?" Charlie asked. "Are you going to a fire?"

"Yeah," John shouted at the top of his lungs, "that's a good idea," and he started walking backwards, doing his *heyoka* bit, turning into an angry maniac who might either dance around backwards, laughing and smoking an invisible pipe, or just kill some unfortunate passer-by for the fuck of it. "Hey, Charlie, a good *heyoka* like myself can walk faster backwards than most men can run frontwards." Then he chug-a-lugged almost all the liquor in his pint bottle without offering any to Charlie, who didn't want any more, anyway, as he was still on the edge of nausea.

"You gotta get ahold of yourself." Charlie said. It frightened him when John acted like this ... John was so goddamn changeable. "Come on back to the room, you need some sleep and then three squares for a while, get you back on your feet."

"Just fuck off, why don't you," John said, "and get the hell away from me." He looked around the parking-lot, located Stephen's two-tone metallic-blue Chevy, and walked directly to it.

Charlie followed, a few paces behind.

"First I gotta consecrate it," John explained as he stood beside the car. Then he unzipped his fly and urinated on the front fender and whitewall tire.

"Stop that!" Charlie said. "What the hell are you, some kind of pervert. Do you want to get us arrested, is that it?" John thought that was funnier than hell, and he was shaking around so much that he urinated all over his own boots. Charlie was disgusted— the Indian didn't have any self-respect.

When John finished, he took out a jackknife and slipped it between the car door and jamb, and with his other hand he opened the door easily.

"What the hell are you *doing*?" Charlie anxiously demanded. He wanted to grab John and pull him away from the car, but he was afraid the Indian would go completely berserk if he even touched him. "The police patrol this area," Charlie said, pleading. "I can't afford to get busted. This is Stephen Isaacs' car, for Chrissakes."

But John wasn't paying any attention to Charlie. He slid into the driver's seat and reached under the dash. The overhead map light seemed to distort the features of his face, making ridges of light along his cheekbones, as if he were wearing war paint. John closed his eyes; he seemed lost in thought.

Suddenly the engine roared to life. It sounded unbelievably loud in the muffled darkness of the parking lot. John looked at Charlie and grinned broadly. "Us *heyokas* do okay with our eyes closed, what do you think?"

"Don't you give a shit for *any*body?" Charlie asked. He was angry and frightened. He didn't want to mess with the law. Joline was right—this Indian was nothing but trouble, and Charlie would be the one who would have to pay! "If you steal this car, they're going to think that *I* took it because I was pissed off at the Isaacs. So turn the goddamn motor off . . ." But Charlie heard the whine that had crept into his voice, and he wanted to crawl away. Joline was right; he wasn't any kind of man or he would have pulled John out of the car by his neck . . . he would have stopped him right away, when the pissing started.

"Calm down, old friend," John said, and he closed the door and rolled down the window, obviously not worried about what Charlie might do. He let his arm hang out the window, his fingers tapping the side of the door. "They're not going to blame you," John continued, "because you're going to be home, safe and sound." His maniacal personality had disappeared, and all the strain and tension was gone from his rough, brown face. "They'll be looking for *me!*" Then he let out a whoop that made Charlie jump backwards." Goodbye, fucker," John said. "If I wasn't dead, I'd pray for you." He gunned the engine. "Go eat shit on Union Street. Kiss ass. Go home." He put the car into gear, and it lurched backwards toward the office buildings on the eastern edge of the lot.

Charlie just stood there, watching. He felt suddenly small, of no account, and he couldn't face the prospect of going home. He couldn't do that now, anyway. He was still too drunk . . .

Suddenly the car stopped. Then the tires squealed as John laid rubber and drove back toward Charlie.

Charlie jumped out of the car's way.

John stopped, reached across the seat, and pushed the passenger door open. "Get in," John said.

"Are you fucking crazy?" Charlie shouted. "You almost run me over and you want me to ride with you?" But the whole thing suddenly struck him as being funny. Maybe he had caught a touch of John's *heyoka* because he couldn't help but smile.

"Either do it now or think about it for the rest of your life," John said. "You're going to be dead soon anyway, so you might as well get blind."

"I'm feeling sick," Charlie mumbled, feeling stupid and foolish even as he said it. For one thing, he didn't feel sick anymore.

"Where are you going?" Charlie asked lamely.

"Get in or go home . . . make up my mind."

On impulse Charlie got into the car.

He felt immediately and wonderfully relieved. He was weightless again. It was as if he were back smoking the pipe in the woods and looking up at the sky and thinking good, profound thoughts and feeling the whole world seeping through his pores as if he were some kind of god or something.

John floored the accelerator and the tires squealed as they drove through the parking lot backwards. John turned onto Avenue A, a narrow, dimly lit street; then he turned onto Main Street tail first, ran a red light, and almost crashed into a black Cadillac. Whoever was driving the Caddy pushed on the horn and didn't let up.

"You can't drive down Main Street in reverse," Charlie shouted, laughing.

"Fuck if I *can't*," John said, and he slid his bottle over to Charlie, who downed it with abandon, just as he had seen John do earlier. The heat of the alcohol exploded in his throat; but he kept it down, even though he wheezed and his eyes watered and burned. But just then he was thrown forward as John sideswiped a parked car and careened to the other side of the street, knocking down a parking meter. Now everyone was blaring their horns, and people were watching from the street and stepping out of doorways. It would only be a matter of seconds before the police were here. Jesus, Charlie thought, how the hell will I be able to face anyone?

"Well," John said brightly, "I guess I *can't* drive backwards on Main Street."

But goddamn if Charlie didn't get the giggles again, right there in the street with all those crazy neighborhood assholes looking right at him. He felt *good*. He was clarity itself. He was perceptive. He was having a good time right this minute. He wasn't thinking about the Old Days . . . he was *having* them! He was so excited he could feel the juice burning in his chest. He was in control. He was quiet. He was calm. Mother-fucker, he was having a good time!

"Switch sides," Charlie demanded in a tone of voice that even *he* didn't recognize, and he scrambled over John's lap and into the driver's seat. He backed the car out into the street—thank God there wasn't any traffic—and took a right turn off Main Street as soon as he could, at the intersection where the record store used to be. He drove over a bridge that wasn't completed yet—only the northbound lane was open—and then took back streets around Harry L. Drive to get to Route 17. If I can only get to the highway, I'll be okay, Charlie told himself.

"Man, you're doing just fine," John said, laughing like hell and leaning half out the window.

Charlie could hear faint sirens.

"If anybody sees this car, we're dog shit," Charlie said, frustrated because so many streets on the North Side were under construction. How the hell am I supposed to get to the highway if I have to detour all over God's half-acre? he asked himself. And they didn't have time to fumble around. The police were looking for them right now; Charlie knew that much.

John was quiet, as if distracted, and looked calmly out the window. He seemed to go from one personality extreme to another. "You're getting nervous," he said. "Slow down, we need to steal another car."

"No way," Charlie said. "We're in enough trouble as it is." But Charlie was in too deep now, and he knew it. One more car wouldn't mean shit to the police. They'd put him in jail for one car or for two. Same difference. Anyway, he rationalized, it wasn't even a felony. He hadn't worked for a lawyer for all these years without learning something about the law. John was right. They needed to park this car, which was bashed up, anyhow, and take out another one. They needed to get up on that old highway and haul-ass away from here. If Charlie was going to be in control for the first time in twenty years, then he'd have to make some decisions.

Charlie parked along a tree-lined street opposite a cemetery.

"What're you stopping *here* for?" John asked, but Charlie only had to nod in the direction of a white frame house with a neat lawn demarcated from the street by low hedges, which were raised and rounded at the corners of the yard. An older model Cadillac was parked in front of a single-car garage. It was a convertible. Charlie had always loved convertibles. Christ, the first car he had ever owned when he was a kid was a convertible. For that matter, he had been driving a red Mercury convertible when he first met Joline; that was all he'd had left after his gas stations had failed. Just looking at this long, red beauty brought back all kinds of memories.

"Now this baby's in good shape," Charlie whispered as they tiptoed into the yard like children stealing rhubarb from a neighbor's garden. The 50's style street lamp gave off enough light for Charlie to see that the car had no rust, although in this light the paint looked faded. The stupid bastard hadn't even locked the car. Charlie got into the driver's seat—he was so excited that his hands were shaking—and unlocked the passenger side for John. Then he just took the car out of gear and let it roll down the driveway's incline and into the street. Charlie felt a tickle in his throat and started coughing. For some reason he felt embarrassed, although he wasn't worried about the police anymore. Right now he had the feeling that he could do whatever he wanted and get away with it. It was like having a run at the crap-table. He was golden . . . and so was the crazy bastard sitting patiently beside him.

When Charlie had finished hacking and spitting—he had opened the door a crack, as the car had power windows—he felt around under the dash and hot-wired the ignition. After a few tries, the engine came to life; it was low and throaty. John unexpectedly let out a whoop, and there was nothing for Charlie to do but get out of there quickly. The Caddy had good response, although it was sluggish around turns. They were built like boats in those days, Charlie thought, as he made his way toward the highway.

Although it was cold outside—not freezing, just a sharp bite to the air—John insisted that they put the top down. Determined, he undid the latches above the windshield and found the switch under the dash. The wind interfered with the convertible drive mechanism, but once the top was down, Charlie felt as if he had taken another drink. He could almost feel he was on that highway already, buzzing along at a cool hundred and ten miles per hour, snapping through the night, going wherever the hell he wished. Driving was like dreaming and motherfucker he was driving.

"It's *cold* out here," Charlie said, and he turned the heat on full blast. John didn't seem to mind. He was quiet again. It was as if John was occupied by two people who were flipping coins or drawing straws to find out who John should be. Charlie liked this "quiet" John, but the other one was always peering out through the eyes, ready to take control any second and start whooping and yelling and doing crazy things—that one was *heyoka*, and Charlie knew that as quiet as John might become from time to time, as pensive as he might seem, John was mostly *heyoka* now. As Charlie's son Louis would say, "That was ruling his sign." Charlie could understand that. Hadn't the booze made him *heyoka* . . . or sort of *heyoka*? That's what he was when he hit that little asshole Joey. That's what he was when he hit Joline. He felt something fall inside him, deep in his chest, when he thought about Joline. But it was too late for that now . . . too fucking late for that.

"We need a drink," John finally said, but the bottle was empty and John tossed it into the street, laughing like a hyena at the smashing noise it made. There was the *heyoka* again, pouring out John's eyes, bright and glowing as that coal clenched between Whiteshirt's teeth.

Charlie felt a chill feather up his back, although he didn't quite know why he should suddenly feel frightened. But the spell passed.

"We need a drink right now!" John shouted.

Charlie wanted to get onto the highway. He wanted to feel acceleration. He wanted to be pushed right back into the cushioned seat. He wanted to drive this mother-fucker to her limits . . . actually, he shouldn't be thinking about this car in that way. He was superstitious about such things. Inanimate objects had personalities, especially cars, and Charlie felt that if you thought bad thoughts about them, or talked nasty to them, they would break down. He should think of this old bloody-red Caddy as a beautiful, mature woman, and riding her would be like humping Sophia Loren.

He was more gentle with the thin, ridged steering-wheel. He drove back around all the construction on Harry L. Drive until he found the highway intersection, where he clover-leafed into the west lane, heading toward Endicott and Apalachin. John complained and insisted that he needed a drink—that they had to stop somewhere and get some *booze*.

But Charlie just wanted to drive ... he couldn't think past that.

He took the Caddy up to a cool ninety, and she still purred right along. The wind mussed his hair and the heater kept him warm. It was like driving through a tunnel: there was only that cone of light ahead and the red dots of tail lights and the high-beams being clicked down to low as cars whizzed past him in the other lane.

Charlie didn't need a drink, although he could feel that nausea lurking right under his throat, building around his hiatal hernia, and if he didn't take a drink, he'd have to stop and vomit and sleep and cough, and maybe John was right—but there wasn't time. He had to drive, that was all that was important: to drive away from Johnson City, to drive away from the Isaacs' family and their properties, away from Joline and the kids, away from everything that was Charlie Sarris. If he could keep drinking and driving, if he could prolong this "right-now" forever, he would never have to cough out his lungs again or smoke cigarettes or feel like shit.

Goddamn, Charlie thought, he needed a cigarette. He worried one out of his pack while he drove, and then he used the Caddy's electric lighter. The smoke made him want to cough, it was strong and harsh, and goddammit, he was alive.

"How many fucking times do I have to ask you?" John said as he moved over across the leather seat and grabbed the steering wheel. He tried to sit right on Charlie's lap. "I need a goddamn drink, I said!"

"Get off me," Charlie screamed. John was pulling the steering wheel, and the car veered to the right. There was a soft bump as the wheels slipped off the pavement onto the soft shoulder, then a pinging and a clattering as the car sideswiped two guardrails before Charlie could regain control and ease the car back onto the pavement.

John was laughing like hell again, completely *heyoka*, and Charlie knew that the crazy bastard didn't care if he lived or died . . . and for an instant, neither did Charlie. That thought was freedom itself.

Charlie pressed the accelerator to the floor and said, "Okay, you crazy red bastard, *you* drive." Then he pushed himself up in the seat and climbed into the back of the car.

The car swerved off the road again, snapping guardrails, but John took the wheel and slid over into the driver's seat. The Caddy slowed down to about seventy. John didn't say a word, and he looked stone-cold sober. But Charlie couldn't stop laughing, and the blood was pounding in his head, and sonovabitch if he wasn't smashed, blotto, drunk-as-a-toad all over again.

This shit must be in my bloodstream, Charlie told himself, gasping for air. He shivered, feeling the wind on his face. If I die right now, fuck it! It's a good time to die. "Hit the guardrails again," he shouted in a hoarse voice, swallowing the tickle and the cough, which were only pushing their way back up again. "Fuck it, this is as good a time as any to die. Might as well do it right. Do it up brown . . . or red!" Charlie started laughing at his own joke, which was only funny to him because of the strange resonance it produced in his mind. It's about time I made an Indian joke, Charlie thought. The fucker's always putting down white people. Goddamned-holier-than-thou-prejudiced Indian!

John took the Caddy back up into the 90's. He threw his arm over the back of his seat and shouted, "Charlie, I think you been reading those books about Indians."

"What the hell are you talking about?" Charlie asked. He climbed back into the front seat; it was difficult and awkward and dangerous, and he bumped his head on the windshield pillar. The warm air from the heater felt good on his legs, but Charlie felt suddenly chilled to the bone. He was also out of breath.

"So you think this would be a good time to die, do you?" John asked.

"I'm not afraid of it, if that's what you mean," Charlie said. "Now let's put the goddamn top back up, I'm freezing my ass off."

"I guess you haven't been reading those books," John said, laughing crazily again, as if he'd told the funniest joke in the world.

"What the hell's so funny?" Charlie demanded.

"Nothing."

"Well, must be something."

"Just what you said."

"What'd I say?"

"About dying, about being a good time to die . . . that's how Indian people think about death. I think you're a goddamned breed, is what I think."

"I'm no Indian, if that's what you mean," Charlie said. "And what the hell is this, anyway? Do you think Indians are the only ones who can die? Everybody does that. Even white folks."

"We're already dead, remember?" John asked. After a beat, he asked, "How the hell do I get to a liquor store from here?"

"You're on the highway, man."

"Well, get me off, or I'm just going to close my eyes and make a turn."

"You would, too," Charlie said; and the crazy fucker *would*, and for all that it might have been a good time to die a few seconds ago, that time was past. John was right: they needed a drink. And Charlie needed to get warm. "Get off at the next exit, and we'll go back on the side road and find a place. But the stores close by ten—it's the law—unless you want to go and sit in a bar. I'm telling you right now that I don't have any money. And we put the top up when we stop, is that clear?"

John didn't answer, but he took the next exit.

"Slow down," Charlie said, as they passed a small used car lot, a roadside diner, several stores, and a pink stucco ice cream parlor that was a landmark around these parts, for the owner made all the ice cream from scratch, from all natural ingredients, and it was a damned-sight better than the crap they sold in grocery stores or in the fast food places. "Slow it down or you'll have a cop up our ass."

Charlie didn't like going back into town. It was bad business. It was going home, and everybody knows you can't go home again. Not tonight, anyway. He felt a heaviness, just going back, even though he was in the next town over, which was not really "home". But it was as if all of his responsibilities were pulling him back, grabbing at him, tearing at him, and once he was caught, they would never let him go again. Tonight was his one chance to beat the Laws, to be golden, and if he fucked this up, it was over. He probably would have been better off if he had died back there when the time was right. But he had missed that. If a rock fell out of the sky and hit him on the head right now, he'd just drop dead like any other asshole. He had missed his moment.

"You got any money," he asked John, "because I sure as hell don't."

"Don't worry, we're all right. We're doing just fine."

"There's a place up ahead," Charlie said, pointing out a liquor store on the right-hand side of the road. It was small, and its neon sign wasn't working, but it was in an old Italian neighborhood and probably did a land-office business, Charlie thought. He had been around here before. In fact, he'd bought a bottle of wine in there once upon a time.

John braked the Caddy, but he sideswiped a parked Oldsmobile before coming to a screeching stop. Then he got out of the car as if nothing was wrong. The Caddy's fins were sticking right out into the road.

"What the hell are you doing?" Charlie asked, getting out of the car, too. He felt dizzy and had to lean against the door. "You can't leave the car here. Do you want to get us caught?" Maybe I should just say fuck it and get out of here, Charlie thought. He could hitchhike home. He could end it right now, and maybe things would just settle out and no one would be the wiser. He realized that he wanted to go home. He wanted to see Joline and the kids. He never really believed that he could just scream out of town like Marlon Brando on a motorcycle.

Yet that's just about what he had done. He had gone along for the ride to protect John, who was crazy out of his gourd. But John was a friend, and Charlie felt he owed him something.

Charlie was woozy and still mellow from the booze—he had tolerated more whiskey than he thought he could, more than Joline would give him credit for, certainly. But the whiskey made him feel that whatever he did could be somehow undone. It was as if he was dreaming and would wake up with nothing more than a hangover.

Charlie started coughing again. Goddamn, he did need a drink to open up his lungs. "Well, how much you got?" Charlie asked, fishing in his pocket for change. He found a dollar, folded tight, and some silver. "I got a buck-and-a-half."

"We're not going to pay for anything," John said matter-of-factly, and then he started walking around backwards again, this time in tight little circles, as if he was a child trying to make himself dizzy. He stopped and asked, "What the hell do you think you can buy for a dollar? Maybe some of that cheap-ass wine *you* drink. But I'm not a goddamn wino. I've got some pride left."

"Screw you, buddy," Charlie said. "If you're not going to pay ... Oh shit, not me! I'll be goddamned if I'm going to rob a store for a bottle of hooch."

"Who said anything about robbing?" John asked. "You robbed this big old Cadillac, not me."

"You crazy asshole. Who stole Steve Isaacs' car, the mice?"

"That wasn't stealing, that was renting because he was going to kick me out. I heard what he said to you about me, so I just used up some of *my* rent money, and his insurance will take care of the tiny bit of damage."

"Haven't you ever heard of a deductible?" Charlie asked, and then he got the giggles again. This whole conversation seemed to come into perspective: here they were arguing about stealing cars and robbing stores as if they were pricing clothes.

"I'll be right back," John said, and he walked backwards in a quickstep into the store.

"Wait!" Charlie shouted. "Come back here, goddammit to hell!" He felt the Laws closing in on him. Suddenly he was anxious and afraid . . . and stone-cold sober; it was as if he had never taken a drink. He had to get John out of that liquor store right away.

When Charlie walked into the store, he found John dancing around backwards and screaming and acting *heyoka*. A black man behind the counter looked terrified. He was stocky, wide-faced, and appeared to be about sixty.

"Look at this," John shouted to Charlie. "How's this for pissing?" Then John unzipped his fly and began urinating on a shelf of expensive cordials. "See? You got to get every *other* bottle—you can't get 'em all wet or you lose the game. That's the trick to creative pissing."

"Cut it out!" Charlie said to John. "You *are* a goddamn pervert. Let's get outa here before we get into real trouble."

"I told him we don't keep any money here," the man said to Charlie. "Just a few dollars in the register, and you're welcome to it. I don't want any trouble. I'm a family man." He talked quickly, excitedly.

"He don't mean any trouble, he's just had too much to drink," Charlie said, trying to calm the proprietor, if that's indeed who he was. He's probably just a part-time clerk, Charlie thought. He couldn't imagine a black owning a store in an Italian neighborhood. They'd skin the poor bastard's ass.

"I heard what you said," John said, zipping his fly. "I'm not drunk yet, at least not nearly enough. Haven't you ever seen a *heyoka* man before?" He walked toward the clerk. His face became hard. He looked big and menacing . . . the clown turned bully.

"He doesn't have a weapon," Charlie said. "Really, he's just fooling."

"Shut the hell up," John growled.

"Let's get *out* of here," Charlie pleaded. "Who the hell knows what they've got in here. It could have some sort of silent alarm built in or something." Charlie just wanted to scare John a bit, prod him to leave the store. But John went completely *heyoka* instead and started screaming and waving his fists at him.

Charlie stepped backward reflexively; the clerk did the same.

Perhaps it was the sudden movement that set John off because he climbed over the counter and grabbed at the clerk, knocking him down. The man made a rasping noise as his head banged against the counter.

"What the hell are you doing?" Charlie screamed.

"He was going for a gun," John said, sitting on the counter. "He was . . ."

"We don't keep a gun here," the clerk said in a quavering voice. "Please . . . just take the money and leave me alone."

John looked at Charlie—and the look on his face wasn't *heyoka*—then he said to the clerk in a soft voice, "I guess we made a couple of assholes out of ourselves. We weren't after your money . . . really. We just wanted some Scotch, you know, something not too expensive. I was going to trade you, so we wouldn't be stealing." John removed a red bead necklace from around his neck, got off the counter, and kneeled down beside

111

the clerk, who looked as if he was too frightened to move. "Here, this is for you," John said, giving the necklace to the clerk. "You know, *wampum*, like in the movies. We just wanted a bottle of cheap hooch. We're not trading for New York City." After a pause, John continued, "Okay, it was my fault, I get like that sometimes. I'm sorry about pissing all over your booze. I'll clean it up for you, how's that?"

The clerk didn't say a word; he just worried the bead necklace through his fingers. His forehead was cut, and the area around it had turned red and puffy.

"You're going to have one hell of a shiner there," John said as he reached over and touched the clerk's head.

"Just take whatever you want and leave me alone . . . please."

"You just cut yourself a little," John said, "probably when you fell. But it's nothing much. You got a first-aid kit here?" The clerk shook his head, averting his eyes from John, as if maybe that would make the Indian disappear. Charlie came around the counter. He felt like a goddamn fool just standing there. It suddenly occurred to him that anyone might walk right in the door.

"Come on, John," Charlie said. "Let's get out of here now."

John ignored him and untied a small leather bag he carried on his belt. He took out a clump of dried-up, brown leaves, which he rolled together in his hands with some spit. Then he applied the paste to the clerk's forehead.

"John!" Charlie said, impatient. "Let's get *out* of here before somebody comes in." But John shook his head at him, and Charlie didn't say any more. He wasn't going to push John, lest he go *heyoka* again and kill the poor black fucker he had just attacked.

"This'll help stop the bleeding and cut down on the inflammation a little," John said to the clerk, "but you've got to get some ice on it as soon as possible. You got any ice?"

The clerk didn't answer, but the look on his face was more amazement and disbelief than fear. "You some kind of Indian doctor or something?" he asked.

"I used to fool around with it a bit," John said. "Iodine and a cold compress would do the trick just as well. But I don't carry iodine around." John laughed; it wasn't his crazy *heyoka* laugh, but a good-natured one. "Remember, you've got to get some ice on that wound, or you'll have a lump the size of a basketball on your head."

"You're like a herb doctor then," the clerk said. It was as if that now he had tagged John as some sort of healer, he didn't have to be quite so afraid.

"I used to be something like that," John said.

"You give it up?" the clerk asked, as if now he had to talk.

"Yeah . . . for white man's fire water."

The clerk averted his eyes from John's, then—as if having made a decision—said, "My grandmother knew about herbs and plants and stuff like that."

"That right?" John asked. "There was a lot of that in my family, too. Come on, let me help you into the chair before we go." The clerk said that he really wasn't hurt and could get up by himself, but he accepted John's help. "Okay, we'll get outa here now. We've caused you enough trouble. We won't take any of your liquor or any of your money, and we'll leave you with our apologies."

The man nodded, as if he was not yet certain that the bad part was over.

"This sobered the hell out of me, I'll say that for it," John said, and something passed between the two men.

"I got a feeling you guys are on a pretty big binge."

"You got that right," John said, chuckling.

As John and Charlie started to leave, the clerk asked, "You want to take a couple of bottles . . . ? You might as well. After all this. What the hell. The boss's insured anyway . . . so what the hell."

"Thanks, friend," John said. He was weaving a bit, shaky on his feet, yet his voice was perfectly clear. Charlie, however, was wired. He paced around as if *he* were *heyoka*.

"Come *on*," Charlie said, opening the door.

"This man says we can take a few bottles along with us," John said, "so let's get us just what we need, and none of that wino stuff either. Whiskey . . . well, maybe one bottle of wine."

"Let's just get out of here."

John grabbed a few bottles as he worked his way out of the store. Once on the street, he said to Charlie, "I got you a bottle of wine. I can't read the label, but it's red. That okay?"

"Fine," Charlie said, although red wine gave him a headache. He was impatient to be on the road. For all he knew, the store clerk could be calling the police this very minute. It was chilly out. There was no one on the street, traffic was light, and the autumn moon was full and large and yellow. When they reached the car, Charlie held the door open for John.

"I still want to drive," John said. "I'm not done yet. I like this big old bird." He walked around to the driver's side, dropped the bottles into the back seat, and got into the car.

"Let's just get out of here," Charlie said, getting into the passenger seat. "Christ, my lungs are *killing* me."

John backed the car into the middle of the road, and then accelerated without laying any rubber . . . without swerving and fishtailing into the oncoming lane.

"We gotta get out onto the highway," Charlie shouted, the wind carrying away his voice, messing his hair and giving him the shivers. "We gotta get off this road or it'll take us right back into Johnson City where we took this car in the first place. And we got to put the top up. I can't take this cold."

Suddenly John cut over to the side of the road, stopped the car on the shoulder, and said, "Before we get out the booze and get all fucked up again, you can still get out of this car right now and walk away from it all. Go home to the wife and kids. Pretend it never happened. Like you dreamed it up, maybe, like that."

Charlie was tired. The booze was working itself out of his system. He had phlegm in his throat and his lungs were raw and he had a headache that seemed to be pulling out his eyes. John was right: Charlie could just go home. He would have had his binge, had it to worry around in his mind when everything came in at him and he had to go into the Isaacs' cellar to get relief. He loved his wife and family, but, Jesus, it would be the same thing all over again. It would be like being dead again. And he was going to get sick unless he had a drink, which would open up his lungs, too.

"Charlie . . . ?" John asked.

Jesus, I'm sitting in an open car—a *stolen* car—right on the road and daydreaming. Get out and go home, you stupid bastard, he told himself. But he said, "We should put the top up while we're here."

"You sure you don't want to take the walk?" John asked. He fumbled for a switch under the dashboard. With a whirring noise the convertible top rose over them. Then they both locked it down over the windshield.

"What the fuck, I already robbed a goddamn store and stole a car," Charlie said. "I might as well go the whole route and have a good time." He reached into the back seat to break out the liquor. He would leave the wine alone—it would only make him sick later, and he couldn't afford to be sick. He chose a bottle of very expensive Scotch instead. He took a long pull on it, choked, and felt the warmth pass down his throat, radiate into his lungs, then down into his stomach. He let his eyes go out of focus, as if that were their natural state, and realized that he had beaten the Laws. "Sonovabitch," he said. "We're getting away with it. Fucking A getting away with it." He had stolen a goddamn Cadillac . . . a

Cadillac, for Christ's sake ... and he robbed a store and sonovabitch if he wasn't alive *right now.*

John was drinking from another bottle. "Just tell me where to go, Charlie," John said.

He put the car into gear, and they screamed back onto the road.

"I'll tell you where to go," Charlie said, laughing and drinking and turning just as *heyoka,* just as crazy-blind-having-a-good-time as John could ever boast. They got on the highway, onto Route 17, going east toward New York. "This'll take us through Johnson City," Charlie said, "but I don't think it'll matter if we're on the highway because I'm going to tell you we're fucking-A golden. Everything's going to work."

Charlie was slurring his words and laughing so hard that he felt as if he were sinking right inside himself. He leaned out the window—which he had trouble getting down because he wasn't used to electric window switches—and shouted to the wind and the cold and the dark shoulder of the road that they were indeed golden.

"Get my pipe out of my bag in the back seat," John said.

"You going to get religion again?" Charlie asked.

"Get the fucking pipe!" John shouted, and Charlie worked loose the laces of the army bag and pulled the pipe out from under some shirts.

"Now just tie it right onto the rear-view mirror."

There it dangled like a rabbit's foot.

"Now we're protected," John said, weaving between cars and eighteen wheelers, cruising along at a cool ninety, and they passed a bottle of Johnny Walker Black back and forth. Charlie drank as if it were the old days, as if he could handle the load ... as if he were still a bull and could drink anygoddamnbody under the table and out of the bar.

"You still believe in that stuff?" Charlie asked, feeling numb and warm. He no longer had the shakes, nor was he coughing, and he could take a deep breath and hear only the slightest wheeze. There was nothing like alcohol for emphysema. In fact, Charlie told himself, this binge was medicinal in nature.

"What stuff?" asked John.

"The pipe."

"Would I hang it on the goddamn rear-view mirror if I believed in it?"

"I dunno," Charlie said.

"Well . . . either do I," John said, laughing. "Either do I. But it worked before. It most likely will work now, although maybe not for you and me."

"I think that's sacrilegious."

"Well, I don't give a *fuck* what you think, but I'm telling you that we're behind an invisible shield like on that television program, and cops or nobody is going to see us or find us till we get where we're going."

He's crazy, Charlie thought, gazing out the window at the shadows whizzing past.

"You're thinking bad thoughts again," John said, "and I don't even have to see your face to know that."

"You're crazy!"

"You been laid since you been married?" John asked.

"That's none of your goddamn business!"

"I don't think you have."

Charlie didn't answer.

"Been a long time for me, too. At least a couple of weeks." John laughed at that. "I just thought you might be interested in the soft touch of a woman, that kind of stuff."

"I wouldn't be against it," Charlie said.

"I didn't mean anything against your wife," John said. "I meant whether you've screwed anybody *other* than your wife."

"I know what you meant, and I don't think it's any of your business."

"It is too my business if we're going to get fucked up together and maybe die together . . . that's the same as a marriage, sort of."

"I think you're . . ." Charlie was going to say "queer," but he didn't want John to go crazy *heyoka* and kill them then and there in the car, so he said, "I only screwed around once . . . and then I never went all the way."

"Well, here's to going all the way," John said, raising the bottle of scotch, then pouring a few drops out on the dash as an offering before taking some himself and passing it to Charlie. "We've got almost a full tank of gas," John said after a while, "although I don't know how many miles per gallon this beast gets."

"Talk nice about the car," Charlie said, "or it'll do bad things." Charlie was sleepy and relaxed, even though John was driving like a maniac—but what the hell, they were protected, they'd beaten the Laws, they were golden, and maybe the pipe would make a difference.

"I think we should follow the birds," John said.

"Whaddyamean?"

"I'm going to take this thing to Florida. You ever been there?"

That woke Charlie up. "Stephen Isaacs' father lives in Florida."

"Well, maybe we should pay the man a visit."

"I don't want to go to fucking *Florida*," Charlie said.

"Why not?"

"Too humid . . . not good for my lungs."

"It's the best thing for your lungs," John said, groping in his pockets for a cigar, which he found and lit. "It's getting cold here. We should go to Florida for the winter like the rich people do."

Charlie opened his window. "That thing is making me sick."

"We're going to make you well. We're going south. That direction has special meaning to an Indian. You know what it means?" John asked.

"How the hell should I know what it means, I'm not an Indian."

"Who knows, maybe you are."

"You're crazy . . ."

"Directions are important," John said. "In themselves. You and me and everybody else has a direction. You have your own. It's a gift, you know, like cigars," and John started laughing.

"You're going off the road," Charlie said calmly.

"South is a good direction, it's the direction of trust and innocence . . . and death."

"I hope you have money for gas," Charlie said, and then he slid into a deep drunken sleep, a wet jolting sleep.

7.

GODS ON A DRUNK

Charlie woke up when the car hit the metal guardrail. He had been sleeping against the door, and it was as if the door had just banged into his head. "Whassimatter?" he mumbled, lurching forward, as John brought the car to a stop by the side of the road. The moonlight gave the forested roadside a silvery cast, and the Caddy's powerful high-beams illuminated the grassy, debris-scattered bank.

"Must've fallen asleep or something," John said. "Maybe you should drive for a while . . . the car's been acting funny, anyway. I think it's probably running out of gas. It's been coughing . . . just like you." John grinned good-naturedly at Charlie, who turned away.

"Jesus, I feel sick," Charlie said. He could feel his stomach clamping up on him, the pain coming and going in spasms, and he felt as if he was going to gag.

"You need some hair of the dog," John said brightly.

"Fuck you. I'll be right back." Charlie got out of the car, stumbled up the bank, and worked his way through the brush and tree branches of the woods. It was windy, and the stunted, grotesque-looking trees seemed to move as if they were animated by dark spirits from the sweat-lodge.

Charlie jumped in fright when he inadvertently kicked an empty beer can. He felt sick again. He leaned against a tree, then squatted down, his back against the trunk, and held his palms tightly to his forehead, just as his mother used to do for him when he was sick. Joline would have done the same thing; he wanted her cool hands pressed against his face. He didn't want to be sick by himself. Just now all he wanted was to be back home in his softly lit living room. He wanted to lie on the couch with Joline and watch the tube. He wanted to feel her soft fleshy body under the blanket beside him; and for a hallucinatory instant he imagined he could smell her hair and her natural, tangy odor. He could even smell her familiar perfume, faint as memory itself; and he imagined he was fondling her breasts, one and then the other; and they were heavy and doughy in his hands, except for the hard knots of her erect nipples. He remembered how she would exhale when he touched her between her legs. Even after twenty years she would become moist at his touch. She would search out his erect penis and slide down on the couch, taking the blanket with her; and she would take him into her mouth, where he would be safe as she worked him until he was shaking and numb in the dream-like wetness of ecstasy; and then she would crawl on top of him and mount him, while he wheezed beneath her, holding her tight, as if he had lifted her over him like a blanket; and she would clench her teeth and make a choking sound as she came.

Charlie coughed and couldn't catch his breath, and for an instant he thought he was really going to choke this time, that this was going to be the big one. He felt in his pockets for his inhaler, found it in his jacket under a pint of Four Feathers that he had taken out of the back seat of the Cadillac, and he sucked its mist greedily into his lungs. He coughed all the more for a moment, and then breathed freely.

After a while, he felt good enough to try to make his way back to the car, but Jesus he was weak . . . and it was cold as a witch's tit out here. His stomach growled; it felt empty. He needed *food*, although he couldn't stand the thought of it; he was sure he wouldn't be able to keep anything down, anyway. But damn if that wasn't what he needed. When was the last time he had eaten? He couldn't remember, but he knew from his younger days that it was dangerous just to drink without feeding your face because all that booze made you think you weren't hungry. Goddamn, I'm weak, he thought, and he was almost going to tell himself that he needed a drink. He zippered up his jacket to his neck. His son had given him that jacket: it was shiny on the outside and soft and warm on the inside. But the chill went right through him and settled in his hollow stomach.

Then he saw something on the road. It was a flashing light, not just the headlights of passing cars. Was there an accident?

Oh, Jesus, Mary, Mother of God, he thought, freezing where he was, then working up the courage to take a few more steps down through the woods to gain a view of the highway. It was true . . . the worst. A green and white state trooper car was parked behind the Caddy, a Plymouth by the looks of it, and its rotating beacon was flashing red and white light all over the road. There was a trooper standing beside the Caddy and talking to John, but Charlie couldn't make out what they were saying.

You got to do something, he told himself, but he was shaking so hard he could hardly breathe. He felt as if he had to urinate, and he automatically tightened his sphincter and pressed his legs together.

What the hell am I supposed to do? Charlie asked himself. If I go down there, they'll only get me, too, and what the hell good would that do? Shit, I could just stay here . . . He could tell John later that he had just plain blacked-out, and when he woke up the car was gone. Just like that. Then maybe he could help John out of the mess. For that matter, he could throw away his pride and call Stephen, who could find a lawyer for John and fix the whole thing up. But that little sonovabitch wouldn't do anything for anybody. No, if Charlie was going to do anything, it had to be right now. After all, he had been a goddamn Marine. He had almost gotten his ass blown off at Guadalcanal in the Solomon Islands, for Chrissakes.

He crawled down as quickly as he could, keeping to the cover, making very little noise as he neared the road. He could hear the police car's motor running. He could also hear its radio, each call sharp with static. The trooper, who was in uniform, but wasn't wearing his hat, stood just to the side of the Caddy's door and was talking with John. John had to crane his neck to talk with the man.

"I don't *know* where my license is," John said. His voice was slurred. He must have been hitting the booze when Charlie left ... before the trooper arrived. "... in fact, I can't even remember if I have a license."

"You don't *remember* whether or not you have a driver's license?" asked the trooper. "Do you have *any* identification? Are you telling me that you don't have your license with you or that you don't have one period?"

"I don't know," John said.

"Oh, Jesus," the trooper complained, impatient. He shone a long, five cell kel-light into the car. "Don't you carry a wallet with you?"

"Nope, I guess I don't."

"You know being a wise guy isn't going to help you."

"I'm not *being* a wise guy, your honor."

The trooper shone his light into the car again, throwing the beam into the back seat and onto John's duffel bag. "What's in there? Would you have identification in there?"

"Maybe ..."

"Well, then why don't we take a look," the trooper said. "And what's that hanging from your mirror there?"

"It's a peace pipe," John said. "Keeps me sober and close to God."

"Let's see that, too."

"I'm too old to smoke pot, your honor," John said. "Of course, all us old Indians drink ourselves dead—you know, because of all those broken treaties and all that stuff. Well, there I done and told you, I let out the red man's secret."

"Just let me see the pipe."

While the trooper inspected the pipe and helped John search his duffel bag, Charlie crawled down to the road. He came out on the shoulder just behind the police car. There was only one chance. If he fucked this one up, he would probably get himself killed. He shivered at the thought.

But he couldn't let John down. Now, it wasn't just John. If Charlie didn't do this, didn't at least take his shot, then he might as well be dead. He wouldn't be able to face himself . . . ever. He knew that most of his bragging was all bullshit anyway, and even the truth was so old that it didn't matter anymore to anyone.

Got to be right *now*! Charlie thought. Oh, God, please let the door be unlocked . . .

He sneaked around to the driver's side of the trooper's car. He was all hunkered over, so as not to be seen until the last possible moment. Then he grabbed the door handle—thank Christ it wasn't locked—and threw himself into the car.

"Hey!" shouted the trooper, but Charlie was already turning the key in the ignition. In his nervousness, he forgot that the engine was already running, and the ignition made a terrible screeching noise. "Sonovabitch," Charlie mumbled as he jerked the gear shift into "Drive."

The trooper dropped his kel-light, which also functioned as a night stick, and was pointing a .357 Magnum right at Charlie's face. "Freeze, asshole," he shouted, "or I'm going to blow you a new one!" He was right in front of Charlie's headlights, and

Charlie could see the trooper's high forehead, his short-cropped red hair and full mustache, his thin, angry face—and the bastard was big!

But the trooper had forgotten about John, who swung his duffel bag at him with all his weight behind it, knocking the trooper off balance. The pistol clattered on the pavement.

"Jesus Christ," Charlie screamed, and he stepped on the accelerator and aimed that police car right at the trooper who was groping for his weapon. The trooper dove out of the way as Charlie brought the car to a screeching halt beside the Caddy. Charlie reached over to the passenger door and pulled the handle as he screamed, "John, get the fuck in here."

But the door was locked. Charlie lost precious seconds as he fumbled it open. "Hurry up," Charlie shouted. "He's going to blow our heads off." John grabbed his pipe and duffel, then jumped into the car, hitting his leg on the rocker panel. Charlie stomped the big Plymouth into overdrive, almost spilling John out of the car.

The trooper fired. The explosion was enormous; it hurt Charlie's ears, and there was a flash of light as bright as lightning.

"Sweet Jesus!" Charlie cried, ducking behind the wheel.

"Watch the goddamned road," John said.

Charlie screamed as another shot tore out a tail light and sent a tremor through the metal of the car. "He's *shooting* at us!"

"He's trying to shoot out the tires, you asshole," John said. "We're far enough away from him now. Calm yourself down. He could have just shot us down dead before, if he'd had a mind to, you know that?" John started laughing, but he didn't slip off into becoming *heyoka*, and he said, "Boy, that poor fucker is going to have a lot of explaining to do." John turned around in his seat and watched the road recede in tail-lit glow through the rear window. Then he swung his army bag past Charlie into the back seat.

"Watch it, I'm trying to drive," Charlie said. "You still got your pipe?"

"It's right here," John said, hanging it on the rear-view mirror bracket. "I may be bad and mad, but I wasn't going to leave a sacred pipe for a honky cop to display above his bar."

"You shouldn't talk like that about white people," Charlie said.

"I suppose you're right. I apologize." Then John started laughing, but he might as well have been screaming because he was making such throat-tearing sounds. "We need a drink, and we don't have *anything*! Goddammit, that trooper's got himself a whole stash of fine booze."

"Here," Charlie said, reaching into his jacket pocket for the pint of whiskey he'd been hiding. "I always keep a little for a rainy day," and then Charlie started laughing. He was *safe*. And he was driving a police car, and that big sonovabitch was back there with nothing but road and his big-dick cannon of a pistol. He opened the bottle and took a good swallow before giving it up to John, who would probably drain the whole damn thing without coming up for air. "Well, we're not *dead*!" Charlie said, feeling the warmth of the whiskey expanding into his lungs, opening them up. He felt warmth in his face and immediately wanted another drink. "You said it, John. We're fucking invulnerable, like on the goddamn television. You were right about that pipe. It's a goddamn rabbit's foot, is what it is."

"Don't talk too soon," John said.

"What do you mean?"

"That trooper is right behind us. He's in the Caddy."

Charlie looked into the rear-view mirror, and sonovabitch if the Caddy wasn't following them, blasting its horn as if it was in a wedding procession; and then there was another explosion and Charlie felt something hit the car. "If he hits the gas tank, we can call it a night. Jesus, he could blow us to kingdom come."

"That's the idea," John said. "I think he's a bit pissed by now."

Another shot, but the Caddy was no match for the Plymouth's souped-up engine.

"He's falling behind," Charlie said, and his hands were shaking on the steering wheel as if he'd been off the booze and taking that emphysema medicine that made him shake like an old man. Thank Christ, he said to himself.

"Shit, we forgot . . . the Caddy was running out of gas!" and John let out a shout and took another swallow from the bottle.

"Don't drink it all," Charlie said, reaching for it. And they polished it off and weaved back and forth on the highway, blowing the horn, and John figured out how to make the siren work.

They screamed down that highway, bathing the asphalt in flashing red light, sirens shrieking, as they soared like gods on a drunk.

8.

KNOCK YOURSELVES

OUT, HONKIES!

"We need booze, and we need to get off the highway," John said. He was wearing the trooper's hat that had been left in the car; the top of the hat was caved in and wrinkled. John had sat on it when he jumped into the car. John wasn't nearly as drunk as Charlie, who was driving, but he was drunk enough to be *heyoka*.

All Charlie could think about as he drove along was that he had done it—he had saved John's ass. The debt was there, and there it was, no matter how much John high-talked. Charlie was golden. He was one beautiful man. He still had the piss and vinegar inside him. He was still a bull. Right now he could drop dead, and it would be fine. He smiled: Let the bastards try to close the coffin on him. The radio dispatcher was talking a mile a minute, and, amid bursts of static, other cars were answering. It was like a goddamn convention of talking robots, Charlie thought, though he had the greatest respect for law enforcement officials when he was straightened out and sober.

"Harrisburg to Five Oh Nine."

"Five Oh Nine."

"Report of domestic disturbance at 3721 Grover Street . . . husband threatening wife . . ."

Charlie took an exit off Route 81 and kept on 34, a two-lane highway where they would be less conspicuous. "Man, nobody'd know we weren't troopers," Charlie said. "We can do *anything* we want!"

John had turned off the siren and rotating beacon, but Charlie was driving as if the trooper was still shooting at him. "Slow it down," John said as Charlie went over the shoulder trying to negotiate a sharp turn. "We've got to find some more to drink and a place to stay for the night. I'm not going to freeze my ass off in a car, or in a barn, or in a field." He took a map out of the glove compartment and discovered a button inside the glove box. He pushed the button and the trunk lid flew up. "Shit," he said, but Charlie didn't seem to notice that he couldn't see out of the rear-view mirror.

"We can rob another liquor store," Charlie said, "but nothing's open this late. We could just break through a window."

"I'm not a goddamn *criminal*," John said. "These things have to be done properly. If you can't trade, you don't do it."

"We'll leave something in return," Charlie said. "Your hat, we can leave that," and Charlie started laughing almost as crazily as John did at his worst and most *heyoka* moments.

John paid no attention to Charlie; he was carefully studying a map that seemed to take up his entire seat from his lap to the dashboard. He had turned on the overhead light, and Charlie complained because it was difficult to see the road with all that light inside. "I've got some people in Hancock, right over here," John said, and he pointed to a town outlined in red at the junction between Routes 40 and 70. Charlie leaned over to look at the map, but he couldn't make out one town or route from another. He slowed the car down to a crawl—he was looking for a good place to pee. He just hoped he could stand up long enough to empty his bladder.

Charlie pulled the car off to the side of the road. "After I pee, we'll go visit your friends," he said, suddenly dizzy. Perhaps it was because he wasn't in motion—that's what he told himself, anyway. Charlie sat quietly for a moment, his door cracked open to let in some fresh air. Maybe it's the goddamn clean country air that's making me dizzy, he thought. "Oh, the hell with it," and he pushed the door open and got out of the car. Leaning against the front fender, he peed right onto the road. He concentrated on directing his stream of urine to make his initials, something he hadn't done since he was a kid.

Everything seemed to be spinning and twisting around. But Charlie felt wonderful. He was light. He was golden. He whispered the word. "G-o-l-d-e-n." Goddamn right, he told himself. He jumped as the dispatcher started talking and making static, and almost urinated on his shoe.

"Harrisburg to Five Oh Seven."

After a long pause. "Five Oh Seven."

"Check for car operating northbound on southbound lane on 83 about five miles south of 76 junction. Possible drunk driver . . ."

"Hey, did you hear that?" Charlie asked, zipping up his trousers. He had to get back into the car before he started feeling queasy—he could feel *that* coming on. But at least he wasn't coughing.

John didn't answer. He'd fallen asleep and was snoring. Well, he had a lot to drink, Charlie thought, and being *heyoka* most of the time would probably tire anybody out. But Charlie had no idea where John's friends lived; and if he, Charlie, tried to look at all those tiny letters on the map, he'd surely vomit. Maybe it's not such a bad idea to just get some sleep here, Charlie told himself. This didn't seem to be a well-traveled road. Christ, there was barely *anybody* driving on it.

Then there was static and the now familiar voice of the dispatcher.

"Harrisburg to all troop cars and stations ... prepare to copy File One, repeat, prepare to copy File One ... Stolen during commission of assault on Pennsylvania trooper 1992 Plymouth police vehicle. Registration number five-oh-nine-one ... vehicle is a marked Pennsylvania state police vehicle, fully equipped ..."

"John, wake up!" Charlie shouted. "That's us, they're talking about us! We gotta do something."

John woke up with a start, shook his head and blinked his eyes and mumbled something that Charlie couldn't understand.

"Listen to this fucking thing, will you," Charlie demanded. We're never going to get out of this, he told himself. Jesus, I don't want to go to jail ...

The dispatcher was repeating the message: "... stolen during assault on Interstate 81, north of Shippensburg, last seen headed south traveling at a high rate of speed, operated by a Caucasian male of approximately sixty years of age. His companion is a male Native American of approximately the same age, gray hair, long, wearing ..."

"Shit," John said, and he started pushing the frequency selectors on the police radio. "It's probably too late, but maybe we can jam the bastard ... one of these buttons is the emergency frequency, and if we can jam that, we'll jam the whole damn thing, nobody'll be able to talk."

"How'd you know about that?" Charlie asked.

"My son-in-law's a cop. There, I think maybe it's the last button." He pressed it and picked up the microphone, holding down the talk switch. "Hello, you dumb sonovabitches," he screamed into the mike. "Knock yourselves out, honkies!"

"Stop it," Charlie said nervously. "We're in enough trouble as it is."

John covered the microphone's grill and said, "You want every goddamned trooper in the state to hear you whining? I need a rubber band or a piece of tape or *something* to hold this thing down, and I'll close it up in the glove compartment." John fished around in the glove box, but there was nothing in there that he could use. He got out of the car and looked in the trunk, which was still open. He found a small roll of electrician's tape in a gray tool-box; he also found two blankets, a pillow, and a riot gun with ammunition. He got back into the car, taped down the talk-switch, and wound the tape around the grill until it was covered and the tape used up. Then he put the mike into the glove box, which he jammed shut over the handset cord. After that he said, "Now look at all the stuff we got."

"We don't need a gun, for Chrissakes," Charlie said.

"One never knows." John was starting to act crazy again. "I've got a present for you."

"Yeah, what's that?" Charlie asked.

John took out a handful of miniature liquor bottles. "I'd forgotten I had these. Even though that guy at the liquor store was being so nice, I couldn't help myself. You know how us Indians are. Anyway, I always thought these little bottles were cute." He gave Charlie two tiny bottles of cognac. "That stuff's good for your lungs," he said. "It'll stop your coughing better than your emphysema medicine. Cure pimples, too. Trust me, I'm a doctor." He laughed good-naturedly. He hadn't reached the nasty, down-cycle side of being *heyoka*. He took one gulp and finished off a bottle of Cherry Herring. He made a sour face and tossed the bottle out the window. "You want me to drive . . . you're still drunk."

"I want you to get rid of the rifle, is what I want."

"Okay, you're right," and John tossed the rifle out the window. "You want me to toss the pillows out, too?" Without waiting for a response, he started throwing out the pillows and blankets, and started pulling buttons off the radios. He pulled the channel selector from the CB set, and he threw out the radar unit, which was on top of the dashboard.

"All right, enough," Charlie said. He finished off one of the tiny bottles of cognac and felt better, but goddamn if he wasn't getting hungry; and if he didn't get some sleep soon, he was probably just going to black out. "We need some candy bars," Charlie said.

John made a face and said, "I'm going to drive. I'm wearing the hat."

Charlie let him drive.

"We gotta get out of here, off the roads, and we gotta get rid of this car," John said. "Then we'll be fine, and I told you I know a place we can go, and I'll get you a candy bar if you're a good boy."

Charlie smiled sleepily. Then John switched on the siren—he had enough sense to leave that unit alone when he was pulling off knobs and breaking levers—and with lights flashing they roared down Route 30. They saw a car ahead, a new Oldsmobile, and John got behind it. The driver pulled over, and John stopped the police car in the middle of the road. "Now we're going to be *cops*," he said to Charlie. "You want to wait here or come with me?"

"Well, I'm not going to sit here in the middle of the goddamn street and get hit by some drunk."

They got out of the car. John walked backwards; the booze must have just hit him again. Thank God I got him to throw away the rifle, Charlie thought. Charlie was having some slight trouble walking. He felt as if he were on a ship; he could feel the ground gently rising and falling. They walked over to the driver's side of the Oldsmobile, John with his wrinkled trooper's hat and Charlie with his vomit-stained shirt and pants.

"You got identification?" John asked the driver, a middle-aged man who was wearing a blue suit and a blue-green tie that didn't match. The driver looked at John and Charlie, obviously surprised. "Well . . . ?" John asked. "Do you have identification or don't you? We're police officers."

"I've never seen . . . troopers dressed like you guys." The man had closely set eyes and jowly cheeks. He looked badly frightened. He was shaking and breathing hard, but he handed John his wallet. He looked to be too nervous to take out his driver's license and registration.

John took the wallet and said, "We work undercover. You know, like on TV."

"Come on," Charlie whispered to John. "Let's just leave him alone and get the hell out of here." He felt sorry for the man and was worried about John. If John was already walking around backwards, he would soon be dancing and screaming and shouting.

"Would you please get out of the car," John said to the driver, who obediently opened the door and stood stiffly beside the car. He was overweight. John took a twenty dollar bill out of the man's wallet and said, "I'm going to requisition this. No, I'm going to trade you this twenty dollar bill for this ring," and John took off a heavy silver ring with a turquoise stone that was set into a worked silver leaf collet. "I think that's more than a fair trade, don't you?" he asked, handing the ring to the man, who, terrified, just nodded his head.

"Come *on*," Charlie said.

John sniffed at the man. "We have reason to believe that *you've* been drinking. There's a lot of that going on, and we're here to put a stop to it . . . that's why we stopped you. Why, you were weaving all over the goddamned road, did you know that?"

"I haven't had a drink," the man mumbled.

"Ah," John said to Charlie, "this citizen says he hasn't had a drink. Okay," he said to the man, "I want you to walk a straight line down the road. So start walking."

Illuminated by headlight beams, the man walked. John paced him. John was unsteady on his feet and made a big show of it; the citizen walked a straight line until he was ordered to stop. When they returned to the car, John said, "You see, you're all over the place. *That's* not what I call walking a straight line, nosireebob it isn't. Not in our book. Right, officer?" he said to Charlie.

"Cut the shit," Charlie said, impatient and ashamed of himself for allowing John to bully this poor man.

Charlie's comment seemed to have a salutary effect on John, for he leaned toward the man and said, "We're going to have to impound your car." The man just goggled at him. "If you don't get it back in a day or so, you should contact our main office in Harrisburg."

Charlie would have laughed at that—John sounded so serious and official—but he felt sorry for this poor fucker who knew damn well he was being ripped-off by a couple of drunk criminals, and was too afraid to protest.

"You should be able to flag down a car without any trouble," John continued. "We would leave you our patrol car, but I'm afraid our present assignment requires two cars. Is that understood?"

The man could only nod.

But Charlie was beginning to worry about John again. Maybe he really did think he was a trooper and that they were going out on some secret assignment. Thank Christ we got rid of that rifle, at least, Charlie thought.

"Officer . . ." John said, meaning Charlie, "you take the patrol car and—no, *I'll* take the patrol car, and you take this car and follow me. Is that understood?"

"Oh, Christ," Charlie mumbled, but he got into the big green Oldsmobile, shifted it into "drive" and followed John. He couldn't help but glance at the man standing alone, back by the side of the road, as he drove past him. The man just stood there, as if he couldn't believe that any of this was happening.

Well, at least he can get himself another car with the insurance, Charlie told himself. Although Charlie never *really* had any dealings with insurance companies, he knew goddamn well that they had a lot of money. He'd known people who had cheated them and come out ahead. Maybe this guy would get lucky. At least he'll have some stories to tell his grandchildren or the boys in the bar. But somehow Charlie couldn't imagine that sheep of a man sitting in a bar telling stories.

Charlie followed John down Route 30 for several miles, and then John turned off the two-lane highway onto a steep dirt road. Charlie followed. They were going north now. They passed a few ramshackle one-storey houses, caught them in the fog-roiling beams of the headlights.

Then there was nothing but bumpy, dusty road ahead and the dark mysteries of the country around them.

Suddenly Charlie was afraid. He glanced into the rearview mirror: nothing but a red halo of tail-lit road. What the hell's the matter with me? he asked himself, forcing a laugh. But he felt as if he was being *watched*. He used to have that fear when he was a child, and it had its long-term effects: He wasn't able to sleep without a night-light until he was almost twenty-five years old. He used to rationalize keeping a light on in the bathroom so he could see where he was going when he had to get up at night to pee. But thank Christ I've grown out of *that*, he told himself. I'm not afraid of any man or any thing!

But he knew he was lying to himself. He was afraid right now.

Then, for one terrible instant, the only working tail-light of the patrol car John was driving became a glowing coal in the darkness. For that instant Charlie forgot where he was and thought he was back in the sweat-lodge. The patrol car had become the face of Joseph Whiteshirt. It was magnified, as if in a dream. It was right there ahead of Charlie, grinning at him again through teeth that clenched a red-hot coal.

Charlie jerked backward, hitting the back of his head on the head-rest, as if he had just awakened from a nightmare. "It's only the goddamn tail-light," he said aloud. He laughed at himself again, nervously. Goddamn, if I don't need a drink, he thought. But John had the booze in the patrol car, or what was left of the booze.

He turned on the radio, tuned in a Willie Nelson song. Charlie loved shit-kicking music, but couldn't abide twanging country-western, which Joline played all day long on her radio.

John slowed down and drove the patrol car off the road into a field. Charlie pulled over to the side of the road and watched John drive the patrol car behind some trees and growth at the bottom of an incline, which might have been a dry stream-bed—it was too dark and far away for Charlie to tell. All he could see were headlights shining dimly through trees; then they went out, leaving Charlie to the glow of the instrument panel, the road ahead lit by high-beams, and the crackle of two stations blending on the radio. He waited for John, who seemed to be taking a long time getting back to the car.

But John stepped into the road in front of the car and came around to the driver's side. "They're not going to find that car for a while," John said, as he opened the door. "Move over," he said to Charlie. "I'll drive because I know where we're going."

"Did you bring whatever we got left of the hooch?" Charlie asked, moving over. He was glad for John's company. "I think I need a drink."

"We've got a little less than half a pint left," John said, sliding into the driver's seat. He gave the bottle to Charlie, who took a long swallow. "You got to make up your mind whether you're sick or hungry or what," John said. He turned the car around, got back on Route 30, and took the Olds up to an even seventy miles an hour. Charlie took another drink. He needed it after seeing that coal in Whiteshirt's mouth again ... even if it was only a goddamn hallucination. Even now, with John sitting right beside him, he felt as if he were being watched.

John drove west, then south and west again, taking a roundabout route to reach Hancock, keeping to the back roads to elude police, just in case. But he drove that Oldsmobile as if it were a stock car in the break-em-up races, and for a new car it certainly rattled enough.

Charlie felt dead-tired and yet revved-up at the same time. He needed to shut down and fall asleep, but his mind was working furiously. He was even seeing little white and purple spots before his eyes, and he had the idea that they were his thoughts. He had felt this way before, and it was always bad. He had ended up in the drunk-tank once, after seeing spots and hallucinating. He couldn't remember much about the incident, except that he'd gotten blasted with a friend when he had the *Lorelei*, and they'd taken some Mexican girls out to sea with them, but he'd continued drinking after he got back home, drinking alone and heavily, and he didn't remember why, but he'd cried his eyes out over something. Never again will I spend another night in the tank with all those stinking, goddamn drunks, he promised himself. "How do you feel?" Charlie asked John. They had finished off the bottle of whiskey together, and Charlie was feeling slightly nauseated again. But at least his lungs were clear and he wasn't shaking.

"What do you mean, how do *I* feel?" John asked. "I feel fine."

"No, I didn't mean it that way," Charlie said. "I mean do you feel sort of . . . edgy, or something?"

"I feel dragged out and fucked up. I want a bed and sleep and a big fat woman to make me happy. Now tell me what the hell you're really trying to say."

"I dunno."

"It's Whiteshirt, isn't it?" John asked, turning down the heat. You either froze or sweltered in this car; there didn't seem to be a middle range.

"What do you mean?"

"I asked *you* that!" John said angrily, swerving all over the road, as if to emphasize his point. "You're seeing things, aren't you, and they're scaring the piss right outa you."

"I didn't say anything about being—"

"You're a liar and you know it. I feel something, as if something's behind me . . . like that."

"Like what?" Charlie asked.

"Just a figure of speech."

"Probably the booze," Charlie said. "But I keep remembering . . ."

"In the sweat-lodge, that's it, isn't it."

"I keep seeing that coal that that guy had in his mouth."

"It works on everybody different," John said. "I shouldn't've brought you with me, got you into this. You're right, we're carrying something heavy."

"What do you mean?"

"Somebody's working on us . . . isn't wishing us well."

"Don't start with that bad medicine crap again," Charlie said.

"*You* brought it up, *you're* the one seeing Joe Whiteshirt, and you tell *me* it's bullshit."

"It's in the mind, that's all," Charlie said.

"Have it whatever way you like."

After a pause, Charlie asked, "What can you do about it?"

John laughed. "Stay drunk and see what happens."

9.

HOW IT WAS IN THE
OLD DAYS

They pulled into the wide driveway of an old farmhouse outside of Hancock at four o'clock in the morning. They were just a few miles over the Maryland border. John had fallen asleep at the wheel several times, but Charlie kept waking him. Charlie was too wired to sleep. He was bone-tired . . . overtired.

It was cold out, and a dog started barking from somewhere in the vicinity of the house. The driveway was lined with cars, as if some sort of convention was going on there. Most of the cars were old beaters, except for a white sports car parked between two rusted-out pick-ups. A full moon, which looked hazy behind the slowly moving clouds, lent the sky some gray, and it *felt* like morning, although it could have easily been ten o'clock at night. An outside light over the doorway cast a harsh light into the driveway and part of the yard, giving the place a desolate appearance. The house looked white in the half-light, and it was long.

"I'm going to stay in the car," Charlie said. "It's four o'clock in the morning, for Chrissakes!"

"*Somebody's* up, there's lights on," John said. "Not to worry. These people are my friends."

"I don't care," Charlie said, but just then a door opened, more lights came on, and someone called, "Who's there?" It was a woman's voice.

John opened his door and stumbled out of the car, almost falling in the driveway. He looked toward the road, hands on his hips, his back to the house, and shouted, "It's John Stone, and he's drunk, and horny as a dog in the rut. And the stupid bastard's backwards and upside-down again."

It was like a goddamn act, Charlie thought. He just turns it on like water from a faucet. But then Charlie remembered that look on John's face when he was dancing around in the cellar, and when he went for that black clerk in the liquor store.

A stocky woman walked down the driveway toward them. She was wearing some sort of sacky dress, and she didn't look like she had a curve on her. "John Stone, you're welcome here, even if you're sick again. But mind you, leave the young girls alone!" She was smiling and obviously teasing him.

John began to laugh. He turned around and let out a whoop. "So you got some college girls for Uncle John . . ."

The woman looked inside the car at Charlie, but didn't say anything to him or acknowledge his presence, if she could even see him. "There's some hot coffee on the stove," she said to John. "And I can make up a fresh pot. There's also bread . . . and *wasna* and *wojapi*. I seem to remember that you like that kind of food. Well, are you going to kiss me?"

John said, "No," and then kissed her.

"God, do you stink!" the woman said. "You'd make a goat smell good."

"Thank you," John said cheerfully.

She stepped away from him. "You're welcome in my house, as always. Your friend, too. But I don't want you drinking. Not here."

"We've mostly run out of booze," John said. "Nothing left to drink, so you're safe." He leaned against the car. "What're all these cars doing here?" he asked, motioning with his arm. "You all going to sun dance?"

"Jesus, you are drunk," the woman said. "This is the wrong season for sun dance. And *you've* already been there."

"Then what's going on?"

"Friend of yours is here. In some trouble. Just like you, except you're too dumb and drunk to know it."

"Who?" John asked. Then his legs seemed to give way, and he slid down the car to the ground. He made himself comfortable and rested his back against the rear wheel. "Goddamn if everything isn't going around and around ever so slowly."

"Are you sober enough to help your friend?" the woman asked Charlie in a loud, raspy voice. Charlie didn't think he was going to like this fat, bossy woman—from what he could see, she was probably fat. But he got out of the car, feeling a touch of nausea and dizziness as soon as he stood up.

"Come on, John," Charlie said. "We're making an imposition on these people. Let's get the hell on our way and leave them alone."

"John's family," the woman said. "And so's anybody traveling with him."

"Goddamn right!" John said, but he wouldn't let Charlie help him to his feet. He pulled his knees against his chest and sat back against the tire. "Now tell me what friend of mine is here?"

"Janet—Joe Whiteshirt's woman. After what happened in the sweat-lodge, she got into it heavy with Joe, and left him. She told him he was acting like a witch. She came here to clean up: We just did a *yuwipi*. She had questions for the spirits, she needed help, like I expect you do, since you're here."

"It was on our way," John said. Then he asked, "Who did the *yuwipi*? And who brought her down here? She doesn't drive."

"Sam."

"What!"

"Sam's a good *yuwipi* man," the woman said. "You ought to know, you taught him most everything he knows."

"But it was *wrong* for him to be bringing her down here," John said. "It was because of her and Sam that this whole thing happened. And Sam's supposed to be vision-questing! What the *hell* is he doing here?"

"Probably same thing you are. He came down off the hill. He couldn't face four days up there after what had happened. It was like a desecration."

"I don't know what that means, but it had nothing to do with Sam. He was supposed to vision-quest! Now he's taken up with another man's wife. This ain't bad medicine, it's just . . . bad!"

"You have a dirty mind, John Stone," the woman said. "They brought people along with them. They haven't been alone for a moment. What happened between them is over. It was a mistake. They both realize that."

"It's just going to make Whiteshirt *more* crazy. I wouldn't be surprised if he showed up here with a gun looking for Sam and Janet. And in a way, I don't know if I would blame him!"

"I don't think you know the whole story," the woman said. "Joe Whiteshirt's practically been living with Violet, the red-headed woman who used to always be hanging out at his camp. Remember her? Things haven't been so good between him and Janet. He's made Janet eat enough dirt for what she did. You can bet on that."

"I already know the story . . . Sam told me. But you can't blame everything on the woman—Violet. There's too much passing the buck going on, and everybody's blaming every human thing on medicine. It's not good, not good at all."

"Well, you're the medicine man. Maybe you can help."

"I'm no medicine man any more," John said.

"Well, if that isn't the biggest piece of bullshit I ever heard," the woman said. "And there's *something* going on. You can call it whatever you like, but it all comes down to the same thing, as far as I'm concerned. I think that woman's a witch."

Charlie felt awkward standing there, privy to the conversation. "Let's just go!" he said angrily. "I've had enough of all this bad medicine and voodoo crap. Excuse me, ma'am, I didn't mean any disrespect," he said to the woman.

"Don't pay Charlie any mind," John said. "He says he doesn't believe in medicine, but he's been shitting his pants ever since he was in the sweat-lodge." After a pause he said, "Lorena, I'd like you to meet my good friend Charlie. Charlie, Lorena. Everybody seems to go to Lorena's when they need some taking care of." He looked up at Lorena, beaming at her, and said, "You might as well become an Indian, for all the trouble you go to for us."

"We talked about that," Lorena said.

"Yeah, Whiteshirt, that stupid bastard, wanted to give her a pipe to carry. It's not time for white people to carry pipes," he said to Lorena. "Even people as good and kindhearted as you. It would have been wrong."

"I still don't understand it," Lorena said, "but I've always trusted what you've told me. Still . . . *you* taught Joe Whiteshirt . . ."

"And I taught Sam, too," John said in a disgusted tone. "And look how that turned out." Then he began to slip back into being *heyoka*. "Maybe you *should* carry a pipe, who the hell knows. Maybe all Indians should go to church and stop sweating and vision-questing and—"

"Stop it, John," Lorena said, looking upset. "You're a crazy-ass drunk, and you're going to say things you'll regret. We have enough trouble already."

"Her husband's a engineer," John said to Charlie. "That's how they can afford to live like Indians." John started laughing, his *heyoka* laugh, and Charlie felt embarrassed for the woman.

"I'll bring you two out some towels and soap," Lorena said,

almost in a whisper. "In the meantime, you can go up to the creek and start getting undressed."

"For what?" John asked.

"You know goddamn well for what, John Stone. You're filthy and you stink. You need some cleaning up and sobering-up . . . both of you, I think."

"It's too cold to wash," John said.

"That never bothered you before," Lorena said. "You used to brag that you were part Eskimo, remember? And neither one of you are coming into *my* house like that. You two are a mess! You should be ashamed of yourselves. Now you *are* going to get washed up and clean." With that, Lorena walked away toward the house.

"I'll be damned if I'm going to jump into your goddamn creek," John shouted. "I'm an *Indian*. It's white folks who need to get themselves cleaned up."

"You're a real sonovabitch," Charlie said to John.

"Lorena's a good woman," John said, as if he had missed Charlie's point. "And she's done a lot for Indian people. But she's trying to *be* an Indian, and she's not. But she'd do anything in the world for anybody. I like her—I'm crazy about her—but I can't stand some of the people she takes in, all those nice middle-class kids looking for gurus, and the weekend Indians trying to *be* gurus. There's always groupies hanging around . . . Wannabees. You'll see."

"You use people," Charlie said.

"You're right, I did wrong. Lorena," John called, "I'm sorry. I'll be a good boy. We'll take our baths."

Charlie helped John to his feet—although Charlie wasn't in any better shape than John—and they stumbled up the grassy stone and dirt driveway. John led the way past the well-lit house and into the back yard, which looked like it was part of a natural clearing in the woods. Charlie could hear the soft gurgling and splashing of the stream, but he couldn't see it. He breathed in a wonderfully damp, woody aroma: the smells of moss and soil and trees. Widely spaced birch and pine trees looked silvery in the moonlight.

Suddenly John broke away from Charlie and started singing and dancing and throwing his clothes all over the ground. Buck naked, he ran toward a grove of hemlocks and jumped down the bank and into the stream below. Charlie heard him belly flop into the water. "Come on," John shouted.

Charlie followed. The stream was about six feet wide and curved into the woods; it looked dark and cold and misty. Charlie remained on the bank, and John stood in the fast-moving water, his hands on his hips, legs apart, as the moonlight turned him to pale stone and shadow. "We're gonna need soap if we're gonna smell good," he shouted loudly enough to be heard at the house. "Now get your goddamn ass in here, Charlie," he commanded. "It's not so bad once you're in."

That was a lie. The water was icy cold, exhilarating, and sobering. Charlie stepped in cautiously, gasped; and for a few luminous seconds, he was overwhelmed with sensation: the sharp bite of cold water, the shivering night shadows, the shattered mirror surface of the stream reflecting silvery-gray moonlight, John's face slipping in and out of darkness, changing each time, as if caught by a strobe light . . . and for those few seconds, Charlie was *heyoka*. He experienced only the moment. The past had sloughed away like old skin. The future was . . . nothing and

Charlie was simultaneously an eagle, wings outstretched. A fish. A bull. The light on the water. The chill in the air. The splashing. He was all that until a callow-looking boy of about nineteen appeared with two bars of soap, which he threw to John and Charlie.

After he left, John said, "See what I mean about groupies? He should be in college smoking pot or something, instead of doing errands for Lorena." John rubbed the large, coarse bar of soap all over himself.

After much splashing and shouting and sobering up, John said, "Damn, that kid didn't leave us any towels." Then in a loud voice: "If Lorena doesn't come right along with some towels, I'm going to walk into the house *naked*."

"Oh, no, you're not," Lorena said.

"Why you sly old fox," John said. "I think you've been standing around here all this time watching us. I'm going to tell your old man you're a Peeping Tom."

"You can tell him whatever you like," Lorena said. "I'm leaving these clean clothes and towels for both of you. When you're ready, there's fresh, hot coffee inside . . ."

It was warm and bright and cozy inside the huge kitchen, which had a wood-burning stove side by side with a gas stove. There was an old oak dining table on the far side of the room and a doorway that opened into a living room. In the middle of the living room was a swing for the children; it hung from the high-ceilinged rafters.

Three young people were sitting at the table—two women and the boy who had brought the towels to John and Charlie. They were drinking Lorena's strong, bitter coffee and eating the remains of a large chocolate cake. They looked wired, as if they were too excited to sleep. Although they were all wearing flannel shirts and faded dungarees, Charlie was certain that the women came from wealthy families. Both of them had almost perfect, even teeth, which Charlie equated as a sure sign of money. The boy, on the other hand, had wide spaces between his teeth. His parents probably worked for a living, Charlie surmised.

Lorena made the introductions: The boy's name was Carl; the tall, lanky, chestnut-haired woman was Sharry; and the intense, nervous-looking woman was Heather. She had short-cropped black hair, and her name, which made Charlie think of freedom and wildness and open country, didn't fit her at all. Then Lorena ordered John and Charlie to sit down, and she served them coffee and cut them some cake. The coffee was just what Charlie needed, but the thought of swallowing that cake made him gag—he wasn't ready for that yet.

John made small talk, and the kids seemed to hang on every word he said—they had obviously been told about what had happened at Sam's vision-quest. Carl and Sharry kept trying to swing the conversation around to religion. They especially wanted John to talk about *yuwipi*'s and about how it was in "the old days". They wanted to hear about vision-quests where medicine men would either hang from the sides of cliffs for days on end, or would be buried alive. John usually persisted, though, in sliding back into small talk, into that smooth and easy, chiding tone of voice that Charlie had heard him use with women before. But John was more animated tonight. He was after something . . .

Although Charlie still felt chilled from the stream, he was sober and comfortable. He was a bit shaky and had that tickle in his throat, but he could breathe and he wasn't nauseated. He was tired, dragged-out-exhausted, and he knew he was going to suffer for the beating he was giving his body—he would pay dues for this eventually! I should go to *bed*, Charlie told himself, but he was wide awake and so nerved-up that everything looked dark and shadowy to him. If he went to bed, he would just lie awake and stare at the ceiling—-but if he didn't get some sleep, he would get the shakes so bad he wouldn't be able to hold a spoon.

As he sat at the table, finished now with his coffee (and he had even taken a mouthful of cake), he found himself watching Sharry. Charlie began to think that she was pretty in her way, even sexy. She wore a cloth headband, as did Carl, who was sitting beside her—-maybe he was her boyfriend. She had such a young, delicate face, and her eyes had a way of narrowing and looking crinkly. Charlie liked that, and he liked the way her mouth would purse. For such a thin girl, she had unusually full, sensual lips. Charlie thought of her as a flower in bloom. She looked so fresh and new. Joline had had that kind of freshness about her, too, but she lost it . . . and just now Charlie realized how precious it had been.

"You know," John said, looking intently at Sharry, "when a man's *heyoka*, he can do anything he wants. He can be perverted and filthy and just plain bad, and yet he's holy all the time."

Sharry looked at Carl and then turned back to John, giving him her full attention. Carl moved slightly closer to her.

"And you never can believe *anything* a *heyoka* says," John continued, "because they lie about everything. Isn't that right, Lorena?"

"I think all of you would be better off going to bed and not listening to this broken-down old drunk of a medicine man," Lorena said, carrying a large bowl of berry soup to the table. "You want some of this?" she asked John.

"I want some dog first," John said.

"You want *what?*" Charlie asked.

"It's probably going to make you sick," Lorena said.

"That's what I want, is there any left?"

"I'll get you a piece from the pot, but . . ."

"Did you eat a piece of dog?" John asked Sharry.

"Yeah, she ate it," said Carl. "We all did . . . one of the harder things we had to swallow."

"Dog meat's not hard," Charlie said, laughing, mocking.

"Well, we did it for the ceremony," Heather said. She was chain-smoking cigarettes, which she kept in a bead-worked pouch. Charlie smoked one of her cigarettes and started coughing again. He embarrassed himself by having to spit up in the sink. No one said a word while he was coughing and spitting, which made it even worse. When Charlie finished and sat back down, Heather said, "Sam didn't tell us at the time that we could have made an offering of the meat to the spirits and wouldn't've had to eat it at all."

John laughed at that and said, "Dog soup is good for you, part of the ceremony."

Charlie couldn't help but stare at Sharry. She wasn't wearing a bra, and he could see the outlines of her small breasts right through her shirt. Charlie usually preferred women with large breasts, but he felt a sudden flush of desire for her, for her youth and innocence. It was overpowering. It was like being sixteen again, when his urges were so strong that he had to masturbate several times a day. Uncomfortable, he pressed his legs together. He thought about Stephie, his oldest daughter. Sharry's probably the same age as Stephie, Charlie told himself. It would be like fucking my own daughter, for Chrissakes. She's a baby . . . Those thoughts brought on the guilt again, and more embarrassment, as if everyone in the room could see just what he was thinking.

But Sharry wasn't even looking at Charlie. She was too taken up with John. She had a look that said if he would've asked her to eat shit, she would have happily done it. Sonovabitch . . .

Just then Janet, Whiteshirt's wife, made her appearance. She walked into the room with a piece of grayish meat in a soup bowl. The meat was in a dirty-looking broth. There was skin on that meat and even some hair, and it made Charlie sick to look at it. He was glad to see Janet; but Jesus, he thought, not *dog*, for Chrissakes. "You're not going to eat that in front of me," Charlie told John.

"I sure as hell am," John said. "It's part of my religion. Don't you have any respect for a man's religion?" Then he looked at Janet, as if nothing had happened at Sam's vision-quest, as if nothing had come between Joe Whiteshirt and himself in the sweat-lodge, and said, "Isn't that right, hon?"

"I knew you'd be coming around," Janet said. She looked as if she'd just awakened from a deep sleep, but her high cheekbones and deep-set eyes could easily give that impression. She had the kind of strong, implacable face that could look mean, yet could also radiate serenity. Charlie liked this woman, had liked her from the first time they met when he was coughing and she gave him sage. She was the only stranger at the vision-quest who had paid any real attention to him. He felt sympathetic toward her, even though he didn't know her from beans. She had a darkness in her, a certain wildness that was at odds with her domesticity; and that attracted him. He felt as if she were family . . . a dark sister. He sensed that the darkness inside her was the same as the stuff inside him, the stuff that made him so angry and depressed that he'd chew up his own family and spit them out screaming.

". . . I sort of expected you to make the *yuwipi*," Janet said to John. "I kept looking for you, figuring you'd show up. I been waiting for you all night—in between cat naps. How's that for faith?"

"You have no business being here," John said.

"I knew you'd say that," Janet replied. "But it's not what you think."

"Don't matter," John said, as he started to eat the meat off the bone, pulling it away with his teeth.

"I can't watch this," Charlie said, getting up. He felt queasy. It disturbed him—the notion that John was almost a cannibal. "You shouldn't be eating something like that," he continued. "It's wrong. I don't care *what* your religion says, it's just not right. I can abide a lot of things, but not that. Eating a dog is like eating something that's human."

"Charlie," Janet said, walking over to him and taking his arm. She pulled him back down into his seat and then rested her hands on his shoulders, calming him. "Give us a few minutes, and I'll tell you about the dog. I love dogs almost more than people, sometimes." Then she said to John, "You are a real bastard, aren't you. Couldn't you tell him what's going on? I thought he's supposed to be your friend?"

"He is," John said. "But fuck him."

"I should've expected as much from you," Janet said. She poured herself a cup of coffee and sat down, pulling a chair between John and Sharry. "I couldn't stay up there. Joe was going crazy, and he scares me. I'm sorry, but I can't help it. I care about him, and I'd do anything for him, but he's into something bad, something dangerous. I'm sure he's been doing medicine. Maybe it's the woman he's living with now, I don't know. But he's doing *something*. What happened in the purification sweat ... that wasn't Joe Whiteshirt. It was like another man."

"Dog tastes good," John said. "Charlie, you want a piece?"

"Stop acting like an asshole," Janet said. "We're in trouble."

"Who was your *yuwipi* man?" John asked, pushing away his bowl of dog and dunking a piece of bread into the sweet berry soup. "I don't know of any around here, except maybe Joe and that skinny Crow guy who dresses up like a goddamn stockbroker."

"Sam did it," Janet said.

"Why didn't you just have Joe do it, or maybe Lorena could've done it. What the hell, maybe women's lib should take its shot at traditional Indian religion." Then after a pause he said, "You're fucking *wrong* to do that!" There was hate in his face suddenly, burning, just as it had been when he'd paced around in his furnished room.

Charlie could in that instant see his strength, could see him as a leader, as a medicine man, but Jesus Lord the bastard was crazy. "Sam should have been up on the hill, not baby-sitting you and the rest of the honky-Indians," John continued. "He had no business doing a *yuwipi* tonight. It's a wonder that the spirits didn't kill him dead ... and the rest of you, too."

"Sam did get hurt," Janet said. "His chest and legs are all black and blue."

John started laughing. "So the spirits did kick the shit out of him."

"The spirits were there," Sharry said, tentatively, as if she knew she shouldn't be speaking, that she shouldn't even be there at all. But she went on. "Everybody could feel them . . . and see them as lights."

"I felt something move behind me," Carl said, "and I felt something against my skin. And then I realized that I was sitting against the wall, and there couldn't be anything behind me but spirits . . ."

"What'd they tell you?" John asked Janet.

"They were just angry, that's all."

Then John started laughing, and he said, "None of them *really* saw or felt anything, did they, Charlie? It's all bullshit, isn't it, Charlie?"

"Is there a place I can sleep?" Charlie asked Lorena. He ignored John.

"Charlie, somebody should've told you what's going on," Janet said. "The *yuwipi* is a ceremony we do when someone's in trouble. We seek help from the spirits. It's a ceremony given to Indian people by God, and to have this ceremony, to bring the spirits down to us, into our hearts, a dog gives up its life. It knows it's going to die, and I've never seen a dog fight . . . it just knows. And we love our dogs, that's what makes this ceremony so hard for us. We give a life—the dog gives its life—so that we may live. It's a gift."

Charlie couldn't say anything. He didn't know what to say. What the hell am I doing here? he asked himself. Next, they'll be boiling up people!

"Don't be angry with Sam for not vision-questing," Janet said to John. "He came down here to do this thing for me—and for you, too."

"For me?"

"Do you have any idea how much my husband hates you? He blames you for everything. Maybe that's because he can't face himself—can't face what's happened to him and everyone around him. He's a dangerous man. And you know Joe . . . he can hold a grudge forever."

"Doesn't matter now," John said softly.

"Why, because you're drunk?" Janet asked. "Because you're pretending to be *heyoka* like you do every time life becomes too much for you?"

"That's right. And I'm not carrying the pipe, either. I'm done."

"You have people that need you," Janet said. "That depend on you."

"Well, fuck them!" John said. "No, I take it all back. I'll help whoever needs to be helped . . . for a drink. Right, Charlie?"

"I'm going to go to sleep," Charlie said. "I don't want to drink, I just want to sleep," and he looked at Sharry and realized that he had a hard-on, and there he was standing up like a dirty old man.

"I'll show you where you can sleep," Lorena said. Charlie followed her out of the kitchen, through the living room and up stairs to a large bedroom off the paneled hallway. The starkly furnished room contained a cot and a bed, several cane chairs, an old worn couch, and a table situated against the wall near the door. On the table were some neatly folded towels and a porcelain basin. "We have no water, except in the bathroom, and you have to pump that—it's a dry toilet, might take a bit of getting used to the smell. You can take the bed here; it's more comfortable than the cot. John's used to sleeping on floors and anything he can get, anyway."

"He can have his choice," Charlie said, but just the same he lay down on the bed. Even though the mattress was too soft and lumpy, he was asleep before Lorena had left the room.

1 0 .

COUNTING COUP

It was after dawn when John brought Heather and Sharry into the room. Charlie heard them snickering and laughing and giggling and making "shushing" noises as they talked among themselves. John sounded drunk, but he might have just been *heyoka*. He'd certainly worked his charm on these two kids because they were as happy as babies with new diapers. Charlie lay facing the wall and listened, not letting on that he was awake. His heart was beating fast. Surely *something* was going to happen.

"So the selfish sonovabitch has taken the bed," John said. There was a puffing noise as he sat down on the couch, and then the clattering of his boots as he took them off and let them drop to the floor. Charlie listened to the rustling noises and the whispers and felt as if he were a kid again, all pimply-faced and ugly and left out—always third man out. He wanted to cough, but he held it back. He tried to breathe evenly, feigning sleep. Although he didn't feel sick, he was shaking. Adrenaline was burning through him, and it was as hot and fast as hard liquor.

"Well, go on over," John whispered. "I told you, you'll be doing a good thing . . . something he'll remember forever."

Charlie heard someone get up and say, "I'm sorry, John, but I just can't do it." Then the clatter-clack of shoes on the hardwood floor. The door opened and closed, and John whispered something that sounded like swearing. "Well, the hell with it," he said. "He's asleep, anyway."

Charlie discovered that he was holding his breath. He exhaled slowly, carefully, afraid they would be able to tell he was awake. He wondered who had left the room. Was it Sharry or Heather? Probably Heather. She was more shy and nervous . . . a good girl.

But an image of Sharry seemed to hang before Charlie, and he could feel his borrowed dungarees become tight. Goddamn it was wrong, but he wanted young flesh, as young as his daughter's. He thought of Stephanie and felt flush with guilt. He had been faithful to his wife Joline for over twenty years; that should count for something. She was a good woman, and had a good body, even if her teeth were bad and her breath had that metal smell. But every day of all those years Charlie had dreamed of other women, women he'd see on the street, or in the apartments when he was doing repair work for the Isaacs', or, worst of all, women he'd had before he met Joline—especially that blue-eyed Mexican whore who had taken care of him for a month after he lost his gas stations, who always used to leave a little money and a bottle of tequila on the tiny bedstand for him when he awakened . . .

Now there was this Sharry, and she was probably going to screw John. She was young enough to be John's granddaughter, for Chrissakes, Charlie told himself. And John was in and Charlie was out, and no matter how good Charlie had been with the women when he was young, no matter how many adventures he tried to convince himself he'd had, he was still in bed alone, odd man out.

More whispering, and then John said, "You're sure you don't mind? I'll go and find Heather, and everything will be all right. I'll talk to her. Charlie heard the rustle of clothes, then heard them kiss. "I'll see you later," John said loudly; perhaps he was trying to wake up Charlie. He put on his boots and left the room, closing the door behind him.

Goddamn if Charlie wasn't scared.

He couldn't sleep, of course, and it would be too awkward to say anything. Let it lie, he told himself. The girl would fall asleep, and so would Charlie, eventually, and then it would be all over— right now that's what he wanted, just to have it all over. But the woman called to him . . . it *was* Sharry.

"Charlie, you asleep?" Her voice had a twang to it.

Charlie didn't answer. He had to go to the bathroom, and he felt nauseated again. He couldn't help it, but he started coughing. Sharry came over to the bed and said, "Charlie? Here, take these," and she put some toilet paper in his hand. "I always carry some . . . you know?"

He coughed into the paper, sat up in the bed and lowered his head toward his knees, which always made him feel a little better. He was shaking, and it wasn't from the booze; he knew that much. He was piss-ass scared of a little twenty-year-old girl. She looked pale in the wan, morning light, a child, except for the red slash of lipstick painted on her generous lips. She was skinny as a rail, not Charlie's type at all, yet he wanted her, as if she could pass her youth over to him as if it were currency or food. He could smell her natural odor; she didn't wear perfume. She probably doesn't shave her legs either, he thought sourly. "What's going on?" he asked. "What are you doing in *here*, and where's John? I thought I heard him come in with you."

It looked gray outside, and the room seemed smoky and muddled and cold, although it wasn't really cold, just cool.

"It was John's idea that we'd all get silly and fool around," Sharry said, "but when we got in here, Heather got scared or something and left. John went after her to calm her down."

"What do you mean, fool around?" Charlie asked.

"You know . . ."

"Jesus, woman, I have a daughter almost as old as you," Charlie said. He fought the urge to touch her hair, which looked clean and soft and thick.

"That doesn't mean anything . . . I have a father almost as old as *you*. So what?"

"So what do you want to be fooling around with old men for?" Charlie asked, and then he asked for a cigarette.

"I think older men are . . . beautiful."

"Cut the crap," Charlie snapped. He must have frightened Sharry because she jerked backward.

"Okay, I didn't mean to get you upset," Sharry said. "John explained what you two are doing."

"What are we doing?" Charlie asked, pulling the strong tobacco smoke into his lungs, feeling its papery tickle at the back of his throat.

"You're taking your last shot, like you're proving that you're still warriors. It's like a holy thing."

"That's just plain bullshit," Charlie said, angry at John for whatever he had told these young girls. John didn't care about anyone but himself, Charlie thought. He's a user, just like I used to be. But I paid for the way I used people. I'm *still* paying for it. And Charlie thought about his two sons from a previous marriage who didn't even acknowledge he was alive.

"John said you and he were counting coup," Sharry said.

"What the hell is *that* supposed to mean?"

"When Indian people fought, in the old days, they would touch the enemy with a coup stick, and that was like killing him, even though you didn't. It was a test of courage, sort of, because it took more courage to get close enough to touch him with a coup stick than to shoot him dead with an arrow . . . you know? And even if the enemy was dead, you could still count coup on him by touching him with a stick, although the first coup was the most important. That's what they did to Custer."

"It's all bullshit," Charlie said. "It's just John's way of making a bender sound holy, and to get little girls like you into bed with him."

"You don't have *any* respect for women, do you," Sharry said.

"I'm sorry, I didn't mean to hurt your feelings, but, shit, you know better than this. Your girlfriend did, that's why she got out of the room quick."

Sharry didn't answer. She just took a long drag on her cigarette and caught Charlie watching her breasts.

"How'd you get into this, anyway?" Charlie asked.

"Into what?"

"This whole Indian thing."

"How did *you*?"

"I asked you first," Charlie said. Sharry grinned.

"I'm looking for something," Sharry said. "I don't know what, yet, but I've found some of it here."

Charlie was going to tell her that she was young, that this Indian business would wear off, that she looked like a nice, middle-class preppy-girl and would probably end up marrying a doctor, but he didn't. Maybe nothing would make any difference. Maybe that's why John was so free and easy about seducing white girls who hang around Indians. But that was John's way, not Charlie's. Charlie had paid enough dues, and he knew the Laws, but it was too late, or too early, and he was too tired to try to explain them to this girl. In fact, he wasn't even horny anymore. Maybe he'd really gotten somewhere. He felt better, but tired. He had to sleep. Right now.

"Do you mind if I stay here?" Sharry asked. "Just to sleep."

Charlie lay on his back and stared up at the raftered ceiling. "Sure," he said, and then immediately realized that he should have said "no".

Sharry got up and closed the thin white curtains over the window, then came to bed. She didn't take her clothes off, and

Charlie let her snuggle against him under the covers, and he felt a thrill run through him, just to have someone this close, someone who wanted him who was not Joline. He felt himself getting an erection again, and he remembered how Sharry had looked downstairs when he was staring at her across the table. She was *supposed* to be with John, but this was the way it had worked out. Chance of a lifetime, but he owed Joline something, didn't he? He'd been faithful for all these years, and he could *still* go back because even though he'd made a mess of everything, it didn't matter as long as he was faithful . . . Joline was like that.

But Sharry was snuggling against him, and he had his arm around her. He let his hand rest naturally against her arm, but he knew that he was also touching her breast—the little brat wasn't wearing a brassiere. Counting coup, he thought, as he started to fall asleep, feeling secure, even if his hard-on was hurting against the stiffness of his jeans. Goddamn he was tired. And she pushed against him, and suddenly the decision was made. He didn't seem to have had anything to do with it. He just did it. He had wronged Joline before he'd begun, and it didn't matter now because he had already jumped into hell with John, and he was never coming out right again. But it *did* matter, and Charlie desperately wanted Joline. He wanted her here right now instead of the little girl beside him. He wanted the perfumed security of Joline. He wanted his life back. But he had lost it. God, he really felt that way right now, and he needed comforting for that thought, more than he'd needed since *he* was Sharry's age.

Then he was massaging her breast, sliding his hand under the rough material of her shirt, and he felt himself descending into a kind of sweet, warm death, as everything he had tried to keep hold of in life slid away from him—his family, Joline, his word as a man.

Now *he* was sliding, falling deliciously, and Sharry wriggled around so he could unbutton her blouse, and she was moaning and kissing him open-mouthed and biting his cheek; and he was grinding against her, pulling at her jeans while she unzipped him. He moaned, feeling as if he were about to come, as if her long fingers were numbing icicles touching him. Sharry's strong, natural smells were like those of the woods. The pale, morning light was a mist in the room, and Sharry's skin was as damp and cool as wet leaves. Charlie lay back as she pushed down against him. She was smooth and tight and young, and she took his penis in her mouth, and he thought of Stephanie and Joey and Joline, and then he remembered various women he had desired over the years. How young and strange this woman was with her warm mouth and even teeth against his penis. It was a fantasy . . . a dream. But it was also a nightmare, for he just could not dismiss the nagging apprehension that tonight he had lost everything forever.

He started to cough. Sharry stopped, pulled back, held him as if he were a child. Angry with himself, Charlie pulled her back down into the bed, kissing her, sucking on her neck and tiny erect breasts; he entered her, feeling that cleanliness he always felt when making love, as if he were in clear warm water. Then followed the terrible wheezing and breathing and hurting to orgasm. Through the cries and hoarse moans, through the tiny, controlled screams and wheezings, he felt the wrongness of what he was doing; and his guilt was as wet and warm as her slippery cunt.

He was raping her, taking her, as if she was Stephanie, as if to punish Joline—and himself, too—by sinning with his cock and with his filthy-dirty thoughts.

He opened his eyes, as if he knew that he had to remember this, take it with him wherever he went, and he saw this young girl, this baby, with her beautifully thick brown hair spread across the sheets, the gray morning light touching her features, making them gentler than they were, flattening out her facial lines, which would deepen with age; and she was for this instant as perfect and unblemished as the picture of the Madonna that Joline had insisted be hung above their bed at home. Sharry was turning her head back and forth, as if she was in great pain, and Charlie held himself up on his hands, as if he was floating above her in clear, cool water, and he lunged inside her. She screamed, as if she no longer cared that she was in someone else's house, that she wasn't supposed to be in this room with this old man, and perhaps her thoughts were of her father, perhaps they were just of Charlie, but she shuddered and pulled Charlie down against her and came. She felt suddenly fragile to Charlie, and the guilt returned, intensified by that same frailty. But such an encounter could only happen to Charlie once. He had sinned against Joline for the first time; and after a while he felt himself stiffen again, inside Sharry, and he took her, as if she could give him back what he'd lost, as if he *was* a bull, as if he hadn't lived his life already.

Then he fell asleep, sweaty and sticky and cold, but he kept jolting out of his dreams, not quite awakening, but caught, drowning and coughing.

Through it all, he felt that someone, or something, was watching him, an eye that was like a hot coal burning malevolently through his dreams.

When he finally awoke, the room was empty and bright.

11.

JIZZUM AND THE
WEIGHT OF THE LAWS

John came into the room with a coffee for Charlie; he was also carrying Charlie's freshly washed clothes, which he put on the table near the door. He placed the coffee mug on the floor beside the bed and said, "Come on, boy, it's past one o'clock in the afternoon, and the birds are singing and getting ready to go south like us." He had shaved . . . if he ever shaved at all; come to think of it, Charlie thought, he *always* looked clean shaven.

But Charlie was hung-over. His eyes were shot, his hair pushed over to one side, showing his bald spots, and his black and gray pepper stubble made him look years older than he was. "The birds have already gone south," Charlie said, feeling every ache in his body.

"Just drink the coffee," John said, and Charlie lifted the stained porcelain mug and took a sip, then looked around the room for something to spit up into.

"I feel like I've been run over by a tank," Charlie said. "Man, am I sick."

"That's what you get for fucking your brains out."

"There's that, too," Charlie said, remembering. "Jesus, I had no business screwing around with that little girl. I'm old enough to be her *father*, for Christ's sake."

"Yeah, she told me you said that. I wouldn't worry, though. She thinks she's done a wonderful thing for you, although by the looks of you, it doesn't seem like it took. She said you were pretty good, you old goat!"

Again people are talking about me, Charlie thought, and doing things behind my back, just like Joline and Stephanie. They didn't even tell me that my own goddamn daughter was pregnant! God damn everybody!

"You mad about something?" John asked.

"Yeah, you shouldn't've set those girls up like you did."

"You didn't have to screw her, either, honky," John said, but he had such a shit-eating smile on his face that even Charlie grinned a little. "We gotta get out of here. I've been hiding out in the woods, pretending I was looking for herbs, for as long as I can."

"I feel terrible," Charlie said hoarsely. He felt the familiar tickle in his throat and started coughing. He motioned to John for a basin or something in which to spit, but John pulled him out of bed and helped him over to the window.

"You got to spit up, do it here," John said, opening the window. "It's all natural, anyway."

Charlie was coughing and hacking, but it was such a strain that he could feel it in his crotch. He hung out the window, and a distant part of him was thankful for the warmth of the sun and the chill of the air—it was cold today. He fumbled in his pockets for his inhaler, and, after a few moments, sank down to the floor. He sat there, his head resting on the edge of the window-stool, and caught his breath.

"I think you need some hair of the dog," John said.

"You want to kill me?" Then after a long pause, Charlie asked, "What'd you mean about hiding out? What do you have to hide out for, anyway?" Charlie kept trying to push away his thoughts

164

of last night, but the guilt kept rising like phlegm. He would never be able to make it right with Joline now . . .

"I just don't want to get into it with Sam, or Janet, for that matter," John said.

"Into what?"

"All the medicine crap. I can't help anybody, much less pretend I'm a medicine man. Let Whiteshirt and the other fuck ups do that."

"So what are you going to do?" Charlie asked.

John took a pint bottle out of his pocket and opened it.

"None for me . . . Jesus!"

John took a pull on the bottle and said, "Then stay here, buddy. Everybody *else* seems to be white, anyway. But I'm taking my ass out of here."

"We can't take that car we been driving. *Every*body's going to be looking for it."

"You're sick with fear, Charlie," John said. "It probably hasn't even been reported yet."

There was a knock on the door, but before John or Charlie had a chance to answer, Sharry stepped into the room and said, "Everybody's waiting for you guys to come down for some lunch." She looked at Charlie tenderly, almost motherly, and said, "Lot's of coffee and jam and home-baked bread."

John said, "Okay, we'll be down soon, as soon as I can put this hung-over drunk together," but Charlie was blushing. Just seeing Sharry brought back his shyness and guilt. And goddamn if he didn't want her again! If she sensed his desire, she didn't show it. She winked at them and closed the door behind her.

"We can't lay over here," John said. "We just *can't*."

"Okay, but I ought to shave or something."

"Fuck that. Let it grow into a beard. Turn you into a new man. If you want to later, you can shave and become good old Charlie Sarris again."

"We going to just walk away, or hitchhike, or what?" Charlie asked, suddenly embarrassed that *he* was acting like the supplicant instead of being a man and telling John how to go about arranging everything. "You ever ride the trains?"

"Some."

"I used to ride them. I was pretty good, and, you know, I liked them. There's something about being on a train, moving along, seeing the world from a boxcar." Actually, Charlie had only jumped a freight once, and that was on a dare with his buddies. But they ran into a bunch of hoboes who told them all sorts of things about that kind of life. Charlie had always dreamed that if things got bad enough, he'd just jump the freights and never look back.

"We don't need to do that," John said. "I can get us a car."

"You're not going to steal—we're not going to take anything else," Charlie said sharply.

"We're borrowing Heather's car. She already said it's okay."

"Are we taking her with us, is that it?" Charlie asked, thinking about Sharry again.

"No," John answered, looking wary. "Look, go downstairs, wash yourself, put on these clothes—Sharry washed them for you—and we'll eat. I'll explain everything later. It's okay ... really."

"You're a bastard," Charlie said matter-of-factly, without malice, although it was disgust that was working through him now. "You're going to take that little girl's car after you've banged her and led her to think you're the great medicine man, aren't you?"

John grinned, no more *heyoka* now than Charlie. "Yeah, I guess you're right, Charlie. That's what I'm going to do."

"You really don't give a shit."

"I do ... I do, but there's a reason for everything, and a lesson in everything. I may be a shit," John said, his voice changing, becoming harder, gritty, angry, "but if that little girl thinks I'm the great red father, that *I* have the answer, then maybe to her I do. I've done a lot of shitty things, but I pay for them; and, unlike you, my friend, I figure out the charge *before* I fuck up. I'm going to take that little girl's car that her Daddy bought her and paid for, and I'm going to teach her a lesson, maybe the best one she's ever going to get."

"What, don't trust an Indian?"

John laughed, but the tension was strong, unbroken. "That's right, honky . . . that's exactly right. She's slumming and probably throwing it up to her parents. She probably even has some half-assed notion that what she's doing here is holy and religious and all that crap. But her way isn't down here. It's with her own people. It's not trying to be a phony down here. Indian people have enough problems of their own; they don't need white kids giving them big heads. Some white kids come here in the right way, and maybe they take something real back with them. But these kids—Heather and Sharry—they came here for a lesson. And I'll give them one they can take back with them. If they can ever get it together in Whiteland, they'll know what I did for them here."

"Then maybe I'd better watch *my* ass, too," Charlie said.

"If you're slumming—if that's how you feel, brother—then maybe you should. But I'll tell you this once, first and last, this is the only time I'm ever going to explain myself to you! Got that? It's my business, not yours." John took another pull of the whiskey. "I don't ask you for explanations about the way you live your life, so stay the fuck out of mine!"

"That's fine by me," Charlie said, looking away from John. He'll keep drinking just so he can stay *heyoka*, Charlie thought. The goddamn chickenshit. He's not man enough to face up to his responsibilities. "Well, *I'm* going home," Charlie said suddenly. He was surprised that he said it; the words just came out, as if he was being given some sort of an okay by God or something. "You go on by yourself. I've had enough of this shit."

He felt lightheaded, relieved. Why couldn't he go home? No matter what he had done, it was still his house and his family. He could just walk in the door big as life. There was no law against that. Pop didn't lose his home and family and life after I caught him fucking that whore, Charlie thought sourly. Goddamn straight he didn't. No, it was *me* who ended up leaving. Well, I'm not going to do that again. I'm going to make things right this time. I'll go home and take my punishment like a man; and Joline, God bless her, will certainly enjoy ladling it out, that's for goddamn sure.

"I'll see about getting you a razor," John said, and he left the room.

Charlie went downstairs to wash. He put on his boots and clean jeans, and carried the rest of his clothes. He could smell Sharry all over him like wild honey. He stank from perspiration and lovemaking, but for an instant he felt elated and fresh and oily-clean and yet also soiled. Part of him felt like a schoolboy who had just gotten laid for the first time. After all these years I can still get it up and satisfy someone else, he told himself. I still have the old jizzum.

But another part of him felt the dead weight of the Laws.

Charlie had broken his vows to Joline, and he had always said that a man's word is his bond. Now he was no better than John . . . no better than his father; in fact he was worse.

He left the bathroom door ajar. Although he wouldn't admit it to himself, he was afraid of being shut in, caught, as he was in the sweat-lodge. He was afraid to look in the cracked, cloudy mirror over the sink, afraid that he would glimpse whoever, or whatever, was watching him. He could feel eyes burning like coals behind him. The same eyes that had been watching him since he had left the sweat-lodge with John. Whiteshirt's eyes.

But that was all superstitious nonsense, he told himself. Too much booze. He was hung-over, and when you're hung-over, your mind thinks crazy things.

As he cleaned his gums with his finger and the last of the squeezed-out tube of toothpaste, he remembered that when he was a kid, no one in his household ever closed the doors. Bedroom doors were always open, except when Charlie's parents wanted to be alone for an hour or so. And even then the younger kids would pester Mom and Pop with a thousand questions and problems that just couldn't wait.

Funny what you think of sometimes, Charlie thought, as he spat and coughed into the sink. Goddamn, if we weren't dirt-poor in those days, but we never had to shut the doors to close each other out. We were a family. But I fucked that up, Charlie told himself, remembering how it was. He thought about his parents, how they looked and acted; and he thought about his three brothers. I wouldn't recognize any of them if they all walked into this goddamn bathroom right now. Christ, I don't even know if they're all alive. The last time he had heard from them was when his mother had died.

I'm going to make things right, he said to himself again. He resolved to try to get in touch with his brothers.

Goddamn if that thought didn't make him feel like crying. But he felt better, stronger. He looked into the mirror. He didn't see Whiteshirt or any of his spirits spooking around.

He saw his father.

Charlie bore a striking resemblance to the old man.

"I guess you got even, Pop," Charlie said, making peace with an old ghost. "We're both whoremasters now."

There was a light knock at the door. Charlie jumped, as if it were his dead father tapping, impatient to get into the bathroom.

Sam pushed the door open and held up a blue plastic razor. "Lorena sent this for you. You'll have to use the regular soap for lather, though. We don't have any shaving foam." Sam was wearing faded jeans, a matching jacket, and a black knit turtleneck sweater. The sweater was at least a size too large, and made his neck look skinny.

Sam laid the razor on the sink.

"Thanks," Charlie said, feeling uncomfortable.

Sam just stood beside Charlie, as if thinking what to say next. After a beat, he said, "You know, I've tried to talk to John, but he won't have anything to do with anybody, especially me and Janet. That's just not like John. No matter what's coming down on him, he always tries to take care of others."

Charlie looked at himself again in the mirror. He looked terrible, but he'd looked worse . . . and he didn't see anything in the mirror flickering behind him. So far so good.

"He's in trouble," Sam continued. "He needs help."

"You must know John better than I do," Charlie said, relieved that he was going home and leaving all this superstition and crazy stuff behind him. "John seems to me to be the kind of man who has to work out his problems in his own way." Charlie was hungry. Goddamn was he going to eat! And so what if I did get laid? he asked himself. Every man slips once in a while. Christ, I've been faithful for over twenty goddamn years. Even God took Sunday off. So I had one small Sunday. Maybe it was a good thing for Joline that I did screw that little girl . . . Now that I feel like a man again, maybe I can treat Joline like a woman. Charlie was pleased with that, even though he knew it was all bullshit.

"I don't think you understand," Sam said.

"What do you mean?"

"It's not over between John and Whiteshirt."

"It sure as hell looked that way to me," Charlie said, but he knew that Sam was right. He had *felt* it, and had denied those feelings. The room seemed to shrink a little. I just want to be home and away from all this crap, he thought. It's all crap. And I'm in it up to my knees.

"Whiteshirt's not going to let him alone," Sam said, "and John's not the kind of man to let himself be beaten and humiliated."

"That may all be true, but Whiteshirt's back there somewhere, and we're *here*."

"Doesn't matter."

"And what's that supposed to mean?" Charlie asked, ready for the answer nevertheless.

"Whiteshirt doesn't need to be anywhere near John to hurt him."

"I'm telling you right now I don't believe in any of that bad medicine business," Charlie said; but after what had happened in the sweat-lodge, Charlie wasn't sure what the hell he believed any more.

Sam didn't reply. He just stood there, gazing into the mirror.

"Maybe something weird *did* happen in that sweat-lodge, but I have to agree with John . . . you can't blame everything on bad medicine."

"Maybe you can't," Sam said, "but you're going to be seeing a lot more of it."

"I'm not going to be seeing *anything*," Charlie said. "I'm going home."

"You're not going with John?" Sam looked anxious.

"I'm going home."

"Did John tell you where he's going?"

"We were going to Florida," Charlie said. But Sam just shook his head and left the room. "What's wrong with that?" Charlie asked, following Sam. Charlie swallowed a bit of toothpaste, and the taste gagged him.

Sam stopped at the head of the stairs and said, "Whiteshirt's camp is in Florida."

1 2 .

WITCHES, ROCKS, AND
MIRRORS

B y the time Charlie shaved and went downstairs, John had left.
Everyone else was in the huge kitchen, drinking coffee
and fresh milk and eating sandwiches made with home-made
bread, while Lorena washed dishes in a large, double-basin sink.
Lorena wore a white starchy-looking dress, which was as baggy
as the one she had on last night. She looked ruddy-faced and
scrubbed; her gray-streaked brown hair was pulled back into a
ponytail. Sharry and Heather and Sharry's skinny, long-haired
boyfriend sat at the table. For an instant, when Charlie walked
into the room, everyone stopped talking; and then the rush of
noise resumed, some of it directed at him. Janet poured Charlie
a cup of coffee and handed it to him, her face showing concern
and curiosity. Charlie's eyes met Sharry's, and he felt his ears
burn. Goddamn she was beautiful. And Goddamn he had been
wrong. But not wrong as John used the term. Charlie had
sinned, and the Laws and the Bible might as well have been the
same damn thing.

Sharry's boyfriend caught something passing between her and
Charlie, and he looked at Charlie with hate and contempt.

Charlie made sure he didn't make any eye contact with him because he had a strong feeling that it wouldn't take much for this boy to lose his composure entirely and take a swing at him. Cause and effect, Charlie thought. Everything had an effect on everything else. John had told him that, although he already knew it. More dues.

For that matter, he'd best not look at Sharry either. But she should have thought about her boyfriend's feelings—*if* he was her boyfriend—before she jumped into bed with me. She was selfish. A typical rich kid. She wasn't trying to help me out for any religious reasons. She's just a goddamn groupie, trying to please John because she thinks he has some sort of magic power. If he told her to stick a balloon up her ass, she'd probably do it.

"John took my car to buy some cigarettes and stuff," Sharry said to Charlie. She looked at him openly, as if she wasn't ashamed or embarrassed. "And he's going to gas it up for me, too. He said to tell you 'bye.'"

"*Your* car?" Charlie asked, surprised. He had thought Heather owned the car, not Sharry.

"Yeah, why?" Sharry asked. "Is anything wrong?"

"I don't mind John buying himself cigarettes," Lorena said. "It's the generic 'stuff' that *I* worry about." When Charlie didn't seem to understand, she lifted her hand to her mouth as if she were taking a drink.

"When did he leave?" Charlie asked.

"Just a few minutes ago," Sharry said. "You don't have to worry. He said he'd be right back. We're all supposed to help him search for herbs later on."

But Charlie ran out of the house. He knew goddamn well what John was up to. He shouldn't have told him he was going home. Goddammit, he owed John *something* . . . to at least stick with him through the bad times. He knew that the reason he wanted to go home was because he was afraid, afraid of what he didn't understand, afraid of what might happen to him with all that bad medicine hanging around like some sort of poison gas. But goddammit he missed Joline and the girls, even though he wasn't ready to face them. He loved and respected Joline and would do anything in the world for her and the girls, but not quite yet. Joline would be waiting for him. He was certain of that. *That* was trust, good and holy and pure. But he was soiled, and he couldn't go back to her until he'd made himself right, until he'd done *something* right. He'd start by helping John. It seemed for some reason John trusted him. Maybe it was because Charlie wasn't fawning all over him like the groupies or treating him as if his shit didn't stink.

But there was more to it than that, something darker. Charlie was afraid that Sharry would think he was in cahoots with John to steal her car. It was pure paranoia, but he was afraid that she'd come after him. She was under age, probably. She'd accuse him of rape.

Somehow, Charlie had to catch up with John. But John could be driving anywhere, in any direction, and Charlie didn't even know what kind of car John had stolen. Charlie fished the keys to the Oldsmobile out of his pocket. He'd take it step by step. First he'd get down the hill, and *then* he'd figure it out. He unlocked the Olds. Charlie always locked up his cars. He laughed at himself . . . even if they were stolen cars, he thought.

Sam ran out behind Charlie. "I had a bad feeling when he left that he wasn't coming back. *Goddamn* that Indian, he'd steal from his own mother, steal her spirit right out of the ground if he could." Sam chuckled. "Sharry's going to have a lot of explaining to do to her folks . . ."

Charlie got into the car and started the engine. He didn't have time to fuck around here while John was probably running himself up a telephone pole.

"You sure you just don't want to stay here?" Sam asked. "It's probably going to get hairy. John's going to get pretty fucked up before he gets right. He's going to have to have it out with Whiteshirt. Do you really want to be around when that happens?"

"What kind of car is he driving?"

"A Toyota . . . the expensive-looking white sports car that was parked by my truck." Sam nodded toward his truck; there was an empty space between two pickups where Sharry's car had been.

"Where's the nearest liquor store?"

"There's two of them," Sam said. "One's in a mall, the other's right on the road. You go down the hill to the main drag. You can turn either right or left."

"That's what I was afraid of," Charlie said, and he saw Sharry step out of the doorway and head for the car. Charlie started backing up the car. He didn't want to make lame excuses for John . . . and himself. He wanted to get out of here.

"My advice is to stay drunk," Sam said, a smile flickering across his face. "Good protection for whatever Whiteshirt will be throwing at you."

"You're all fucking crazy," Charlie said. "And so am I. I don't have a prayer of finding John."

"You'll find him," Sam said. "If that's what John wants you to do . . ."

"Hey, Charlie, wait up," Sharry called. She started running.

But Charlie pulled away quickly, almost hitting one of the trees that edged the driveway, in his rush to get away from Sharry.

Charlie found the white Toyota on the first try. He had turned left onto the main drag and passed truck-stops and gas stations and motels and roadside inns and fast food places. He saw a small mall and drove into the parking lot, which was about half-full. The stores and restaurant fronts were redwood, and the place looked expensive. And there was Sharry's shark-shaped car, parked between a delivery truck and an older model sedan. John's pipe was hanging from the rear-view mirror.

The liquor store was two doors down.

Charlie prayed that John wasn't robbing the place, or pissing on the floor, or beating up the manager. When John was *heyoka*, he really didn't know right from wrong. Goddammit, that's just what I should do, Charlie thought. It would be like being a kid all over again, being able to do anything that comes into your head—time-out, they used to call it.

As Charlie rushed to the liquor store, it occurred to him that that was exactly what he had been doing. Except Charlie knew better. There was no time-out. The dues would get you.

The liquor store was deceptively large. Rows and rows of various wines from France and Italy and Germany and Spain and Yugoslavia and New York and California took up most of the floor space. Hard liquor and liqueurs lined the walls. Expensive porcelain bottles molded into various shapes were displayed on the wide ledge of the front window. There were dull-finished statues of George Washington and Andrew Jackson and Benjamin Franklin, a shiny horse, a fire engine, and a bust of Elvis Presley (the collector's edition). There was a replica of a foreign sports car that must have been three feet long. And standing in the middle of them all was a statue of Sitting Bull. A tag around his neck said he was hand-painted. Sitting Bull didn't look a bit like John, who was standing at the counter with a dozen bottles of hooch. He had pushed all the bottles together. There were four bottles of Four Feathers, which was always on sale, a few bottles of cheap red wine, some rye of unknown label, and a bottle of Johnny Walker Black. It was as if John was preparing for all contingencies: cheap booze to get shitfaced on, wine in case Charlie showed-up, and the Johnny for a celebration, should the sticks fall that way, as Charlie's son would say. John was smiling at Charlie, beaming, in fact; it was as if Charlie had showed up just in time to be best man at John's wedding.

But Charlie didn't smile back. He was waiting to see what John was going to do. John did nothing untoward. He just pulled out three crisp twenty dollar bills and gave them to the cashier, who looked a bit queer to Charlie, but somehow all tall, gangly boys in their twenties looked queer to Charlie, as if the quintessential fag had to be tall and skinny and neatly groomed. The young man rang up the sale and handed John his change, then carefully put the bottles into two large bags with carry-handles attached.

Charlie knew that John had stolen that money, but he also knew better than to mention it. He didn't want John going blotto again. And what's done is done, he thought.

"I figured it could go fifty-fifty," John said, handing one of the bags to Charlie.

"What do you mean?" Charlie asked as they walked out of the store. He was relieved that they had gotten out of there without incident.

"I was waiting around for you. Not really *waiting*, but I was sort of expecting you. I don't know why, but I couldn't see you going back home yet."

"Someone has to look out for you," Charlie said, and it came out as it was meant: seriously.

John nodded and gave him the keys to the Toyota.

"Let's just leave the Toyota here," Charlie said. "We can just as well take the Olds." He lowered the heavy shopping bag of bottles onto the sidewalk in front of Sharry's Toyota.

"Look," John said, "we're going to talk about this just one last time, so you have this one last chance to make up your mind. Remember what I said in the bedroom? That still holds. We're taking the Toyota, and that's final. Think of it as part of God's plan. Anyway, I already consecrated this car. Can't you see the pipe?" John chortled at that, and then continued. "Everything's going to get bad. We're going to have a good time, the best time you ever had, you can fucking bet your ass on that, but it's going to get bad."

"I don't know what you mean."

"You sure the fuck do!" John said loudly. "Turn around and go back home. I'm sorry I got you into all this."

Charlie took the keys from John and got into the Toyota.

"Don't forget the booze, for Chrissakes," John said, picking up both bags and putting them on the floor behind his seat.

The inside of the Toyota was like a cockpit. Charlie felt cramped. It took him a minute to get the car started. "I hate these foreign cars," Charlie said. "Nothing's in the right place."

John opened a bottle of Four Feathers and started drinking.

Charlie finally got the car into gear and drove out of the parking lot and onto the highway. But Charlie wasn't going to drive like a maniac. He wasn't drunk and didn't intend to get that way. He had a mission. He was going to take care of John. If he drove slowly, like a normal person, he'd lessen the chances of getting picked up by the police. He was in control now. Goddammit, he was going to make the Laws work for him.

But he wasn't on the road five minutes before somebody in a red Plymouth convertible back-ended him. Charlie wasn't going to wait around and compare insurance companies. Fuck Sharry, he thought, as he ground through the gears. Let this be a lesson to her. Maybe John was right. At any rate, this Toyota could certainly fly. If it had wings, he'd be halfway to Florida by now. I've flown airplanes that are slower than this, Charlie told himself.

John was laughing all the while, drinking and laughing.

Charlie finally managed to find his way back to Route 81, and when his heart slowed down, so did he. He drove at a comfortable speed through Maryland, past Falling Waters and Martinsburg and Harper's Ferry. He kept his eyes out for cops. He was still in control.

John confessed that he had borrowed money from Sharry and Heather outright, and then riffled their pocketbooks for the rest of their stash, which was considerable. He even took two rolled marijuana cigarettes, claiming that it was an ancient Indian remedy. He offered one to Charlie, who refused, and smoked the other one himself. Maybe it was smoking marijuana that made John *heyoka*, Charlie thought. Maybe he's been smoking that shit all the while. And there was no way that pot was some ancient Indian medicine, Charlie told himself. That goddamned Indian was worse than the Russians . . . he'd probably claim that Indians invented the telephone!

But they had money now to buy gas and stock up on junk food and candy bars and cans of beans and soup: John liked all the Progresso brand soups. You didn't need to add water. He claimed they were good cold, right out of the can. They also bought a can opener.

They passed Stephens City and Middletown and took 66 back up north to Marshall in Virginia where they picked up 17, which John said was faster than pissing around Washington on the Loop. Charlie just drove, a cool sixty-five, which was just about legal. No self-respecting trooper would pick you up for that. John was being good company now, for a drunk. He didn't seem to be *heyoka*. No crazy outbursts. No pissing out of the car or screaming at young women. He was just getting numb, which in itself worried Charlie a bit, but Christ, Charlie told himself, you can't have it both ways. They didn't talk much and Charlie had time to think. He daydreamed that he was sitting home and watching quiz shows— Joline was a crackerjack at coming up with the answers to the questions. If he could get her on one of those shows, they'd be goddamn millionaires. It's crazy what begins to look good after being alone a while, he told himself. He always used to complain to Joline that he hated those afternoon television programs. Now he'd like nothing better than to be home watching them.

It was late afternoon, and a beautiful, clear day. The Blue Ridge Mountains seemed to shimmer in the distance, each curving shape a different color, from gray to its namesake blue. Route 17 was a trucker's route, and even though it was in God's country, there was a honky-tonk flavor about it, something like a countrified Paramus, with drive-up Pig stands and gas stations and cheap-jack steak restaurants as plentiful as chain stores were in New Jersey.

Charlie took it all in, but he was nervous. He couldn't shake the anxiety that seemed to come upon him; and it wasn't John, who would doze and drink and yawn and then find a more comfortable position. John spoke once in a while, but to himself; and once in a while he'd speak in what Charlie assumed to be Sioux. Perhaps John was praying, even without the pipe. Damn, if Charlie didn't have the urge to smoke that pipe. When he'd smoked it alone with John that first time in the woods, it seemed to make everything all right.

Maybe everything was all right *before* they had smoked the pipe, Charlie told himself.

He wondered if Sharry had called the police. Certainly no one would be able to stop her from doing that. Charlie smiled: Lorena and Sam and Janet must have their hands full with her by now. Christ on a crutch!

Charlie looked into the rear-view mirror and realized that he had been doing that every few seconds. That's natural, he told himself. It was a part of driving, making sure no one was tailgating you. But there was more to it than that. Charlie felt someone, or something, watching him. He had had that same sensation back in the sweat-lodge. He was suddenly afraid, even with John sitting right here beside him. The hair on the back of his neck started to prickle.

Now he was afraid to look in the rear-view mirror, which to his mind was an even more fucked up thing to do than looking at it constantly.

Goddammit, though, there *was* something behind him, watching . . .

What the hell have I gotten myself into? he thought. He pushed the rear-view mirror out of the way so he couldn't see into it. "You're going crazy, Charlie Sarris," he mumbled to himself.

John was awake and staring right at him.

"What'd you say?" John asked.

"Nothing," Charlie replied, defensively.

"You should have a drink," John said, opening a bottle of rye. "It's gonna get worse."

"Sam told me that Whiteshirt lives in Florida," Charlie said.

"Don't feel bad, you would've figured it out eventually."

"If he's there, why the fuck are *we* going there?"

"Sometimes you can't run away or pretend something doesn't exist," John said. "Some things have to be taken care of because they won't get better. You had your chance to go back home, but you wanted to see this through, isn't that right?"

"I wasn't going to just pack up and leave you in the cold," Charlie said.

"Because you knew that *something* was coming down . . . right?"

"I don't know what the fuck I think anymore. The whole thing's crazy."

"Then why do you have the rear-view mirror twisted around?" John asked. "Afraid of what you may see behind you?" After a beat, he said, "Witches use mirrors. Did you know that?"

"You're fucking crazy," Charlie said, but without conviction.

"You're going to feel Whiteshirt, the closer we get to Florida."

"Maybe Whiteshirt isn't going home. Have you thought of that?"

"Then we'll wait for him," John said. "But he'll be there . . ."

Charlie thought he could understand what John was feeling. John had been humiliated by Whiteshirt in front of his own people. In front of Charlie, too. John had to get even. That was it, Charlie told himself, even though John was trying to charge it all up with that bad medicine mumbo-jumbo. He was just trying to make everything seem larger than it was. But Charlie had made up his mind to stand by him, no matter how crazy it seemed.

"You know," John continued, "it doesn't matter if Whiteshirt's even there. It's his place, it's got him all over it. Sometimes a man's possessions, his objects, his land, are more powerful and more dangerous than the man. You know why?"

Charlie didn't answer.

"Because a man can put himself into an object and hold right onto it, even after he's dead. He can do it with land, or a ring, or even a stone . . . There are places where it's dangerous to even pick up a rock because those rocks hold power, and they're at war with other objects. I know a place like that in Tula, in Mexico. You get in the way of those things, you can get killed."

"Christ . . ." Charlie muttered under his breath.

"Here, take a drink," John said. He seemed oddly ebullient. "You're going to need it." He tried to pass Charlie the bottle, but Charlie shook his head.

"I don't want to drink," Charlie said. "You're drinking enough for both of us. One of us has to be in control."

"The booze is medicine," John said. "It's protection, like a warm coat in the winter. Protect you some from whatever Whiteshirt's doing. You're going to need it." Then John started laughing, as if he were *heyoka* again. "Why do you think I stay drunk all the time? It's medicine . . ." Suddenly, he seemed as if he was going to fall back asleep. But he focused again and asked, "Where are we?"

"Close to Fredericksburg," Charlie said, relieved to stop talking about medicine. "We should hit 95 pretty soon now."

"Take us straight down to Florida."

"Where does Whiteshirt live?" Charlie blurted out before he thought about it. He should have just left well enough alone, and then maybe this whole thing would come out all right by itself. The more John talked about Whiteshirt and bad medicine, Charlie thought, the more real it all became.

"He lives somewhere around New Smyrna Beach," John said. He was leaning back in his seat, his head against the headrest, his eyes closed. "There's a reservation around there, but he don't live on it."

"Jesus . . ."

"Whatsamatter now?"

"That's where Nathan Isaacs lives," Charlie said.

"You mean the old man lives on the res?" John asked, smiling.

"Cut the shit, you know what I meant."

"So we'll settle all our scores." Then John fell asleep. It was almost as if he had been talking in his sleep all along because he started snoring again immediately.

But Charlie felt something behind him, a pressure on the back of his neck, a tingling. Still . . . he wouldn't look into the rear-view mirror. He wouldn't adjust it.

He wouldn't give in to it.

13.

SOMETHING
PSYCHOLOGICAL IN
THE COFFEE MAKER

It might have all been bullshit, something psychological in his head, but John was right. Charlie couldn't deny that. It did get worse as they drove south. Charlie became increasingly nervous, as if Whiteshirt was sitting right there in the back of the car weaving spells and casting the evil eye. Charlie's mother had believed in the evil eye, but Charlie had always thought it was all nonsense. He still thought it was all nonsense, but he was nervous just the same.

It was funny the things you remember when you're sitting in a car, Charlie thought. He felt as if he was alone; John made his presence known by snoring, but that was all. When Charlie was little more than a baby, his mother used to curl his hair like a girl's, and she had made him wear a loop of red ribbon pinned to his shirt. She even made him wear it when he was in bed. She said it kept away the evil eye.

Maybe he needed one of those ribbons now. And goddamn if he suddenly didn't miss his mother, God rest her soul. I should have gone back to see her after Pop died, he told himself. But he just couldn't bring himself to go back home. He couldn't face her . . . maybe Pop's stroke *was* his fault. Charlie had called her every Christmas Eve, but that was all—no cards, no visits, and when she died, Charlie didn't really cry or mourn. He knew she was dead, yet he wouldn't, or couldn't, accept it. But now, somehow, he did. Mom was dead and he was alone.

Nothing he thought about seemed to help his state of mind, not even trying to get into the state of the cow, where everything was straight lines and calmness. He *felt* something, something heavy and deadly and evil . . . and it was getting stronger. It might all be bullshit, but it was real bullshit, he told himself. He shivered, even though it was warm in the car. He leaned over toward John, and pulled the bottle of rye away from him.

From there on it was numbness and nausea and easy breathing and the plashing of tires along the highway, until Charlie missed his exit for 95 and found himself on secondary roads, passing by pig farms and run down gas stations selling cheap cigarettes and fireworks. Frustrated, he turned the car around and backtracked until he found the exit. Once on 95, he drove like hell, as if troopers were after him—and he might actually have a chance to outrace them in this car. The damn thing could certainly move, even though it was the silliest goddamn piece of engineering he had ever seen. Although the windows had to be manually raised and lowered, the side view mirrors were electric. Only the Japanese could think that one up, he thought. And there wasn't enough room to pick your ass; if you were going to sit in the back seat, you'd better be a dwarf or something. Well, that wasn't really fair to the Japs, Charlie thought. All cars nowadays were being built for people the size of midgets.

But Charlie had never had to worry about that before, since he could never afford anything but old beaters, big old gas-guzzlers that had enough room in the back seat to play pool.

Charlie was all right through Richmond, and John was awake enough to give him money for tolls. Knowing John, Charlie thought, he'd probably robbed *everybody* at Lorena's. It was getting dark, and the traffic was quite heavy, three lanes' worth of it, but then they were back on open highway. It was as if they were moving backward through the seasons. The trees were greener; autumn had not yet taken its full bite. They drove through woods and rolling farmlands punctuated by gas stations with signs on high poles and eateries that seemed to repeat themselves such as Stuckey's and McDonald's and Burger King and Hardees and Dairy Queen and Wayfara. And Charlie felt alone again. He had to keep drinking to keep himself from suddenly turning around to see whatever it was that was watching him. He wasn't going to be able to keep this up, he thought. Not for long. But the booze did help.

"You want to stop for a while?" John asked. He'd been awake for a time, but hadn't spoken.

Charlie was weaving all over the road. It was just past dusk when what light was left seemed refracted into the blue. It seemed dusty, as if they were driving through a mist, or a dream—he wished it was a dream. "No, I'm doing just fine."

"Doesn't seem that way to me."

"Maybe we should get some coffee," Charlie said.

"I'm in the mood for pizza."

Just the thought of pizza brought a bitter, metallic taste to Charlie's mouth, but he found a sign for Pizza Hut, and then had to drive two miles from the highway before they found the place. It was across the street from a Day's Inn and a McDonald's.

They went inside. The restaurant was decorated like every other Pizza Hut, which made Charlie feel suddenly depressed. He could almost be back home in Johnson City. They walked past the video games and the coat closets and the wood and plastic salad kiosk, and took a booth against the wall. There was raunchy rock-and-roll music coming from speakers in the ceiling, and the place was empty, except for six punk-looking high school kids sitting at a table on the other side of the room.

Charlie felt dizzy. It had to be all that booze. He looked out the circlehead window beside him and saw his own reflection in the dark glass. He turned away quickly. "You know," he said to John, "I think this medicine stuff is all in our heads. If we could be strong enough, it wouldn't bother us. I think we hypnotized ourselves, or something."

John smiled wanly. "You got some of it right. Of course, it's in your head, where else do you expect it to be? In your pants? But we didn't do it to ourselves. Once you get over thinking *that*, you can start to fight what's really after you. Then, if you're strong enough, it *won't* hurt you."

A waitress in a brown uniform gave them menus and asked if they wanted coffee. She appeared to be in her late thirties; and she was pretty, but it was a tired, faded beauty. Her long blond hair was pulled back into a ponytail; and, although she was very tall, she wasn't a bit awkward. She had a smooth, experienced way about her and looked a little like Charlie's first wife, Ruth. Charlie had run out on Ruth thirty years ago. But it was her own goddamn fault, he told himself. I wouldn't have fucked around on her so much if she would have just stopped hammering and nagging at me all the goddamn time, every minute of the day. I was a good provider for her, and things might have been different if she'd acted like a woman instead of my mother. Charlie was surprised at what he was thinking—Christ, he hadn't thought about Ruth for years; he'd put her completely out of his mind. Joline and he never talked about her, and Joline never mentioned his two children from that marriage. Ruth had set those kids against me, Charlie told himself. That's why they never called, would never return my letters. Well, it's like they never were. It's like you never were, Ruth. Goddamn your eyes. And now I walk into a pizza parlor in the middle of nowhere and I find your goddamn ghost. Charlie wanted to get out, but he had just got here, and there was no way that he could pull John away from the waitress.

John seemed to come to life as soon as he saw her. He was at it again, smiling and looking all over this woman. All Charlie could do was put it all out of his mind—Christ, he'd been putting Ruth out of his mind for thirty years. Now she was a ghost, is all. A few memories of regret and guilt well-layered with rationalization.

Immediately and unabashedly, John let it drop that he was a medicine man. Charlie could feel something quick pass between John and the waitress, and that made him jealous and insecure. Goddamn if she wasn't flirting back at John.

He didn't understand his feelings, but it was as if *Joline* was flirting with John.

"I'll be right back with your coffees," she said to John. She spoke with a slight, but noticeable southern drawl.

"We should take her along with us," John said as he watched her walk away. He smiled. "Make this trip more interesting."

"Maybe I should order some orange juice, the booze makes me thirsty," Charlie said, looking at the fold-out menu. Fuck John and fuck the waitress . . . and fuck Ruth, too, he told himself. I don't need this shit. Then he thought of Sharry and felt ashamed and embarrassed and angry. *She* had been interested in John, too. She only fucked me because *he* told her to. God damn him! But Charlie was even more disgusted with himself for being here— his place was with Joline and the kids. They were his only salvation. Sonovabitch if that hadn't come to him as a shock after all these years.

"You're crazy," John said. "You drink orange juice and you'll be barfing all over."

When the waitress returned with their coffee and silverware, John said, "You know we been drinking ourselves numb, and

188

doing some pretty mysterious things, and my partner here wants to order orange juice. Can you believe that?"

"I don't know about the mysterious things," the waitress said, "but if you've been drinking, I'd advise you to stick with the coffee. Juice might make you sick."

But Charlie insisted, as if he had to save face.

After she brought Charlie his orange juice and went back for John's pan pizza, John coaxed her to sit down. "The place is empty, anyway," he said; and then he began his routine, working her, as if he were reeling in a sunfish from the ocean. He asked her name ("Kim") and where she was from ("Right here"), and they talked about the loud music and the high school kids who were trying to look like punks. John talked to her about medicine and vision-quests, and she seemed interested in everything he had to say. He talked about Whiteshirt and how they had to stay drunk because booze was protection. Then he started talking dangerously.

"Now you should have seen Charlie, he's a regular hero," John said. "He stole a goddamn patrol car right out from a trooper. That trooper got himself so bent, he started shooting at us."

"Jesus H. Christ," Charlie said. "Shut the hell up! What are you trying to do, anyway?"

"She's okay," John said. "Trust me, I wasn't a medicine man for all those years for nothing." And he continued talking. He had her. She was laughing with him as if she'd been through it all with them.

"Is this for real?" she asked.

"If I really try to convince you, you're still not going to believe me," John said. "So what's the point? But even if you don't believe it, you gotta admit it's a helluva story."

"That it is," she said. "Are you really a medicine man?"

"If you're not going to believe the story, why would you believe I was a medicine man?"

"Good point," she said, smiling at him. "You know, I did some traveling once upon a time. I hitchhiked out west, got pregnant, and rode back home on a Harley." She laughed at that. "I just never could get comfortable out there. All the rocks seemed to be shaped funny, you know? I have a sixteen-year-old boy . . . he's taller than me, if that's possible. Don't you guys have any family?"

Charlie averted his eyes from her gaze, but he noticed that she had a faint tattoo: three dots on the knuckles of her right hand. An old boyfriend must have done that. Or who knows, maybe it was her husband's work, Charlie thought.

His first wife never would have done anything like that, that was for damn sure. She used to tell Charlie that he had disfigured himself—turned himself into a circus freak—just because he had a Marine insignia tattooed on his right arm. The tattoo had faded, but, dammit, he was still proud of it.

"Well, *he's* got a family," she said, meaning Charlie. "Why're you doing this, drinking and stealing cars and all that?"

"Why'd you go cross-country on a cycle and get knocked-up?" John asked.

"I was a kid. Eighteen years old."

"Just like us," John said. Even Charlie smiled at that. But Charlie was nervous. He wanted to get out of here. He wanted to get John out of here—alone.

"That's not good enough," she said. She was suddenly serious, earnest.

"Okay, so we're two old fucks," John said. "But by the time we're done, we'll show the whole world we were alive. You married?"

She looked surprised. "No."

"Then why don't you come along with us? Your son would be okay for a while by himself, wouldn't he?"

"We gotta *go*," Charlie said, and he stood up. The sooner they were back on the road, the sooner Charlie could pay off his dues, try to get Whiteshirt out of his life, and go home to Joline. But that might not be possible, he thought anxiously. If Whiteshirt wins, he'll probably kill us both or turn us into spirits or something. Christ, he thought, I'm getting as crazy as John.

"Why don't you guys stay here for a while?" Kim asked.

John seemed to be considering that. Charlie touched his arm and said, "Come on. We got enough problems as it is. You can't bring anybody else into it."

"We're supposed to be having a party," John said, and his eyes looked hard, as if he could go *heyoka* right here in a snap. He could go either way. But he said, "Okay, Charlie, you're right. We could have showed you some time, though," he said to Kim.

"I'll bet you could."

"Can we have the check?" Charlie asked, changing the mood.

"Wait one sec," and Kim went into the kitchen. When she came out, she had a large soda container capped with a white plastic top. "This is for the road, and don't shake it or open it here."

"What about the check?" John asked.

"On the house," and she turned and walked away to wait on the high school kids.

It had started to rain while they were in the restaurant. It was drizzling now, and the air was heavy with mist. The parking lot was dappled with puddles.

John insisted on driving.

When they got inside the car, he started the engine and turned on the heater—it was cold tonight. Then he shook the soda container. "This sure as hell isn't filled with water." He opened it and started to laugh. "Well, bless her heart."

"What is it?" Charlie asked.

"Protection."

"What?"

"Good old homegrown. And she even dropped in a pack of Zig-Zag."

Charlie reached over and took the container from John. It looked like it was filled with tobacco. He smelled it. "I know what this is. I'm not smoking that crap, and either should you."

"That a fact," John said, taking back the container. He expertly rolled four joints, licked them, and twisted the ends. "We need all the help we can get." He lit one joint and put the others in his shirt pocket. After taking a drag and holding it deep in his lungs, he passed the marijuana cigarette to Charlie. Charlie refused it. "Indian people been smoking this stuff for hundreds of years," John said, exhaling smoke.

There he goes again, Charlie thought. Now he's got Indians inventing pot. The pungent odor of the marijuana made him feel queasy—or maybe it was that orange juice. "You can't drive on that stuff."

John laughed and said, "Hell if I can't!" He threw the car into gear and drove like a wild man, puffing and coughing, trying to find the interchange. Charlie had to tell him to turn on the windshield wipers. John must have taken a wrong turn, for they passed what seemed to be miles of broken five-rail fences and dilapidated farm houses painted in several colors; and it seemed that rusting appliances and used tires were strewn around every house and farm, as if they were part of the southern flora like jimson weed and trumpet vine and kudzu.

"I *told* you, you can't drive on that stuff," Charlie said, and they both started laughing uncontrollably. Charlie began to choke, and he opened up his window. He felt slightly numbed. Probably all that pot smoke, he thought; but he got the giggles, just as if he had been smoking the pipe with John. And that old pipe was still hanging from the rear-view mirror, sliding back and forth on the dash as John rounded one turn and then another.

John lit a new marijuana cigarette and passed it to Charlie.

"This'll open up your lungs. And you can't just turn down a present. This is holy shit."

So Charlie tried it, just to show John that he was in control. He gagged trying to hold the burning, sickly sweet smoke in his lungs. It didn't have much effect on him, he thought, except to make him a bit sleepy. But he didn't get sick—orange juice or not. It was a question of mind over matter. He could be in control, no matter how fucked up he got.

John found the interchange and got back on 95. Charlie slept some, although his thoughts seemed to be going every which way. He dreamed of Ruth and Joline and Sharry, and they all got mixed up in his mind. He awoke feeling gummy. He smoked and drank some more, as did John. Maybe the pot counteracted the booze, Charlie thought.

But even with the pot, this driving through the night became monotonous: the same sounds of tires rolling over the long blocks of concrete, the moon sliding out from behind curtains of clouds, and the monochrome shapes of corn, cotton, and tobacco country all around them, flattened out by the night. Charlie remembered passing through Rocky Mount—an exit sign and a small constellation of lights flickering by—but he dozed through Benson, Dunn, Godwin, Wade, Fayetteville, and Lumberton. He woke up with a full bladder, and made John stop so he could piss by the side of the road ... he even tried to "hang it out the window", as John had suggested, but there was no way he could manage that.

Charlie played a game with himself: He'd try to stay awake until he came to the next billboard advertisement for *South of the Border*, a motel, shopping complex, and amusement park located on the northern edge of South Carolina. Each successive sign seemed to be grander and bolder than the last. But Charlie would nod out between signs nevertheless, dazed and drunk on drugs and booze.

He dreamed of the sweat-lodge . . . he dreamed that the rocks and stones in the pit had turned into eyes, unblinking coal-red eyes watching him.

He awakened with a jolt.

"Whiteshirt at it again?" John asked.

Charlie nodded. He might as well accept the inevitable, no sense calling an elephant an apple. *Somebody* was doing *something*. It *had* to be Whiteshirt. Charlie thought such thinking was crazy, but if he didn't believe what was happening to him, then he'd certainly be crazy. He should make John give up the wheel, and then he could turn this car right around and go back home. That would save both their asses, probably. But it wouldn't be so easy to get John out of the driver's seat. It was too late, anyway. They were too far gone. If they didn't face Whiteshirt and get it over with, those goddamn eyes would be watching them for the rest of their lives. It wouldn't even matter if Whiteshirt dropped dead, probably, Charlie thought. If what John said was the truth, then Whiteshirt could put himself into rocks or the goddamn coffee maker, for that matter, and haunt John and Charlie forever. Charlie chuckled, thinking about Whiteshirt in the coffee maker, yet it also scared him that nothing was safe, not even those things he was most familiar with. Christ, for that matter, Whiteshirt could take over Charlie himself . . . or he could take over John. That thought shook him, removed his smile.

"What's funny?" John asked.

"Nothing."

"Was something . . . must have been *something*."

"I was thinking about Whiteshirt being dead and turning into the coffee maker Joline uses to make coffee every morning."

"So you're finally believing what you see," John said seriously. He was still drinking hard and smoking pot. How he was managing to keep the car on the road and talk like a sober person, Charlie had no idea. Then John started laughing. "I kind of like that ... Whiteshirt ending up as a coffee maker. Beats turning into a rock, I guess."

Charlie was relieved that John had restrained himself from going *heyoka*. Every time John laughed or chuckled, Charlie wondered if he was going to go over the edge again. In spite of all the bad medicine crap—and with the help of all the booze he'd been drinking and all the pot he'd been smoking—John actually seemed to be sober. Goddammit, Charlie thought, it's *him* that's in control. Charlie could feel the marijuana working through him like Novocaine, maybe shielding him from whatever half-assed, crazy medicine stuff was going on around him; but dulling him just the same, giving him cottonmouth and cottonbrain.

"It's good to turn things into laughter," John continued. "It's power. A good medicine man can usually laugh his ass off, no matter what, no matter how bad his situation might be. He could be dying and still laugh his ass off. You wanna be a medicine man?"

"I'll leave all that to you," Charlie said. Then, after a beat, "Let me drive for a little while now ..."

"You're too drunk to drive, honky," John said. He gently pressed the accelerator to the floor, and they passed the neon carnival that all the signs had pointed to: *South of the Border*. It glowed in the darkness like an image in a junkie's dream.

1 4 .

GETTING GAS, JEWS,
AND *HEYOKA*

John went *heyoka* when they hit Savannah, sometime around two o'clock in the morning.

Charlie had been catnapping, waking up bleary-eyed and nauseated, then slipping back into dream-haunted sleep. There wasn't much traffic; although what there was moved along quickly, as if no one had to worry about police in that town. John was wide awake and still drinking. It seemed that the more he drank and smoked dope, the more sober he became. He drove slowly in the right-hand lane, squinting ahead as if trying to work something out. The faster-moving cars sighed past him in the other lane.

But just as they passed the Philip Morris factory and its giant smokestack that was painted to look like a cigarette, a car appeared out of nowhere behind them. It was tailgating them almost bumper to bumper.

"Will you look at those assholes," John said.

Charlie was awake and had been taking in the scenery. That smokestack reminded him that he needed a cigarette. "You got any cigarettes?" he asked John.

"What the fuck are they *doing*?" John asked, agitated. "There's two goddamn lanes, why don't they just pass?"

"Who?"

"Turn your face around and look, those assholes behind us." John kept looking into the rear-view mirror, which he had pulled back into place when he had taken over the wheel.

Charlie turned around. The car behind them looked like a Pontiac station wagon, probably, maybe an '82 or '83, but it was difficult to tell, especially at night. He could see that the car had been in an accident: its grill was twisted and broken. There was once a time when Charlie could have told you anything about any car by just glancing at it, but he'd been out of the business too long for that anymore.

One thing, though, it looked like there were a fuck of a lot of people in that car, Charlie thought. Or maybe he just wasn't seeing right. "Why don't you just pull over on the side of the road?" Charlie asked. "I gotta piss, anyway."

"Why should I pull over? Let the assholes pass me." Then John started mumbling something in Sioux, or some other gobbledygook language Charlie couldn't understand . . . and Charlie could see that it was something more than the tailgater that was bothering John.

Charlie motioned to the tailgaters to back off and said, "Well, just gun the fucker and move over into the passing lane. Let's get the hell out of their way. They're all crazy, anyway; that's how they are down here."

But John just kept looking into that rear-view mirror. He had both hands locked on the wheel. He was starting to shake. Charlie didn't notice, however; he was still turned around in his seat trying to wave the tailgaters back. And he was trying to guess the year of the car. "There are certainly enough people crammed in that car," Charlie said. "What the hell are they trying to prove?"

"Well, we're sure going to find out," John said.

"Just step on the gas. That goddamn Pontiac, or whateverthehell it is, can't go very fast."

"Hold on," John said, and he started laughing, that explosive laughter fraught with craziness.

Charlie had just enough time to turn around in his seat. He jumped when John laughed. It was as if lightning had struck the car. In that instant, John went completely *heyoka*.

This wasn't a simple change of masks. This was completely crazy.

Instead of accelerating, John jammed on the brakes. "You fucking witch!" he shouted at the rear-view mirror.

"Jesus Christ in Heaven!" Charlie screamed, as he was jolted against the dashboard. He reflexively threw out his arm, which thudded achingly against the windshield; at least he didn't hit his head against anything. The car behind them braked, but not quite soon enough, and immediately Charlie felt another jolt as the car banged into their rear bumper. Charlie felt disoriented. All he could hear—all he could sense around him—was John's high-pitched, crazy-assed howling that passed for laughter. John was lit, on-fire insane. He was acting like Whiteshirt, Charlie thought. He was acting like a witch. Those crazy fuckers might have been wrong to tailgate, but they didn't deserve to be smashed up for it. "Please try to come out of your trance or whatever the hell it is," Charlie said. "You're going to kill us all dead." Charlie tried to use some psychology. He knew something about that: he had read some books when he was taking care of The Middle School. "If you want your chance at Whiteshirt, you'd better get us the fuck out of here now, or we're going to either be dead or in goddamn jail." For an instant Charlie thought his words had taken effect because John seemed calm, in control again. He was driving slowly . . . much too slowly.

The other car switched lanes and was trying to pass them. It was the filthiest-looking car Charlie had ever seen, but that was nothing compared to the people inside. They were the weirdest-looking things he had ever seen in his life, which is saying something. There must have been four people and a baby just in the front seat, and maybe six or even seven people crammed into the back. The men wore wide-brimmed black hats and had long, curly beards and sideburns. They were all looking at John and Charlie, and their lips were moving, as if they were arguing and shouting at each other.

John looked intently ahead, and he suddenly jerked the Toyota into the passing lane, crashing into the Pontiac, hitting it just in front of the door. There was a terrible grinding sound, and the Pontiac careened off the road onto the grassy median.

Charlie watched as if it were happening to someone else, as if it was something on television. An instant later he saw, almost as an after-image, the passenger who was closest to the window. His round eyeglasses seemed to be the only thing distinguishing his bearded face from the others. He just stared out the window at John and Charlie, blinking in utter astonishment.

Charlie imagined smoke and fire and Hell.

The car was left behind as John burned away, his foot pressing the accelerator to the floor. Charlie looked behind, but couldn't tell if they were all right back there, or whether the car had burst into flames, or rolled over, as he had once seen a Volkswagen Bug do on the highway.

"What the fuck are you trying to *do*?" Charlie screamed at John.

"It was Joe Whiteshirt in that car," John said calmly. "Couldn't you see that?"

And goddamn if it wasn't Whiteshirt in that car, Charlie thought, his chattering teeth sounding like a pinball machine. It didn't matter what they did now. Whiteshirt had won. John had turned into some sort of crazy-assed *heyoka* witch who only wanted to hurt people. John was turning into Whiteshirt! And everything else was a reflection of Whiteshirt, too, as if the fat medicine man had swallowed everything up.

Everything was dark edges. Everything was burning like coals in the sweat-lodge. Yet everything was cold . . .

They were trapped inside Whiteshirt's medicine bag, and he was shaking it like a rattle.

Those are crazy thoughts, Charlie told himself. It's John. It's *us*! *We're* fucked up. And we're over the edge. Christ Almighty, those funny-looking people behind us might be fucking dead for all we know. And yet Charlie felt paralyzed. He couldn't get it up to start yelling and shouting at John to turn the car around so they could check on those people.

But someone will. Someone will stop. Surely they're all right . . .

Charlie started drinking, fast, gulping down the fire, feeling it come back up on him; and he leaned out the window, thankful for the wind, which had just a bite of the north to it yet.

John didn't speak for miles. He just drove hammer-down through the still-urban area, then down, down past Richmond Hill and Riceboro and South Newport and Eulonia, down I–95 along the east coast, the black ocean to their left, invisible beyond upland and scrub and dense pine forest. They crossed level tidewater, passed the moonlit trees blighted by Spanish moss.

They had driven over the edge. Charlie knew that as certainly as he knew the Laws and the Book. Before it had been a ride. Charlie was just a passenger, tagging along. But all that changed somehow when John hit that car. That was vicious. And Charlie hadn't been able to do a thing, or say a word. He was *part* of it, and now there was nothing left to do but see it through.

It was warm, and they had the windows down. They'd driven into a black nightmare of a summer, a fever-dream that might have been glimpsed only in a sweat-lodge, and goddamn if Charlie wasn't sick. He was sick right down to his gums. Everything ached. He was past vomiting, past choking with dry-heaves. If he'd had the words for it, he would have said he was sick in his soul. He knew the Laws. He would pay for those people in the Pontiac.

Then suddenly, as if John had just shaken himself out of his *heyoka* trance, he said in a calm voice, "Don't worry about those people, Charlie. They're all right."

"How the fuck do you know whether they're all right or not?" Charlie snapped. At this point he didn't care if John went *heyoka* again. The damage was already done. There was no turning back. Sonovabitch if I'm not in hell, Charlie told himself. Joline was right: I'm a stupid bastard. But it was also funny how he seemed to be noticing everything: all the sounds and smells and sights and memories that could be stuffed into a single minute; the shadow shapes beyond the road that suggested country different from the kind they saw in the north; the special headlight green of the roadside foliage; John's even breathing, and his own, sharp and raspy and plosive; Joline in the front of his mind while that bastard Whiteshirt was in the back. Goddamn if this wasn't hell. It was sick and fucked up and full of vomit. But Charlie *knew* he was alive. He felt every tickle, every ache and pain and tearing cough.

"I just know they're all right, that's all," John said quietly, contritely. "I've still got some medicine left, even if I am all fucked up and wrong."

"Is that why you bashed the shit out of those weirdoes' car?"

"I was *heyoka*."

"That's just an excuse to do whatever you want," Charlie said. "I can just see Hitler explaining to the Jews in Heaven, 'Oh, I'm sorry, Jewpeople, I was just a little *heyoka*.'" John chuckled at that, and Charlie could sense a sadness in the car. Maybe it was just because it was warm and dark and they were moving as if through a tunnel that could go on forever . . . more likely, though, it was John's presence. He seemed to broadcast feelings sometimes, Charlie thought, as if he were a television set or something.

"I guess I earned that one," John said. "So you knew about those people."

"What do you mean?"

"In the car, the Chassidim."

"The *what*?"

"They were Jews, they live in a traditional manner . . . maybe they're what Jews are supposed to be. Just like traditional Indians are what Indians are supposed to be. I guess both kinds are hard to take." He laughed softly at that.

"Are you ready to go back now?" Charlie asked. "Before we kill somebody . . . if we haven't already."

"You know where we're going," John said. "You should have been smart and stayed at Lorena's, fucked that little girl some more, ate yourself fat and then went home to Momma—*that* would have been smart. But it's too late for that now."

"I think we should call it a day, we've had enough," Charlie whispered, thinking about that car full of Jews careening off the road and into the median. Didn't matter if they were crazy-assed-looking Jews. John shouldn't've done that to them.

Then John started laughing, as if he were going to turn *heyoka* again. It was that quick, cruel laugh, full of body and life, even now. "If I'd've been drunk enough, that wouldn't've happened," John said. "It's Joe Whiteshirt, and he's not going to let go of either one of us, no matter where we go. You can get out of the car now. Hell, I'll *give* you the goddamn thing so you won't have to dirty your clean-living hands stealing another one."

Charlie didn't say anything.

"I've got to finish this thing out," John continued. "And so do you, whether you know it or not."

"I think it's a lot of bullshit in our minds," Charlie said.

"That's probably so. But it still doesn't make any difference."

Charlie snorted, but everything felt dark and hollow again. That asshole Indian was right, and that was just plain crazy thinking. They were both plain crazy, and as lost as two goddamn rats in a maze. Sonovabitch, Charlie thought, frightened. Fucking crazy . . .

"And I'll tell you what I'm going to do whether you stay in the car or not," John said. "I'm going to smoke up this pot and drink up this booze as fast as I can"—he lit a joint and reached into the back seat for the bottle of Johnny Walker— "and then I'm going to stop at a service station and get gas, and then I'm going to get completely fucked up and *heyoka*. But *I'm* going to get myself *heyoka*. I'm not having any asshole Joe Whiteshirt phony-ass medicine man working medicine on me to make me *look* like I'm *heyoka*."

"What?" Charlie asked.

"Don't matter, I know what I mean."

"Why don't you just try to lay off it a little, maybe you'll feel better."

John took a large swallow from the bottle. "I told you the booze was a screen from bad medicine. It helps you out. If I were as stinko as you when Whiteshirt started working his medicine on me, I wouldn't've hit those poor Jew-bastards. I would've just screamed a little."

"So now you're telling me that you go *heyoka* when somebody is doing bad medicine on you?" Charlie asked sarcastically.

"I've never been mean-crazy before like that," John said, as if the dope and the booze had once again made him stone-sober. He took another puff from the marijuana cigarette and inhaled deeply and noisily. After that, he seemed to breathe heavily, like Charlie.

Maybe my emphysema is catching, Charlie thought; and he felt the urge to laugh, just as he had after he first smoked the pipe with John. Maybe I'm like some sort of goddamn Typhoid Mary, except that everybody who gets near me gets emphysema. He had to laugh as he imagined everyone he'd ever met coughing their asses off. Serve the bastards right . . .

John's right, Charlie thought. I do need a drink, and maybe even a little more of that weed.

"You think that's funny?" John asked.

Charlie nodded. He couldn't stop laughing.

John got off at the next exit and found a gas station (STUCKEY's TEXACO—VIDEO GAMES FIRECRACKERS CIGARETTES). "Gas it right up," he told the sullen-looking attendant who wore his thick black hair greased-back in a duck's-ass like Elvis. "I don't want to go near that gasoline," John said to Charlie. "There's so much medicine going on around us that it might blow the goddamn thing up."

Charlie turned away, disgusted, and said, as if he were talking to the window, "Let me drive for a while. It's my turn."

The attendant walked across the narrow concrete service island to take care of a woman in a yellow Mercedes. She had a dark tan and bleach-blond, shoulder-length hair. We sure as hell must be getting close to God's country, Charlie thought.

"Well, are you going to get out and let me drive?" Charlie asked John. But John keyed the ignition and blew out of that Texaco station, waving a ten dollar bill out the window as payment. The gasoline nozzle spout was torn out of the Toyota's tank, and the bill ruffled off like a piece of newspaper in a hurricane.

John screamed onto the secondary road and laid rubber up the access ramp to the highway. As he fishtailed back onto I–95, he said, "You're too sober to drive, honky!" Then he shouted some Indian oath and opened the window wide so that the spirits sitting on the wind or wherever they sat could come right into the car and shout along with him.

15.

WEARING THE
EMPEROR'S CLOTHES

Everything seemed to have weight: the night, the flatlands, the air—and it was getting warm. John and Charlie had opened their windows, but the muggy air only made Charlie feel even more dirty and grimy and slippery-sweaty.

They were in Florida, passing through Jacksonville, which looked like something out of a postcard, not a real city in the real world. Lit like a large-scale *South of the Border*, it looked like a glittering futuristic city.

They blew past Jax at a hundred miles an hour.

They felt Whiteshirt's presence everywhere. They saw him in every light and flicker. Every taillight was a coal-red eye watching . . . waiting. It was as if John and Charlie were driving themselves crazy. This warm country wasn't *real*. It was just that dark, blind state that John called *heyoka* . . . They were being pulled right through Florida, a speck of Japanese tin drawn to a magnet. That John was driving and pressing down hard on the accelerator wasn't as real as the sensation Charlie had of being pulled along, of being sucked into the dark. They passed Neptune Beach, Jax Beach, Ponte Verdra Beach, Vilan Beach, Crescent Beach . . .

Charlie thought of the ocean. He thought of getting clean and leaving behind everything wrong and dirty and fucked up. He could feel that ocean all around him, even if he couldn't actually see it from the car. He could smell it everywhere, and it was wonderful, the only *real* thing in this dark, shadowed, moonlit country.

Every once in a while they'd pass palm trees standing in the median, lit by passing cars, but the trees were scrawny and dying: there had been some sort of desiccating tree plague hereabouts.

"I'm hungry," Charlie said, the first words he had spoken to John in a hundred miles. John was quiet, almost pensive, but there was a tension in the car, for John was still *heyoka*, only quietly so. He could still burst open and go completely crazy-ass crazy, Charlie was sure, but he didn't have any idea when that would happen. Charlie had discovered that when John was *heyoka*, even when he seemed as calm as a clear sky, John would breath deeply, just as he was doing now. That was the giveaway that he could be smashing, blotto, pissing-on-the-wall crazy at any moment. And Charlie had the chilling thought that what had happened with those Jew tailgaters was only the beginning.

"You should've had something to eat in that pizza place," John said. "You shouldn't be hungry now, anyway. You're too drunk."

"What I *should* be is fucking seasick, the way you're weaving from one side of the road to the other."

"Then don't tell me you're hungry, honky."

Charlie let that one pass.

"Take one of the cans in the back seat, or on the floor here." John suddenly let go of the steering wheel to search for the cans. Charlie took the wheel. He didn't complain. He was used to it by now. But goddammit, Charlie didn't want to eat something cold out of a can. He wasn't a bum. He wanted a good portion of Joline's meatloaf, or some steaming hot chicken chow mein on those crunchy noodles. He wanted to be home where he could sit back on the couch and watch television and maybe cop a tender feel from his wife. He wasn't horny—he'd been horny enough with Sharry—he just wanted this to be done with. He was as homesick as when he'd left his parent's home—some forty-odd years ago.

"Here," John said, sitting up, a can opener in one hand and a small tin of beans and bacon in the other.

"You want me to eat this shit?" Charlie asked.

"We're all out of the soup."

Charlie dutifully opened the can, but the smell gagged him, and he felt the vomit coming up again. He wasn't going to be able to eat. He couldn't shit, he couldn't eat, all he could do was drink. Goddamn if I'm not going to turn into a skeleton or something, he told himself. And then he did get sick, just when he was about to take a short nip to keep the tickle back from his throat. He learned out the window, and the canned beans spilled on his lap.

"Jesus Christ," Charlie said after a time. "We gotta stop. I gotta clean up." He wiped up the beans as best he could.

"How'd you get those burns on your face?" John asked happily.

"What?"

"The burns on your face. I never asked you about them before."

"What the hell has that got to do with us stopping so I can wash up?"

"I just wanted to know, that's all," John said petulantly. "Don't try to tell me you got them in the war because you would have told me that already, right?"

Charlie grinned in spite of himself. John certainly had his number. Charlie was an old bullshit artist ... he had been fabricating his past for so long that he could hardly remember where the bullshit ended and the truth began. John was smiling, too, and for a minute everything was all right. The weight had lifted. But then Charlie felt it back there again, hanging over him, as heavy as the air in the sweat-lodge. "I was on my way to a beauty contest and an oil can blew up in my face," Charlie said.

John didn't laugh. He was nervous again, weaving all over the road.

"It was a factory accident, in Louisiana, machine exploded and I was sprayed with hot oil," Charlie said.

After that, John started laughing. So did Charlie. Charlie suddenly felt that old freedom he'd experienced when John backed up to him in Stephen Isaacs' car. It was a feeling like flying, like being in a dream and extending your arms and rising into the sky. It was the feeling of being able to do anything you want. It was what had started Charlie on this trip, but that wild, berserk freedom had been swallowed. That freedom was just a tiny crack in the Laws, and its consequences of Threes followed every damn crazy thing they did. You couldn't get out. You could only *pretend* you could. Whiteshirt was another crack in the Laws. Or maybe he was just another consequence. One of God's consequences.

They came upon an overhead green sign that said BEACHES-A1A, and John took the exit at about sixty miles an hour. That little Japanese car could certainly take the turns, Charlie thought, even if it was built for midgets. They drove over a long, fog-covered bridge, and went south on A1A, which looked deserted. There were a few expensive homes on their right and the dark smashing of ocean on their left.

"Let's get over on the beach," Charlie said, impatient to get out of the car, to be free of it all . . . goddamn, if he was going to die anywhere, he thought, it should be on the beach, by the water, away from metal parts and contraptions.

"Can't drive on the beach, we'll sink in the sand," John said, and as soon as he said that, he jerked the wheel to the left and rolled the car right over the shoulder. There was a tearing sound as the bumper smashed into a stone downgrade, but John kept his foot on the accelerator. The car lurched, and then they were driving across the flat, even beach toward the water. The closely packed sand made a firm surface; the Toyota wouldn't get stuck unless John drove too close to the ocean.

The horizon was beginning to turn gray, which made the water seem an even deeper black by contrast, and angry, somehow. Moonlight skipped like stones across the cold, dark surface, and Charlie imagined that the pounding, breaking ocean was waiting to take him under. He was in no hurry just now to step into that water.

But suddenly John slammed on the brakes. He turned off the engine and got out of the car, leaving Charlie where he was, his lap starched with the still-sticky remains of a can of pork and beans.

This was a bad idea, Charlie thought as he got out of the car. His legs were stiff, and his stomach growled and burned, as if he'd swallowed acid. Charlie was awed and frightened by the combined immensity of the starry sky and the ocean, which seemed to be as deep as the world was wide. Thank God that the sun would soon be coming up. There was safety in daylight.

"Well," John said. "I thought you wanted to take your goddamn bath?"

"It's cold out here."

"Cold? It's fucking hot. Hurry up, we got a date to see your old landlord and my old student, you might say." With that, he laughed. John walked along the shore, his boots in the water, as if he was oblivious to the surf . . . as if he were walking along the desert back home. Then he wandered away and disappeared. Charlie wasn't sure where he could have gone. Probably away from the beach. The fucker's probably robbing some rich honky's house.

Why did I say that? Charlie asked himself, now laughing, feeling the booze he had drunk pumping through him again, giving him a second wind. *I'm* a goddamn honky! He started laughing at that, and he felt the freedom. Perhaps it was the coming of the light that made him brave. He pulled off his clothes as if they were some sort of reptilian skin; and his own skin, white and pallid-looking and soft, was like a new babe's. It was as if *he* was new, as if he were being given a second chance. Or maybe this was his one chance to flout the Laws with impunity.

He went into the dark water, taking his chances with whatever might be in there—sharks, rays, squid, jellyfish, all the creatures of his imagination that might be lurking on the furrowed sandy floor. He ventured in up to his ankles, feeling the cold, and goddamn it was worth it all just to be here, just to be in the water, alive . . . fucking alive! He bellyflopped into the shallow water, scratching his chest on shells and stones, and pulled himself along on the bottom, feeling wonderful, strong, virile. Those creatures of the deep better not fuck with me!

Everything turned gray, except for the ocean, which wasn't going to give up its darkness just yet. It was like swimming in clouds, in the sky. That's it, he thought, belching, I'm swimming in the goddamn sky! He let out a whoop. Honkies could whoop, too, he thought, laughing, then coughing as he inhaled some salt water. But he was only wading in water up to his knees. There was hardly an undertow here. His thoughts drifted free, and he remembered that woman in the Mercedes. Then his mind flashed back to Sharry, clutching him as he banged into her just like those crazy Jew tailgaters. He remembered her face, beautiful in agony, flushed because he was fucking her, because he was pumping her like her own heart, and he realized with drunken logic that this was God's country, where anything could happen. Freedom, goddammit! he told himself, and he shouted again.

The cold water seemed to bring the booze to his head, warming his face, while goosebumps formed all over his body.

One last whoop, which was answered by John, who had returned. It took practice to whoop properly, Charlie thought, standing up and pressing the water from his hair. His eyes burned, and he couldn't focus well. Perhaps that was the booze; most probably just the salt. He let out another whoop. With every one he felt stronger, younger.

"Hey, John, what are you doing?" Charlie called, "Come on in you goddamn Indian chickenshit." John was walking around the beach where Charlie had thrown his clothes. Then there was a roar as the engine of the Toyota came to life. "Hey, what's going on?" Charlie shouted, wading his way out of the water. He slipped on a smooth stone and stubbed his foot on a shell. By the time Charlie could reach the beach, John hit the accelerator with that lead foot of his and roared away, spraying sand in all directions.

"You goddamn fucker!" Charlie screamed, but then he began to get sick, and he was so dizzy that he fell to the ground. Then he couldn't stop coughing. What the hell did John do that for? Charlie asked himself, once his coughing had subsided. He was still dizzy. The coughing had pumped more of that booze into his brain, or so he thought.

He's letting me go. He's letting me out of it. But I'm *not* out of it, Charlie told himself. I was going through to the end, goddammit! Does he think he can take care of Whiteshirt by himself? Probably get himself killed, the stupid fucker. And then I'll find his ghost popping out of the goddamn coffee percolator or something. I was *supposed* to go the whole route. *He* told me that himself.

Suddenly, though, Charlie felt relieved. It was out of his hands. He *could* go home. His job was finished. He would live to talk about it. He got up and stumbled around looking for his clothes. Charlie thought about John, about the way he'd been acting, like a goddamn psycho. But, through it all, John had been a friend. A good friend. And John needed Charlie. If I could find him, Charlie thought, I'd go with him to the end of the goddamn world. I'll fight that red bastard Whiteshirt. I'm not afraid of him.

Jesus, he was tired, relieved and tired, and how the hell was he going to get home? He'd worry about that later. First he had to find his clothes. He recoiled at the thought of putting them back on, but he could wash them out in the salt water, after all. He could just wear his pants after he washed them out, and he could carry his wet shirt and underwear until they dried. (He knew that wearing anything wet on your chest would give you a cold.)

But he couldn't find any of his clothes, not even his brown, lace-up workshoes. He walked around in circles looking for them, and then it struck him with the soberness of a morning after that that sonovabitch Indian bastard had taken them. He wasn't trying to save my ass. He wasn't trying to keep me from getting hurt at Whiteshirt's colony or commune, or whatever the hell you call it. He was just plain asshole *heyoka* again. The sonovabitch was crazy, and dangerous. He had tried to kill those poor Jews. And this just wasn't fucking funny. "Do you hear that, you red bastard?" he shouted. "It's not fucking funny!"

Christ, I'm completely naked, he thought. And it's daytime. And that sonovabitch John Stone won't be back. It just isn't his way.

Maybe the Indian bastard would crash up the car and kill himself, Charlie told himself. But he regretted that thought, It was a bad one. I'm sorry, he mumbled, as if speaking to the gods. I'll bet that asshole Whiteshirt would enjoy this.

Charlie started walking between the tire tracks in the smooth, hard sand. Jesus Christ, he thought, people are going to be coming out to the beach soon. Very soon. What the hell am I going to do? He could hide in the bushes, maybe steal someone's towel. That was as much of a plan as he could formulate.

A horn blared somewhere ahead. It sounded like the Toyota . . .

1 6 .

GETTING IT UP

Charlie found the Toyota, and then he made out the shape of an airplane sitting on the beach like some great big frozen seagull. At first he didn't believe what he saw. He didn't blame the mirage on the booze; just that everything hereabouts was so flat and even and gray. It was like Kansas with an ocean, for Chrissakes. But then he saw John sitting in the plane, hunched under the overhead wing, his elbows on his knees, and the cabin door wide open. John was either praying or thinking or more likely sleeping. That fucker could probably sleep upside down like a bat, Charlie thought.

What the hell is a plane doing *here*? Charlie asked himself, forgetting he was naked, forgetting he was pissed off at John. How could you be angry at a crazy person, anyway?

The plane looked like an old Cessna, maybe an '82. Charlie had learned to fly on an old Aeronica Champ. But this plane ahead of him didn't even have a tailwheel; it just sat straight up like some sort of alert dog or something. What the hell is it doing here? Charlie asked himself again, admiring it, even though it had not been well kept. It was, in fact, filthy, and the registration numbers on the rudder and engine cowling had been spray-painted out. But Charlie could make out the numbers: N6259N.

The plane was white with brown stripes; the silvery propeller blades were nicked and slightly bent.

Charlie walked quickly toward the plane. He was almost running. Without realizing it, he held his penis and testicles—not so much to hide them, but it was difficult to move around without underwear or pants. Goddamn that John!

"What the fuck have you done with my clothes, you asshole!" Charlie shouted as he came upon John and the plane; and then he immediately noticed that his shirt, pants, and underwear were neatly draped over the wing. His boots were set side by side in the sand. Clothes and boots were soaking wet.

John laughed and shook a bottle of bourbon at him as if it was a rattle. "You're a regular sleazeball, you are. I figured that if I didn't up and steal your clothes and wash them out, you'd just splash around in the water and put your stinking rags right back on."

"Just fuck you," Charlie mumbled as he put his wet clothes on. They'd dry off fast enough in the sun. He wasn't going to let John catch him out again.

John was rocking back and forth as he sat half-inside and half-outside the cabin, and Charlie thought better than to provoke him. He was on the edge of meanness, Charlie could plainly see that. John was shaking, as if he had that old man's disease that makes you tremble like a piece of paper held in the wind. It was sure as shit that he was going to go *heyoka* again.

John got out of the plane and told Charlie to take a look.

Excited, Charlie climbed inside. He found that the plane had been gutted. Two of the three Navcom radio units had been removed from the instrument panel, and seats had been ripped out to hold extra fuel tanks. Whoever had flown this bird had not intended to fly it again. But Charlie was impressed anyway. This was, or had once been, a *plane.*

"Well, what do you think?" John asked.

"What do you mean?"

"Jesus, man, do you think you can fly it? You told me you had your own plane back in the old days, remember?" John had that look on his face: he knew that Charlie had been bullshitting. But he didn't leave any way out for Charlie. "Well . . . ?"

"I don't even know if the goddamn thing has any gas," Charlie said. He got out of the plane and, mostly to impress John, he stepped up on the wing strut, his elbows pressing on the top side of the wing. Then he asked, "Get me a twig or something."

"What do you want a twig for?" John asked.

"For a dipstick, what the hell do you think I want a twig for?"

Charlie felt better, more in control. "The tank is in the wing, here." John brought him a long twig, which Charlie dipped into the tank. "Well, it has fuel. Now let me check the oil. Also, there might be a lot of water in that gas, you know, condensation. Who the hell knows how long this plane's been sitting here."

"I wouldn't expect it's been too long," John said, nipping at the bottle of bourbon, his eyes half closed, as if he were planning something.

Charlie made the most of a good moment: He had found the checklist book in the cabin, and so he strutted around the plane as if he'd been flying this particular model for his whole life. He checked the wings and ailerons, the rudder and elevators, the tires, and he even drained a small quantity of fuel from the quick-drain valve on the fuel tank to check for water and sediment. John seemed properly impressed.

"You think this plane was stolen?" John asked, giggling.

"How the hell should I know? They certainly didn't want anybody to see them or they wouldn't've sprayed out the identification numbers."

"Smugglers, then?"

"I would expect so, with that added tank in the cabin," Charlie said. Sonovabitch, he thought, angry at himself. That had all passed him by. He was so shocked to find a plane out here in the middle of nowhere that nothing else had occurred to him. Of course the fucker was used by smugglers. Probably to smuggle pot or cocaine or heroin, or whatever the hell they smuggled these days. He'd read about it all in the papers. These bastards make so much money it wasn't even funny. They could afford to buy a plane, fly it once, and leave it for the police. "Yeah," Charlie said definitively, "it's smugglers, all right." He suddenly felt lightheaded. "We could fly this!" he said, without thinking. He was flushed with excitement, not because he could actually fly this plane, but simply because it was here, ready to be flown. It was like finding a cigarette dispenser with the door open.

"Could *you* fly this?" John asked, almost in a whisper, his face looking hopeful, as if for the first time he really expected something of Charlie, and Charlie *couldn't* let him down on this one.

Of all things, Charlie felt embarrassed. If he were any kind of a man, he told himself, he'd just tell John that he didn't know how to fly this plane. But, goddammit, here was the fucking plane, sitting in the sand like a gift from the gods. And Charlie *had* flown planes. Of course, he hadn't actually owned one, as he had said. He used to hang around with a gang who'd all bought into a plane; they divided the air time between all the members, and Charlie had gotten his chances to fly. He'd flown, all right. But he wasn't a pilot. And for Chrissakes that was over twenty years ago . . .

"Yeah, I suppose I could fly it," Charlie said to John. "I can probably fly anything. But I've never flown this particular plane."

"I know that," John said.

"I mean this particular brand—Cessna. Nothing was so fancy when I used to fly. I'd have to get used to all the controls all over again. When I used to fly my old Champ—and that was one hell of an aircraft—it didn't have these goddamn steering wheels. It had a stick. You flew by your wits, by your ass. You didn't have all these twirly instruments to take you home."

John gave Charlie the bottle, and Charlie started drinking. Just drinking and talking and being so close to this airplane was like getting laid, somehow, Charlie thought. It was as if the airplane gave him power, pumped him up. But goddammit there's no way I'm going to fly this plane, he told himself. He took another drink. Maybe I *should* fly it, though. Maybe that's what I came all these miles to do. Maybe this is *my* test. Maybe I'm *supposed* to tell John I can fly this dirty fucker, and we'll either turn into goddamn birds or die. One or the other. Find out once and for all whether or not the Laws are with me. And if they aren't, I might as well pay all the goddamn dues in one shot. Charlie started laughing; he was drinking much too fast.

John laughed, too; then he started screaming and acting *heyoka*. He ran around in the sand, then ran to the shoreline, where he kneeled and patted something on his face.

I've got to stop drinking one of these days, Charlie thought as he watched John. Here I'm about to go and kill myself, and I don't feel a thing. It was just another day. Just another morning. But what a morning! It wasn't beautiful, or colorful, or much of anything; but Charlie had swum in the ocean and wasn't afraid of the monsters swimming under there. He had proven *that* to himself.

This was a good day to die, he thought. He and John were going to go up in the air like birds, and what happened after that didn't matter. He wasn't even afraid. He'd been afraid for too many years, and that was wrong and stupid. Now that death might be right here, it didn't matter a dime. Not a goddamn dime. Charlie started laughing, but didn't know if he was laughing or crying. Then he had a thought that made him laugh even harder: I'm not laughing or crying, he told himself, I'm fucking *dying*! I'm as *heyoka* as John. No . . . more *heyoka*.

Then John turned around. Half of his face was smeared with what looked like pitch. It was thick, and black as coral. He walked back to Charlie, who was flabbergasted. Something about seeing John covered up that way was deeply frightening. It was as if John really wasn't John now, and all because he'd painted his face with that sludge washed up on the shore. It was *pollution*, for Chrissakes, Charlie told himself. *Dirt!* Probably from some leaking oil tanker. But with that dirt on his face—and that look of determination, as if he was some wooden cigar store Indian— John appeared to be larger than life. He seemed to be a part of something else, but Charlie didn't know what.

"What the hell did you *do* to yourself?" Charlie asked.

"It's just a thing we crazy, drunken Indians do," John said, but he didn't smile.

Charlie was more afraid of him when he'd do something crazy and then pretend to be sane. This was dangerous crazy. But what did it matter? Charlie asked himself. What the fuck did it matter one bit if they were both going to die, anyway? Once again, Charlie wasn't afraid. He wasn't afraid of *anything*. Goddamn, he told himself. *Goddamn!*

"I know you can fly this plane," John said. "And I'm just getting ready to fly, is all. You know, you came down here to Florida to visit your old friend and landlord. Well, I'm going to visit an old friend, too. But as a warrior." Then John began singing a song. Every note sounded off key. In its own weird way, it was beautiful . . .

"That's a black-face-paint song," John said. "It's as old as the ground. If we're going up there like goddamn spirits"—he looked up at the clear gray sky—"then I'm going to need to be a warrior."

Charlie laughed at that, but John was serious because he went back to the car and got his star blanket and his pipe. He wrapped the blanket around himself and said, "Let's fly this fucker."

"First we have to turn it around," Charlie said. What the hell am I doing? he asked himself. I can't fly this aircraft. But it wasn't up to Charlie; it was up to the Laws now. If John thought they could fly, they could fly, goddammit. They *would* fly.

Charlie pulled on the propeller blades; maybe he did straighten them out a bit. Then he showed John how to turn the plane around by leaning on the tail section and just walking it into line. They climbed into the cockpit, and John hung the pipe on the overhead panel. "Might as well be safe," John said, and laughed.

Charlie was excited. The booze was a warm glow. He felt as if he were lit up inside, as though if some doctor opened him up, he would radiate light like a goddamn saint or something. This was it, right now. This was fucking wonderful. He was *doing* something. He wasn't living his life through old memories. His whole goddamn life had been just old memories. But not now. Not fucking now! He was alive again. Even John seemed to catch it, the brightness. Maybe this was what happened before you died. If so, not bad. Not fucking bad.

"What do we do now?" John asked.

"Hot wire the fucker, that's what we gotta do," Charlie said.

He turned on the master switch; there was a whining noise as the gyros wound up. "Fucking A," Charlie said, looking at the lighted gauges. "We've got fuel and battery power. Fucking A. Okay, cross the wires and let's see what we're gonna do." Charlie set the fuel mixture to rich, and the prop to high RPM. "Let's see," he said, talking to himself while he checked the procedures book, "we'll close the throttle, switch on the auxiliary fuel pump. Okay, let's start the fucker."

Charlie pressed the ignition switch, and the engine cranked, but wouldn't fire. "Goddamn, I flooded it," Charlie said, grabbing John's hand. The wires came away and everything was quiet, except for the hiss and static of the radio. "Turn that thing down."

The radio was crackling and a voice said, wavering in and out, "Eight-two Alpha Aztec turning right and—" Charlie flicked switches until the radio was quiet. This aircraft has *got* to start, he thought. It was as if the plane was a manifestation of the Laws. If it wouldn't start, then that would be a sign that the universe was against them, that Charlie and John were *wrong*, and there would be nothing but dues.

He set the mixture to the idle cut-off, and pushed the throttle wide open. "Okay, *now* try it," Charlie said, and the engine raged into life. The whole plane was shaking, and Charlie kept his feet on the heel brakes and let the engine crank. He pulled back the elevator control, holding it by the yolk; it looked like a broken-off steering wheel and responded as if it had been oiled. "Are you fucking ready?" Charlie yelled to John. The windows were broken, and the engine noise seemed to be everywhere. But right now Charlie didn't feel any sense of inside or outside. *He* was going to fly, never mind that he was inside a machine.

John shook his pollution-smeared face at him, looking like something Charlie would see in a nightmare, and Charlie held back the elevator control as far as she would go and stepped off the brakes. He held back the control because he was afraid the plane would nose over. In the old Champ that's what you had to do if you didn't want a broken prop.

Charlie screamed for joy. But then the plane started veering left. He stepped hard on the right rudder pedal, overcontrolling, and the plane veered right, toward the ocean. "Sonovabitch!"

"Whatsamatter?" John shouted.

They lost momentum when the aircraft drifted left and almost got stuck in the soft sand. Then, with Charlie overcontrolling, they almost drove into the sea. But now everything was perfect. Throttle full out. Going in a straight line. The sand was like a runway, but Charlie had to toe the line: too far to either side and the wheels would pull into the sand. With all the noise and vibration and the wind whistling as if through a football helmet, with that nose pulling up so smooth, and even with John shrieking, Charlie felt like a god. He was a bird. He was something fucking perfect. "Come on *baby*," Charlie coaxed the plane. "Get it up . . ."

He was getting the feel of it, but when that nose came up, the plane started drifting left again, and he had to touch the right rudder pedal to control it back on line. Fucking A . . .

Then they were lifting. You could feel it. It was as if a great gentle hand was holding the fuselage, lifting it ever so smoothly, and Charlie's heart was pumping right there in his throat, pumping with happiness for a change.

But they mushed back to the ground with a lurching.

"What the hell's going on?" John shouted. "I want to *fly!*"

Charlie held that elevator control wheel back as if he could somehow pull the plane off the ground by his own sheer will. They hit a sudden bump in the ground where the sand was high, and then they were airborne.

It was perfection. All sounds melded into one, just the rushing of perfect air. And the sky, it was clear, like a huge crystal ball. Charlie noticed it, even though he had other things working through his mind. He *had* pulled this thing up into the air. His trembling arms strained, and his hands gripped that black control wheel.

Goddamn if everything didn't look different, as if Charlie was looking down at a giant game board. The land was laid out in perfect squares; and the ocean was cellophane, and it went on forever. And for a long lasting moment of clarity and beauty, he felt as if he had slipped right out of his body. He escaped thought and doubt and guilt. His arms were wings, his eyes were mirrors, and he roared above the earth, skimming over it like the shadow of a storm.

They were about seventy feet into the air when the plane started mushing back toward the ground, drifting left. Charlie had pulled the elevator control too far back, had pushed the wing at too high an angle. It didn't help that the propeller blades were bent and not fully efficient.

"Watch it!" John shouted, although he was still slogging down the whiskey even as they were crashing.

"Don't worry, I know about these planes," Charlie said, manipulating the controls, as the aircraft tilted left, drifting for a few peaceful seconds, almost touching down gently on the sand, before crashing into a thick palmetto that reached out from the scruffy, gorsed rise where sand ended and habitation began. There were green lawns above—that thick stuff that passed for grass, but was really some sort of weed that needed to be almost constantly sprinkled with water.

"Sonovabitch," Charlie mumbled, still trying to control the plane. There were brushings and scratchings and then, sliding and jolting, the plane came to a halt. Charlie just sat behind the controls and stared out the cracked windshield at a tiny twig on the cowling, as if he could concentrate himself into that tiny area, as if all that existed was one timeless twig on the cowling.

"You all right?" John asked, trying to get the door open. Branches and bush pushed against it.

"Yeah," Charlie said, as he reached over to turn off the switches. "Pull the ignition wires apart, just to be safe."

"Why don't we just get the hell out of here?"

But Charlie was stunned, somehow shocked that they weren't still in the air, floating over the sand, working their way up into the clouds. How could it be that they were alive and on the ground, and not a fucking thing had changed, nothing had been determined? He didn't know if he had broken the Laws or just paid some more dues. Maybe the whole thing was bullshit, he thought. Maybe *nothing* meant anything.

But he didn't want to leave the plane. He *had* flown it.

"Charlie?" John asked, working the door open. "Let's get out of here. This whole thing could blow up or something."

Now that would be proof, Charlie thought. It wouldn't be perfect, but maybe it would still be a good day to die. Charlie felt as if *he* was *heyoka*.

John pulled him out of the plane.

Charlie drank some more bourbon, which had a woody taste, and walked around, looking at the plane. He felt disgusted, as if he had wounded one of the seagulls on the beach. The tip of the left wing had been torn and was dripping gas; and the aileron had been ripped away.

"Maybe we can still fly it," John said. "Maybe fix it up somehow."

Charlie couldn't control himself. He started laughing, and John did, too. They put their arms around each other and laughed. "Oh, sure," Charlie said after an attack of coughing and wheezing, after he finally caught his breath, "we can fly it. We don't need wings or gas or a goddamn motor. We can just use your prayers." John slapped him in the face, but that just got them laughing again, and they drank some more. Charlie tried to bend the propeller back into shape. He was compulsive about it, even though he knew the thing would never fly again.

But then John cleared the branches and brush away from the door and crawled into the plane. "Come on, honky," he shouted, "we're *going* to fly this thing on prayers!"

Charlie laughed, but John was already hot-wiring the ignition, pushing in the throttle, and cranking up the engine. Miraculously, it started without any trouble. Charlie ran over to the plane. Sonovabitch if that bastard didn't see everything I had done, he thought. "What the hell are you trying to do?" he shouted at John, but John couldn't hear him over the noise of the engine—or he pretended he couldn't hear him. Charlie got into the cabin.

"How do I make it work?" John asked.

"What do you mean?"

John started laughing hysterically. "What if I lift my feet off these pedals?"

"Nothing," Charlie said. He had set the brakes before.

"Come on, you asshole," John said. "I thought you said you wanted to *fly?*"

"You won't even get this thing out of the bushes, and I never heard of anyone flying with one wing, no matter what that song says."

"Come on, we'll drive it back to the car. You're not in any shape to walk, anyway."

Charlie released the brakes and said, "Gun it, maybe we can just pull out of the bushes. Here, I'll do it."

"Oh, no," John snapped. "My turn, remember?" and he throttled up the engine, and there was a tearing noise, and the plane seemed as if it was going to pull apart under the strain, and then suddenly they were free, cruising along the sand, zigzagging, all the while Charlie was giving John lessons on how to control a small aircraft. "You got to toe the line, or you'll sink into the sand." Goddamn if John didn't look like some sort of demon or witch or *some*thing, with all that glop smeared over one side of his face, Charlie thought. Maybe he, Charlie, should have smeared some on, too. Maybe it was some sort of talisman to protect you or something. But goddamn they were going like hell in that airplane, even if they were going in the wrong direction to get to the car. "Turn around," Charlie shouted. "The car's t'other *way*," and Charlie pressed the right rudder pedal. The plane turned, and they were off in the other direction.

There was almost something sacrilegious about driving a plane that couldn't fly. It was like a bird that couldn't fly, like a goddamn chicken or something, for Chrissakes, Charlie thought.

But there was also something relaxing and reassuring about driving in the sand like this, driving and drinking, especially since he didn't feel as if he was riding with John. It was like riding with some goddamn sweat-lodge spirit or something, that's what it was, Charlie told himself. Charlie was protected, fucking golden again, and he felt lightheaded. He couldn't feel the heavy presence of Whiteshirt. He didn't feel those coals, or feel afraid when he thought of Whiteshirt's eyes burning into him in the sweat-lodge.

"Okay, there's the car," Charlie shouted over the roar of the motor. The engine was not firing smoothly enough to take them into the air again, even if they had wings or prayers. But it still felt good to hear that roar. That's what driving a car in the old days used to be like, Charlie thought. Goddamn straight it was.

The Toyota gleamed on the flat, wide beach. It was banged-up, filthy, and part of the passenger's door just below the window was encrusted with vomit, as if covered with barnacles. A man and woman in their forties, both dressed in white tops and shorts, both wearing rubber clogs, were examining the car. At this hour they were probably beachcombing, looking for rare shells before the hordes of tourists took them for souvenirs or crunched them underfoot. Egrets and herons flew over the ocean, searching for breakfast, and dirty-looking white gulls walked along the edge of the beach. It was as if the whole world in that instant could only consist of coquina rock, sea oats, sandy beach, and the frothy wave lips of the deep-blue Atlantic. Only the Toyota and the roaring Cessna speeding toward it were out of place.

John was steering straight for the Toyota at full speed. He wasn't slowing down one bit.

The couple looked at the plane, stunned, and then ran toward the coquina barrier that divided beach from road and expensive vacation homes and condos.

John swerved the plane and headed toward the couple—perhaps to frighten them; perhaps he intended to actually hit them—when Charlie stepped on the brakes. John screamed something in Indian, and punched Charlie viciously across the chest. Luckily, Charlie's arm was in a position to break the blow. "I'm driving this, remember?" John shouted above the roar. "Don't you *touch* those fucking brakes!"

"You're fucking crazy!" Charlie screamed. "I'm not going to let you hurt those people!" Charlie stepped down hard on the right rudder pedal and took hold of the control yolk before him, taking control away from John. But John punched at his legs. Charlie felt something thrum, and he thought a bone had broken. Reflexively, he lifted his legs toward his chest, banging his knees on the dashworks of the plane. John laughed that *heyoka* laugh of his. He was completely gonzo, right over the edge again, and still shooting toward that poor couple.

Luckily, they found a cement stairway up and away from the beach; and they just kept on running toward a white, three-storey condominium that wasn't completed. The grounds had not yet been landscaped, and the condo looked for all the world like a beach front penitentiary, its small dark windows staring out to sea.

John lifted his foot from the pedal and turned the control yolk. The plane's wing tip grazed the retaining wall. John turned the plane around, sending clouds of sand into the air, and he drove toward the Toyota. He almost hit it the first time; then he came around for a second run, shattering the car's windshield with the tip and leading edge of the wing.

Charlie was screaming and crying. He was going to die, and he wasn't in control. John hardly looked human, and he screamed and shouted and chanted unearthly, ungodly music. He's become Whiteshirt, Charlie thought feverishly. That's it. He's Whiteshirt again. He's the goddamn devil. Fucking Satan. And Charlie had made his choice, and was now going to be dragged ass-end first into hell!

John was goosing it, and the plane was picking up speed again, making a straight line down the hard-packed beach. John had stopped screaming, but the engine was screaming and wheezing and clanging as if it was some *heyoka* spirit that had escaped from the sweat-lodge with John and Whiteshirt and Charlie.

"Goddammit, God*dammit*!" John said, a grin splitting his half-painted face. "Can't you feel it, Charlie?"

That tar was doing something to John, Charlie thought. That crazy Indian was always on the edge of being dangerous, but now he was dangerous, murderously dangerous. He'd do *anything*, no matter who might get hurt.

"You got that bad face on again," John said. "Come on, lighten up. This is fucking wonderful! Can't you feel it?" At least John had stopped breathing heavily. Perhaps the spell had passed.

"I don't know what you're talking about," Charlie ventured nervously. "But I think you broke my leg or something is what I think."

"I'm talking about being alive. Right now, you stupid sonovabitch, right now you're fucking alive! This is all there is. This is the juice!"

"You were going to run those people down . . . you didn't even give a shit," Charlie said.

John laughed; it was the good-natured laugh that had attracted Charlie to him in the first place. "I wasn't going to run them down. I was giving them something to tell their relatives and children, something to take to bed with them when they're old farts like us. And I can bet you those two are going to be jumping on each other's bones today—we probably gave them the first thrill they've had since he first put his pinkie finger into her pussy." After a long pause, John said, "Yeah, maybe I was going to run them down."

Charlie started to say, "You're crazy," but he thought better of it. Anything could put John back over the edge. Every time John had gone *heyoka*, he'd changed some, become wilder, more removed from everything that was right and made sense. He was becoming whatever it was that he looked like: some sort of half-and-half spirit.

He would have run down those people, sure as anything, Charlie told himself. He would have . . .

"Look, I got the pipe hanging," John said. "I can't be all bad and have the pipe right here."

"Whiteshirt could."

"Yeah, you're right about that. I can't fool your ass, can I? Look," John continued, "you wanna drive this now. How's that for good faith? That way we won't run anybody down, and you won't be so nervous."

Charlie took over the controls and slowed down the plane. What are we going to do now? he asked himself. Just drive on forever? That was no answer. John would only get crazy again, and someone would certainly get hurt.

"Charlie, you want to leave?" John asked, as if he was reading his mind. "Nothing stopping you. You got something nobody can take away from you. You can go back to the wife and kids and die with a smile and a hard-on!"

"I think you broke my leg," was all Charlie could think to say.

"It's not broken. I only tapped you, you candy-assed honky." John broke out laughing, and Charlie caught it too, like the flu, and they roared down the beach again, kicking up sand, laughing and pulling on the bottle, as if they were drinking airplane fuel and flying just inches off the ground in this great broken bird, coming in for one last big fuck-you-world landing.

The pipe swung back and forth from the cabin panel. The whole world looked blue. But it was getting darker, as clouds pushed heavily across the sky, and somewhere over the ocean, clouds were boiling, turning black, charged with electricity.

"Going to rain," John said matter-of-factly, as if nothing unusual had happened, as if they weren't coasting down the beach in an airplane left by some drug smugglers, as if they hadn't almost killed that couple back on the beach, as if they hadn't almost killed those Jew-people on the highway, or stolen five cars, and fucked up who knows how many people on the way; and Charlie had made the big break from everything that was normal and safe and real; he had banged Sharry and felt like a man for the first time in who-knows-when; and sonovabitch if John hadn't been right, if Charlie hadn't been living, really living, for the first time since he wanted to remember. Man, he had felt *everything* for the past day and night, and it wouldn't've mattered if he had bought the farm and died anytime during the trip, except now. Now it was different. John had changed too much, had become too wild. And Charlie was afraid that they had gone too far and would never be able to make anything right again.

Maybe he should leave John. But if he was going to do it, he would have to do it right now.

Something had to be done, and quickly, because the beach was coming alive with people: retirees who sunbathed in the morning and napped indoors in the afternoon, couples with their children searching for shells, surf fishermen with their pails and rods and rubber boots, lovers with arms locked around each other. Blankets and brightly colored towels appeared on the sand. A frisbee arced over the ocean.

But everything stopped as John and Charlie roared down the beach. Everyone stared at the broken plane passing by. People pointed, ran out of the way, even though most of them weren't in any danger. The world seemed to be starting and stopping in freeze-frame spurts, and John and Charlie were the center of it all. It was as if a flying saucer was zooming over the beach.

Certainly John and Charlie were the aliens, the bug-eyed monsters out to destroy everything in their path.

It would only be a matter of time before the police came. They just didn't allow planes to joyride around on the public beaches, leaking gas and oil all over the goddamn place and scaring the shit out of all the residents and visitors. No, Charlie thought, the police would stop them.

And that would end it. End it good.

17.

GHOST VOICES

Charlie made that Cessna do everything but fly. He pushed the engine until the whole plane was shaking, but strong winds made steering difficult and slowed them down. The storm at sea had infected the sky above, which was now layered with steel-wool clouds that moved against each other as if they were magnetized. Lightning flashed nearby, and there was a great peal of thunder that could be heard over the roar of the motor. John seemed agitated, excited, and he began laughing and shouted, "This is wonderful, this is fucking wonderful." He started breathing heavily again. "Goddamn spirits love this shit, this is Indian weather, none of that soft-shit honky weather like we've been having for the past few days. You're gonna see the spirits in the air. You're gonna *feel* the fucking things like they were electricity. *Now*, motherfucker, right now is when you should be shouting 'This is a good day to die!'"

John was right about it all: The rain came pelting down, and Charlie could have sworn he heard sounds like bells. Maybe the crazy Indian bastard was right about there being spirits after all.

It was getting darker and darker. The beach was empty; Charlie hadn't seen a car parked on it for miles. There was nothing but hard-packed wet sand, patches of sea-oats, and a few brave sandpipers scurrying around. To his left were sun-bleached wood and glass houses and high-rise condos, their cement balconies giving them the appearance of ancient ziggurats. It was as if the developers were trying to create a science-fiction version of Cape Cod.

This darkness and rain is a bad sign, Charlie thought. He didn't know why, but it felt bad. It should have been good, though, Charlie told himself, because if there wasn't anybody out on the beach, they would at least have a chance of getting away. Of course, all they had to do was ditch the plane and just walk away. But Charlie *couldn't* bring himself to do that. That's why he knew the Laws were at work, working themselves out through him and John. So he did have control after all, because without him they'd be working themselves out another way, maybe in a worse way.

The weather turned suddenly cooler, almost cold, and it began hailing. Hailstones the size of pingpong balls beat on the skin of the Cessna, bounced on the wet sand. It was as if God was throwing glass down at them from Heaven or something, Charlie thought. That was a sign, too—if he could only figure out what the fuck it meant.

John seemed to love it all. He was shouting and singing and leaning out of the plane into the wind and hail.

It was then that Charlie saw Nathan Isaacs' house atop a gentle rise. The house looked just as it had in the Polaroid photographs Nathan had once proudly shown him. Charlie would have recognized that yellow stucco castle with the monogrammed chimney anywhere. Who the hell else but Nathan would think to have a fireplace in Florida, anyway? Charlie asked himself as he braked the plane, turned it around, and taxied in the direction of the house. Leave it to Nathan, he thought. A goddamn castle, for Chrissakes.

But just looking at that chimney made Charlie laugh.

"What's the matter with you?" John asked. "What the hell are you looking at? That house over there is nothing but some honky's idea of prison, is all."

Charlie couldn't stop laughing . . . it was that goddamn chimley, as he'd always called them.

"Ah, so *that's* the place," John said. "You see, we are golden. What did I tell you? We ran right into your destination. Well, let's go and pay your friend a visit!" John took over control of the plane before Charlie could even think to stop him. The next thing he knew, they were bouncing and jumping and riding over a shell-shelf, up an incline, and then they were rolling over grass, John just heading straight for that house, ignoring everything in his way, shearing more metal from the useless wings against palmettos, cutting deep ridges into Nathan's immaculately kept lawn, knocking down plastic pink flamingoes, scattering lawn chairs, and smashing through a combination fountain and bird-feeder.

"Stop it!" Charlie screamed. This was, after all, Nathan Isaacs' home.

"You're still afraid of him, aren't you."

"I'm not afraid of any man," Charlie said, holding onto the control panel to keep himself in the seat. But he was afraid, afraid that Nathan would come running right out of the house. Charlie suddenly began to have trouble breathing. He started coughing. It was nerves, but he couldn't stop coughing, not even long enough to stop John from revving the engine and driving the plane behind the house. There was so much jarring and bumping that Charlie couldn't even manage to reach for his inhaler.

John tore through hibiscus bushes and Nathan's long narrow garden of marigolds, petunias, dusty miller, and geraniums. Then he just closed his eyes and aimed that crippled, flightless plane toward a row of oak trees that probably made up the eastern boundary of Nathan's property. There were palms in that grove also, but all the trees were twisted out of shape, as if a hurricane had once blown and bound them together, shaped them grotesquely.

Charlie managed to catch his breath. "What are you *doing?*" he asked, wheezing. "You crazy fucker, are you trying to kill us?"

"That's the general idea."

Charlie jammed his foot down on the brakes, but it was no use.

The plane crashed through the trees, losing both wings and the right stabilizer. The propeller was smashed to pieces. And as if by a miracle, the plane came to a bone-jarring, shivering halt. Everything was suddenly quiet. Charlie was wheezing again. Reflexively, he worried his inhaler out of his shirt pocket and took a few breaths of the choking mist. He felt numb. He was afraid to open his eyes. Maybe I'm *dead*! It's possible, entirely fucking possible, he told himself. He had been in accidents before. There had been no initial pain, just a concussive shock and an odd kind of flowing, a floating. Then he would wake up in a room as white as heaven and try to breathe. He would feel the world cracking open inside him, and then he would feel overwhelming pain.

Charlie smelled gas.

Christ, he thought, bolting upright, if they didn't get out of the plane, it could fucking *explode*. "Got to get out of here," he mumbled to John, but Charlie couldn't seem to get the words out properly. He felt dizzy and sleepy, as if he were nodding-out, as if he were having a dream. Everything was moving slowly, passing before him, around him, through him. Time was like taffy, and he was caught in it. He couldn't get out to scream or jump out of the plane.

He heard glass breaking, and he dreamed of crystal Christmas tree ornaments sparkling, catching the light, slowly drifting . . . falling to earth. It was only static from the Navcom unit. Charlie could make out words, but he was dreaming, and the words sounded like glass, and they were made of light. He heard banging, too, as rain—or hail—pelted the cabin. Rocks falling from the sky, he thought.

He could open his eyes, but it seemed dark. Could the morning have turned back into night? he asked himself, mumbling, trying to give form to his thoughts.

A voice crackled over the Navcom: "*Daytona Beach Tower, this is Cherokee Six-four-three-five-Zulu, ten miles south, inbound for landing Daytona. You painting weather over you, too?*" Charlie listened, vaguely aware of what he was hearing. He was going to try to open his eyes again; once he could do that he'd be fine, and then he'd get the fucking hell out of the plane and save John and Nathan and Stephen and Joline and the kids and himself.

John started howling and shouting. Charlie could hear that, and it seemed to bring him back to the surface, back into the world.

"You ain't no fucking Cherokee Indian, that's for goddamn sure," John shouted into the Navcom microphone. He was slurring his words. "I've seen enough goddamn airplane movies. I'm going to help you to crash, you sonovabitch honky bastard."

"*Say again, somebody covered you up. I think a couple of kids got hold of a Navcom. I don't know. But I can't make you out. Six-four-three-five-Zulu.*"

Charlie looked over at John, whose wet clothes sparkled with glass splinters. John had been drinking from a bottle of bourbon; he must have banged it hard against the control panel. John was stinko. He might even be too drunk to be *heyoka*, Charlie thought. John didn't even look like himself, not with that tar all over his face and the glass on his clothes. He sounded different, too; of course, that could be because Charlie was groggy.

John was shaking the Navcom mike, as if the voices would fall right out of it. A peal of thunder seemed to shake the plane. Rain pelted down; the drops hitting the fuselage sounded like pebbles striking a tin roof.

"What the hell are you doing with *that*?" Charlie asked, meaning the microphone. "We got to get out of here, can't you smell the goddamn gas fumes? You want to get your ass blown sky high?"

John laughed at that.

"Well, I'm getting the hell out of here," Charlie said. Then the Navcom cut in: "*Daytona Tower, this is Six-four-three-five Zulu. I couldn't read your last transmission. I'm low on fuel, requesting landing clearance. Please come back again.*" Charlie listened; he could hear the anxiety in the pilot's voice. John was laughing and holding that mike, his finger pressing the button again. After a beat, he released it.

"*Daytona Tower, can you read me? Please come in. This is Six-four-three-five Zulu requesting landing clearance. I'm low on fuel and experiencing weather difficulty. I repeat, can you read me?*"

"I can't read a fucking thing," John shouted into the mike. "You fucking honky!"

"*Look, whoever's on frequency One-two-three-oh, please release your mike button. This isn't funny. I'm in trouble here! You could get yourself into—*"

"I think it's funnier than shit," John said, and he kept his finger on the button, preventing any further communication.

"What the hell are you *doing*?" Charlie asked John. "Put that thing *down*. Didn't you hear what the man said? He's in trouble."

"Everybody's in trouble," John said. "Look at us, we're out of booze. Damned bottle smashed, all by itself. I was just lifting it up to take a short one and"—he lifted the mike as if it was a bottle—"bang!"

Charlie grabbed at the mike, but John held it out of reach and then swung at Charlie, backfisting him smartly in the face. Charlie tasted his own blood, but didn't feel any pain, just the

236

blinding shock; and suddenly, as he recovered sight and thought, he saw that the man sitting beside him was not John, but Whiteshirt. Whiteshirt in the spirit and the flesh. Under John's tar face-paint was Whiteshirt grinning . . . just as he had inside the sweat-lodge. Whiteshirt had won. He had completely taken over John. And now he was trying to make John fuck up that poor bastard in the plane who was flying through the storm.

"You're not going to make that plane crash, not while I'm alive," Charlie said, launching himself at John. He didn't care if he got hurt; he was *doing* this for John! Charlie grabbed him by the shirt, but John broke his grip and pushed him away. He tried to punch Charlie in the face again, but his elbow struck the control yolk. He recovered and struck Charlie again, connecting with Charlie's chest. All the while, John held onto the mike. Charlie tried to tear out the Navcom unit, and John struck him again, this time on the collarbone. Screaming with pain, Charlie started punching wildly, ferociously, striking out at John with the strength and intensity of a man half his age. He was pummeling John. It was as if he were striking back at everyone who had ever fucked him over, everyone he loved and hated . . . *everyone.* He was hurting John. Enraged and completely *heyoka*, John threw himself against Charlie with such force that Charlie struck the door, which wasn't latched. Charlie grabbed at John. Punching, biting, and screaming, they both fell out of the plane.

It was over as soon as they hit the ground.

Soaked and chilled from the rain, Charlie rolled away from John.

But John was coughing and vomiting blood.

"Jesus Christ," Charlie said, watching John. He moved to help John, but John waved him away.

John's breathing was shallow. He wheezed and held his side, and his face was contorted in pain. "Get me the pipe . . . and my duffel." He seemed suddenly calm. He managed to stand up by himself, although he was bent over with pain.

Charlie stepped over to him, supported his weight, and said, "We've got to get away from the plane. It's not safe. Gas all over the place. Can't you smell it?"

"Then I'll get the pipe myself," John said, pulling away from Charlie.

"I'm not letting you go back into that plane."

"Now let go of me, old friend," John said gently. "Some things I just need to do." It was the old John. It was as if the binge had never happened, as if John had never been *heyoka*, as if the very idea of John going *heyoka*-over-the-edge was just crazy.

"I didn't mean to hurt you like that," Charlie said. "But . . ."

John chuckled, then winced and held his side. "I owe you one, Charlie. Thanks." He leaned against the plane, positioning himself to try to climb inside.

"Oh fuck it," Charlie said. "If the plane blows up, then it blows up. But we can't stay around here because one way or another the police are going to be peeking around."

John nodded to Charlie, then folded up in pain. He sank to his knees. "Charlie," he said, "wipe this shit off my face. I'm not in any shape to do *those* kind of dances right now." He smiled at that, but tears ran down his cheeks.

Charlie pulled his handkerchief out of his back pocket—it wasn't clean, but it was better than nothing—and tried to wipe the tar from John's face. "It won't come off."

"Try some gas."

"Come on, John, I'll take care of this later."

"Now . . . please. Dip your rag in the gasoline. But get me the pipe first."

Charlie complained, even as he climbed back into the plane. He retrieved John's pipe and duffel, then soaked up some gas into his handkerchief, which he gave to John. "Come on, you can wipe the tar off while we walk. But we've *got* to get out of here."

John leaned on Charlie, who could barely hold him up and carry the duffel at the same time. "I've got my pipe," John said. "All else I need is my blanket," which he carefully took out of his duffel; his sage and tobacco and eagle feather were neatly rolled inside the blanket. "Get me the fuck out of here, old friend. Now there's something *I've* got to do."

"You're not going to do anything until I take you to a doctor or something."

"Too late for that honky bullshit, my friend. Just steal us a car for old time's sake."

"I *am* getting you to a hospital, and that's final!"

"I'll be all *right*," John said, but Charlie knew he was lying. He must have done something to himself when he fell out of the plane. Or maybe I accidentally punched him in the wrong place, Charlie thought, rationalizing. In fact Charlie knew someone who had accidentally killed somebody in a brawl . . . just hit the fucker wrong and smashed out his kidney or something. Suddenly, Charlie felt tears well up in his eyes. He heard thunder, which was inside his head this time. When he was a kid, he always heard thunder when he was about to cry. But there was nothing to say, not one fucking thing. If John was hurt, then that was that. Charlie understood that he had to leave John alone, or help him do whatever it was he wanted to do. Even if it killed him.

The sky cleared, and it became bright and hot and humid almost instantly. It was as if God had forgotten he'd made a storm, or simply changed his mind. This place seemed like a dream to Charlie, as if it were dreaming itself, changing instantly from darkness to light, from New York gray to Florida blue. Only the waterlogged clothes, the scattered, melting hailstones, the wet ground, and rain-shiny leaves reminded Charlie that only moments ago he had been in the middle of an angry storm. Soon all the evidence would be baked away, dried out by the post card sun.

Charlie helped John across the lawn and away from the plane.

Just then a drenched Nathan Isaacs approached the house from the beach. He looked angry and disgusted. Nathan had always been one to walk, and an early riser, so he had probably gotten himself caught in the storm. He was with his paramour, a red-haired woman, who looked to be thirty years his junior. Her hair hung in ringlets from the rain. She was tall, well tanned, and wore a pearl-colored, one-piece swimsuit and a soaking-wet terry cloth beach coat. Nathan had a shock of white hair that was too long on the top, a handsome rugged face that was only now going to ruin; he wore blue shorts and a matching polyester shirt opened three buttons at the chest. Undoubtedly he had looked pressed and neat when he had left the house; now the wet shirt was almost transparent. Charlie thought that Nathan looked thin, even though he had a potbelly just like his own. He could hear Nathan and the woman arguing.

"Well, you didn't have to come along," Nathan said.

"But I didn't mind taking a walk with you," said the woman. "It's just your constant bitching. So you got a little wet, you won't melt."

"I just don't like imposing on my neighbors."

"Well, I'll be damned if I was going to stand out in the open in a hailstorm," she said. "Anyway, the Ross's were happy for the company. They're your friends, aren't they?"

"They're neighbors," Nathan said. "Nothing more."

"They were awake. Christ, they're up earlier than you are."

"That's not the point—" Then Nathan's tone of voice changed, as he surveyed his grounds. "What the hell is going on around here," he said, hurriedly walking around the lawn, following tracks left by the plane.

Charlie and John were safely hidden behind hedgerow.

"It's those goddamn kids with their dirt bikes," Nathan said, "I'll have their asses thrown in jail." When he saw the damage to his trees and the wreckage in the back lawn, he seemed beside himself. "Sonovabitch!" he shouted.

Charlie felt a rush of fear pass right through him. He was still afraid of this man, even now, with John doubled up beside him, probably dying or something, for all he knew . . . even now when nothing mattered anymore. But there it was: old habits die hard. And he still respected the man, even though Nathan had fucked him over good, the rich-ass Jew-bastard. Almost as a litany in his mind, Charlie thought, God forgive me for thinking such a thing.

"What the hell happened here?" Nathan shouted. "What the hell's going on!"

"It looks like a plane crash, honey," the woman said. "Maybe somebody's hurt."

"You stay just where you are, I'll call the police. My God . . ." Nathan said and hurried back to the house. The woman remained outside. After a pause, she started walking toward Charlie and John and the plane to investigate; but Nathan came to the door and shouted, "Get inside here this very minute! That thing could explode."

"Not what I'd call a curious man," John said. He was curled up beside Charlie, his knees against his chest; and he was shivering. "Apple doesn't fall far from the tree."

"What the hell is that supposed to mean?" Charlie asked as he watched the woman go into the house. He knew that he had to do something, and quickly, or they'd have their asses hauled into jail. The police wouldn't give two shits if John was hurt and dying; they'd let him rot in a cell.

"The son seems just like the father."

"Son's not nearly so bad," Charlie said, but he was preoccupied.

"Let's do it now," John said.

"Do *what?*" Charlie asked impatiently. He was in no mood to have words with John. He just wanted to get him away from here and to a hospital. What Charlie really wanted to do was leave him in some clean, disinfected room and go back to Joline and the kids and be done with this whole fucking thing.

"This is the only favor I'll ask you, Charlie. Get me out of here. I've got an appointment I've got to keep."

"You're fucking crazy," Charlie said. "Do you think you can walk?"

John stood up with Charlie's help, although he couldn't stand erect. He rested most of his weight on Charlie, and they worked their way to Nathan's gold painted, silver-flecked Lincoln Town car, Nathan's pride and joy, which was parked in front of the house. The car had just been repainted. Perhaps, for all Nathan's bullshit, he wasn't willing to shake out the big bucks for a new one.

A siren sounded in the distance. It was coming closer.

This was a real chancy one, Charlie thought, because Nathan had probably locked his car. Well, maybe John could do his knife trick with the door ... if he could stand up long enough to manage it. But the passenger side was unlocked. Charlie got in and pulled John into the car beside him. He fumbled under the dashboard, found the ignition wires, and started the engine. It came to life with a shiver. This car ran so smoothly that the steering wheel hardly vibrated.

"Get it moving," John said hoarsely, as if under his breath. His face looked pasty. He rested his head against the window.

The sirens were nearby now. Charlie could hear them even with the windows closed and the air-conditioning on—Nathan always kept the air-conditioner working full blast. But the moon-roof was cracked open, which was why the seats were soaked. They smelled of mildew. Just as Charlie shifted into Drive, he saw Nathan coming out of the house. Maybe he's checking on the car or the plane or just waiting for the police, Charlie thought. Who could know? he asked himself. But there he was, big as fucking day, and looking right at Charlie, recognizing him, then running toward the car.

"Charlie? Charlie? What are you doing here?" Nathan asked, surprise quickly turning to anger. "Get the hell out of my car, what the hell are you trying to do?" Before Nathan could reach the car, Charlie floored the accelerator and fishtailed out of the driveway.

"I'll bring it back, Nathan," he shouted. He could see Nathan in the rear-view mirror: the man was running, actually trying to chase the car. Christ on a crutch if this Lincoln didn't beat the hell out of all them Cadillacs put together, Charlie thought. He felt calm, even though his heart was up there, beating in his throat. John sat quietly, looking down at the floor, as if none of this were happening. Maybe he was praying.

Charlie passed two police cars followed by an ambulance, their sirens blaring and beacons flashing. He slowed down until they were out of sight, then drove as fast as he could. If he didn't get out of here quickly, he knew he wasn't going to get out of here at all. He turned onto Third Avenue, which took them east onto South Bridge. There weren't any boats cruising the intercoastal waters just now, and the long, straight bridge with its evenly spaced, modern lamps seemed to stretch on forever.

The Lincoln whispered through the streets of the town, quiet as an expensive gold watch. Charlie drove it flat-out, past the early morning beach-bum hippies and locals and tourists, past the tourist traps—the antique shops with cane chairs on the lawns and bric-a-brac in the windows, past seafood restaurants and family luncheonettes and fast-food places filled with senior citizens having breakfast on the cheap. Cadillacs and BMW's and Mercedes and Lincolns were parked along the streets, as were old Volkswagen Beetles and curtained Chevy vans. The sky was clear, and the streets were drying up.

Charlie felt the old surge of youth as he passed a young woman sitting on the curb, her long legs akimbo. She was dressed in shorts and a revealing halter top, and she gazed sleepily at the cars plashing by, as if that was the only thing in the world that she had to do. And that feeling stayed with him as he drove through the town. Perhaps it was just seeing this woman on the curb. She triggered old, clear memories; and Charlie imagined that if he just drove this car, it would be as if he were young again. He forgot about his emphysema. He forgot about not having teeth or money. He forgot he had a family. He was just old Charlie, built like a goddamn tank, horny as shit, with a wad of bills in his back pocket that could choke a horse and a million places to spend them in. That's how he remembered the old days: a skein of well-worn lies. But the lies had always been real enough to satisfy him. And just look at this car, he told himself, it's a living room, complete with shag carpet, a goddamn apartment on wheels is what it is. Then he glanced over at John, who looked broken, somehow smaller or thinner. Fragile.

"If I hurt you, I'm sorry," Charlie said as he drove out of town on Route 44, heading west toward Crows Bluff and Altoona, the bottom-side of Ocala National Forest. Forty-four was a two-lane state road, cutting straight through the country. There was hardly any traffic.

John tried to shift position. He made a face and groaned. "What're you sorry for? Man, you got more guilt than a Catholic. You did exactly the right thing, for Chrissakes. You knocked some sense into me."

"You don't look right. You're all scrunched up and you're white as a sheet."

John chuckled, then winced in pain. "That's what I get from hanging around with honkies." Once again he tried to find a more comfortable position; his face contorted in pain, and he remained as he was.

"You need to go to a hospital, Goddammit!"

"I'm not *heyoka* anymore, Charlie," John said. "And there's something I've got to do first."

"What's that?" Charlie asked.

"I gotta make things right with Whiteshirt, and I need your help. I need you to drive me to Whiteshirt's."

"You're fucking crazy, and you're sick. If you don't see a doctor, you're going to die is what I think."

John suddenly laughed and held his chest.

"Maybe you broke a bone, that would give you a lot of pain. Is it a sharp pain?"

"Don't you worry."

"Whaddyamean?"

John laughed again, grimacing. "I'm already dead," and he fell asleep right then, his head resting on the window, the grease from his long white hair smearing on the glass.

And for a second, Charlie got scared, thinking John might really be dead.

But John was breathing, snoring, and later on talking in his sleep, talking Sioux or some foreign language that was sharp and labored, talking to the spirits, perhaps the ones whispering in the air-conditioner.

18.

LISTENING TO THE PIPE

John held the pipe on his lap, touching it, stroking it as if it were some live thing. The time was past when it would hang on the rear-view mirror like sponge dice in a teenager's hot-rod. John had been quiet for miles, and Charlie left him alone. There was something almost hypnotic about the day: the clear blue sky; the preternaturally bright sunlight; the large brown dashboard curling before them, all plush leatherette; the whirring of the air-conditioner; the coolness inside separating them from the blisteringly hot "outside". The Lincoln was a world in miniature, a cozy minute-by-minute world that *had* to be shattered, but for the time being was indeed perfection. Although Charlie felt a bit sleepy, he wasn't having any trouble keeping his eyes open. He didn't even know what he was thinking about; but thoughts flittered and flickered past him, sharp shadows fleeting, freighted with anxiety, all forgotten as soon as they passed.

Charlie just drove, keeping off the main drags as a matter of course now. They were in "Cracker" country, poor country, not so different from parts of New York, not so different from rural life around Charlie's hometown. They passed gray wooden houses with rusting corrugated tin roofs. Around these houses, like totems, sat old automobile hulks, washtubs, and scrubboards. People sat in their yards or rocked back and forth on their unpainted porches. Charlie imagined that these people had nothing but time. It was as if they owned time. They had time to count all the cars roaring by. Time to drink beer and swat flies and read magazines.

Charlie had once had that kind of time . . .

"You want to know something, Charlie?" John asked, breaking the silence.

"Yeah?"

"Did I ever tell you about this pipe?"

"We smoked it, remember?" Charlie said. "You told me some things, and a lot of stuff I felt, just smoking it."

"Well, you said that right," John said smiling. He was sitting up and looked a bit better.

Charlie glanced over at him and grinned. Goddamn, I said something right. About fucking time, he thought.

"Man, this pipe is going to make me pay out the dues. Probably turn me into some asshole spirit heavy as this car after I push over."

"What do you mean?" Charlie asked.

"After I'm dead, asshole!" Then John continued, "This pipe is really old. We were given the original pipe by the White Buffalo Woman." John started laughing, then coughed just like Charlie. "Don't make sense to tell you anything. You don't believe in anything, except what you can see, do you? Well, if we had the time, I'd *show* you the pipe she gave us. We've still got it. Can you believe that?" Charlie just stared straight ahead, feeling a bit nervous, as if maybe John could get *heyoka* again, except this time he'd probably just drop dead or something. "When the White Buffalo Woman came to us she was walking and singing a song. You wanna know what she was singing?"

"If you want to tell me," Charlie said.

"I like it that you don't ask questions all the time," John said. "It shows you have a good way of being here, like Indian people. You see, what fucked you up is that you're white—no offense meant, don't get yourself stirred up—and the white world doesn't work in a natural way. But one day it will. By that time, we'll both be under the daisies."

Charlie didn't ignore John, but he didn't act as if he was exactly paying attention. He just let him talk.

"Well," John asked, "do you want to hear that song or not?"

"I said yes."

"She was singing, '*Niya taniya mawani ye.*' You know what that means?"

"Yeah," Charlie said sarcastically. "Have a nice day."

"It means I'm walking with visible breath. When we smoked that pipe together, we were breathing the life of all our people. And there's something else—that smoke from the pipe is like thought. If you're praying right, you can hear the thoughts all around you. You can hear the thoughts of the trees, of the stones. You could hear my thoughts, too. For holy people, just thinking is praying. It's smoke from all the pipes. Smoke from this pipe right here. You think I'm crazy, don't you?"

Charlie couldn't help but burst out laughing.

"Well, you're probably right," John said, "but that doesn't mean that what I just told you isn't true." John chuckled. "Anyway, the White Buffalo Woman gave us the pipe and then turned into a buffalo. You probably don't believe that either, you stupid honky, do you? Doesn't matter. Indian people are part buffalo. We depended so much on the buffalo—she fed us, clothed us, the whole nine yards—that we *became* part buffalo. See that? I'm a goddamn buffalo man. Can you see me like that?"

"I see you as one crazy fucker," Charlie said.

"You smoke the pipe enough and you'll see," John said. "Indian people and buffalo share the same destiny. Right now it looks like they're both extinct almost. But when you see those buffalo coming back, man, then you're going to see real Indians again, wild and crazy like God. Goddamn!" Then John started laughing. Pale and bloodless as he looked, he clutched his stomach and laughed. He leaned toward the door, then pushed himself away, as if he were rolling around like a child who had just thought of something hilarious.

"You okay?" Charlie asked, concerned. I should just take him to the hospital, he told himself. But that would never work. You didn't fuck with John when he didn't want to do something. And he always had his reasons, even if they were crazy as shit.

"Maybe you don't want to hear about the White Buffalo Woman," John said quietly, seriously, "but I'm going to tell you something you can, and better, believe. Remember when I told you how power can attach itself to things? And those things, or places, can be dangerous, or they can also be holy. I guess I didn't tell you about the holy part . . ." John smiled weakly.

"I think you should go to the hospital," Charlie said.

John just shook his head and continued. "Well, it's the same with the pipe. This pipe's pretty old. Been held by a lot of medicine men." He laughed. "And a lot of fuck ups, too. I could probably tell you about every one of them, but we don't have that kind of time. When I told you about that smoke stuff, well, it's like the pipe thinks at you. That smoke is everyone who's ever prayed or used the pipe. I can see you in the pipe. I don't have to smoke it to see who's been here. So now this pipe is a part of you, too. What do you think of that?"

"I dunno," Charlie said.

"Well, I can hear the pipe," John said. "Sonovabitch, it's been a long time since I could hear the pipe." Then John pressed a switch on his armrest and lowered his window. He leaned his head out. A rush of humid air screamed into the car.

"What the hell are you doing?" Charlie shouted. "We got the air-conditioning on."

"Fuck the air-conditioning. Roll down the windows." John leaned out the window and looked upward. The wind whipped his long hair about and seemed to push back the skin on his face.

Charlie grabbed his arm and pulled him back into the car. Then he pressed one of the switches on his armrest and raised John's window. "You're fucking crazy, you know that?"

"I thought I was crazy enough to see an eagle out there."

"Did you?" Charlie asked.

"Not yet," John said. "But I got a good feeling about it all."

"About what?"

"My medicine."

"You mean, it's coming back, your healing powers?" Charlie asked.

"Maybe on loan for a while," John said. "You see, maybe you punched those *heyoka* spirits right out of me." Then, after a pause, he asked, "Are you going to drop me off at Whiteshirt's or are you going in with me?" He stared intently at Charlie, as if trying to read something in his face.

"I already told you," Charlie said. "I've come this far, and I'm going all the way. But I'm telling you right now, I think you're fucking out of your gourd is what I think."

John didn't smile, but he seemed to relax. Then he started talking in earnest, as if they only had a little time. "Like I said, power can attach to things. A man's whole life, his whole spirit, everything, can be shut up inside a rock or a tree . . . or a pipe. That power could be good, like you feel when you smoke the pipe and your prayers are right, or it can be bad. It could be a spirit left over by a witch, and just taking hold of that rock or tree could bleed out *your* spirit. Could kill you. You following me?"

Charlie nodded, but it was as if he was resisting any acknowledgment of medicine or magic.

"Well, that's what I meant about the pipe. It has power. When I'm clean, I can feel it pouring into me. All those men who had this pipe before me—those old, strong, wild warriors—they poured their spirit into this pipe, blended it right in; and when I smoke the pipe, they all help me. They helped you a little, too. I could tell when we smoked the pipe together."

Charlie remembered. He had felt close to everything, as if he were made of air or light. And the pipe and prayers had made him feel clean.

"That power in the pipe is stronger than any witch," John said. "You can bet your ass on that. But it wasn't working for me for a long while, none of it was, because I was all backwards and fucked up."

"You say it's working for you now?" Charlie asked.

"It's not working against me. Maybe it'll help me for a while before I pay off the dues."

"I guess you believe in the Laws, too," Charlie said.

"I guess I do," John said vaguely; he stared out the windshield. After a long pause he said, "But even though the pipe has power, Whiteshirt might still be able to break me in half. You gotta be right to use power . . . to carry the pipe."

"Well, you said you felt right, didn't you?"

"I been wrong before, lots of times, honky."

"Don't call me honky," Charlie said.

"We been through enough by now that I thought you'd appreciate it."

Charlie smiled faintly. He was nervous, but not scared, not flat-out scared as he'd been before just thinking about Whiteshirt. Maybe a lot of this shit is in our heads, he told himself. Maybe it could be made right . . . But then he remembered John trying to kill those Jews, remembered the look on his face. That wasn't John, goddammit. It was Whiteshirt. Or maybe Charlie just thought it was Whiteshirt because he was shitting-his-pants scared.

"Make no mistake," John said, "Whiteshirt's got it on for both of us. If he fucks me up, he's going to fuck you up, too."

"I can take care of myself."

"Cut your bullshit, you know what I mean. He'll come for you in your dreams, he won't stop until he's fucked you up. Or do you still think this is all superstitious bullshit?"

"Yeah, I do," Charlie said. "But I'm not stupid enough to go looking for more trouble. If you say that's how it is, I'm willing to consider it."

"My advice is to haul ass out of Whiteshirt's camp if anything seems to be happening. Don't worry about me, just get the fuck out."

"Then what?" Charlie asked. "You just said he'll keep looking for me."

John grinned, which seemed to give him pain. He looked exhausted. "I guess you should go see a priest . . . and stay away from your family."

1 9 .

THUNDER BEINGS

John remained awake and alert; he squinted straight ahead out the windshield. His rough skin looked grayish and glossy, as if there were a sheen of oil rubbed over it. Charlie kept east on 301, away from Gainesville, and passed through Payne's Prairie, which was a lake of grass, dry and green and flat. Below Cross Creek, John directed him to get off 301 by Island Grove, and they drove through forest land on a two-lane black-top road. Most of the trees were slash pine and stubby scrub oak. They passed the occasional farm. There were areas where forest suddenly ended, having been cleared and burned by lumber companies; and there were other areas, where the companies had planted pine in precise, even rows like uniformly dressed soldiers standing at attention.

"You feelin' okay?" Charlie asked.

John smiled wanly. "Yeah, I'm just fine."

"We must be close to Whiteshirt's by now, aren't we?" Charlie asked, feeling nervous and claustrophobic.

"Yeah, I guess so." John seemed distracted, as he'd been for the past few hours.

"Any of this familiar to you?"

"I guess so."

"That all you can say?"

"Pull over when you can."

"Why?"

"Just pull over," John said. "I got to smoke the pipe and think for a while."

Charlie pulled off the road where scrub pine and blackjack oak gave way to a lush island of live oak and long-leaf pine. Before Charlie could put the car in 'park', John had the door open. He grabbed his bundle—his blanket which contained his pipe and medicine bag—and made his way into the woods. He was bent forward, and he held his stomach with his left hand and his bundle with his right. He might be hurting, but he could still move. Charlie followed him, but he was in such a hurry to get out of the big, heavy Lincoln that he forgot to shut off the engine; he had to open the door again and pull the ignition wires apart.

"You know, this isn't such a good idea," Charlie shouted after John. "We're just leaving the car parked on the road. Anybody can see it there. And then come looking for us. Doesn't make any goddamn sense to me at all." He caught up with John, who was still walking hurriedly, almost in a half-run. "Where the fuck are you going?" Charlie asked. "You're supposed to be sick."

John didn't answer. He stepped through the thin undergrowth easily, walking between oak, red bay, holly, hickory, and wild cherry. It was dark and cool; sunlight shafted through the ceiling of treetops and the smells were moist and delicious. Then John found a small clearing, a natural haven, and he dropped to the ground.

"What in the hell is your rush?" Charlie asked.

"I had to find a good place to be for a while," John said, unrolling his star blanket, taking out his pipe and medicine bag. "I had to do it quick, before I thought about it too much, or I wouldn't have gotten five steps away from the car."

"As it is, I'm going to have to carry you back," Charlie said as he helped John spread out the blanket.

"Well, you do that, Charlie, and I'll have to owe you another one."

Charlie sat down on the edge of the blanket beside John and looked at the woven star in the center. He remembered the night they had gotten drunk and stole Stephen's car, the night that John had thrown his holy pipe at the wall and it had landed right on that star. This blanket had come all the way with them, Charlie thought. It had been in Johnson City, where Charlie's family was, and now it was here. And everything had changed. His whole life had broken up. He was separated from his wife and family. He had done everything wrong and might never see them again. Even if he could go home, they might not ever want to speak to him. But here was that blanket and John's pipe and medicine tools.

They were the same. They were the *only* things that were the same. Charlie remembered breaking the glass pane of the office door, remembered punching his daughter's boyfriend in the face. He remembered John running that broken-down airplane right through Nathan Isaacs' lawn. He chuckled. Sonovabitch if it somehow wasn't worth it all just to do that!

John burned some sweet sage and purified his pipe in the smoke. He seemed more comfortable here in the woods than anywhere else. "You know, I lived around here for a while about thirty years ago, although I've been back off and on to see old friends. That's how I discovered Joe Whiteshirt." He smiled, as if he had invented the man. "But it takes a while to feel settled into a part of the country you've been away from for a long time. It used to be different here back in the old days. Maybe not better, but wilder, freer. There were still leopards and bears walking around. You ever see bears walking down the street, dancing around, forgetting they were bears?"

John lit the pipe, and Charlie just sat there taking in the smells and the wonderful damp coolness. Jesus was it quiet. Not even the bugs were clicking. The doves and jorees and red-birds and bee-martins were all quiet, as if the earth's blood had slowed down. It was noon. Only a hawk screed; and then he, too, was quiet, as if ashamed of breaking the silence. Charlie stared into a shaft of sunlight that cut through the trees before him. He was mesmerized. He felt that everything was right just now. He realized that this was a special time. He hadn't felt this quiet, this filling-up of himself with the world, very often. At least, not that he could remember. Once was with John that first time smoking the pipe. And once before, in Long Beach, California, where he used to spend a lot of time by himself near the water. He recalled that it had been a perfect day. He had been out on the *Lorelei* alone. He hadn't even taken any booze along. And he just lay down in that big, beautiful boat of his and looked up at the clear sky. Goddamn, I can remember that as if it was yesterday, he told himself. How the hell could I remember that sky so well after so many years? But he could: The sky had been clear and light blue with strands of cirrus pulling across it. He had felt that special way then. It was as if he had been a bottle filling up with color and air, with the ocean and the sun and the whole goddamn sky all at once. Maybe it was the sunlight—too much sun, probably. But Jesus Christ was that it? he asked himself. Had he only felt peace three times during his entire lifetime? He looked into that shaft of sunlight coming through the trees and heard the thunder inside his head that always presaged tears. Goddamn, I'm fucking crazy, he told himself.

He was crying over a piece of fucking sunshine.

John passed him the pipe, and he took it and pulled on it, drawing in the sweet tobacco, thinking about Joline, and Whiteshirt, too. But he felt abstracted. Although he was terrified of Whiteshirt, he could think about him now without fear. All the fear and bullshit was back out there on the road. This place that John chose exuded its own power. It seemed almost magical. Who the fuck knew, maybe it was chosen by God.

Charlie took a deep breath, as if it would be his last, and passed the pipe back to John. He inhaled the odors of sage and tobacco, and here in this dark place, he felt himself filling up with that shaft of light, as if he were drinking it through the air, through the pipe, through the soil. Charlie was drunk on it, and right there he fell asleep. He had questions to ask John. He should be taking care of John. But he slept, dreaming of sunlight and fire . . .

When Charlie awoke, he found John all hunched up over his pipe. John was rocking back and forth and praying. Charlie stretched out, yawned, and watched the petals of chinaberry blooms falling to the ground. It was windy and there was dampness in the air, perhaps presaging a storm. The light cutting through the trees was gray; it was hard to tell what the weather was going to do around here. Charlie waited for John to stop praying and said, "You look a little better, you know that? You feeling better?"

"Why don't you go back to sleep, old friend?" John said. "I've still got some praying to do before we visit Whiteshirt."

"I just woke up," Charlie said. "How long you think you're going to want to pray for?"

"I'm getting ready. Getting my strength back. You should do the same."

"You mean I'm not praying enough, is that it?" Charlie asked.

"You're going to need to rest up," John said. "I'd get as much sleep as I could if I were you."

"And what about you?"

"I need praying. I'll have plenty of time to sleep later."

John prayed for the rest of the day. He sang in an off-key and rocked back and forth like a Jew in a synagogue. He would doze, too, and then wake up with a start, as if he'd seen something—for all Charlie knew, maybe he did. Charlie was feeling better, although he had had a heavy bout of diarrhea, and was sore from wiping with leaves. The diarrhea was a result of the booze working its way out of his system; it was always the same for him. John was right about laying over in the woods here, Charlie told himself. He was feeling better. But he was starving. John wouldn't even let him go to the car for the crackers and candy bars they had lifted from a gas station counter. John said that they were going to go to Whiteshirt's "clean". He said that's where the power lay, or some bullshit like that, Charlie thought. Charlie couldn't remember exactly.

"Okay," John said suddenly, giving Charlie a start. "We might as well do it as not." He grinned. "I'm about as strong as I'm going to get." Then he carefully took apart his pipe, cleaned it, patted down the little mound where he had buried the tobacco ashes, and rolled his pipe, eagle's wing, sage, and tobacco into his star blanket.

"What are you going to do when we get to Whiteshirt's?" Charlie asked.

"You'll see soon enough," John said as Charlie helped him back to the car. The sun was low in the sky, near setting, and behind them the forest creatures became noisy. By sunset they would be frenzied: squirrels would run up and down the trunks and jump through the fronds while jays and red-birds screamed and flapped their way from tree to tree. The small animals did this when the day opened, and when the day closed, as if shouting for joy for the sun's safety, and then screaming in terror for its passing.

John directed Charlie from black-top to winding, gravely dirt roads. "Do you have any idea where the fuck you're going?" Charlie asked.

"I think I can remember," John said absently. There was a blueness in the air; even the forest had caught it, was darkened by it. "This is the time when I wanted to get to Joe Whiteshirt's," John said. "I always like to use the blue time when I can. It has a power for me," and he lowered the window and looked up at the sky.

"Come on, close the window," Charlie insisted. "I got the air-conditioner on. It's humid as hell out there."

"Didn't seem to bother you before," John said, pressing the switch that raised the window.

"You looking for eagles again?"

"Certainly would make me feel a fuck of a lot better if they were up there."

"Did you see any?" Charlie asked.

"Not yet, but I got a good feeling they're going to come back. I feel good. Strong. Those eagles better not fuck with an old fool." John laughed at that, and bit his lip in pain.

"We got to get you some help," Charlie said. "This is plain crazy."

"You got that right, Charlie. But you're helping me right now. I owe you one for this. But don't get smug—your ass is in the same sling as mine. Whiteshirt would like to see both of us dead and buried."

"This would be as good a day to die as any, I suppose," Charlie said. Now that they were almost at Whiteshirt's camp, now that it was about to happen, Charlie felt calm. He was resigned, and almost relieved. "I think maybe praying in the woods, sitting around all day, helped us some. Relaxed us, I mean."

John nodded and then seemed to withdraw into some special part of himself, and Charlie felt alone. The blue haziness, this special refraction of light that occurred only twice a day, in the morning and just before dusk, made everything seem cool. Perhaps it was the air-conditioning that fooled Charlie into feeling a chill, but that blue made everything appear sharp, as if etched. In a few moments, the blue time would be over, and then the world would melt into darkness.

"You know, everything *does* look blue," Charlie said, as if speaking to himself.

"Yeah," John whispered. "This time of the day works like the eagles for me . . . was part of my vision. Now that's something I've never told anyone before."

Charlie felt the bond between them. Even though John had told him about something that didn't really make much sense in the real world, it was special and privileged . . . and John had told him. Maybe all that had happened, even fucking that little girl, was all meant to be. Maybe in a way it would make him better. Jesus, there you go again, he told himself. You're so full of bullshit, you'll explode! You did wrong by fucking Sharry and stealing. Maybe it was all right for John, but you did wrong, Charlie Sarris.

"There's something that's been on my mind," Charlie said.

"Yeah, what is it?" John asked.

"I was wrong to come along on this thing with you. Cheating on my wife and stealing and everything." Here he was confessing, as if John could absolve him of his sins. And Charlie wasn't even Catholic.

"So . . . ? At least you *did* something. You've got something to remember now. Half those stories you told me about the old days, *you* didn't even seem to believe."

"That's because I don't fucking know what's true or not anymore," Charlie said. "I've told those stories so many times that they sometimes feel like the truth and then sometimes they feel like bullshit."

"What do you feel about them right now?" John asked.

"I feel that some of it was true, but I exaggerated everything so much that it wasn't. It was all bullshit, I guess." Charlie felt the emptiness, the old emptiness; there was no other way he could describe it, except that, like tears, it was always accompanied by a thunder sound. Then he said, "It was all to make myself feel like something, all that talk about having had it all once and enjoying it." Charlie laughed. "I never had much of anything when I had it."

John grinned. "I like that."

Charlie felt a burden lift. He had never talked about such things to anyone. Well, if he was going to make a fool of himself, he might as well go all the way. "You know, sometimes when I really feel sad, like right now, I hear thunder. Do you hear it ever? I always wondered if everybody else heard it, but just that nobody ever talked about it because it would sound stupid."

"You heard the thunder beings," John said, and then he laughed. "You pay attention to them. They're powerful creatures."

Charlie felt his face grow hot with embarrassment. *Goddamn I shouldn't have opened my mouth*, he told himself. *I'm talking like an asshole. I deserve to be laughed at.*

"You're special, Charlie," John said in that low, gritty voice of his. "I've never heard of anybody who could hear the thunder beings, except Indian people praying for them. You've got the big birds. You've had them and didn't even fucking know it. All I had were the eagles. But nobody can take those birds away from you, and they're strong spirits. You can bet on that. Maybe *that's* why I wanted you along on this trip."

"You're so full of shit," Charlie said, still feeling like an asshole.

"Maybe I am, but you listen to the thunder. When you're hearing it you're on the right track. It's when you *don't* hear the thunder beings that you're fucked up."

John directed Charlie onto another dirt road, this one narrow and rutted, nothing more than a path. The Lincoln wasn't built for this kind of use, and it bounced slowly on its heavy shocks as if it were a great liner heading into a storm. The atmosphere grew heavier as they drove ... as if the blue-tinged atmosphere was solidifying into glass, hard, brittle, pop-bottle glass.

They drove right into the middle of Whiteshirt's camp.

It was a run-down farm, in its way like Sam's farm, where Sam had tried to vision-quest, where it had all really started. The main house was large, and on concrete blocks. There was a barn behind it, and a gray weather-beaten smokehouse and a chicken-pen. A few old battered cars were parked on the edge of the clearing, as were two trailers and a truck with an attached plastic enclosure. Of the trailers, one was small and rounded, probably 50's vintage, and the other was large and more modern; a dancing Indian design had been painted on its rear wheel cover, obviously hand-done.

Then the blue time was over. It was as if the world had shifted without any warning, and everything seemed dark, somehow two-dimensional. The evening darkness was like a heavy, poisonous cloud, a miasma, and Charlie could feel it pressing against him . . . against his chest, even though he was inside the car. It was difficult to breath. He felt his glands open up, adrenaline burned inside him; his composure had passed along with the blue time. He took a deep breath and let it out slowly. His heart was beating fast, and there was a metallic taste in his mouth: fear.

The door opened to the main house, and a heavyset man stepped outside. An outside bare light bulb backlit him, and his shadow shot along the driveway almost reaching the Lincoln. Charlie jumped, for he thought that the shadow itself was alive. It moved too quickly and had the wrong shape . . . it had the shape of an animal, a raging beast, a demon. A spirit. It was Whiteshirt, wearing dungarees and no shirt. His belly drooped over his pants and his arms were large and muscular. Charlie couldn't make out Whiteshirt's face. But he could *feel* Whiteshirt looking at him, just as he had in the sweat-lodge. He could feel those hot, feral eyes boring into him.

Charlie was terrified. He wanted to run. He wanted to leave John here, sitting in the car by himself, but he would be even more vulnerable out in the open; and the beast would devour him, burn him, tear at him, transform him, as it had John.

Jesus Christ, I don't want any trouble, he told himself; and he remembered John trying to crash into those Jews. But that was Whiteshirt. Whiteshirt was there, in the car with them; and now John and Charlie were here, face to face with him. Whiteshirt might as well have brought them here. Maybe he did! Charlie thought, and the dead weight of the night seemed to be suffocating him, crushing him, as if it was just an extension of Whiteshirt's ill will. Charlie's blood was pumping and his heart was beating way up in his throat now. He thought he was going to have an emphysema attack. That *would* be the way Whiteshirt could take care of me, take me right out! But that was crazy thinking, he told himself. Whiteshirt's nothing but a fucked up Indian . . . like John.

But goddamn he was afraid anyway. Maybe there were such things as medicine and spells and witches and all the rest. Right now he could believe in them. Damn if he didn't! Charlie tried to catch his breath.

"Take it easy," John whispered to Charlie. "You better be listening to those thunder beings of yours." Then he opened the door and got out of the car.

Charlie sat and stared out the window before pulling the door latch.

He couldn't hear a goddamn thing!

20.

INDIAN GIVING

Whiteshirt walked down the driveway, flanked by two men, and two women walked behind them. John and Charlie stood beside the Lincoln; both front doors remained open, as if to create a barricade. Charlie felt his hands shake. He was still having trouble breathing. The background chittering of insects sounded deafening to him, but the noise seemed to modulate with every shallow, gasping breath he took.

As Whiteshirt and his coterie approached, Charlie recognized the young man who had offered Charlie his pipe at Sam's vision-quest. His name was Keith, and he was dressed in a T-shirt and faded dungarees, just as he was when Charlie first met him. John had called Keith a "Wannabee". To Whiteshirt's left was one of the Indian brothers who had sung the ancient songs at the sweat ceremony before Sam's vision-quest. The man glowered at Charlie; in the moonlight his face looked as if it had been sharply modeled from dark clay or sculpted from pipestone. It was a face hardened with hatred. But Charlie looked away from him, for he recognized Whiteshirt's wife, Janet. So she's come back to Whiteshirt, after all, Charlie thought. He was surprised to see her; she couldn't have been here very long. Janet looked tired, worn out. Charlie was relieved to see her, certain that she would be an ally. He nodded to her, but she averted her eyes; there was too much tension and imminent danger for contact. Whiteshirt's woman, Violet, stood beside her. Exuding possessiveness, she stepped forward to stand between Whiteshirt and Keith. She wore a plaid shirt and stiff new jeans. She seemed as arrogant and hard-faced as she had when Charlie first saw her at Sam's, and she had the same strong erotic presence now. Although she wasn't pretty, Charlie could see why men liked her . . . why they called her a witch. He felt her attraction; he could sense her wildness, her feral nature.

And Charlie suddenly had a hallucination, probably brought on by the booze and fatigue and tension.

He saw Violet as some sort of wild vulpine animal—that was her natural basic form: her human form was like an ill-fitting dress that she wore so as not to shock strangers with her raw nakedness.

Whiteshirt stood before John. He was tight-lipped, and his eyes were squinted-up in glowering, cold hatred. He looked as if he would shatter from the tension of being so tight. A smile would break his face, leaving only those haunted eyes set in his skull like brown marbles. Charlie imagined Whiteshirt's flesh lying on the ground like pieces of a broken gourd. He recognized that look on Whiteshirt's face: it was the same crazy, dangerous look that John took on when he was about to go *heyoka*.

In fact, *Charlie* felt *heyoka*. He felt a vertiginous shifting from mind to muscle. But this wasn't just craziness; it was another mode of seeing . . . of being. It was clarity itself—

Or it was just another fatigue induced hallucination.

But Charlie could glimpse them in all their animal forms. It was like images seen with peripheral vision: as fleeting as the flickering spirits he saw in the sweat-lodge. He could smell their animal presence, too, strong and wild in his nostrils. Charlie imagined Whiteshirt as an elk or a buffalo . . . shaggy and horned and dangerous as a trapped boar. John was weak, yet focused and clear. A wounded eagle with great invisible wings. Charlie thought he heard a flapping noise like the beating of wings . . . he could *feel* them thrashing. But there was only the gusting of wind, the raspy sounds of his breathing, and the roaring of insects.

"What the fuck do you want here?" Whiteshirt asked John, almost in a whisper. "Haven't you had enough? You want more trouble, I'll give you more." Whiteshirt's eyes glittered like a forest animal, as if they were radiating a cold light of their own. John and Whiteshirt were already locked in battle. Although Whiteshirt breathed slowly and deeply, he was shaking, shivering as if he were cold. "Say your piece, or whatever, and then get off my land."

"*Your* land?" John said, surveying the camp. "I suppose it's good for a holy man to own things . . ."

"I don't have to take any shit from you, John Stone." Whiteshirt moved closer to John. "And that's right, *my* land."

"I have a present for you," John said, smiling weakly.

Whiteshirt laughed, looking to the others for support, focusing on Violet, saying, "He's got a present for me. I think we've had enough of your presents to last us a lifetime." He glanced at his wife Janet, who flinched.

But John paid no attention. He leaned into the car and, after a few beats, came out with his pipe, eagle feather, and medicine pouch, which he usually wore on his belt. His pipe was assembled. He closed the car door by pushing against it with his body. Then he faced John directly. He held the pipe and ceremonial objects out to Whiteshirt. Everyone was dead quiet. Even the insects seemed to have stopped buzzing and chittering for an instant. Charlie held back a cough.

"You're a pipe-carrier," John said to Whiteshirt. "Here, I'm giving you my sacred pipe and my medicine. I'm passing it on to you to keep, or to bury. You can think of it as proof that you've beaten me, if you like."

Whiteshirt blinked in surprise and bewilderment. He started to say something, but stopped.

And Charlie saw Whiteshirt as a man again. The animal image dissolved, as if it were being completely absorbed into the darkness.

"Don't take that pipe!" Violet snapped, pushing past Whiteshirt, closer to John. "Can't you see, he's trying to kill you!"

Reflexively, Charlie took a step backward. He saw her as a wolf, or maybe a fox. She looked so smooth and hungry and quick. He felt her power, feral and strong and sexual.

But John still held out the pipe and ceremonial objects. He looked at Whiteshirt, as if there were no one else there.

"That's not so," Janet said, following Violet and grabbing her arm to hold her back. Violet shrugged it off, but Janet stayed close to her and seemed ready to pull out Violet's hair, if necessary. "Look at him, for Chrissakes," Janet said. "He's sick, and he's hurting. What *happened?*" she asked Charlie, but then she looked away from him: it had not been a question to be answered.

"You bet you ass he's sick," Violet said, "and that's why he's giving you his pipe because it doesn't matter if he dies or not . . . he'll hold onto you." She looked at Whiteshirt, and they seemed locked together for an instant. Charlie, for his part, could feel the tension and frustration and just plain ugliness, as if they were noxious fumes. He felt caught where he was, as were the others around him. Something was being played out, and he was powerless to affect it in any way.

"I told you," Violet said, still facing Whiteshirt, "he's using bad medicine on you. And he has been all along. He's a witch!"

"Shut your mouth!" Janet said.

"Well," Violet said nastily, "if he isn't a witch, then you're a whore!" That caught Janet, for she just stood there, her face white and taut, her hands in her jeans' pockets; her fists were working under the tight material. But Violet had her. As violent as Janet might be, she did not seem ready to strike out for herself, and Violet used that against her. She just stared Janet down, and once Janet lowered her eyes, Violet looked back at Whiteshirt and John.

"Is Janet right?" Whiteshirt asked John. His voice was soft.

John ignored Whiteshirt's question. "I expect your friend Violet is right about this old pipe," he said. "After all the years I've carried it, I'd guess that there's something of me inside it, clinging to it. I tried not to carry it when I was fucked up, but, then what can you do? Sometimes I was so fucked up that I carried it anyway, you know what I mean?" John pulled the pipe and bundle to his chest. "You know, maybe I'm not in such good shape." He chuckled to himself. "You going to take this stuff or not?"

Whiteshirt turned to Violet, as if he was suddenly angry at *her*, more likely he was ashamed of himself. "A man doesn't give away his pipe and his medicine," Whiteshirt said. "I don't fucking care *what* you say. No medicine man would give away his medicine."

"That's the whole goddamn point," Violet shouted. "He's not a medicine man. He's a goddamn witch!"

Whiteshirt shook his head. It was as if the scales had suddenly dropped from his eyes. "You're a cunt," he said softly, almost in a whisper, "and you're running a game on me. Not even a witch would give his medicine away to his enemy. John Stone isn't so stupid that he wouldn't know what you'd try to do with it . . . if I let you!" He turned to John, dismissing him, and said, "You might be a pretty stupid Indian, but you ain't no witch." Then Whiteshirt took the pipe, holding it reverently in the traditional manner—pipestone bowl in the palm of his right hand.

"Throw it *away*," Violet said. She looked distressed, frightened. The insect sounds seemed to be reaching a crescendo, as if they were registering what was being said . . . and felt.

"I always thought that this pipe had something special working inside it," Whiteshirt said to John, ignoring Janet. He was gentle with the pipe, holding it, touching it as if it were a live thing. "You know, when we used to smoke this pipe back in the old days, I could always feel the spirits coming out of it like—"

"You stupid bastard!" Violet shouted, and she reached over and grabbed the pipe by its stem, yanking on it, trying to pull it out of Whiteshirt's hands. For a second, Charlie thought the pipe would break in half, but Whiteshirt held onto it.

"Let *go* of the pipe!" Whiteshirt said, and when she wouldn't give it up, when she challenged him, her eyes snapping, her bloodless face tight and taunting and mocking, he slapped her hard in the mouth. He had exploded into quick-firing rage, but in that instant the knot of hatred and pride and bad medicine seemed to break. Whiteshirt was a man overcome with simple, white-hot, elemental anger, that was all.

This was not the practiced, dull, malicious hatred of ceremonial magic.

Violet staggered backward, holding her jaw; a bruised redness began to spread over the area, and her mouth was bleeding. A trickle had run down her chin and stained her blouse. Her jaw would soon puff out and turn blue, unless she took some ice to it. She stood calmly now, radiating the same hatred that had burned John inside the sweat-lodge. "You're going to blame *me* for what you are, for what you've become, aren't you?" she said to Whiteshirt. "Well, go ahead and keep the old man's pipe. And you can let your wife here keep the door for you." Violet turned to Janet. "Now you can start worrying again about who she's going to fuck next," she said to Whiteshirt while she tried to stare down Janet, who, although blushing and trembling, didn't back away or take her eyes off Violet. Violet broke it off by turning to Charlie and saying, "Who knows, maybe it'll be John Stone's friend over here. Maybe she'll fuck him next. She seemed to be liking him at Sam's vision-quest."

"That's enough," Whiteshirt said.

"I haven't even begun," Violet replied. "And what are you going to do, you fat fucker? Hit me again?"

"So that's how it is," Whiteshirt said. His face and ears turned red, but he kept his composure. "Maybe I should give the pipe to *you*, witch."

That seemed to drive her crazy, and she went after Whiteshirt. But Janet came between them. When Violet tried to push her out of the way, Janet struck her hard in the face, knocking her down. Violet remained on the ground for a moment, staring downward as if meditating, and then stood up, without looking at Janet or Whiteshirt. She called to Keith. "Will you give me a ride into Gainesville?"

"Is that okay with you?" Keith asked Whiteshirt. Whiteshirt didn't answer him; he just turned back to John. "Yeah, I'll give you a ride," Keith said.

"Well, come on," Violet said, walking away. "There's nothing I need but what I've got on."

"No," Janet said, following her. "You can take everything . . . that or I'll burn it."

"Then fucking burn it!" Violet said. She walked with Keith toward the vans. Whiteshirt watched them, then turned his attention back to John. He looked pained, yet his face had softened. Finally, Janet turned away from Violet and Keith, who were now inside the van, and she walked back to stand beside Whiteshirt. There didn't seem to be any tension between them; nor did there seem to be any warmth or closeness either. Charlie felt relieved, for everything seemed to be normal and real again. He was thankful for that. But being *heyoka* had left him exhausted and wired at the same time.

"Why'd you really bring this to me?" Whiteshirt asked John. "No matter what, you've never given up your pipe."

"Violet said it right," John said. He was sweating, and his breathing sounded funny to Charlie. "I'm not exactly giving it up . . . I'm passing it on."

"Why . . . ?"

"You're pretty fucking thick for a medicine man," John said. "Too many honkies around here. Melting away your spirit."

"And what do you call *him*?" Whiteshirt demanded, pointing his face at Charlie. Charlie jumped. Whiteshirt certainly still had something, a raw animal strength, a power. Goddamn, there had to be *something* to that medicine stuff. Christ, I've seen it myself . . . but now that it was over Charlie wasn't really certain what he had seen.

"An old man like me's allowed a honky once in a while," John said, smiling; but his face was tight with pain, especially around the eyes and mouth. "Anyway, Charlie's my friend, and he just sort of got caught up in all the bullshit."

"What'd you expect?" Whiteshirt asked, but there was a hint of humor in his voice. "He was with you, and with all the medicine that's been done . . ."

"Wasn't just medicine," Janet said. "It was weakness. My weakness."

"It was medicine," Whiteshirt said to Janet. He was a stubborn hard man. "I guess I owe you for putting up with the likes of . . . her."

"No, you owe her for putting up with you!" John said.

Whiteshirt's face turned mean, and Charlie was afraid that he, Whiteshirt, would do something, although Charlie wasn't quite sure what. But John was grinning, and that grin of his was infectious.

John really does have power, Charlie thought. And somehow he knew that John was a medicine man again. The others seemed to acknowledge it, too. Sonovabitch if this John wasn't the same John who got fucked up all the time—Charlie couldn't quite verbalize to himself what he had in mind. Perhaps it was that even though John could be drunk and fucked up most of the time, he could suddenly become like some sort of great man, powerful like . . . Geronimo or somebody. Like the old Indians with feathers and all. Those old Indians probably had the gift of eagles too. And sonovabitch if it didn't make Charlie want to cry, which was a stupid reaction anyway, he thought.

But he was proud to be John's friend.

Whiteshirt looked at John, and then nodded, acknowledging wrongs he had done. And then they both started to laugh, just as Charlie had when he had first smoked the pipe with John. It was release, a joyous confession. Charlie could understand that.

Keith honked the horn, and everyone moved out of the way as he drove an old gray van slowly down the driveway and out onto the dirt road. Violet stared straight ahead.

"We haven't heard the end of her," Janet said, moving closer to Whiteshirt. "I'm going to have to tear the house apart. You can bet your ass she left something behind just to fuck us up . . . something to poison us."

"Do what you have to do," Whiteshirt said to Janet, "but don't mention her name again. You remind me too much, and we'll be taking separate paths again." He squeezed her hand and then said to John, "I don't think we're going to be seeing Keith around for quite a while . . ."

John leaned against the Lincoln; the color was draining out of his face.

"Come on, honey," Janet said to John. "Let's get you into the house. I'll make you some coffee that will take the hair right off you."

But John's head nodded forward, and he fainted. Charlie tried to break his fall, but John felt as heavy as wet earth.

A bird screeched in the distance. It was probably an owl, but Charlie had it firmly in his mind that it was an eagle. He could visualize it as being black with huge wings, and Charlie heard the thunder in his ears, and realized that he was crying for his friend.

2 1 .

SLIPPING AWAY

John insisted on sweating.

"I'm a goddamn medicine man," he said and refused to go to the hospital. He sat on the ground, leaned against the Lincoln's tire, and smiled. He was sick as hell; Charlie could see that. John needed help right now, Charlie thought. But John was in control now, not Charlie. Everyone deferred to John.

They did a sweat-lodge ceremony out in the woods, in a beautiful, alien place beside a natural whirlpool turned opalescent by moonlight, where sand swirled around and seemed to form animated Indian designs. The whirlpool was fed by a clear spring; the banks around it were dark and verdant. The sweat-lodge, a skeleton of branch and sapling, was hidden, unless one knew where to look. It fitted right into this place.

The women brought blankets and tarpaulins; the men brought rocks for the fire. John sat down under an old tree webbed with Spanish moss and watched Whiteshirt and his people prepare the sweat-lodge and build the fire. He had a pained expression on his face. Charlie sat down and fidgeted beside him.

John . . . ?" Charlie asked.

"Forget it," John said. "Go with the flow."

"I don't like this. I don't like it a'tall.

"What the fuck do you think they're going to do for me in the hospital?" John asked in a low voice.

"Save your goddamn life, for one thing."

"How do you know I'm that sick?"

"I've got eyes, don't I?"

John chuckled and nodded. "Well, this is the way I want to do it. You going to sweat with me?"

"I dunno."

"Maybe be the last time we get to do this together . . ."

Charlie nodded.

"I'm going to stay in the sweat-lodge, stay the night, try to put everything to right. You know, clean myself out."

"Yeah," Charlie said, not knowing what to say. Once again he had the feeling that something beyond his comprehension was being played out. He felt powerless to do anything but nod and say, "Yeah."

"We'll all sweat together, make like a family, heal the wounds, all that shit, but later—after it's over—I want you to stay." John laughed. "I need someone to pray over me."

John made it hot in the sweat-lodge. Charlie wasn't used to it and felt so much pain that he started praying for everyone. He screamed so loudly that Whiteshirt had to wrestle him to the ground where it was cooler and press sage against his mouth and nose. The other Indian sang the ancient songs. Janet kept the door and brought in shovelfuls of glowing rocks when asked.

Time blinked by. Hours or minutes, Charlie couldn't tell. And then it was over, and everyone was crawling out of the sweat-lodge, dipping themselves into the spring water, shouting.

John and Charlie sat across from each other in the darkness of the tarp covered sweat-lodge.

"You wanna stay inside or go out with the others?" John asked.

"What do you mean?"

The rocks were still glowing—Janet had passed in more rocks for John.

"Why didn't you get out with everybody else?" John asked.

"Maybe I blacked-out, fell asleep or something. I don't know."

"Well, old son, you wanna stay? We'll sweat a little, pray a little, and make a night of it. If not, get the hell out now because I'm getting a chill, and I think I'll put some more of this water on the rocks. Well . . . ?"

Charlie didn't answer. He felt weak and tired and cramped, and he was suddenly afraid of the darkness again in this place where all time and space seemed to get tangled and stretched.

"I'd feel you'd be doing me a favor, though, if you stayed close," John said. "You know, maybe outside the lodge, if that's what you want to do."

"What about everybody else?" Charlie asked. "Whiteshirt and Janet . . . ?"

"They'll be up at the house, praying, working things out for themselves again."

"I thought you wanted to be alone, isn't that what you told everybody?"

"That's right, honky, I do. I sure as hell don't want you blathering away all night in my ear. But you're my friend."

"I'll stay," Charlie said.

With that, John poured cold water over the rocks, and John and Charlie screamed together.

Nothing but darkness and night sounds. The rocks were dead, not an ember alive, but the steam seemed to have soaked into this place, leaving Charlie wet and chilled. Yet his lungs felt clear. Janet came by and asked if they needed anything, but John wouldn't answer her, so Charlie told her everything was fine.

Charlie listened to the sounds of John's labored breathing. Branches rustled. An owl hooted. Small animals scurried. Insects buzzed and chirruped. John prayed, chanted songs, touched Charlie with his eagle feather, and passed him the pipe, which Charlie took and smoked.

Charlie slept and dreamed about eagles and Joline. Waking up with a jolt, he found himself in the darkness and screamed because it was as if he could not wake up . . . could not separate waking from dreaming.

All the while John chanted, until he, too, finally slept.

"Charlie? You awake?"

Charlie opened his eyes. He discerned tiny sparks of light in the darkness. Maybe he was seeing spirits. Most likely, though, his eyes were playing tricks on him. "Yeah, I'm awake."

"Tell the others I want to be buried in the natural way. You got that?"

"What the fuck are you talking about?" Charlie asked.

There was no answer.

"John?"

Charlie heard something. It sounded as if John had farted, and then Charlie smelled feces. "John?" He crawled over to his friend, then pulled down the tarps and blankets and shouted for the others.

John was dead.

Moonlight illuminated him like a ghost. He was bent forward, his sacred pipe clenched in his hands on his lap. Whiteshirt and Janet and the others had been nearby, after all, for they were there in a minute, all standing still, looking stricken.

"Did he say anything to you?" Whiteshirt asked.

"He wanted me to tell you that he wanted to be buried in the natural way."

Whiteshirt nodded.

"Come on out," Janet said to Charlie, coaxing. The others carefully removed the rest of the blankets and tarps from the sweat-lodge. The slight breeze was cool on Charlie's skin. He looked around. Everything seemed milky, bathed in wan moonlight. The pool and stream were silver. This place had become hard and cold and dead.

"I think we should pray for John and have the ceremony at dawn," Whiteshirt said. "We have some work to do."

Charlie noticed for the first time other people standing around, people he had not seen before: two white boys who looked to be in their early twenties, and an Indian boy who looked like a younger image of the man who had sung the old songs in the sweat-lodge; probably his son. There were also children peering in at him, two nut-brown ragamuffins of about eleven.

"Come on, Charlie," Janet said gently; tears streaked her face. "Come out with us, honey."

But Charlie just sat there, dazed, shocked, although to his mind he just needed some time here to figure things out. John had just up and died. That was all there was to it. No drums or whistles. Nothing profound. Just a fart and bango. Charlie felt tears running down his cheeks, although he didn't *feel* any different. He was shivering with sweat. John *couldn't* be goddamn dead. Charlie didn't have to believe John was dead. After all, everything else was still the same. He, Charlie, felt the same. He heard himself say to Janet, "If it's all right, I think I'll just stay here for a while."

The others left, and after a time Charlie could see a fire burning in the distance and could hear chopping and sawing. Maybe they're building another sweat-lodge, he thought. Crazy fucking Indians. If John had taken my advice and gone to the goddamn hospital, he wouldn't be dead here in the sweat-lodge and bent over like a statue or something.

Charlie couldn't help but laugh. Goddamn if it didn't make any sense, yet somehow it was funny . . . but Charlie didn't know if he was laughing or crying. It was all mixed up inside him. He knew something that he couldn't express: that in some terrible sense it didn't matter. Yet he heard the thunder again and cried. It was all for this. To sit here with his dead friend in the middle of goddamn nowhere. Again he laughed; he laughed and cried and the tears ran down his cheeks to drop on his stomach.

He put his arms around John. John's skin was cold and clammy to the touch. Charlie held him, to warm his friend. "Goddamn you, you sonovabitch," he mumbled, slurring his words. "Goddamn you."

Charlie looked up through the willow skeleton of the sweat-lodge at the sky. Not a fucking thing had changed. Not a fucking thing . . .

They came for John at dawn, just as Whiteshirt had promised. Charlie was still holding him, and didn't want to give up his friend. Janet and Whiteshirt had to pull John away from him. Charlie felt neutral, as if he were watching the whole scene from far away, watching himself making a fuss, making an asshole out of himself.

Charlie got dressed; and then he was walking beside Janet, who held onto his arm as they followed behind the others. It was a procession, just like the one at Sam's vision-quest. Charlie wondered if Sam ever did get to do his vision-quest. Probably not, he guessed. Charlie wasn't thinking about John; he was looking around; it was like watching a movie from a distance. Until suddenly he snapped back, and was again himself, and everything was real and deadening.

"Where are we going?" Charlie asked Janet.

"We built a thing for John to lay on."

"What do you mean?"

"Right there," and Janet pointed to what looked like a bier attached to four trees. It was about six feet high, a platform made out of saplings and tied with rope. Small pieces of colored cloth hung from its sides like an uneven fringe. A rough circle was cleared around and between the trees. John was laid out on the ground.

"What the hell are you going to do, burn him?" Charlie asked. There was a salty taste in his mouth, and his heart was beating in his throat again. He watched Whiteshirt and two other men lift John onto the platform. There was no ceremony. Just silence. And it was done.

"We're just going to leave him there," Janet said a moment later. "That's what he wanted."

"Just to rot?"

"The birds will get him. It's the natural way."

Charlie looked up toward his friend. The sky was taking on color, and the leaves seemed to be shining with dew. This place seemed to be filled with a green haze of moss and grass and branch and leaf.

Better to have it up in the air, Charlie thought, then to let the worms go at it. He looked around, his neck craned.

"What are you looking for?" Janet asked.

"Eagles . . . I figured they'd be here by now, if they were going to come at all."

But there wasn't a goddamned bird in the sky.

They didn't make a big deal out of it afterward. No rending of garments or loud crying. Whiteshirt said a short prayer to *Waken-tanka*, lit some sage and sweet-grass, passed around the pipe, and they all left, walking away quietly as if that was that. People lived, people died. There were chores to do. Janet took Charlie by the hand and led him to the house for coffee and breakfast. But Charlie wouldn't go inside, even though he was hungry. He didn't feel it was right for him to eat yet. He still had John and the sweat-lodge with him. If he ate anything now, he'd be right back in the world again; and he had something to do first. He had to make something right.

He told Janet Goodbye.

"Wait, let me get Joe, he'll want to at least say Goodbye."

"Let's not make a big deal," Charlie said. "I just want to sort of just slip away, you know what I mean?"

Janet smiled. Charlie saw her as beautiful, even with her missing tooth. "John didn't like fusses either," Janet said. "Except when he was drunk."

"We did a lot of that," Charlie said, and they laughed together and then embraced.

"I don't think we'll see each other again. I have that sense."

"I guess," Charlie said. He held her, then broke away. He walked down the driveway, got into the Lincoln, and connected the ignition wires. The engine turned over, and the air-conditioner seemed to fill the car with sound. "John, you're a stupid asshole," Charlie mumbled to himself. "Goddamn you, Goodbye."

Charlie's eyes were moist, his vision slightly distorted. But he shifted into reverse and roared out of the driveway, stomping down on the accelerator as if he were *heyoka* and full of belly-rotting bourbon. He turned into the dirt road and shifted into drive, not knowing if he had even turned in the right direction. He didn't look around, didn't peek into the rear-view mirror. He just drove the car, letting the shocks take the bumps and stones and potholes. He drove like a crazy, drunken Indian, stirring up a golden tornado of dust in the road.

And all the while he talked to John, as if John were sitting right there in the car beside him.

Charlie was in a hurry now. He had somewhere to go, and something to take care of.

22.

GHOST VOICES . . .

AGAIN

Charlie took one dirt road and then another, until he finally found a paved two-lane highway that cut through slash pine. Charlie drove as if in a trance. He remembered driving through a blizzard in Canada once with a friend. They had been drunked-up, and Charlie was driving. But Charlie could hardly see the snow-covered road ahead and had to guess where it was. Somehow he'd guessed right. He'd say, "Goddamn road must turn right . . . *here,*" and he'd turn the wheel, and they'd still be on the road.

Goddamn if right now I don't miss the snow, and Christmas time with Joline and the kids, Charlie thought.

Charlie was driving as if he was in that blizzard with his friend. He didn't care where he was going. He just knew that somehow he'd get where he wanted to go, and in quick-time, too. Which he did. Somehow he managed to get back on 305 going south, which he took down to Ocala.

There he turned east on Route 40 to Daytona.

"I know my goddamn way," he said. "I just follow the signs. That's a fuck of a lot more than you ever did." Charlie listened to his stomach growling. He stared out the windshield at the road ahead and then leaned forward, craning his neck to see the sky. "I don't see no eagles," he said. "Not a one." He pressed the window switch, and the window buzzed down, letting in a scream of air. Charlie stuck his head out of the window and looked up into the clear sky. Then he leaned back into his seat and put the window back up. "Still don't see any," Charlie said. "Where the fuck are they? And don't give me that shit about how they're flying over your body back there, 'cause I didn't see them there neither. Not even sparrows or anything."

Charlie listened, as if expecting the space in the seat beside him to become John and answer.

And it did.

Charlie heard the words in his head just as he had when he was a kid. He used to look up at the bedroom ceiling and transform the cracks and peeling plaster into animals, grotesque faces, women with large breasts, gnomes . . . anything he could conceive. He would create them, and they would talk to him, keep him company.

"I'm dead, you stupid asshole."

"No, you're not," Charlie said. "You're in the car, right here with me. You think I'm going to face Nathan Isaacs alone?" Charlie waited, and he heard the thunder noise, which sounded like laughter. A smile crossed Charlie's face, wide as his skin would allow.

"Don't be so happy, honky. The eagles are eating me, all right, but I'll tell you what . . ."

"What?"

"I'm giving the eagles to you . . . a gift. Right out of the box."

"Yeah. Thanks."

It was somewhere around Emporia and Barberville that Charlie felt John leave him.

He mourned him by driving flat out. That's how John would have done it. It's a good day to die, Charlie thought, and he wondered if John would be crying like a goddamn baby if the tables were turned and it was Charlie up there in the woods being eaten by eagles.

23.

SMART BUSINESS AND
REGULAR DEBTS

Charlie arrived in New Smyrna around eleven o'clock in the morning.

He got off I–95 and drove down the North Dixie Freeway, past the seemingly endless fast-food restaurants, steak houses, diners, malls, and beer gardens. But the sky was a cloudless blue, and Charlie turned east and drove over the span of South Bridge, over the intercoastal, and then south along A–1-A. The ocean was to his left. Although it was placid and beautiful with the gulls and the beach and the expanse of turquoise water meeting the sky at the end of goddamn forever, Charlie knew he could never live here. Even with the beautiful summer houses to the right and the rich, happy-looking people walking along the road and playing and sunning themselves on the beach, there was something about the flatness and the immensity of ocean and sky that made him feel completely alone.

He drove directly to Nathan's house.

Better to face him and be done with it, Charlie told himself. He'd be back on the beach soon enough, although he wouldn't be driving this big Lincoln and listening to the comforting hum of the air-conditioner.

Goddamn! Charlie thought. John's dead. How could that *be*?

Well, if it all goes against me, as I expect it will, I can always fucking just walk into the ocean. Charlie laughed at himself. He remembered a sign he'd passed along the beach: WORLD's SAFEST BATHING. Shit, I'd have to walk out to the goddamn horizon for the water to be over my head.

If you're going to do anything, he told himself, you've got to do it now. You could drive this fucker right into a wall, flat out. Wouldn't feel a goddamn thing. We should have done it in the plane. Now *that* would have had some elegance.

But Charlie didn't do any such thing. He found Nathan's house and drove right up the driveway.

Several gardeners were working on the lawn. In a few hours, no one would ever know that Charlie and John had counted coup all over the fucking place here.

Nathan Isaacs opened his polished, inlaid front door and took a step backward. "Jesus *Christ*!" he said. "What the hell is going on? What have you done with my car?"

"It's right here, Nathan," Charlie said, pointing toward the driveway. "It even has a full tank of gas in it." Nathan seemed satisfied that his car was unharmed, so Charlie continued. "I'm sorry I had to take it like I did, but my friend was . . . ah, fuck it. I took it and brought it back. I'll try to pay you off for whatever damage we did to your lawn when I can get up the money."

"*That's* costing me over a thousand dollars," Nathan said. He was back in control, for his voice sounded artificial, pompous; he was speaking to Charlie as if he were a client.

"Well, you can call the police," Charlie said. "That's your choice. At this point, I don't fucking *give* a good goddamn."

"Just watch your language," Nathan said. "There's a lady present."

Charlie could see Nathan's girlfriend Helen standing behind him and off to the side. She was part of the reason for all Charlie's trouble. Before she persuaded Nathan to move away to Florida, she was always badmouthing Charlie. She would tell Nathan that Charlie wasn't a "professional", that he was a cheap-jack handyman. Since she was a fair-to-middling handyman herself, she started taking over Charlie's jobs. She shoved Charlie out of the business little by little. She had broken his pride.

"Pardon me," Charlie said, almost slipping back into his old, obsequious role. But he caught himself and turned away. He'd go back down to the beach and think. He'd figure out what to do next.

"Charlie, you look like hell. You want to come inside?"

"No, I really think I should be going," Charlie said.

"I think you at least owe it to me to come into my goddamn house when I invite you, don't you think."

What's the harm, Charlie told himself. He did owe Nathan, in a way. Although Nathan had been a bastard, he didn't deserve to have his car stolen and his lawn fouled. So Charlie followed him into the house. The door opened into a large, airy living room. Two bay windows partially covered with puffy, translucent curtains let in the sunshine. On the wooden parquet floor was a long white and blue Persian carpet. Along the wall nearest the driveway were a set of carved Italian-looking credenzas, a white couch that faced two chairs, and a Louis XV ornate commode veneered with ebony and Boulle marquetry. At the far end of the room was a writing table of the same full-blown style. In the middle of the room was a Sony portable television on a white plastic stand. A dingy, pink stuffed chair and a card table seemed to divide living room from dining room. There was a phone and assorted papers on the table. This was obviously Nathan's private space. Just as obvious, the rest of the furniture, with the exception of the television and *maybe* the couch, was there for show, not use.

"Here, have a seat," Nathan said, but he led Charlie into the dining room, which contained four high-backed, rounded wicker chairs and a large table. Glass doors opened onto a deck that overlooked an oval, blue-tinted pool. The outside pool area was enclosed by a patio wall that gave it the look of a Greek temple. Every four or five feet near the top of the wall was a lamp with a red bulb. It's a regular whorehouse, Charlie thought, but he was impressed nevertheless.

"Charlie, can I get you some coffee or a soda?" Helen asked. She wore a mint-green cotton poplin dress that flattered her ample figure, but Charlie noticed a varicose vein on her leg.

"Coffee'd be very nice, thank you," Charlie said, feeling uncomfortable in the wicker chair.

"I think you owe me an explanation," Nathan said.

"Nathan, I'll admit to you that I was wrong in doing what I did, but other than that, what I did was my own business."

"Stephen called me and told me about how you broke the glass in the office door and took *his* car. You did over a thousand dollars worth of damage to that car, do you know that?"

"I'll pay back every nickel," Charlie said. "I'll make right whatever damage I caused, you can believe that, Nathan." Then Charlie checked himself. Fuck it, he thought. I have nothing to lose now. At the very least, he could afford a little honesty. "Look, I'll do whatever I can. I'll pay you back as much as I can if I can find work. I'll *try* . . ."

"We can discuss that later," Nathan said. "Right now I want to know what happened." Helen brought Charlie his coffee in a china cup on a saucer. Charlie didn't ask her for a bowl to cool off his coffee; he just thanked her and waited before he drank it. Helen prepared to sit down with them, but Nathan asked her if he and Charlie could be alone for a while. Helen left without a word, but Charlie was sure that there would be hell to pay later.

"Would you like some cognac or an aperitif with your coffee?" Nathan asked tentatively, as if one drink would turn Charlie back into a raving lunatic. But Charlie had to hand it to Nathan: Nathan was giving him respect by making the offer.

"No thanks, Nathan," Charlie said. "I've done all the drinking I'm going to do for a while."

Nathan nodded and fixed himself a drink.

"If I were you, I'd be a lot more pissed off than you seem to be," Charlie said. "You're a better man than I am."

"Joline called me as soon as you left," Nathan said.

Charlie felt himself getting hot in the face. He should have known that she'd be calling Nathan every five minutes. "Is that why you didn't call the police?"

"She loves you very much, you know."

Charlie looked down into his coffee cup. Goddammit, Joline should have just left everything alone, he told himself. Maybe it would have been better if the police had caught me. Then I could have paid my dues up properly.

"She wants you back," Nathan said.

Charlie just shook his head. He had gone past the point of being able to go back. Who the fuck was it who said "You can't ever go home?" Charlie asked himself. Maybe Plato or somebody like that. He thought about screwing Sharry. He could see her head on the pillow right now. He could see that look of pleasure and agony on her face. Sonovabitch, I've lost everything! Well, fuck it, it's done.

Then Charlie told Nathan the whole story, everything that had happened. Let him tell that to Joline. Maybe if she heard the worst she'd forget about him and make a better life for herself. Maybe she'd find another man who could take care of her. But Charlie couldn't stand to think about that.

"So your friend is dead?" Nathan asked.

"That's it," Charlie said.

Nathan seemed to show Charlie a new respect. He was treating Charlie as an equal. It felt like the old days to Charlie. When he had his gas stations, he used to talk with lawyers and doctors. He used to meet them in clubs. They used to buy him drinks. But fuck that, Charlie thought. None of that mattered now. It was all bullshit. Except for Joline and the kids, his whole life had been bullshit.

"Do you want to call Joline?" Nathan asked.

"No."

"Are you telling me that you're just going to leave her out in the cold?" Nathan asked.

"She's better off without me."

"Well, either way, I'm going to have to call her. You owe her that much."

"You're right, I do," Charlie said, and he sat down in Nathan's pink, stuffed chair and picked up Nathan's remote telephone, which had an antenna.

"Joline, I'm at Nathan's."

"Thank God. I thought you might end up there. I've been calling him every day."

"He told me."

Then there was a long pause. Static on the line. And Charlie felt awkward, just the way he had felt the first time he had made love to Joline all those years ago. For that instant he remembered the past with such clarity that he almost forgot he was in Nathan Isaacs' dining room with a phone pressed against his ear. He stared out though the glass patio doors at Nathan's pool. The breeze-textured water sent sunlight flickering into his eyes, flashing . . . and then everything dissolved into a sun-filled room in the Hotel Bainbridge. He was in bed with a seventeen-year-old woman named Joline, whom he had just met in the country store/post office. She had long legs and her hair was loose and so full of electricity that when he stroked it, it would stick to his hand like a dry cloud. She had freckles on her face and a pimple on her chin, which she said embarrassed her; Charlie had never met anyone so wholesome and open and fresh. There was also something else about her—a directness—that made Charlie nervous, and that was unusual because Charlie was *never* nervous around women.

Joline smelled like bread and like sweat and her breath was warm and tangy. She lay in bed on her side, her head propped on her arm, and she gazed at him, as if he were somehow the most wonderful goddamn thing that ever was. Her breasts were high and the nipples still pink, and her skin seemed so tight on her large bones . . . yet she was a big, soft woman. Charlie touched her slowly; the bright sunlight turned the blond downy hair on her arms white as chalk. She had taken off the lipstick and make-up that Charlie had said he didn't like, and he kissed her, pushing past her slightly uneven teeth with his tongue, tasting her, feeling his erection against her thigh. Charlie was going to make it good for her; he was going to be the best she'd ever had. This was the part of sex he had always liked best, the foreplay, the sense of complete control, of knowing that a woman wanted him so much that she would cry out and dig her nails into his back as if he was a tree that she was clinging to for her life. This was the mechanical part; he didn't have to think about where to touch a woman. He had it all down. Goddamn, he'd had enough practice at it. He'd fucked enough women in his life to populate a small town.

She tried to pull him against her, on top of her, but he held her back as he worked his fingers around her insides. Charlie thought that sex was something like fighting, only in slow motion. Joline was strong . . . but Charlie was stronger. He touched her clitoris, and she said, "I want you," but Charlie was slow and confident. I might be a fuck up, he told himself, but goddamn I can do this right. He pretended he was in a room by himself. He tried not to think about Joline too much, or start sucking on her breasts—it was important not to get too involved at the start, or you'd come too early.

"Charlie," Joline said, staring at him intently, as if she had just come out of a trance and was wide awake . . . as if she was trying to read his thoughts through his eyes and face. "I get this feeling that you're . . . I don't know, far away or something. Don't you want me?"

"Yes, of course I want you," he said, suddenly feeling awkward and embarrassed. She had seen right through him. And goddammit his thoughts and the way he did things were his own business. But he knew that was bullshit.

"Then make love to me," she said. He felt a warmth in his penis as she touched him, squeezing him until pain was indistinguishable from pleasure. She looked right at Charlie, as if she were having some sort of a conversation with him, as if she were silently telling him that she loved him.

And the crazy thing was that he wanted to tell her that he loved her. He wanted to let everything go—he had fallen for her. That was dangerous, but it was true. This wasn't some slut he was banging for a buck; this was the woman he was going to marry. He knew that when he saw her in the store; it was love at first sight just like in the magazines was what it was. That hadn't ever happened to him before, not with his last wife, and certainly not with any of the whores he'd lived with in Mexico after he lost his gas stations and all his money.

Everything had to be perfect. This was the most goddamn important moment in his life, and here he was fucking it up.

Bad thoughts flashed through his mind: He wasn't good enough for Joline, he really was a fuck up and a shit, just like Ruth, his last wife, had told him. He was no better than his father; and Ruth, God damn her eyes, was just like his mother. He had played out his parent's marriage all over again. Ruth was just like his mother—she didn't understand shit; she was just there to take it. Charlie had fucked around on her, had done everything his father had done to his mother. It was as if he had had to repeat the pattern. Because he was like his father. Because he was a shit. Because he was nothing.

Right then and there he thought about his father, remembered a day as warm and sunny as this one. His mother had sent him to find Pop at his friend's apartment, where he was supposed to be playing cards. He remembered knocking at the door and waiting. He heard noises inside, and instead of knocking harder on the door, he just walked in. He snuck in like a thief to find his father cheating on Charlie's mother, fucking that other woman, who was probably a whore. The worse thing was the woman's face. It had been burned into Charlie's thoughts. It wasn't a beautiful face. The mouth was crooked and she wore red make-up on her cheeks. But the goddamn woman looked like his mother. She had similar features, and the same long, thick, auburn hair.

Those thoughts intruded like leering strangers and now, when it really counted, Charlie lost his erection. He was mortified. This had never happened to him before. Never. Now he'd fucked up because of his bad thoughts. When push comes to shove, I'm not even a man, he told himself. He sighed and fell away from her. He lay on his back and looked at the cracks in the ceiling. He saw faces looking down at him. One looked like a young woman. It could be his mother or Joline. But he blinked his eyes, and it changed into an old man smiling. It looked like any old man, but Charlie knew it was his father.

Joline continued to caress him, investigating, even though he was limp. She leaned toward him, her face close to his, and said, "Sometimes that happens. Maybe it means you really like me." Then she smiled, as if it really didn't mean anything.

"I'm sorry," Charlie mumbled. "That's never happened—"

"Was it something about me that you didn't like," she asked nervously, drawing away from him. Her hair was unkempt, pushed over to one side, as if it was a variation of a style fashionable ten years ago.

"No," he said, "it wasn't you." But he couldn't believe that. It *had* to be her fault. He wished he were back on the road. Anywhere but here.

But he needed to be here. He needed to be with her. Yet he couldn't bring himself to reach over and touch her. He couldn't even look over at her.

He listened to the cars swooshing by below. He could hear street conversation—a couple having an argument over finding a baby-sitter: the window was open wide, for it was a warm day. He felt isolated, ashamed of himself. He had fucked it up and now he couldn't work his way out of himself, couldn't make it up, couldn't fix it. It was as if they'd had their first big fight, as if silence lay between them like some hard, cold object.

"I want us to feel close," Joline said after a few moments had passed. "That's why I came up here with you. Don't shut me out because we fucked up in bed. I'll try again whenever you want to. It's not that important."

"It sure as hell is."

"Why is it?" she asked.

Charlie didn't have an answer for that, but he said, "Because a man's supposed to be able to satisfy a woman."

"That's bullshit."

Charlie didn't respond.

"You don't have to try to impress me, I told you that before we even came up here."

"I don't have to impress you or anyone else," Charlie snapped. Then after a pause he said, "This never happened to me before, is all."

"Maybe I was wrong about you," Joline said, her face flushed with anger; it was as if she hadn't even heard what he had said. "Maybe you think I'm just some country bimbo who you can impress the hell out of. I didn't come here just to get laid and find out if you're the best fuck in the universe. Maybe you are, but I came up here because I felt something special between us. I'd feel it if we were just holding hands."

"I feel the same way," Charlie said, blurting it out. "I love you. I know that sounds crazy. I wanted everything to be perfect. Christ, you shouldn't even be here with me. I'm old enough to be your goddamn father, and I've fucked up everyone and everything I've ever touched."

"That's a bunch of bullshit. If I thought that's the kind of man you are, I wouldn't have come here in the first place."

Charlie felt better, lighter. Maybe he could try again . . . and, goddamn, she *was* a good looking woman. "You've got beautiful breasts," Charlie said, watching her.

She grinned. "My best part . . . it's certainly not my face."

"You've got a beautiful face."

"I want to talk," she said. "I want to know everything about you, secret things, stuff you wouldn't tell anybody else." She looked at him again, as if she could read him, as if his thoughts and memories were more important than anything written in history books. She didn't seem to be embarrassed about being naked before him, and yet he could sense her shyness. She was a good girl.

He talked to her, at first about how he'd won his boat—the *Lorelei*—in a card game, and how he'd lost his gas stations trying to be a big shot. He told her about his drinking and whoring and bad business decisions; he told her about Ruth, whom he had never spoken about to anyone, and he told her he was a whoremaster like his father. He talked about his family and his recollection seemed clear and fresh, if not without bitterness.

He couldn't stop talking, even though it embarrassed him. He had to keep talking, for he knew that if he stopped, he'd never be able to open up like this again. He had never revealed himself to Ruth, nor had she ever really tried to know him. But maybe she did try, Charlie thought. Maybe I was so wrapped up in myself that I just hadn't noticed. Maybe I haven't seen anything right.

But just talking to Joline now, looking back into his life, made everything seem different.

"I couldn't get away from my father, even after I left," Charlie said. "He stayed right with me, sort of in my mind—even after he died. I can't help it, but I still hate him."

"You're different than him," Joline said. "He never even talked to your mother, or treated her like a wife."

"I didn't do any better with Ruth."

"But you are with me . . ."

She held him and listened and told him she loved him. They looked at each other, and suddenly they both started crying. It was the craziest goddamn thing that had ever happened to him, and Charlie felt as if he had given himself to her, as if he was something fragile and delicate—yet he was safe. This was the safest he'd felt since he'd left home. Sonovabitch if that wasn't the truth.

And then they were pushing against each other, unable to get close enough, and Charlie felt hard and hot and strong, felt stronger and better than he'd ever felt in his life, and he made love to Joline with an intimacy he'd only known in his most private thoughts.

"Charlie . . . ?" It was Joline's voice on the telephone. Only a few seconds had passed.

"Yeah," Charlie said, yearning for her, remembering, wanting to come home. But all that he could say was "yeah".

It was as if the old silence was between them again, and he couldn't break through it.

"Can you come home?"

"You sure you want me to? I've been pretty f—messed up."

"Come home."

"John's dead."

"Come home, Charlie. I love you."

Nathan gave him a hundred dollars for a bus home. Charlie could work it off later. He could work for Stephen. He could pay off all his debts in bits and pieces, and perhaps Nathan and Stephen could recoup some from their insurance. Or maybe they could call it a tax loss. Or do whatever it is smart businessmen do.

"I guess I owe you one," Charlie said.

"I guess you do," Nathan replied, but there was a knowing between them. Perhaps it was because Nathan owed one to the world, and in his way he was trying to pay it back now.

So maybe Charlie did owe him one, but that was just a regular debt.

Even if it was his fucking life.

24.

HEARING THUNDER
AND TASTING SALT

Charlie walked down to the beach. He had refused Nathan's offer to drive him to the bus terminal. When Nathan looked pinched-up and leery, Charlie told him that he, Nathan, would have to trust him—if he couldn't, then Charlie would give him back the hundred dollar loan.

It was a clear, blue, beautiful day. The sand looked like it had been raked and seemed to stretch on forever. There were more swells than spindrift breakers; the ocean was quiet on this beach. Children splashed in the water with their parents and built sandcastles on the beach face, while senior citizens sat on folding chairs and took in the air, the conversation, the good life. They probably lived in the apartments and condos behind them.

But Charlie was in the same place he'd always been. He wasn't ever going to have a dime. He'd still be living in that slum on St. Charles Street. He'd have Hell's Angels for neighbors, and that fucking filthy slob Clifford, who lived next door, would probably never move out.

Charlie kept walking—miles, it seemed—until he came to a deserted stretch of sand. The sun was hot on his face, and his skin felt tight and dry. It was so bright that it was difficult to look across the beach. He couldn't see any houses from here and the sea oats on the banks, as brown and burnt as the old men who had retired here to die, added to Charlie's sense of desolation. He had lived the compressed life with John. He had done the whole nine yards. Come around full circle. Yet something worked at him . . . something he had left undone. The past was still eating him. He was still the whoremaster he had thought his father to be. He was still a nothing, even if he could hear the thunder once in a while.

He wondered if he was really going home . . . if he could go home. But all he could do now was walk, take one step and then the next. He felt he was in a trance. It was like driving.

If he did go home, though, he wasn't going to tell Joline anything that would hurt her. He'd done enough of that.

But then again, maybe he would just keep on walking.

The day passed as if he were in the sweat-lodge. It was hot enough, but that wasn't it. He had no sense of time. He was just being carried along. He wasn't feeling sorry for himself. It was as if he was looking for something, something magical right here on the beach—a polished pearl-surfaced shell that when put to his ear would whisper all the answers, would tell him what the fuck it all meant and why he was here. If he could find that magical thing, maybe he could go home.

But all he could do was walk.

He walked the day away. He didn't even know where he was. Just on the beach somewhere in Florida. Walking. Fucking walking. He even picked up rounded, striated pebbles and shells, and he remembered what John had said about things containing power. But nothing spoke to him. The sea whispered, but it was talking to itself. He listened, though, and heard his feet scrunching in the sand. . . . heard the blood pumping through his body.

And as if in a dream, the blue time came upon him. Everything shifted, became softer, fuller, more real. A chill came into the air, turning clarity into shadows of possibility. Perhaps Charlie had gotten too much sun, for he saw everything as a quiet explosion of luminescence. It was in the water, in the sand. It was the magic he had not been able to find before in the seastones and shells and afternoon whispering of the sea.

Charlie's stomach had stopped aching. He still had not eaten; now he wasn't even hungry. He was tired, but he couldn't stop walking. In a few moments it would be dark. Then what . . . ?

He listened and walked and waited. His thoughts came to him as flashes of memory, deep and clear and luminescent. There was an equivalence of his memories and the sand and breeze and whispering life around him.

He remembered John telling him in the sweat-lodge about the rock people. He sensed the inorganic life pulsing all around him.

And as the world slipped into evening, Charlie saw his father.

The old man was standing right there on the blue-tinged beach, waiting for him. He looked like Charlie, same rough-set face, same tousled hair, same wiry body. He had his hands in his pockets. He nodded to Charlie in recognition.

Charlie walked up to him. The old man was a shadow, a mirage . . . like John was after he had died, when he had continued talking to Charlie in the car on the way to Nathan Isaacs.

"You're dead," Charlie said to the ghost.

Pop nodded.

Charlie stood before his father and felt an overwhelming sadness come over him. Recognition and sadness. He wanted to cry, right there on the beach in front of a goddamn hallucination. "You were a sonovabitch."

Again, Pop nodded. And Charlie couldn't help but smile sadly. "So am I."

"It's not the same," Pop said.

"You were a shit to Mom."

Pop just watched Charlie.

"You never gave a shit about any of us."

"Yes I did," Pop said. "I just fucked everything up."

"You didn't talk to us ... you didn't cry," Charlie said. Goddamn that's a crazy thing to say, even to a hallucination. Especially since Charlie was crying. "It would have been all right to cry when you fucked up, Pop."

And then Pop just smiled and disappeared. Without a word, without a tear.

But at least he had smiled; that was something.

Charlie looked up at the sky, which was darkening. The moon was pale, gray; soon it would be white and the sky would be filled with stars. He stretched out his arms and shouted, "Goodbye, Pop. Goddammit, I forgive you. I didn't do so hot myself."

There were birds flying overhead, but they were gulls.

Charlie started laughing. So what if they were gulls? It didn't matter. "Goodbye, John, I'm going home. I love you, you crazy fucking *heyoka*!"

But Charlie's words were swallowed. There was too much of the world, and his lungs were bad. But something had changed, he told himself, even though nothing had changed. He laughed at that and kept walking, walking right into the night. He knew what he was going to do. He would go home and get drunk once in a while and do some things wrong and fight with Joline and sleep with Joline and take on odd jobs and pay back what he owed to Nathan and Stephen and make his peace with that little asshole Joey who would most likely marry his daughter.

That would all be the same.

He would be the same, too ... but he would be different. He imagined Pop and John as ghosts hanging around in the air, eavesdropping, talking together, getting drunk and laid and *heyoka*.

Charlie thought that was very funny. As he walked, the ocean turned dark. He saw the first stars and began to yearn for Joline and his home.

He lingered for a bit, but he knew he had heard the last of the voices.

It was time to go.

He needed something to eat. Somehow it would be all right to eat now. The birds were most likely done with John, and his spirit was . . . could be anywhere.

But Charlie couldn't stop himself from laughing. He left the beach for A–1-A and took a shortcut through someone's lawn. He heard something above. It must be a bird, he thought. He didn't allow himself to look up, but he could imagine its huge eagle wings flapping, pumping the clear night air like a bellows.

Charlie heard the thunder and tasted salt. He laughed and cried and shouted for John and Pop and Joline and the whole goddamn world.

Goddamn he was hungry.

AFTERWORD:

A GIFT OF EAGLES

The past—or our memory of it—is indeed another country.

In another life in a far land I was in a sweat-lodge being led by a medicine man who, it was claimed, had the gift of eagles. It was explained to me that that was his medicine, his power. In that sweat lodge where it was so hot that your skin could suddenly crack, I remember the steam coming up so hot that it actually felt cold; I remember trying to hunker down into my blanket, and in that moment of sensory deprivation, in the intense heat and darkness, in that small space with eight other men . . . a space that seemed like miles of darkness . . . I heard a giant bellows working, felt something flapping inside the lodge, felt the touch of feathers, as something very large frantically flew about, trying to get out of that dark.

The bellows was probably my own blood pounding.

The medicine man had an eagle's wing, and was slapping it against my thigh, probably waving the wing in the steam-black air. I know that now, knew it then; but I remember that on one level, it was an eagle loose in the sweat-lodge. I knew it was a trick, but a trick played by the Trickster, one that had resonance on a level beyond the rational. For in that instant I had felt the eagle, not the medicine man's feathers, but the eagle.

It was a shared hallucination. I remember shyly asking someone who had sat next to me in the sweat-lodge if he felt anything strange in that session. He laughed and said, "Yeah, you mean the eagle in the sweat-lodge."

Why was I in that Indian sweat lodge?

I was researching an idea I had for a novel, of course.

Counting Coup.

However, traditional Indian religion is not often accessible to non-Indians, and I've been told that most accounts of Indian religion are not entirely accurate. Traditional Indians are wary of "Wannabees," ie., groupies who see Indian life as glamorous and want to be close to it. How did I get in? I got lucky, I wasn't a "Wannabee," and . . . well, it's too personal to put to paper.

But those experiences subtly changed the way I experience the world. I recall being at a friend's vision-quest where everyone was "giving flesh," a ceremony in which the medicine man cuts the supplicant's skin with a razor and drops the tiny pieces of flesh into a colored square of cloth, which the participant later ties to the branch of a nearby tree as a totem. I asked the medicine man why people were doing this, and he looked at me as if I had just asked the most stupid question imaginable. He laughed and answered, "Because that's the only thing you've got to give. Your skin is the only thing you really own. So you give a little of it to your friend, to help him. You give a little of yourself. You take a little pain for him."

And so I gave flesh.

For my son Jody. For my friend Albert. For all of us. And for a little while I lost hold of my ego. There and in the sweat lodge where I burned for a few minutes, or a few hours, I had the revelation—or aberration depending on your point of view—that perhaps down deep in the quick of our unconscious our basic impulses are not selfish and self-seeking.

Of course, back then I also felt the wings of eagles beating in the sweat-lodge.

My characters often have different "intentions" than their author, who often sits bemusedly in front of the laptop while the characters engage in their own conversations and take the "plot" in directions *I* never intended. I had intended *Counting Coup* to be a straight-forward road novel, a novel about two men who are at the end of their lives and decide to show the world that they are still alive, still vital, and can still drink, shout, and shake the trees. I thought I'd write a novel in the tradition of Jack Kerouac's *On the Road,* or John Steinbeck's *Cannery Row.* Originally, I thought it would be interesting to explore the interaction of two men from different cultures in similar circumstances. But once again the research changed the story . . . and of course my life.

The elements of magical realism in *Counting Coup* are close to the truth of my own private experiences. I have found as I enter my more mature, reflective years that my "real" life is scattered with these small bits of magic realism. Or perhaps it's just that as I wander through that distant country that is my past, I recast the ordinary into the numinal.

For me fiction has always been a way of ordering and remembering experience; and I came closest to remembering the sight and smell and "feel" of those experiences when I wrote *Counting Coup.* Once again I could hear the spirit voices and feel the steam that's so hot it's cold. Once again I remembered what happened when everything soured and turned into "bad medicine."

Once again I remembered being on the road, living without impediment . . .

And once again my fiction and my personal life blurred, one folding into the other.

ABOUT THE AUTHOR

Jack Dann has written or edited over fifty books, including *The Memory Cathedral*, which is currently published in ten languages and was #1 on *The Age* bestseller list, and most recently *The Silent*, which *The Australian* called "an extraordinary achievement." He is a recipient of the Nebula Award, the World Fantasy Award, the Australian Aurealis Award (twice), the Ditmar Award (twice), and the Premios Gilgamés de Narrative Fantastica award. He has also been honored by the Mark Twain Society (Esteemed Knight). Jack Dann lives in Melbourne, Australia, and "commutes" back and forth to Los Angeles and New York.